Praise for Dreda Say M‗‗‗‗‗‗ ‗us books:

'The best reflection of re‗‗‗‗‗‗‗‗‗ ‗ seen in a long time . . . A book's "v‗‗‗‗‗‗‗‗es its greatness and Mitchell's voice is ‗‗‗‗‗‗‗

Lee Child on *Running Hot*

'*Killer Tune* is sharpl‗‗‗‗‗‗‗ncisive and a moving story of conflicting loyalties and ‗‗‗shed business.'

Guardian

'Dreda Say Mitchell confirms her position as a hot new name in crime writing with this taut novel.'

Elle on *Killer Tune*

'Brilliant – a gripping roller-coaster for the reader'

Independent

'*Killer Tune* lays the breezy musical name-checking of Hornby's *High Fidelity* over a well-crafted murder mystery.'

Financial Times

'The narrative throbs with energy and has a refreshing directness.'

Sunday Telegraph on *Killer Tune*

'Confidently paced tale, told in language both lyrical and salty'

Daily Mail on *Killer Tune*

'Sharp-eyed, even sharper-tongued chase story . . . distinctly different; well worth seeking out'

Literary Review on *Running Hot*

ALSO BY DREDA SAY MITCHELL

Running Hot
Killer Tune
Geezer Girls

ABOUT THE AUTHOR

Dreda Say Mitchell grew up in the east end of London where she continues to live.

GangSTER GirL

Dreda Say Mitchell

HODDER

First published in Great Britain in 2010 by Hodder & Stoughton
An Hachette UK company

First published in paperback in 2010

6

A CIP catalogue record for this title is available from the British Library

ISBN 978 0 340 99320 0

Typeset in Rotis Serif by Hewer Text UK Ltd, Edinburgh

Printed and bound in the UK by CPI Mackays, Chatham ME5 8TD

Hodder & Stoughton policy is to use papers that are natural, renewable and
recyclable products and made from wood grown in sustainable forests. The
logging and manufacturing processes are expected to conform to the
environmental regulations of the country of origin.

Hodder & Stoughton Ltd
338 Euston Road
London NW1 3BH

www.hodder.co.uk

This one's for Auntie Lydia

ACKNOWLEDGEMENTS

A massive thanks to Kate Howard, Justine Taylor and the team at Hodder, Stephanie Glencross, my agent Jane Gregory and her team.
To my geezerettes.
And as always to the fabulous Tony.

now

one

Daisy stared at the dead body.

At the growing pool of blood.

At the compact pistol in her hand.

'*Whatever you do, never run*', she heard his earlier warning beating once again inside her head.

But she ran. Shot out of the room. Down the corridor. Took the stairs two at a time. Hit ground level. The sweat trickled down her face from the heat. From the fear. Her breathing cut up the air. She looked straight ahead. More blood on the floor. Red, wavy lines this time. She kept up her pace. Dodged the blood. Reached the glass front doors. That's when she stopped. Gulped in a steady stream of uneven air. One . . . two . . . three. Shoved the gun into her pocket. Rolled the balaclava off her face until it lay under the low hanging hood she wore. She hesitated at the door as his words came back to her:

'*Whatever you do, never run.*'

She took deep breaths. Pushed her head down and the door at the same time. Stepped outside into one of London's busiest business districts. The light from the June sun struck her eyes, blinding her. She rapidly blinked trying to flick the glare from her eyes. Trying to find out if she could make it without being seen. Her vision cleared. And what she saw horrified her. The area in front of her was filled with crowds of people, workers enjoying a drink and chat in the still bright evening light.

'*Whatever you do, never run.*'

A deafening, high-pitched, wailing noise screamed blue murder from the building behind her.

She ran.

Her heartbeat kicked into overdrive. She didn't look left. Didn't look right. Didn't look at the City workers who she knew were now gazing up at the building rocked by the alarm. Didn't look at the people who were staring after her running figure. Didn't look at the people who were now pulling out their mobiles to call the cops.

Sprinted around a corner. Kept motoring forward until a hand snatched her arm swinging her against a hard wall. The air slammed out of her body in a savage whoosh sound.

'Where the hell have you been?' Relief washed over Daisy as she stared at the familiar face. She opened her mouth to respond but the other person got there before her. 'Get your arse into gear, we need to get to the car.'

Heads down, they bolted towards the waiting car. They kept going until they saw it in the distance. Saw the figure who waited for them in the driver's seat. As they got closer the gun nose-dived out of her pocket. Clattered onto the ground. Daisy skidded to a halt. Whirled around.

'Leave it!' the other person yelled as they kept running forward.

But Daisy knew she couldn't do that. She grabbed it. Rammed it back into her pocket. Twisted towards the car at the same time the other person reached the passenger side. She sprinted towards the car. The driver blocked the other person from her view. A police siren wailed between the city blocks somewhere in the distance. She ran harder. And harder. She was almost there.

Then there was a loud rolling rumble of thunder.

That's all she heard. A terrifying boom tore through the air. The car she'd been running towards, exploded outwards and into a fireball. Daisy felt the shock go through her body as if she'd touched a live wire. She somersaulted through the air like a circus acrobat. She landed on her back, winded, as parts of car and street lamps came down around her until she was covered in debris and glass. She could feel something seeping down her face. Blood. Through her hazy vision she saw the shattered and twisted remains of the car as red and orange flames belched with smoke high into the air.

Her vision became fainter and fainter. Her mind started to slip. She heard The Mamas And Papas singing 'Dedicated To The One I Love' as her mind slipped further back. Back to two weeks ago. Back to the day her life had changed forever. Back to a day that had started with a death . . . .

two weeks earlier

Two

He's dead.

Twenty-six-year-old Daisy Sullivan's mind reeled as she read the note the security guard had handed her. Daisy was tall, slim, with porcelain white skin, a beauty spot just above the right side of her pouting Angelina Jolie-style lips and hair that fell to her shoulders like a newly pressed black curtain. But it was her eyes that stopped both men and women in their tracks. Bright and blue. Eyes that mostly twinkled with laughter. Eyes she'd inherited from her long-dead gangster father, Frankie Sullivan. Of course. not many people knew who her dad had been and they never would if she was going to make it as a lawyer. Not that she was ashamed of her dad because she wasn't. She was ashamed of the terrible things he'd done, but he'd been the best dad in the world to her. But at the same time she'd worked her knickers off to get this far as a lawyer and she couldn't afford for anything to get in her way. And if that meant keeping quiet about who her dad had been, then so be it. Besides, who was going to find out? Sullivan was a relatively common surname.

The note shook in her hand as shock settled with disbelief. No way. This couldn't be true. He couldn't be . . .

'Miss Sullivan.'

Daisy raised her head. For a few seconds she was disorientated. Didn't know where she was. Didn't know who was calling her name so impatiently.

'Miss Sullivan?' The voice came again, with more urgency this time.

She turned her head towards the voice. She was sitting at a table, sitting side-by-side with a young lad with shy looks and big hands. In front of her was a stack of papers. Shit. She bolted out of her seat. She remembered where she was. Youth Court on a Monday morning. Courtroom number four at Thames Magistrate Court and Judge Morgan was about to read the verdict on fifteen-year-old Lee Moore, who she was defending on an ABH charge. The note still in her hand she addressed the judge, who looked back at her as if he wanted to send her down to do a lengthy stretch.

'Pardon, your Honour.' Her voice was husky and smoky and somewhere between upmarket London with a dollop of her cockney heritage rolling in it. She nodded her head respectfully.

'Not keeping you from your life I hope, Miss Sullivan?' Judge Morgan's voice dripped with sarcasm, his thin head moving loosely between his shoulders making him look like a dead ringer for an irate, ageing Thunderbird.

Without responding Daisy turned to her client. Nodded briskly. Biting his lip he got to his feet. They looked at the judge who was ready to dispense justice.

'Lee Moore, this court has found you not guilty of the offence . . .'

Daisy turned to the defendant and smiled. Another case won. At the firm they called her 'Got Off Daisy' because she had a knack of getting defendants acquitted. The other lawyers were desperate to know what her secret was. Simple: hard work and a great mentor. Her face sagged as she thought about the note. Her mentor was gone. Charlie was dead.

'Thanks, Miss Sullivan.' Lee Moore stretched out his hand

She clasped it. 'Behave – you might not be so lucky next time,' she whispered.

He blushed at that. She knew he was as guilty as hell. But the truth never came into it. Her job was to defend her clients, not establish the truth. That was the one of the first things that Charlie taught her about being a lawyer. Charlie. Her heart lurched.

She needed to get out of here. Find out what had happened to Charlie. As soon as her defendant was gone, she quickly gathered her papers and pushed them into her briefcase. She snapped it shut. Picked up the lonely note on the table. Her mouth went dry as she reread it.

'Miss Sullivan?'

She looked up to find a stocky man on the other side of the desk. He was slightly shorter than her but had the build of a human mountain, tough and hard to take down.

'I'm Lee's friend, Mr Doyle.' His voice was cockney to the core, but low and light. She looked at him some more. She knew a villain when she saw one; it was in her blood. Hadn't she been brought up by one of the toughest Faces London had ever known? Frankie Sullivan might've been dead and buried going on eleven years now, but his name still sent chills through certain parts of the capital.

'I help run the boxing club that Lee goes to,' the man continued. 'Just wanted to say thanks.' He didn't offer her his hand. 'Lee knows that if he steps out of line again I'm going to give him a cuff.' She smiled at that. He didn't. 'Cos you've helped my boy out, anytime you want anything just let me know. Not that a woman from your stripe would need any help, of course.'

She smiled, but as soon as he'd gone she forgot about him and grabbed her case. Entered the corridor, which was more or less empty except for a few people sitting silently on benches outside courtrooms. Her gaze darted around trying to find another lawyer, her best friend Evangeline Spencer-Smith, or 'Angel', as she was known. She found her. Angel was pinned up against a wall by the tongue-lashing she was receiving from a pockmarked faced man in his early twenties. Next to them stood a group of three men, who seemed to be modelling themselves on bit-part players from a naff gangster flick.

The man growled at Angel, 'If I end up doing a stretch in Brixton I'm gonna make sure that you get sorted out, you get me?'

Oh, Daisy got it. No one treated her friend like that. No one. She moved over using the walk that her dad had taught her to use when she meant business: shoulders back, long strides and with a slight scowl about the lips. As her old man had always pointed out, if you can fake menace, you can get away with anything. 'Gents . . .'

The way she said the word carried all the sarcasm she felt. 'What's the problem?'

The man harassing Angel whirled around. His bloodshot eyes gave her the once-over like she was trash and then he sneered. His mates snickered. 'Do you want some?'

Go fuck yourself, she wanted to snarl at him. He wouldn't be giving her a load of verbal if he knew who her dad had been. But instead she said, '"Want some?" No, not me, but I think security might. They're ex-cops with friends in the force. So you know what that means? You're going to find yourself banged up on a bad wing.' Her eyes didn't waver from his.

He stood his ground for a full thirty seconds. Then backed off. 'Remember what I said, lawyer lady.' He pointed menacingly at Angel, then took his posse and left.

'You alright?' Daisy took a step closer.

Angel collapsed against the wall. She was petite, with a fake all-year tan and platinum hair that bobbed around a gorgeous face that most men stared twice at, and a wicked nature that Daisy said would one day get her into a wagonload of trouble.

'Yes. That was Johnny – Johnny Digby – one "those" Digbys . . .' Daisy knew who she meant. The Digbys were one of East London's low-budget underworld crews. 'He's the youngest member of the gang. Just showing off to his associates.'

'The tart. But then I suppose without those sort of tarts we'd be unemployed,' Daisy muttered.

'I know.' Angel responded as if she'd just finished eating the most delicious cream cake in the world. Her eyes danced with delight. 'If only he were a few years older . . .'

Daisy shook her head. Angel might have the poshest voice in town and come from a family who had more money to burn than accountants to keep track of it but she loved her men rough and with no class at all. Although they were complete opposites – Angel the ultimate fun-loving party girl and Daisy, who some called the hardest-working lawyer in the law firm of Curtis and Hopkirk – they had bonded together like two long-lost sisters on their first day as lawyers two years ago.

Daisy shoved the note at Angel. 'Ohmygod,' her friend let out after reading it. 'What happened?'

'I don't know. But I'm heading back to the office to find out. Randal wants to see me.' Daisy couldn't wait to head back to her car, a molten red, Trident sports car, she was barely keeping it together as it was. As least in the sanctuary of her car she'd be able to let out the grief she felt at Charlie's death. She turned on her heel and strode down the corridor. Angel followed, her stilettos click-clacking against the concrete floor. Daisy passed two men in suits, the taller of the two wearing Gucci shades and with a tattoo of a piano on his neck. As she neared the exit she heard a cry behind her. She twisted around to find Angel on her knees, desperately clutching her open briefcase with papers strewn on the floor around her. The man with the shades and tattoo was on his hunches beside Angel with his arms loosely around her.

'So sorry,' Angel apologised to the man. He gave her a crooked, cheeky smile.

Daisy made a move towards her friend, but stopped when she saw the look in Angel's eyes. Lust. Nothing Angel liked better than being in the arms of some fella. Daisy rolled her eyes. Angel and her men.

'I'll see you back at the office,' Daisy called quickly. She flipped around. She didn't have time to waste, but needed to get back to the office pronto to find out what had happened to Charlie. Mind you, she thought sadly, did it matter? The outcome was going to be the same. Her mentor, Charlie Hopkirk, would still be dead.

The driver of the black van with tinted windows looked at the sobbing woman in the red sports car beside him at the red lights and tutted. Bloody birds, always blubbing about something. The sound of the weeping women holed up in the back of his van intensified. Fuck, it was no concern of his. His job was to drive them and dump them off at some place in Whitechapel and take the fat, brown envelope bulging with cash, no questions asked. Mind you he didn't envy them who they were about to meet. He switched the radio on to drown out their noise as the lights turned to green.

*   *   *

Curtis and Hopkirk Associates was slap-bang in the middle of London's bustling Holborn and was one of Britain's top law companies. Usually the second floor was a hive of activity as the lawyers and their assistants got cracking with winning their next case. But not this afternoon. It was bleak, with a hush that was unnatural. Daisy knew that every eye in the room watched her as she walked into the room. Everyone knew how close she and Charlie had become during her two years here.

'Daisy.' She let out a huge sigh of relief on hearing her name, only realising then that she hadn't been breathing properly. Her eyes softened because even without turning around she knew who it was.

Jerome McMillan. He was the same height as her, with floppy bronze hair, sharp hazel eyes and a voice that had been culti-vated at one of Britain's top public schools. But what she loved about him most of all was his laughter. He was one of Curtis and Hopkirk's rising stars and hailed from a family who had statutes and torts running through their veins; his father was a former QC and his grandfather had been an attorney general. And Jerome had chosen Daisy Sullivan to be the girl he wanted to be seen around town with. They'd been dating for just over a year now and she still couldn't believe it. Jerome was one of the most generous, kind-hearted men she knew, and suspected she would ever know. He was the kind of man she'd never have met in a zillion years, had her dad still been alive. That's why she'd never risk telling him about her background. Men like Jerome didn't come to girls like her every day of the week and that's why she was going to do everything on God's earth to keep him.

'Is it true?' he let out when he reached her.

'Charlie? Gone to the great Bailey in the sky?' She nodded. 'Yes.'

Immediately he wrapped his arms around her. She sank grate-fully into him. Trust Jerome to know what she needed at that moment, someone to lean on.

'How are you bearing up?' He stared gently into her face.

'I feel like I'm the one getting ready to be buried, not Charlie.'

His smooth palms gently ran down her arms. She flinched when his hands brushed the chunky, gold bracelets that she always wore on her wrists. Daisy hated anyone touching them, even Jerome. She eased her arms from his embrace. 'Well, I'm here,' he said soothingly, 'so any time you need a shoulder to cry on I've got two waiting for you.'

That almost made her start blubbing. How had she ever deserved a guy like this?

'I hope this doesn't sound too insensitive darling,' he continued. 'But I was going to meet Charlie today to discuss the Woodbridge class-action case.'

The firm were involved in a high-profile lawsuit against Woodbridge Council for its handling of child-abuse allegations in its care homes in the early nineties. A group of adults, who had once been in its care system alleged that the council had turned a deaf ear to their cries for help. Now they were suing the council for a record four million pounds, one million for each of the claimants. The case would have come and gone with little media attention, except one of the adults was the lead singer of one of Britain's top pop girl bands, Electric Star.

'He said that he had something that might help me with the case. Something to do with Maxwell Henley, former leader of the council, who disappeared twenty years ago and is now believed to be living in Spain.'

'I can't help you I'm afraid.' She took a step back from him. 'Randal wants to speak to me, so I'd better see him. If I hear anything about what Charlie was going to tell you, I'll let you know.'

'Don't forget that you're meeting my parents next Wednesday at their cocktail party. They're eager to meet you before they fly out to their place in Florida on Thursday.'

This would be the first time she'd be meeting his parents and she was dead scared. What if they saw right through her? What if they could spot a chav at forty paces, no matter how well dressed she was? Although being fingered as a council estate girl was better than the real story . . .

'Don't look so worried.' He squeezed the top of her arm. 'They are going to adore you, just like I do. And when am I going to meet your people? We've been hitting the town for a year now, so don't you think it's about time?'

The thought of him meeting Jackie – the woman who'd taken her into her home after her dad's death – and her surrogate aunts scared her even more than it did meeting his parents. Jackie and her aunts had once led troubled lives. Lives that had, once upon a time, been mixed up with her dad's. She'd even heard it whispered that Auntie Ollie had been a child soldier in the African country of Sankura. Perhaps he'd think that was cool? Perhaps he would, but only if he was reading about it in the papers. No, she couldn't see Jerome meeting them being a party made in heaven. And as for him meeting Misty . . . she took her mind swiftly away from that thought.

'Let's see how I get on with your parents first, OK?' Her eyes flicked to the large double doors at the end of the corridor. 'Got to go.'

He gave her a swift peck on the cheek, then was gone. Daisy stared nervously at Randal Curtis's office door. Meeting this man always made her nerves feel like electric wires since the day she'd learnt Randal believed her dad had murdered his son.

'So, how did he go?' Daisy quietly asked the older man sitting at the desk in the huge, plush, but businesslike office as she stood in the doorway.

Randal Curtis was still an impressive figure in his late fifties, with a full head of dyed brown hair and a body he kept in good condition in order to keep up with the many affairs he had behind his wife's back, and a brain that made him a legend in courtroom brawls. He sat in a leather swivel chair in front of a huge glass window that had an eagle-eye view over this corner of the capital.

Daisy eyed the surviving senior partner of the firm nervously. She always got the jitters around him. When she'd first started at Curtis and Hopkirk she'd liked Randal Curtis, ignored the nasty nickname the other lawyers called him behind his back – Randy Randall. She had heard on the office rumour mill that Randal had come from a working-class London family and had grafted his way, through sheer hard work, up the rungs of the law establishment. She'd liked that because it made Randal sound a bit like her. That is until the day Charlie had told her to never mention who her father was. It wasn't as though she had been telling everyone the news, but when she'd asked him why, his answer had frozen her to the spot. Randal believed her dad had killed his son. His eldest boy had pegged out on a speedball in a Whitechapel bedsit fifteen years earlier. In his grief Randall had convinced himself that the East End's then leading criminal, Frankie Sullivan, had supplied the drugs. On no account, Charlie had warned her, should she ever mention who her dad was to Charlie's partner. If she did then Randy Randall was going to return a very guilty verdict on her career and there wouldn't be any appeal. That warning made her realise that her old world and her new one were very different and should be kept apart, as much as she possibly could.

'Take a seat.' Randal waved his hand at the single leather chair on the other side of the desk.

Daisy closed the door, crossed the room and took a seat. She brushed her long hands down her tailored black skirt, made by an up-and-coming designer who had a stall in East London's Spitalfields market. She turned her blue gaze to him as her thumb anxiously rubbed against the cold bracelet on her left wrist.

'I'm afraid it was the usual end for the super-fit, non-smoking, trim professional – a heart attack,' Randal said wryly. 'Apparently he was having an early morning game of squash and collapsed.' Daisy's teeth clipped her bottom lip as a disturbing image of Charlie in pain on the floor shook her mind. 'There was nothing they could do for him by the time they got him to the hospital.' Randal coughed, clearing his throat, clearing the image of Charlie from Daisy's mind. 'This is a sad day indeed, not just for us, but for the whole of the justice community.'

Daisy nodded, not wanting to be in here any longer than she had to. She half rose out of her chair.

'One minute, please.' Shit. She sank back down in the chair.

He pulled out the top drawer of his desk. Took out a long, thickly rolled Cuban. Clipped the end and lit up.

'You don't mind, do you? I know it's against the legislation, but I'm trying to avoid a heart attack . . .'

He leant back in his chair as he puffed once. Twice. The third time he gazed intently at Daisy through the rising smoke. 'This is all such an unfortunate business. Death you know. I don't suppose someone as young as you has had many dealings with the grim reaper yet?'

Oh, but that's where you're wrong mate. She knew all about the grim reaper, in fact he was virtually a friend of the family.

'No, can't say I have.' Her eyes darted to stare out of the rain-soaked window and settled on a magpie that sat on the window ledge. She shivered as if she was the bird sitting in the unseasonably damp June air, gazing in from outside.

'Do you know how long myself and Charlie had been in business together?' She knew because Charlie had told her. But she didn't say that. Just shook her head because she knew the man opposite her wanted to tell his story. 'Thirty-three years. Not many people realise this but we started out representing some of the less savoury characters in the world. The scum that no one else wanted to touch. But we kept going until we'd established a name for ourselves. That's what you're going to have to do, Daisy, get your hands dirty sometimes, and work hard.' He sighed and tipped the cigar ash into the chrome ashtray on the desk. 'Now that silly bugger has gone and left me. His wife's going to want all his stuff and that's where you come in. I need you to go through his office with one of those fine combs you ladies like to use and find out what belongs to the firm and what the wife can have.'

Daisy shuffled urgently onto the edge of the chair. 'But Mr Curtis, I'm due to start assisting Jerome on the Woodbridge class-action case . . .'

The older man waved his large hands in the air sweeping her words aside. 'I know that you're eager to prove yourself, but don't forget that it was Charlie who picked you out of all the students for a work placement here two years ago and he went out of his way to make sure that you understood the business inside and out. Is it too much to ask for you to pay him back by sorting through his life?' He leant back and stabbed her with a look that made her feel like she was in the dock. 'Besides,' he carried on. 'I need that office if I'm going to install a new partner in there soon.'

The heartless bastard. They'd hardly pulled the sheet over Charlie's head and this wanker was already measuring the curtains in his office.

'When do you want me to start?'

He picked his cigar back up. 'A lawyer strikes while the witness is wobbling in the box, does he not?'

'I'm sorry?'

'Now would be a good time.'

Daisy nodded as she stood up. She turned and quickly moved towards the door, eager to get out.

'Oh and Daisy.' She stopped, mid-stride. Shit, what now? Turned back around. 'If you should come across anything that's, let's just say, "interesting", you will bring it to me, won't you?'

His statement startled her. 'What do you mean "interesting"? Charlie was a straight-up type of guy . . .'

But before she could finish, they were interrupted by a knock on the door. It opened to reveal Randal's PA in the doorway. The woman was a young kitten, just the way Randal liked them. 'I'm sorry to interrupt . . .'

'This had better be good, my girl.'

'There are two men to see Mr Hopkirk.' Her plucked eyebrows shot up. 'Two policemen.'

Three

'Welcome, ladies! But I'm afraid you've heard wrong. The streets of London aren't paved with gold. They're paved with bloody needles and old condoms . . .'

The terrified group of eight women huddled together as they knelt on the dirty floor. They were in the basement of a Victorian terrace around the back of Whitechapel station, where the prostitutes and junkies picked up their punters and fixes day and night. And it wasn't the dank smell that terrified the women. It wasn't the narrow confines of the room. It wasn't the tough muscular man and brassy-looking woman who stood on either side of the locked door. It was the woman who stood towering over them. And the unforgiving knife she held in her hand.

And they were right to feel shit scared. Wised-up Londoners belted in the opposite direction when confronted by forty-two-year-old Stella King. She bossed the gang that was usually described in the local papers as 'well known to the police'. She stood six foot in her heels, with blond shoulder-length hair that bounced off her shoulders when she got really pissed off, and a face that she was the last to admit had seen enough nip and tuck over the years. Her densely powdered skin set her face into a frosty, icy mask. But her light grey eyes had a little spark, so people who didn't know her too well took her to have a kind heart. Stella King hadn't had a kind heart since she was fourteen years old.

Her heavily painted, cherry-red lips spread into an easy smile as she watched the women's reaction. A knife was a knife in any language. The women had been unloaded from the van a few minutes ago, a shipment of illegals from the Ukraine. They had left their country, having paid through the nose, thinking they were on their way to jobs as dancers in London. Only they'd been misinformed. As soon as they arrived, two men had escorted them to the basement in Whitechapel. A couple had to be roughed up along the way when they started making noise. Now they realised that it wasn't the men who controlled their future, but Stella and her knife.

Without speaking Stella leant down and grabbed the nearest woman by her ponytail. The woman screamed as she was yanked to her feet. Stella twisted her around to face the group. With easy, cutting motions she used the blade to tear through the woman's blouse. The woman trembled as the knife cut through her flimsy bra. Soon her naked breast quivered for all to see. The woman sobbed when Stella placed the blade under her nipple. Without a flicker of emotion Stella turned her head to the side and with a quick nod motioned for the woman standing with the man near the door. Tatiana, who had been one of Stella's girls for over a year now, came forward.

Stella tightened her hand on the captive woman's hair and spoke in that gravelly voice that most people never forgot once they heard it. 'I learnt this trick from a pimp I worked for when I was about your age.' Tatiana translated her words into Ukrainian. She was one of Stella's girls from her main brothel in Finsbury Park. She'd been in the terrified woman's position once. Knew the score. She kept the emotion pinned back as she repeated Stella's words.

'He showed me once that it don't take much to hack a nipple off. See it ain't got any bone. He had this girl by her throat on the floor, just like where you are now. Took out this fucking wicked looking blade. You wanna know how many cuts it took to take it off?' She stopped, letting her words settle over the women like poisonous gas. 'Three.'

She shoved the sharp steel into the woman's skin. Not too far, just enough so that a thin line of blood began to form. The woman groaned in pain. 'Now, I don't do that to my girls. I look after them. That's why you've gotta count yourself lucky that you're under my wing now.' Her voice grew harder. 'But my wing don't come cheap. And that means that things could go either way. You can either end up dead, sliced up, floating down Father Thames – or you can do an honest day's collar in one of my high-class houses of entertainment in this fair city. Subject to a licence fee, of course. We British are into free enterprise, not that clapped-out Communism you're used to.'

As the Ukrainian translation rang across the room some of the woman began to weep.

'Now the men who come to my houses expect to find nice young ladies who are more than happy to show them a good time. Don't forget you can't go nowhere because I've got your passports. But if you do the proverbial and go to the cops I will find you and cut your tongue out with my little friend here and you won't be speaking to no one again in your life. So it's simple: you talk, you're dead.'

Abruptly she let the woman go. As the sobbing woman fell back in amongst the other women the door flew open. Another man, his leather jacket flapping around him, stepped into the room.

Stella's mouth twisted as she stared at her twenty-two-year-old son Tommy. Typical Tommy, didn't even apologise for being friggin' late. He was a few inches shorter than her, with closely cropped brown hair, a tattoo of a black and white piano on his neck and a slim, sullen face that most women found good-looking. It was only when people got to know him better they saw the brutal side of his nature. He was a dead ringer for her old man, Stevie 'Crazy' King. The man who'd run the King empire with an iron grip and even tighter fist at home. Together she and Stevie had grown the family business from a van-load of toms, giving men a grope at their fantasies in dark alleys and cars, to one that dealt drugs, trafficked people and any of the other crimes on the cops' top-ten list of what not to do with your life. Then the stupid bastard had gone and got himself knifed to death by some tart he was seeing on the side. Of course Stella had known about the other women, but she was the one he took down the aisle, his number one, and after the nightmare of her childhood that had been good enough. Besides, when he was pawing other women, he wasn't pawing her.

She gave Tommy the once-over and mentally shook her head. He wasn't a patch on her Stevie. Both Tommy and her daughter Jo-Jo were a sorry lot. They had brought enough grief to her door to last a lifetime. Then she remembered another little girl with piercing blue eyes . . . She shook the image from her mind because it was a time in her life she'd fought long and hard to forget.

'I hope you ain't been sniffing around those posh birds again?' Stella bit out. 'I've warned you about that. You fuck up again I ain't clearing up the mess for you this time.'

Tommy had the grace to look away from his mum. He'd steered clear of posh birds for a few years now, but Stella was continually reminding him of how close he had come to going down for murder. The last bit of posh he'd slept with had disappeared off the face of the earth. He'd only meant to go out with the girl, do the usual partying and snorting the night away on coke and sex. But somehow the girl had ended up with a broken neck. That's just how it got with him sometimes, totally out of control, no idea what he was doing until it was too late. The big mistake he'd made was not checking out who the girl was before. She'd turned out to be the only daughter of some company director with friends at the top of the Met police, out for a night on the razzle looking to see what the wild side of town had to offer. So with her being from a nice family and everything, the police were very interested when she didn't come home. If a bird from down their street hadn't come home, the police would have one of their dogs to look into it. Stella had cleaned the mess up and muddied the water, as usual, and had the body disposed of in a chemical plant out Canvey way, with all traces of Tommy removed. Everyone knew who'd done it. But the cops hadn't been able to prove a thing. And since then they'd vowed to take Stella and her crew down. Mind you she still had a few influential cop associates, who still visited her numerous brothels to get their tackles-tickled.

'I ain't too late to try one of them out?' Tommy finally said, looking over at the women, his tongue flicking against his bottom lip.

Stella balled her hands and shoved them onto her hips. 'You know what the going rate is, Tommy. If you've got that in your pocket, next to your stash of Charlie, you can have a pop.'

Tommy curled his lip. 'Fuck. You.'

'Watch your mouth around your mum, son,' the other man near the door said, his voice low and menacing.

He stepped in front of Tommy, and got right into his face. Fifty-three year old Billy had been Stevie King's right-hand man and now he was Stella's. Built like a heavyweight boxer, with a bruiser's face that showed every hard knock experience he'd ever had, he took his job seriously. Very seriously. If anyone tried to get to Stella they had to come through him first. And that included her kids.

'Calm down, Granddad, I'm family. Are you?' Tommy sneered.

'Shut up, Tommy,' Stella ordered.

She turned back to the women. Looked them over. She pointed at two of the women. One at the front and one in the middle. Two of the prettiest women there. 'I want those two in my place in Finsbury Park. Divide the others between the houses in Bow, Spitalfields and Leyton.'

Tatiana nodded. Stella turned back to Tommy. 'Stay here and help her sort this out. And don't, for fuck's sake, do anything stupid. Billy we're out of here,' she said, already moving for the door.

Once inside Stella's four-wheel drive, Billy drove them through London's hectic streets. Towards her headquarters in her brothel in Finsbury Park. Stella slipped her hand under her blouse and touched her breast. The one with the nipple that had been hacked from her body when she was seventeen years old. Mind you, that was nothing compared to the pain she'd felt every time her mum had demanded she 'entertain' some dirty geezer in the bedroom of their flat on the Caxton estate when she was fourteen years old.

Screw you, Mum, Tommy thought as he did one of the women up against the wall. If she found out about the bit of posh he'd met earlier she'd bitch slap him until his head was ringing like the sound of Bow Bells.

*   *   *

'I understand you're here to see Mr Hopkirk?' Daisy greeted the two policemen who sat on the grey sofa near Charlie's PA's desk. Daisy had volunteered to speak to them instead of Randal as her way of showing the firm's remaining senior partner that she was serious about taking care of the last of Charlie's affairs.

They sprang to their feet.

'Detective Sergeant Clarke,' the shorter of the two men introduced himself. He was stocky, with a sweaty face attached to a balding head, with one too many pounds sloshing around his middle and tiny purple veins on his nose that said he liked a jar after clocking off every night.

'Detective Inspector Johnson,' the other detective said. He was tall, black, wore a neat fitting suit over a well-kept body and a face that was probably the same age as his partner but looked years younger. Daisy noticed that, unlike his partner, he wore a ring on his wedding finger.

'I'm really sorry, but Charlie . . . I mean, Mr Hopkirk, won't be taking any appointments today.'

The two detectives looked at each other. Looked back at her.

DS Clarke shuffled slightly forward, his face splashing with waves of red. 'We're on urgent police business, Miss, so if you just tell us . . .'

'Unfortunately . . .' Daisy gulped. Shit this was hard to say. 'Mr Hopkirk passed away earlier today.'

'*What?*' Clarke's voice rose in disbelief, the force of his words making his balding head rear back.

'What happened?' Johnson cut in, his voice way calmer than his partner's.

Daisy quickly explained, then added, 'Maybe I can help you instead. If you tell me which case you wanted to see him about maybe I can find the paperwork . . .'

'No need for that.' Johnson held up his hand. 'We're really sorry to hear about the firm's loss. We'll be in touch.'

Before she could say another word they walked off. She watched them go, with a puzzled look on her face at the speed with which they were moving. Then a voice beside her asked, 'Did you find out what happened to Charlie?'

She turned to find Angel. Daisy sighed. She was getting tired of explaining what had happened.

As if reading her thoughts the other woman continued, 'Why don't we have a couple of lattes at that Italian place around the corner and you can tell me all about it?'

Daisy shook her hair back. 'Randal wants me to go through Charlie's things. I should . . .'

Angel placed her finger on her friend's mouth. 'Sh. Sh. Sh. I'm taking you out.'

Angel's finger dropped away. Daisy noticed the smile playing at the other woman's lips. 'You've got that I've-met-a-tasty-bit-of-male look on your face.'

Angel just smiled and hooked her arm into Daisy's.

As they walked Daisy whispered, 'Randal said something really strange to me. He said that when I look through Charlie's things if I should find anything "interesting" I should let him know . . .'

'Bitch. Bastard. Bitch. Bastard. Bitch.'

Detective Inspector Johnson cursed as he beat the living shit out of his steering wheel with his fists. He sat next to Clarke in their car parked in a side street two minutes' drive from the law firm.

As Johnson turned the air as blue as a serge suit, Clarke pulled out a hip flask of whisky from his breast pocket. Took a double shot. They'd been partners back in the old days, starting out as PC Plods at the now defunct Bethnal Green station. The days when it was usual practice to get a confession by banging a suspect's head against a cell door. Both men had prided themselves on never being part of the bully-boy-brigade. They were cops who took their vow to uphold the law seriously. Until that night twenty years ago . . .

'If only we'd got here a day sooner,' Johnson seethed, as he examined his bruised hands.

'Yeah, and if my auntie had balls she'd be my uncle. So let's not worry about the "ifs".'

'So what are we going to do now?'

'Well, let me think . . .' Clarke replied sarcastically. 'Why don't we go down the morgue and slap Charlie Hopkirk's corpse around until he sees sense and comes back to life.' He held up his hip flask and gazed into it.

Johnson slapped the flask out of his hand, and it landed in Clarke's lap. 'You're being very unprofessional – and we're professionals remember?'

'Professional? May I remind you that we may end up kipping on Charlie's slab if we don't find it.'

Silence descended as they both thought about what *it* was. Charlie Hopkirk had something that could put them both in the slammer slumming it with criminals they'd put inside.

'Anyway,' Clarke started. He picked up the bottle and placed it back in its hiding place. 'It ain't just down to us. If we go down so does our "friend".' The word friend was soaked in sarcasm.

Johnson wiped his hand over his mouth. Pulled out his mobile and punched some numbers into it. Before he could utter a word the voice on the other end of the line calmly asked him, 'Did you get it?'

Johnson shook his head. 'No. And you know why? Charlie Hopkirk has gone and kicked the bucket.'

'When?'

'Apparently he dropped dead on a squash court early this morning.'

'His ticker must have had a double fault . . .' Clarke sniggered.

Johnson shot him an evil look. Turned his attention back to the phone. 'What do we do next?'

There was no reply for a few seconds. Then, 'We meet. Tonight on the South Bank. In the meantime I'm going to find out as much about Charlie's Hopkirk's affairs as possible.'

The line went dead. Johnson looked at the mobile for a while and then shoved it back into his pocket. Without any warning he twisted around and grabbed Clarke by the front of his ill-fitting jacket. Rammed him into his seat.

His voice was tense as he inhaled the booze fumes coming off Clarke's sharp, erratic breaths. 'I've come a long way since that night twenty years ago. I don't know if you've noticed, but it ain't easy for people with my colour skin to get doors to open in Her Majesty's police service. I'm what they call a fucking role model. I'm the Met's fucking poster boy for recruiting more ethnic minorities. And you know something? I like being a role model and I want to keep it that way. So while me and you are handcuffed back together again, you knock the sauce on the head. Keep that,' he tapped Clarke in the temple, 'clear. I've come too far to let an unfortunate incident from 1990 fuck up my life.'

'You ever wish we hadn't done it?' Clarke's voice was quiet and calm, just like the days before he found refuge in a bottle of booze. Johnson gazed at his former partner, knowing that Clarke hadn't touched a drop of liquor until that night twenty years ago. None of them had been the same since. You do something bad, for whatever reason, you live your life dreading the day you might have to pay the price. That's what they always said to murderers on those TV appeals – give yourself up, what's the point? Waking up every morning, worrying whether today will be the day, there's a knock on the door? But that wasn't going to happen to him, no fucking way.

He gently let Clarke go as he vowed, 'I don't know about you, but I'm prepared to do anything to stop it rearing its ugly head again. And that means we need to find it before someone else does.'

Four

She didn't want to do it.

Daisy stood on the threshold of Charlie's office not wanting to take a step further. The room was neat and tidy, not fussy and showy like Randal Curtis's. Surprisingly it was one of the smaller offices on the floor. Daisy smiled as she remembered the first piece of advice Charlie had given her – *'You don't need to be big to show quality.'* It was rectangular with a well-trodden wooden floor and shelves stacked high with files and books. Another door, positioned in the right wall, led to a private bathroom. Daisy's eyes scanned the room and came to rest on the one place you could always find Charlie – at his desk. It was wooden and littered with papers, a phone, a small reading lamp and photos of Charlie's family. She imagined Charlie sitting in the leather chair, sleeves rolled back, smiling and chatting away as if there would always be a tomorrow.

She still couldn't believe that her mentor was gone. Her fingers tightened around the set of keys that Charlie's PA had given her, which gave her access to all his cupboards and drawers. She stepped inside. Closed the door. The first time she'd met Charlie was while she was still at university studying law. The legendary lawyer Bell Dream, her auntie Anna's girlfriend, had introduced them in order to set up a work placement for her at his firm. When Bell let it drop that she'd told Charlie all about Daisy's history she'd become scared silly that Charlie would withdraw his offer. But the opposite had happened, with Charlie declaring that the sins of the father should never be visited on the daughter. After her course had finished Charlie had offered her a job. Charlie had watched her back in the two years she'd been here and the least she could do was to now pack away his things.

She moved towards his desk and stared at the framed family photos. One showed Charlie with his arm slung casually around his twenty-four-year-old daughter Jennifer, who Charlie always claimed was a dead ringer for Daisy.

The door opened making Daisy flick her head up. Charlie's PA stood in the doorway holding a stack of bright red plastic packing boxes in her hand.

'I'll get you more of these tomorrow,' the woman said, tears still glittering in her eyes.

Daisy pressed her lips together as she nodded sadly. *Well, better get to it girl,* she told herself once she was alone again. She put her emotions aside and got on with the job of clearing Charlie's life away. She started on the desk by using the keys to unlock the drawers. She sorted and stacked, two piles: Charlie's personal belongings in the packing crate; anything of the firm's on the desk. Next she approached a locked cabinet next to the window. Charlie's legendary drinks cabinet. She found the correct key in the bunch in her hand and opened it. She smiled when she saw bottles of champagne and other drinks. Charlie certainly knew how to enjoy life – Champagne Charlie, indeed! She closed the cabinet, deciding to leave the booze as Charlie's welcome to whoever next occupied his office. She moved across the room and opened the door to the private bathroom. Small and square, with a surprisingly modern sink, shower unit, wall cabinet and frosted window. The scent of the soap Charlie used hit her. A spiral of memories washed over her. She pushed them away. Shut the door. The air seeping in from the window added a chill to the room. Daisy shivered as she moved towards the steel medicine cabinet on the wall. She caught her sad reflection in its mirrored twin doors before she tried to open them. She tugged hard but they wouldn't budge.

She frowned. Lifted the bunch of keys. Tried the first. No luck. The second. No luck. She tried all of the keys but the lock wouldn't move. She peeped nervously over her shoulder at the door because she wanted to check no one was there to see what she was going to try to do next. She opened her bag. Took out her purse. Took out a credit card. This was a trick she'd learnt from her dad. She slid the edge of the card with ease between the lock, but it didn't work. The doors stayed closed.

She sighed as she stepped back. Briskly she turned and moved out of the room, across the office and opened the main door. She pushed her head out and called across to Charlie's PA, who sat tapping away at her computer.

The woman raised her head. 'Have you got any other keys of Charlie's?'

'No.' Her hands fell away from the keyboard. 'Is there a problem?'

Daisy opened her mouth to start telling the other woman about the cabinet, but she saw how tearful she still looked and clamped her mouth closed.

'It's nothing. We'll get it sorted out after the funeral.'

As soon as the word 'funeral' sprang between them new tears trickled onto the woman's face. Just looking at the other woman's emotions made Daisy feel choked up all over again. She couldn't go through Charlie's things anymore, she felt too upset. She stepped outside. Quietly closed the door. Walked away from Charlie's office. As she shoved the bunch of keys into her pocket, her mind wondered why Charlie would keep his medicine cabinet locked. She stopped abruptly as a terrible thought hit her. What if Charlie had been into some hard drugs? That was nonsense of course. But then it was surprising just how much nonsense some of these respectable middle-aged suits could be into, so what on earth could be inside that cabinet?

Randal Curtis's words rang in her head. *'If you should come across anything that's, let's just say, "interesting", you will bring it to me, won't you?'* Shit, maybe he was right and Charlie did have secrets. No, she wasn't going to allow anything to sully Charlie's reputation. Charlie had given her a chance when most wouldn't have. He'd hidden the fact that she was Frankie Sullivan's daughter. She'd do anything for Charlie. Anything. And that included finding the key to the medicine cabinet before someone else did.

* * *

Deadwood Hotel.

That's what the huge white building was called in Finsbury Park. It advertised itself as an impressive B&B accommodation made up of thirty clean and bright rooms, with twenty-four-hour security and private parking. The other B&Bs and hotels that lined the street offered mainly places of rest for homeless families working their way up the council housing list and recently arrived refugees and asylum seekers. But Deadwood Hotel was different. The only accommodation it offered were to men looking for an appointment with their sexual fantasies for an hour or two.

Stella King stood in the large main room, or the Meet 'n' Greet room as it was called. It was situated at the front of the house, but with discreet light blinds always down to ensure that privacy was the brothel's number one priority. It had pastel coloured walls to create a calm, kick-off-your-shoes-and-chill-out feel, with huge comfy red sofas, a large plasma TV screen mounted on the wall and a bar that served hard liquor and softer refreshments. A black grand piano sat neatly in a corner. It was the room where the clients were introduced to the toms. And currently Stella stared at a group of three women who were huddled, comforting one of the other girls. She looked at them with a miffed expression. If there was one thing she hated it was a woman boo-hooing as if the world was coming to an end. Gave the establishment the wrong atmosphere. The Deadwood was, as far as she was concerned, a top of the range brothel in London town. None of that dark shabby, get your dick in-and-out, hole-in-the-wall type of joint. This was a place where men came to forget the world outside. A place they wanted to come back to again. And again. And again.

And there wouldn't be coming back if they saw girls showing how they actually felt.

'What are you bawling your eyes out for?' The women all looked at her. 'Are you watching the end of *Four Weddings and A Funeral*? For fuck's sake . . .' She slammed the door on her last word, just so the girls knew she wasn't pleased.

The women stepped back. Away from the woman in the middle they had been comforting. Stella was shocked to see that the one blubbing her eyes out was one of her most popular girls. Crystal to the blokes who came through the door, and Belinda to the world outside. Stella stared at her run mascara and red nose.

'The rest of you go and get cracking for later.' The others followed her command quickly and left her alone with the round and curvy Crystal.

Stella plonked herself down by the distressed woman. 'Did your old man find out what you do to top up his dole money?'

Although Stella used illegals from the former Eastern bloc, most of her girls were women who lived regular lives. Who woke the kids up in the morning and took them to school, who did the laundry and the shopping, who tried, well some of them, to study for higher qualifications.

Crystal gave her head a tearful shake.

'So what's all the noise about?' Stella persisted.

Crystal wiped her nose with the back of her hand. 'I've just found out he's dead.'

'Who? Father Christmas? Come on, spit it out.'

'Charlie.'

Stella reared back in her seat. 'Charlie flamin' Hopkirk?'

Crystal nodded. Shocked, Stella just looked at the other woman. Charlie was one of the brothel's most popular clients. Always cheerful and respectful of the girls, he often came for a quick poke and a longer chat. He'd been seeing Crystal for a good three years. But what Crystal and the other girls didn't know was that Stella and Charlie went back a long way. Back to when she was fifteen. The day of her first ruck with Old Bill. She'd been arrested, along with everyone else, inside a brothel that had been so unsavoury that even Stella did her best never to think about it. Once down the nick Charlie had been assigned as her solicitor. Back then she thought most older blokes were just dirty old men. And when she'd met Charlie she'd stuck him inside the same box. But he'd proved her wrong, alright. Got her a minimum fine. Right on the court steps she'd offered to show him a good time as a thank you. He'd laughed and declined, gave her his card and said she should go home to her foster mum. She'd done that but was back on the streets in two weeks flat. When she was arrested the next time she knew just who to call. And that's how it had gone on for years until Charlie had set himself up in partnership in the city.

She hadn't charged Charlie a penny when he first came through her door. It was her quiet nod to him for being there for a young girl when most hadn't given two fucks. Mind you, after that she'd made him pay through the nose like everyone else, just so he understood she was no pushover.

'How did he go?' she asked, slipping out of her memories.

'His heart gave out.'

'His heart? Well, at least that's one organ most of our punters don't have to worry about.' Stella stood up and looked down at Crystal. 'Look, babe, you know the rules, we don't get attached to the sad sods who come through the door do we? Unless they're promising to take you away from all this and prove it by bringing you a large rock and a cheque for your auntie Stella.'

Crystal stood up sniffing. She gave the taller woman a funny look. 'Everyone's dead frightened of you, ain't they? But you're a softie underneath it, ain't ya?'

Stella shot a look back that was so sharp and piercing Crystal thought she'd been stabbed by steel. Stella's next words twisted the knife. 'Oh yeah, I'm a real softie, me. Just ask anyone who's got in my way. They'll tell you, the ones that are still alive anyway. And especially where family's concerned, I'm a regular Nelson Mandela.'

Crystal knew who Stella was talking about straight away. Her daughter Jo-Jo. That had been a bad business, one that those in the know had whispered about for the last couple of years.

'And she was my own flesh and blood. You ain't, so if you know what's good for you, you'll get up those stairs and get that little toosh of yours made up.'

Crystal belted out of the room. Stella's mouth twisted. She hated hearing anyone talk about Jo-Jo, hated even the most oblique references to her daughter. Everyone knew never to mention that name in her presence. She'd done everything for that girl and what had she done time and time again? Spat in her face. Bitch. She'd overstepped the mark the last time. She'd been gone for two years and could stay gone. Why hadn't she been like that other little girl who'd been in Stella's life? Black-haired and blue-eyed. A real cutie. And who did as she was told.

Stella closed her eyes and soaked in the memories for just a few seconds.

Her eyes snapped open. She flicked her hair off her shoulders as she made her way to the door. Soon she was marching across the lightly lit hallway towards the receptionist's desk. The desk was where all the money and bookings changed hands and where the new clients were told that house rule number one was to treat the girls with maximum respect. Abusing them was the management's job. She passed the ATM which she'd had installed in case clients needed extra cash and looked over at the desk. Molly, the young receptionist, was laughing loudly with Clive, one of the security men who also drove the courtesy Mercedes if wealthy clients needed picking up and dropping off. Seeing her approach, Clive straightened up and nodded silently at Stella and moved back to his chair near the front door.

'Shame about old Charlie boy,' Molly whispered to Stella.

'I want you to order a mega bunch of flowers and send them to Charlie's widow.'

'What shall I have put on the card?'

Stella mulled over the question. 'Put . . . *He was one of the best. From an old friend.*'

'Talking about flowers . . .' Molly started as her hand reached below the desk. She pulled out a simple bunch of red carnations. She said nothing as she handed them to Stella. The flowers were delivered twice weekly as regular as clockwork. Stella made her way up the stairs towards her office. Her hand caressed every petal as she thought of the grave she always put them on. The grave of the only man she'd ever loved.

Five

'Rumour has it that Charlie Hopkirk kept a safe-deposit box.'

'So what? I've got a safe-deposit box.'

'Yes, but I expect you keep sandwiches and crisps in yours. Charlie Hopkirk may have kept rather more serious and incriminating material in his. Do you see where I'm going with this, gentlemen?'

Clarke and Johnson considered the words spoken by the person opposite them. They were seated on a bench by the river on the South Bank later that evening. The Thames shifted in front of them, dark and moody, while high-energy music played behind on a ghetto blaster belonging to youths showing off their skateboarding moves.

'We can't proceed on a rumour,' Johnson snapped.

'Well it's more than a rumour really,' the person opposite him and Clarke answered. 'Apparently during that big robbery case last year, the leader of the gang's phone was being tapped. He mentioned that his solicitor kept sensitive documents in a deposit box . . .'

'And his brief was Charlie Hopkirk,' Clarke finished quietly.

'In the end the investigation found all the evidence they needed without requesting to see inside Hopkirk's box.'

'We're fucked,' Clarke responded harshly. 'If this all comes out I'll lose my pension.' He pulled out a flask and took a deep drink.

The other person looked at him with open disgust. The three of them went back years. The person opposite had gone on to greater and bigger things and he'd, well, he'd just sunk deeper and deeper into the hole the alcohol had dug in his life.

'How do you know he kept it in this safe-deposit box?' Johnson asked.

'I don't for sure but I do know that Charlie was no fool. He wouldn't have kept anything of a sensitive nature just lying around. That's why he lasted so long in the game because he knew how to play it. He wouldn't have kept it at home as it could put his family in danger; keeping it in the office runs the risk of someone stumbling across it. Really, it's a simple case of elimination. A safe-deposit box is the simplest solution. Our job is to find it before anyone else does. The deposit box might be mentioned in his will, which means his wife could get it. We can't afford for that to happen.'

Johnson leant forward. 'So what do you suggest we do?'

'First we need to find out where he kept the information about the box. It's either going to be somewhere safe in his office or at his home.'

'We can't just go stomping off into his office . . .' Clarke cut in.

'Just listen. Someone in his firm will have been given the task of packing his personal effects away. Most probably his PA, but we can't make that assumption. That's going to be my job to find out. I've got friends inside the building and I'll get them on the case straight away. In the meantime I want both of you to spin his drum.'

Johnson snorted. 'And how the fuck are we going to do that?'

'Easy. You get into his home at a time when no one's around.'

'Now he's dead his house is going to be swarming with people holding his grieving widow's hand. That's going to be morning, noon and bloody night.'

'No it isn't. There's going to be one time when no one will be around.'

'When?'

'When Charlie Hopkirk's being lowered into the ground, being laid to rest.'

*   *   *

For the first time in ages Daisy thought about popping one of her happy pills. She sighed as she leant heavily against the back of the lift taking her to the second floor where her apartment was located and absently rubbed her fingers over the large, gold bracelet on her left wrist. She looked down at the bracelets that rested on both her wrists that she rarely took off. They were made of thick, pale gold with a large golden daisy moulded on the top. They were a gift from Jackie, her adoptive mum, when she was fifteen years old. Instantly her mind shot back to that dreadful night, the first night she'd stayed with Jackie. The night when the pain of losing her dad had become unbearable. The doctor had prescribed anti-depressants and therapy. Jackie had been happy for her to do the second, but not the pills. Jackie hated any types of drugs. But Daisy had taken the pills just to get through each day. That was until the weird things they did to her mind got too much. She started hallu-cinating and seeing her dad, having those painful dreams about a little girl . . . Now she only took them when she was really stressed out, and boy had Charlie's death knocked her for six. No, she shook her head, she wasn't going to take them. She could get through this without them. All she had to do was get through Charlie's funeral in four days' time and find what was inside his medicine cabinet.

The lift opened and wearily she stepped into the second floor of Nutmeg Wharf in East London's fashionable dockland district of Wapping. Perched on the edge of the river it was an immaculately maintained, sprawling, four-storey former warehouse built of red brick, with an uninterrupted view of the river. Disused and aban-doned in the 1970s, it became a hang out for squatters, but then it was taken over by developers at the height of the property bubble, and now it was a place that the offspring of many generations of families that had grown up in Wapping couldn't afford. Jackie had purchased the apartment for her on her twenty-first birthday. Where Jackie got that kind of dough Daisy would never know.

She pushed her key into the door. Stepped inside. Instantly froze because the light in the hallway was on. She hadn't left the light on. Then she heard a noise in the kitchen. Someone was in her home. *Shit.* She didn't need this after the day she'd had.

She had two options – either get out of there and find help or stay and defend her property. It was a no-brainer. Frankie Sullivan had taught her everything she needed to know about fighting. He'd made sure that his daughter could drop kick a man the other side of Christmas by the time she was thirteen; punch someone's lights out in two quick moves by the time she was fourteen; put a man down with a bullet by the time she was fifteen. Frankie Sullivan had made sure that his little girl was ready for all those little things that life throws at you.

She kicked off her heels. Moved forward, softly on the balls of her feet. She reached the lounge doorway the same time a tall body popped out of nowhere. She didn't hesitate. Flicked her foot straight into a forward kick. Caught the intruder in the stomach. With a groan the person crashed to the floor. Daisy rushed forward. Stopped dead in her tracks when she realised who it was.

'Jerome!' Her fingers fluttered just over the beauty spot above her lip. 'Shit. Sorry.' Quickly she crouched down beside her boyfriend who looked at her with pain in his eyes. 'I didn't know it was you.' She had given Jerome the spare key to her flat only weeks before, and she was still unused to the fact that he would let himself in without arranging it with her first.

'"Hi honey, I'm home" would have done,' he said weakly as he struggled into a sitting position.

She winced at that. 'Sorry. I'd forgotten you were coming around tonight,' she said as she helped him to his feet.

'Where did you learn to do that?'

'From my–' Abruptly she stopped and changed tack. 'My self-defence classes. There was a string of attacks on girls when I was at college. The students' union organised them,' she finished weakly, casting her eyes down so he wouldn't see her lie.

'That's a relief, I was just wondering what on earth they taught you in the Girl Guides.' His hands caressed her face as he gently smiled. 'I thought you could do with some TLC after hearing about Charlie.'

That's what she loved about Jerome, he always knew what to do to make her feel safe and secure. Made her realise that the reality of having her own family was in her reach.

'I love you,' she said simply.

'Good.' His fingers continued to feather her skin. 'Because I'm planning to stay with you for the rest of your life.'

A thrill ran through her at his words. Maybe, just maybe he was going to ask her to . . . *Don't get ahead of yourself, girl*, she warned herself. He might not mean marriage and babies, he might just be chatting away like men do when they want to protect their woman. But she wasn't like the other women she knew. She hadn't been the same since the day the kind-faced policewoman had told her the devastating news that her dad wasn't coming home. Shot to death on a summer afternoon when she was fifteen years old. She hadn't seen her real mum since she was four years old, could pass her on the street without recognising her. The only thing that had saved her from ending up in the care system was being adopted by Jackie Jarvis, the woman her dad had appointed her guardian. Even though Jackie had done a terrific job of bringing her into adulthood, Daisy had always felt like an orphan. No mum. No dad. That's why she worked 24/7 to prove she was the best at her job because it was her gateway to having a decent family life when the time came. And she couldn't have asked God for a better man to send her than the gorgeous man standing in front of her. She knew that one day that she'd have to level with him and tell him all about her dad, but not yet.

'I've cooked your favourite,' Jerome said leading her towards the lounge. He moved to the stereo and put on the soundtrack of the classic fifties' musical, *Calamity Jane*, that Daisy loved. Doris Day's regretful, haunting voice singing about a 'Secret Love' pulsed around her. This was the room she loved the best because she'd modelled it on the main room of Calamity Jane's cabin in the movie. A blindingly bright yellow door with the names *Calam and Daisy* printed in fancy black, fancy script. Exposed brick-work on all four walls and wired-brushed oak floors. The fabric of the white curtains, dotted with brightly coloured flowers, also covered the long soft, sofa. The warmth in the room came from the artificial log fire and the golden light that seeped from the old-fashioned lamps fixed to the walls. Daisy even pretended that the river Thames outside was just like the creek that was at the bottom of Calamity's cabin. Scattered around the room were photos of her adoptive family. But there were none of her dad.

Her face lit up with delight when she saw the small dining table positioned on the open-air balcony that looked out across the river. Laughing, they walked hand-in-hand outside and stared at her favourite dish: bangers and mash. Jerome had prepared something completely different for himself because he didn't care for bangers and mash. But she'd get him into it one day.

Later they were back inside, snuggled in each other's arms on the sofa as they watched the final minutes of *Calamity Jane*. It didn't matter how many times she watched this film, it always brought a smile to her face. Tough gal gets her man. Just like she'd got hers. She pressed a few kisses against Jerome's jaw line.

As his arms tightened in appreciation around her he asked, 'Did you have a chance to look through Charlie's things?'

She cuddled deeper into his side as she thought about the locked medicine cabinet. 'I started but I couldn't face it.'

'If you find anything to do with this class-action case let me know. He said he had some information on a character called Maxwell Henley.'

'Who?'

'He was the leader of Woodbridge Council, so as far as my claimants are concerned the buck stops with him about what happened in all those care homes.'

Daisy sighed. 'I don't want to talk about work anymore.' But even as she said the words an uneasy feeling crawled in her stomach. She knew she had to get the key that opened Charlie's medicine cabinet.

A boat ride away, up the river, in a penthouse in London Bridge, Angel wasn't being any angel. She pulled down the red, satin straps of her bra with one hand as she stood on top of an electric blue grand piano. The tune 'Big Spender' pumped from the piano as the man's fingers glided across its black and white keys. He looked up her and smiled, passion flaring in his eyes, as his fingers didn't miss a beat. Angel shot him a wicked grin as she continued her striptease. Soon she stood only in her suspenders and eye-blinding pink high heels. She tossed back the remaining champagne in her glass. Threw the empty glass across the room. Giggled as it smashed into the wall next to a ridiculously huge painting of a horse. Shit, she was high as a fucking out-of-control balloon, which had less to do with the coke she'd snorted earlier than with the man who played the piano. A man she'd met only hours before at the court-house. But if there was one thing that Angel loved it was danger. And she knew that this man was dangerous. Rough, from the other side of the tracks, with gangster oozing from every pore of his tough body. She couldn't resist it when he'd whispered in her ear 'Meet me at eight, Merchant's Quay.'

He hadn't disappointed her. Coke and sex, sex and coke. Bloody hell, he'd blown her mind with the lethal combination. And now she posed, almost in her birthday suit, excitement rumbling under her bold boobs, waiting for his next move.

Abruptly his fingers ceased moving. The music stopped. He stood up. Began to undress. She knew what he wanted her to do. She slid down until she was positioned on her back on the piano. He scrambled up next to her. She saw the small, transparent bag of coke he held in his hand. He turned the bag upside down and sprinkled the coke around her belly button. Then he dipped his head and began to lick the drug slowly and slickly from her body. The sensation of his tongue against her skin made her sigh as she moved her hips. She gripped his hair with her hands. Pulled his head up.

Her question was thick and hoarse with desire. 'What's your name?' He knew who she was, what she did for a living. That was her only problem with coke, it made her chat away like there was no tomorrow. But he'd been more cagey.

He grinned back at her, lips smeared with cocaine. 'Tommy.'

Six

Three days later, on a cool, blustery Thursday morning, Clarke and Johnson watched the grieving widow and the funeral procession leave the detached house in Hampstead. The house was big, red bricked, raised high over three floors and with a solitary aspect that suited Clarke and Johnson fine because they didn't need anyone beaking around while they went about their business. They were parked up on the opposite side of the street under a large tree with sprawling branches that cast massive shadows over their car in the gloomy, grey morning light.

They gave it one minute. Two. On the third they looked at each other. Nodded and then pulled down their hoodies like two South Bank skateboarders. Johnson asked, 'Have you got your warrant card?'

'Yes.'

'Good. We can flash it if anyone disturbs us.'

They gazed at each other again. Nodded once more. Then eased out of the car. Heads down they ran towards the side of the house. They stopped beside a white box, positioned on the brickwork underneath a slim, stained-glass window that held the wires to the security system. Johnson pulled out a pocket-knife. He flicked the steel blade out. Jammed it inside the box and wedged it open. He lowered his head and stared at the criss-cross of wires. Gently he pinched one of the wires and eased it towards him. With a single cut he disabled the system,

'The silly sod should have got himself a decent system. He could have asked me, I'm a security consultant on my days off these days.'

'Maybe he wasn't expecting the police to break in. People are funny like that.'

He tilted his face towards Clarke. Then at the large black fence that led to the back of the house. Clarke moved towards the fence, but was stopped by Johnson's irritated command.

'I'd better do it. All that booze you've downed over the years has turned you into a total slob. If you climb that you'll most probably have a heart attack on the other side, the local coronary unit will start wanting overtime. And how tasteless would that be when the mourners came back and find another stiff in the back garden?'

Clarke showed him the finger. Johnson ignored him as he shoved the knife back in his pocket and then scaled the fence. Less than thirty seconds later he was on the other side.

'Meet me at the front in one minute. If I ain't there, get the fuck out of here.'

Sweating like a pig Clarke leant up against the wall. Took out his hip flask. Pulled off his hood. Greedily swallowed the throat-burning booze. He clasped the flask to his chest as his heart thundered inside his unfit body. He didn't want to be here. If he had his way he'd have turned his back and walked away. He took a few calming breaths and then made his way to the front of the house. Johnson was already in the open doorway. He quickly ushered Clarke inside the grand looking hallway.

'What took you so fucking long?'

'You said a minute—'

'It's two minutes over.' Suddenly he stopped as he leant closer to Clarke and sniffed. 'You've been at the sauce again. If we fuck this up because of you . . .'

'I thought you were in a hurry? But you've got time to give me a health and safety lecture? You worry about his safe-deposit box, not my liquor intake.'

Johnson checked his watch. 'We're in here twenty minutes tops. I need to be back at base because I've got a meeting to go to. I'll do upstairs, you do down here.'

Johnson followed his words by flying upstairs. Clarke pushed the first door he came to. He wasn't sure what room it was but it was long, with fancy artwork on the wall, and French doors leading to the garden. A long table, with a pretty tablecloth was laid out with food and refreshments for the wake. He reached the table. Picked up a cracker with cheese and a pink sauce he didn't like the look of. Popped it in his mouth anyway. Not bad, he decided as he munched. Using his arm he savagely knocked over the vase in the middle of the table. Flowers spilt across the table, along with a card that read: *He was one of the best. From an old friend.*

'Earth to earth. Ashes to ashes. Dust to dust.'

Daisy stood between Jerome and Angel, under darkening clouds, with the other mourners around Charlie's graveside. Charlie, being the popular guy he was, had a great turn out. Opposite Daisy, Charlie's widow, Priscilla, stood sniffing, with a handkerchief pressed to her nose, leaning heavily on her daughter Jennifer. The daughter Charlie had often told Daisy she reminded him of. Sure, they had the same-shaped face, were of a similar height and age, but Jennifer Hopkirk had her blond hair cut in a bob while Daisy's hair was black and hit her shoulders. On Priscilla's right side stood Randal Curtis with his arm around her. Daisy held back her own tears as she remembered another funeral at this cemetery. Frankie Sullivan's. That funeral had been big as well. If there was one thing cockney gangsters enjoyed more than killing each other, it was burying each other. The road leading to the grave had been jammed with Mercs, Jags, Bob Marleys and other flash motors that had brought men who were decked out like Italian football managers. And the flowers. She'd never forget the flowers. Huge wreaths, with flowers arranged into words like The Face, The Don. The massive one that had been shaped into a double barrel shotgun. That must've pissed off the cops who'd gathered on the other side of the graveyard.

'Come on.' Jerome's whisper interrupted her thoughts, bringing her back to the present.

He took her hand as he steered her away. As she moved she noticed a woman wearing a distinctive uniform, with a flat-brimmed cap under her arm, talking to Charlie's widow. She was tall, somewhere between fifty to fifty-five, with deep black hair that framed her long face in a short cropped layered style, with arched eyebrows and a face that drew you to its toughness. She wore no make-up. No jewellery. Not even a wedding ring.

'Who's that?' she whispered.

Jerome looked over. 'Barbara Benton. Or "Basher Babs", as she's known at the Yard.'

'The Yard?' Daisy looked back at Jerome.

'Yeah – you know – New Scotland Yard. She's the deputy commissioner. And they're saying that when the commissioner steps down next week she's going to be named as his successor at a gala dinner at City Hall. She'll be the first police chief to wear women's clothes since J Edgar Hoover.'

A sad smile crept across Daisy's face as an image of the long dead former head of the FBI and the rumours he liked to doll himself up in women's clothes. 'Charlie knew everyone didn't he?'

'You find anything yet to do with this Maxwell Henley and the class action while you were packing up his stuff?'

Honestly, Jerome, this isn't the time or place, Daisy almost said, but she checked herself. Jerome was just doing his job, and Charlie would want to know that he was trying to get justice for victims in the Woodbridge abuse case. An image of Charlie's medicine cabinet loomed unbidden in her mind. She still hadn't found the key to it. Still didn't know what was inside. Maybe she should tell Jerome about the medicine cabinet? As she opened her mouth Jerome's mobile pinged in his pocket. He pulled it out and swivelled away from her as he read the text message. She clamped her lips tight together. No, she wasn't going to tell him about the medicine cabinet. He had enough on his plate.

He twisted back around when he finished his call and said, 'We should go.'

The wind flicked up, shooting a surprisingly cold pulse of air over Daisy. As she crossed her arms over her black coat her eyes spanned the distance. Spanned over the other graves. Her chill increased and it had nothing to do with the wind.

Eyes still firmly fixed on the distance she said, 'I'll see you back at the car. I've just got something I need to do.'

She left him and strode purposely for a few minutes to a part of the cemetery where the graves were older. A wind chime hanging from a tree tinkled in the cold summer breeze as she nodded briefly to a tall woman she passed as she zigzagged through the graves. She stopped when she found the grave she was after. A grave she hadn't visited in nine years. Not because she hadn't wanted to but because it was so painful. Black marble, gold writing.

FRANKIE SULLIVAN
A HARD MAN ON EARTH
AN EVEN HARDER ONE IN HEAVEN

She'd chosen those words herself. She knew her dad would have approved.

The grave lay next to Frankie's mum. When she was young he would take her to visit his mum's resting place. It was only years later she learnt that he hated his mum with a vengeance. She opened her bag and pulled out a single red rose. She got ready to crouch down but froze when she looked down. When she saw what was on his grave. Fresh carnations organised in a tidy arrangement, attached was a card: *You're always in my thoughts big guy, xx.*

Someone else hadn't forgotten her father either. But she couldn't think who that might be. Her dad didn't have many close mates, the only two he'd kept close by his side had gone the same way as him and all his women were long gone once the will had been read. It should've been her tending his grave.

'Love you, Dad.'

As the wind chime sang its lonely song in the distance she laid the rose tenderly on his grave.

The blast of the car horn made Daisy jump. She turned to find Jerome staring at her through the open window of his metallic-silver sports car. She turned her back on her dad and made her way towards Jerome. Got into the car.

'You can't honk your horn in a graveyard. It's disrespectful.'

'Why not? You can't wake the dead . . .'

A ripple of pain shot through Daisy. When she was fifteen that's all she'd wished for.

'Whose grave was that?' Jerome asked as he drove the car forward.

Daisy bowed her head. This was her moment to tell Jerome about her dad. *Go on, do it. Do it.* But she couldn't. 'No one, really. Just someone I once knew.' She lifted her head and pulled down the make-up mirror. She checked out her face. She looked like what she felt, absolute crap. Pasty, blotchy skin and bloodshot blue eyes. Even her fading lipstick looked like it wanted to run a mile from her face.

They didn't talk for the rest of the journey as they followed the procession back to Hampstead. Less than half an hour later they pulled into the huge driveway of Charlie's home. Jerome pulled the car to a stop as Daisy watched Charlie's wife get out of her car, supported by her daughter. They walked slowly towards the house. Daisy stepped out of the car. Took a huge breath. She couldn't wait for this day to be over. As she moved towards the house a scream came from inside. Daisy sprinted across the driveway. Ran inside the house. What she found made her gasp.

Seven

Thirty-three-year-old Ricky Smart wasn't sure who threw the first punch in Belmarsh Prison's shower block, but he made sure that the next one came flying courtesy of his fist. He had a face girls had gone gooey-eyed over all of his life. The best blend of his Jamaican and Irish heritage – bronze skin, dark smooth and shaded eyes, full lips that moved from cocky grin to menacing snarl in seconds, a six-two frame topped with a number one cut that kept his hair painted to his skin. He landed an almighty blow on the bridge of the man coming at him like a bull let loose in the street. Blood spurted out of his opponent's nose as he crumpled, groaning loudly, to the concrete floor. One down, one to go, Ricky thought as he eyed up his next opponent.

His eyes skated quickly towards his cellmate, Paul King, who lay prone on the floor clutching his stomach. Ricky had walked into the shower room to find his teenage cellmate receiving the kicking of his life. They'd been sharing a cell since Ricky had been transferred from Brixton prison to Belmarsh two months ago. It didn't take Ricky long to hear the whispers that Paul was connected to one of London's most feared gangland families. Stella King ruled the roost, with her son Tommy close by her side. Paul was Tommy King's cousin on his dad's side. Most of the prisoners feared the Kings, so they stayed well out of Paul's way. But there were those who had close ties to a rival gang and Paul's appearance in Belmarsh was their chance to get even. But Paul just wanted to do his bird quietly and liked talking about his baby son and girlfriend. He was no fighter.

The other man charged. Ricky let him get within a couple of inches, then neatly twisted on the back of his right heel, stepped to the side. As the man staggered towards thin air Ricky grabbed his arm. Twisted it behind his back. Marched him, struggling, towards the wall with the sinks and a single mirror. Ricky gripped his hair, yanking his head back. He whispered, 'Spread the word – anyone touches that lad and it won't just be their remission they're losing, you get me?'

Ricky rammed his head into the mirror. The glass cracked as a single stream of blood poured down it. A noisy blast of pain shot out of the man. But Ricky didn't let him go. Ricky slammed his head into the sink below and let him drop unconscious to the floor. Ricky spun around the same time the other thug got to his feet. The man took one look at the fury on Ricky's brown face, then hightailed it out of the room. He had reason to be scared. Ricky's prison record stated he was inside for GBH of a very aggravated variety.

Ricky walked briskly over to Paul, who still lay on the floor. He crouched down. 'We need to get out of here.'

Paul nodded as he rose shakily to his feet. Ricky gave him a quick once-over, but didn't touch him. In prison, regardless of the situation, you soon learnt that you had to stand on your own two feet. They walked steadily out of the shower area, Ricky moving with his usual swagger, back towards the block. It didn't take them long to bump into one of the screws. A prison officer who all the inmates nicknamed Robocop because he truly believed in the principles of his job.

'Problem, lads?'

Ricky gave him a lazy smile. 'No, sir. You know us prisoners, we can't resist a little bit of handbags now and again.'

The screw gave them a long, penetrating look. He flicked his head to the side indicating that they should hop it. Ricky knew their attackers would keep their mouths shut. The first rule of being inside was to never give anything up to the screws. The two men walked back to the block. Up to their landing. Once they were back in their cell, Paul groaned as he lay on the bottom bunk. Ricky crouched down and pulled up the younger man's prison regulation top. He winced when he saw the purple bruises covering Paul's stomach and rib area.

'You might need to see the quack.'

Paul briskly shook his head. 'I'm alright. Compared to the stuff I used to take from my fuck face step dad, this is a picnic.' He shifted his head so that he gazed straight into Ricky's eyes. 'I owe you one though.'

Ricky didn't answer as he stood back up. He heaved himself up onto the top bunk. Pulled his stash of tobacco and Rizlas from under his pillow. Lay down as he began to make a roll up on his chest. He sprinkled some grass into it, a drug easier to get inside prison than out of it. Four more days and he was out of this human cesspool.

'You got anything lined up when you get out?' Paul asked.

Ricky sank into his pillow. 'Yeah, some people to go and see, a few favours to call in.'

Paul snickered. 'So you've got nothing then?

'I'll manage.'

'I'm sure but in the meantime perhaps I can help you out. I've got a cousin who can always use a guy who's a bit handy. He goes by the name of Tommy King.'

Tommy King. The name hung in the air as tension tightened Ricky's lips. He raised the spliff to his mouth, licked the edges and sealed it. He eased his head up and looked under his pillow. But didn't pull out his matches. Instead he took out a small photo. He eased back down as he gazed at the picture. Ricky finally answered. 'You sure?'

'Yeah. No problem.'

Ricky nodded. That was the great thing about prison; it was so good for networking. His thumb caressed the face of the woman staring at him. A woman who had disappeared twenty years ago. And he knew that only one person had the answers to the questions about what had happened to her. And now his cellie was opening the door that would lead him to this person.

*   *   *

Daisy walked the police officers solemnly to Charlie's front door. They had arrived on the scene soon after Barbara Benton had contacted the nearest station. With the call coming from the deputy commissioner herself, the police had arrived at top speed five minutes later. Daisy closed the door, looked around still reeling at what had happened at Charlie's. Someone had gone through his home like a category 5 hurricane, turning out drawers, cutting through fabric, overturning furniture. The house was such a mess that Charlie's widow had fainted after letting out that single anguished scream.

Daisy made her way back to the sitting room where Priscilla Hopkirk was being comforted by her daughter and Randal Curtis on one side and Barbara Benton on the other. The other mourners had long gone.

Jerome stepped behind Daisy. 'We should go.'

Daisy turned her head halfway towards him. 'You go. I'm going to stay and help tidy up. It's the least I can do for Charlie's wife.'

His fingers caressed her cheek. 'Alright, darling. I'd stay and help, but there's people I need to see about the class-action case.'

After he'd gone Daisy stepped into the room. 'Mrs Hopkirk, why don't I help tidy up?'

The older woman raised bloodshot eyes towards Daisy and sniffed. 'I'd be really grateful. I just can't do this at the moment.'

Barbara Benton stood up. Although Daisy was tall she immediately felt intimidated by this woman's height and power. No wonder she was tipped to be the face of the capital's police force.

'Why don't I help you?' Daisy was surprised by how light and soft her voice was, like her words barely touched the tip of her tongue.

'I can do this on my own. I'm sure you've got more pressing business to take care of,' Daisy responded.

'Not on Charlie's day, I don't. Why don't you do upstairs and I'll sort it out down here.'

It took Daisy over an hour to rearrange the two bathrooms and three of the four bedrooms. The last room she tackled was the master bedroom. Old-fashioned, with its antique furnishings and littered with the loving touches of a couple who had been together for more than thirty odd years. She let out a long sigh as she took in the destruction. The sheets had been pulled from the bed and the mattress slashed. The drawers of the dressing table and the bedside cabinets had been pulled out and their contents lay strewn across the pale, blue carpet. The doors of the built-in wardrobe that stood next to the window with a great view of Hampstead Heath and Highgate village had been flung open and the clothes chucked below.

She started with the drawers. Over half an hour later she was on her knees picking up the last items of clothing. A pair of trousers, jacket and a handful of socks. Crazy patterned socks. Charlie had loved his socks. She bunched them under her arms as she carefully and lovingly placed the trousers and jacket back in the wardrobe. She let her hand smooth over the linen jacket remembering the last time she'd seen Charlie wearing it.

She pulled the top drawer inside the wardrobe. As she threw the socks inside two odd socks, one grass green, the other jet black, tumbled onto the floor. She leant down. Grabbed them. As her fingers closed around the fabric of the green sock she felt something bumpy and hard inside. Curiosity pushed her across the room to sit on the slashed mattress with the sock in her hand. She tipped the sock upside down. A small, silver key fell into her lap. As she picked it up the door swung open.

Eight

Across town the screams echoed around the room as Tommy played Gershwin's 'Rhapsody In Blue' at the piano in his office at his main club in Mile End. The area of Mile End was, some said, divided into two. The posh lot that lived in the grand houses and Georgian squares across from the tube station; and those who dwelt in the housing estates that sprawled on the other side of the Mile End road. Tommy's club, The Pussy Hound, was on the other side of the road.

As the screams continued Tommy shut his eyes and soaked up the drama of the music. He'd been playing the piano since he was eleven years old. It was the only thing that made him calm down, feel human again. The only thing that had made him stop wetting the bed. One of his mum's ladies, a Russian immigrant who needed to top up her music tuition, had taught him between punters. Once Stella realised he had talent for the ol' Joanna she'd paid the prostitute proper money to teach him. The pro had given up lying on her back and Stella, Tommy was sure, hoped that his mood swings would go. She'd been wrong.

Tommy snapped open his eyes and kept playing. 'Bring her here,' he said.

The screaming stopped. A young woman, about Tommy's age, was dragged by two heavyset men towards the piano. The men doubled up as bouncers in the night and Tommy's gorillas in the day. He stopped playing. Rested his fingers lovingly against the keys. Then turned around. He stared at the bleeding mess that had once been a very beautiful woman. One of the men grabbed her long hair and yanked her head back.

'No one comes in here and sells dodgy gear in my place.'

The woman had been employed as one of Tommy's pole dancers. Everyone knew, including her, that he didn't tolerate anyone coming into his yard and selling drugs. That honour fell to him alone.

'The only thing you were employed to do was sell yourself.' He looked at one of the men. 'Do it.' The men pushed the woman to the floor. Spread her face down. One of them grabbed her arm and stretched it out until it lay under the piano near Tommy's feet. He trapped her hand by the wrist so that her hand lay flat. Tommy didn't get up. Instead he began to hit the room with some more 'Rhapsody In Blue'. He swayed with the music. And then with no warning, at the same time the clash of cymbals would come in, he raised his right foot and stamped on the terrified woman's pinkie. The scream she let out stopped all the human activity in the adjoining rooms. He leant back into the piano, heard the imaginary cymbals and raised his foot again and did the next finger. This time the crunch of bone was audible in the room. Piano, cymbals, he did another. And another. As he raised his foot one final time his mobile rang. He eased his foot back down. Took the call.

He smiled when he heard who it was. 'Paul. How's life in Her Majesty's dope palace?'

They chit chatted on while the woman on the floor moaned and grunted. Then Paul got down to business. 'I've got a mate in here who's been looking out for me. I just wanted to know if you can take care of him when he gets out on Monday?'

'What's he been doing?'

Paul told him. Tommy was impressed.

'Can you do it?' Paul asked.

Tommy thought for a while. Then looked down at the woman on the floor. He moved the phone away from his mouth. Twisted his mouth as he gazed down at the shattered woman. 'You better tell the Digbys that I'm on to them.' He stamped on her last finger, with no music this time. Stamped again shattering her bone. His victim passed out.

He moved the phone back to his face and finally answer, 'Yeah. Why not? That's the trouble with this country, no one will give an ex-con another chance.'

Daisy tightened her hand around the key and shoved her fist into her lap as the Deputy Chief Commissioner of the Met police stood gazing at her from the doorway. Barbara Benton stepped inside, minus her jacket and with her sleeves rolled up in a no-nonsense fashion.

'I was just wondering how you were getting on.'

Daisy pushed herself to her feet, her fist falling tight by her side. Flustered, she picked up the sock that had fallen. 'Fine. I'm just finishing up.' She turned her back and walked quickly to the wardrobe. She leant over to put the sock in its place. She took a deep breath, praying that the woman behind her wouldn't see what she was about to do next. She pushed the fist that held the key deep into her front trouser pocket. She sighed with relief as she turned back around.

She found Barbara looking with murder in her eyes at the slashed mattress. 'I'm going to make it my business to find out who did this and when I do . . .' She left the words hanging in the air. Daisy understood why her nickname was Basher Babs. 'I think we should go now and let them have some privacy.'

'Do you think whoever did this will come back?'

Barbara shook her head. 'Most break-ins are opportunistic crimes. Whoever did this probably saw the hearse outside the house, waited for everyone to go and took their chance.'

'That's horrible.'

'No, that's the world we live in today.' She gave Daisy a slight smile. 'Is your car outside?' Daisy quickly explained that she would get a cab. 'I'll give you a lift back.'

Daisy nodded and followed the other woman out of the room.

'I just need to use the bathroom and get my jacket.' Daisy nodded absently at Barbara's words. She turned one last time to look at Charlie's room. Then her thumb pressed against the outline of the key in her pocket. The key she hoped would unlock Charlie's medicine cabinet.

*   *   *

Daisy had never felt comfortable in the company of coppers, a leftover from her days as Frankie Sullivan's daughter. And now she sat in the passenger seat next to the second in command of the country's strongest police force. They sat in silence for the first leg of the ride. Daisy was the first to speak.

'I hear that you're going to be wearing the chief's cap soon,' Daisy said.

Barbara's face split into a crooked smile. 'I hope so, but you can never tell what's been plotted behind closed doors. It's all politics. But hopefully I will be presented to the world as the new commissioner at a gala dinner at city hall next Thursday.'

Daisy sank deeper in her seat beginning to feel more comfortable in the other woman's presence by the minute. Suddenly she felt in awe of this woman's immense achievements. Barbara was the type of woman she could look up to. A woman that all women could look up to. 'Is that how you got to know Charlie, through your work?'

'Charlie was the brief on the first arrest I made as a green WPC. He did quite a number on me, spinning this law in my face until I was so confused I almost let the suspect go. Over the years we worked well together. It was a bit cat and dog sometimes but he was a friend and I will miss him.'

They both sank into memories of the man who linked their lives. Then Barbara flipped the radio on. Chrissie Hynde's husky, mellow voice, midway through singing 'Brass In Pocket', eased effortlessly into the car.

'I hear that you're helping out on a high-profile class-action case we've taken,' Daisy said a few minutes later.

Barbara's hands tightened on the wheel as she took a sharp turn that bought them into the heart of London. 'Yes. I got my stripes leading one of the Met's first units on child protection. It was a hard slog getting people to take child abuse seriously and if we had we wouldn't be in the position of having this class-action case now.' She peeped a quick look at Daisy. 'Are you working on the case?'

'Not really, but my boyfriend . . .' She blushed. 'I mean, my partner Jerome McMillan is the lead barrister.'

Barbara's instant grin softened her features. 'Young love.' Daisy's blush deepened, but her lips tugged into a tiny smile.

Daisy was starting to like this woman. 'You married? Got kids?'

Barbara took the car into a deep turn, not answering for a few seconds. She shook her head. 'This is where I'm meant to say I never got around to it, but the truth is I never saw domestic bliss as being part of my life. All I ever wanted to do was be the best copper in town. I hear that Charlie was your mentor.'

Daisy straightened slightly in her seat. 'How did you know?'

'His wife was telling me about you when you were upstairs. She's really pleased that you're the person going through his things at work. You remind me of someone I mentored years ago. Someone who grew up on the streets.' Daisy tensed at her words. 'Don't worry, I think I'm the only person who can suss out which end of town you're really from. You know why? It takes one to know one. I came up the tough route as well. I grew up on a real rough estate in London. The Caxton, which I'm pleased to say has now been pulled down. I worked hard and kept going. So will you, Daisy.'

They drove the remainder of the way in silence until Barbara stopped the car outside Curtis and Hopkirk's in Holborn.

'It was great meeting you.' Barbara gazed at Daisy smiling. 'What's your last name?'

Barbara may have figured out where she came from, but Daisy knew if she supplied her surname the other woman might put two and two together and come up with Frankie Sullivan. Daisy hustled to open the door as she quickly said, 'I've got to run. See you again sometime.'

'Wait,' Barbara said. Reluctantly Daisy turned back around. The older woman pushed her hand into her jacket pocket and held out a white business card. 'If you ever need me . . .'

Daisy nodded as she reached for the card. As she took it the other woman's hand caught her own. Held on to it.

'Take care of yourself,' Barbara whispered simply.

She let go of Daisy's hand. Daisy tightened her grip on the card and got out of the car. Without another word Barbara roared off into the distance. Daisy quickly fished in her pocket for Charlie's key. Stared at it for a few seconds as it lay in the palm of her hand. She curled her fingers around it as she decided to go straight to the office to see if it would unlock Charlie's medicine cabinet. As she stepped forward her phone pinged. She took it out and read the text.

```
Need u pronto
```

Of all the times for her adoptive mum Jackie to call her it had to be now. Jackie most probably wanted a blow-by-blow account of the funeral. Her hand tightened on Charlie's key. She should go to the office, but she knew if she didn't go and see Jackie now she was in for a mouthful the next the time she saw her. When Jackie called you bloody well better move your arse sharpish. She pushed the key back in her pocket. Whatever secrets Charlie was keeping in his medicine cabinet would have to wait until tomorrow.

'We found fuck all.' Johnson rammed his words down his mobile.

He sat opposite Clarke at a round, scratched table in The Merry Swan boozer in Bethnal Green. The pub had once been their favourite haunt when they both worked at the now closed Bethnal Green police station back in the eighties. The pub was already filling up, even though it was only minutes to three. Thin Lizzy's 'The Boys Are Back In Town' threw a wild, hectic beat over the place.

But neither Clarke or Johnson got in the groove. They were too anxious about not finding any information about the safe-deposit box in Charlie Hopkirk's home.

Johnson carried on talking into the phone. 'We tore the place apart and didn't come across a dickie bird.'

'I think I know who's clearing away Charlie's stuff at his office.' The voice on the other end of the line said.

'Who?' Johnson replied eagerly. When he heard the name he started with surprise. 'You're pulling my dick . . .' He stopped abruptly remembering who he was talking to. 'I mean joking.'

'I wish I was. Ain't life a bitch sometimes. You know what this means? We've got no alternative but to involve Stella—'

'No way,' Johnson kicked in, half lifting out of his chair. 'I ain't going down that route again.' Clarke looked up in surprise.

'Believe me, if there's an alternative to getting involved with that woman again I'd be taking it. She was involved in this as well. If I've got the person going through Charlie Hopkirk's belongings right, then she is the only person who can get to her.'

Johnson fell back into his seat. 'What do you want us to do?'

'You need to get the ball rolling tonight.' Then the line went dead.

Johnson cupped his hand over his mouth, letting out a shaky breath as he caught Clarke's worried, bloodshot eyes. 'What's going on?'

Johnson stood up, pushing his mobile into his suit pocket. 'I'll tell you about it in the car. And you ain't going to like it any more than me.'

As Clarke eased to his feet the barman's voice bit out like a human Rottweiller, his words now commanding the attention of everyone in the room. 'I've told you already that I ain't serving you. Why don't you go home and remind your neighbours why they're trying to get a house transfer.'

Johnson was too unsettled by the latest twist to events to pay much attention to the disturbance, but Clarke looked over and saw who the barman was yelling at. A woman. Small and as dainty as a child. Her size reminded him of his little girl when she was twelve, the last time he'd seen her before his two-timing bint of an ex-wife had taken her to live in Portugal with the guy she'd been fooling around with behind his back. Said she couldn't live with him anymore, couldn't stomach the drinking. Clarke moved towards the bar.

'What are you doing?' Johnson asked angrily.

Clarke turned back to Johnson and the pain he saw in Clarke's eyes made him swallow. 'I was a good cop once, you know.' Johnson said nothing because he knew the other man was right. 'I'll meet you at the car,' Johnson said and then made his way outside.

Clarke reached the bar, his eyes switching between the stocky barman and the woman. 'There a problem?'

At the sound of his voice the small woman wobbled to face him. She was a pretty little thing, Clarke thought. Short, black layered hair, with purple streaks at the front, a silver nose stud and a delicate bone structure that put him in mind of a ballerina. Big caramel-coloured eyes shimmered back at him in her pale, white face. Compassion washed over him as he stared at the haunting hurt look that lurked in her eyes.

'You alright, love?'

She tottered towards him and peered up at him. He could smell the drink on her. 'Love?' she threw back in a thick cockney voice. The twisting shape of her mouth removed the image of the ballerina instantly from his mind and instead he saw the seen-too-much-of-life mouths of every tough woman he'd ever arrested. 'You saying me and you are in love?'

The barman sniggered at that. Clarke ignored him. 'Look—' he started to say, but she cut him off.

'I can't imagine being in love with a tub of lard.'

That bought more laughter and not just from the barman this time. Clarke took no offence at her words. He'd been called much worse in his years patrolling the streets of London. Without responding Clarke grabbed her arm and marched her towards the door.

'Oi,' she shot out as she tried to wriggle out of his grasp. 'Get off me, you gorilla.'

But he just tightened his grip muttering, 'Let's find you a cab.'

They stepped out into the drizzle. Realising that she was not going to escape she quietened down as they made their way to the bright lights of Bethnal Green High Street. Clarke checked the street.

'Does your mum know you're out?'

The word mum seemed to set her off because she began to laugh in a raucous wild fashion. Crazy girl, Clarke thought. As her laughter rang in the air he spotted a black cab. Hailed it. He opened the cab door and threw her into the back.

'Where do you live?'

She mumbled an address somewhere in Bow. Clarke slammed

the door shut and made his way to the cabbie up front. He told him the address and pressed some money into his hand.

'There's an extra fiver there to make sure she gets to her door alright.'

Clarke watched as the cab drove off into the distance. Little girls always caused trouble. If it weren't for little girls he wouldn't be trying to erase fresh footprints that led to a crime he'd helped commit twenty years ago.

Nineteen-year-old Jo-Jo slumped drunkenly against the back seat of the cab. She twisted around and watched the tub of lard disappear in the distance. She couldn't remember the last time some bloke had been kind to her. Men were usually after one thing. No, she corrected herself. Usually after two, the second of which was to impress her mum. She stared out of the window at London, as it whizzed by in a blur of hellish colours before her eyes. Streets she'd once known like the back of her hand. She'd been away for two years now. Hadn't wanted to go but her mum had put her on the first train out of here and told her not to come back until she sorted her shit out.

She lurched as the cab hit a bump in the road. She pulled out a half bottle of vodka from her bag. She knew she'd already had a skin-full but what the fuck. She tipped the bottle to her lips. Her face twisted as the neat alcohol burned a path down her throat. She gulped more as she thought about her mum. A woman, she knew who would most probably do one thing when she clamped eyes on her – throttle her to death.

Nine

Daisy stared at the only woman who had ever been a true mother to her. Jackie Jarvis. Thirty-six, five foot two, pixie red hair and freckles that some people mistook for cuteness, but those that got to know her knew she was one of the gutsiest and most caring women around.

They were together in the small, cosy kitchen of Jackie's second home, her flat in Ernest Bevin House in Hackney. Daisy sat at the table while Jackie bustled around making a brew for both of them. Daisy remembered the first night Jackie had bought her here. It was a month after her dad had died, a hot, sticky evening in August. While Daisy unpacked her belongings in her new bedroom she'd heard the rising voices. Jackie and her new husband, Elijah 'Schoolboy' Campbell. Talking about her.

'Are you off your head bringing Frankie Sullivan's girl here?'

'And what the hell did you expect me to do? Just leave her? Abandon her into the care system like I was when I was fifteen? She's here for good and if you don't like it you know where the door is.'

'Alright, but you better not forget that she's Frankie Sullivan's daughter and always will be. Whether you like it or not, she'll always be a gangster's girl.'

A gangster's girl. The words had run around, like hot ashes, in her mind, until the pain was too much to take. She'd gone to her bag and taken out her penknife . . .

'What's that mind of yours ticking away over?'

Jackie's voice brought Daisy back to the present. She looked up at Jackie who stood with her hands jammed in her jeans pocket leaning against the edge of the sink. She didn't tell Jackie what she'd been thinking because she knew that Jackie still felt guilty about what had happened that night.

'Wishing this day would be finally over,' she replied instead, her fingers rubbing her left bracelet.

Jackie moved and sat down besides her. Her green eyes twinkled as she asked, 'So when are we gonna meet that young fella of yours?'

She said what she always said. 'I just want a bit more time with him and need to meet his parents.'

Jackie shifted forward, the twinkle in her eye disappearing. 'You ain't ashamed of us or something? It has been a year now—'

'How could I be ashamed of a woman like you?' Daisy quickly denied.

'You told him about your dad yet?'

Daisy said nothing, dropping her gaze from her adoptive mum. Jackie grabbed her hand, careful not to touch her bracelet, and caressed the inside of her palm with her thumb. 'The past has a way of coming back to bite you in a very painful place, I should know. Your Jerome may be alright about it. You should tell him.'

Anything else they might've said was stopped by the sound of the front door opening. Female chatter swarmed inside. Daisy smiled and got up knowing exactly who the new arrivals were; her surrogate aunts, Anna, Roxy and Ollie. When they saw her each of them gave her a hug like she was five years old. Anna was black, the tallest of the trio, with a beautiful face and a girl-about-town nature that made Daisy easily understand why Anna and the legendary lawyer Bell Dream had been lovers for over ten years now. Ruby was white, with a body shape that could best be described as homely and loved to chat about anything on God's given earth. Ollie was the quiet one, who'd arrived in Britain as a shell-shocked child soldier from the African country of Sankura, but had transformed herself into the director of two well-respected organisations helping refugees. Daisy knew they had all ended up in the care system when they were fifteen and became fast friends. What happened to them while they were in there they wouldn't say. And she never asked. Everyone was entitled to their secrets.

'You all packed?' Roxy asked Jackie as the women settled themselves in the sitting room.

Tomorrow the women were off on a much-needed two-week holiday to Spain. Roxy owned a luxurious villa there.

'Bloody case won't close,' Jackie groaned.

'That's because you're taking far too much with you,' Ollie chided in her soft, lightly accented voice.

'A girl can never have too much. Besides I've got to take stuff for the boys as well.' Jackie had three sons, sixteen-year-old Ryan and her eleven-year-old twins, Darius and Preston, otherwise known as Little Whacky and Little Mojo in honour of two close family friends.

Anna settled her brown face into a beaming smile as she looked at Daisy. 'You could still come with us. You work way too hard. Chill out, girl, and have a break.'

Daisy gazed back at her knowing her aunt was right. She did give Curtis and Hopkirk more hours than a person should give any job, but only hard graft was going to get her where she wanted to be in life. Anna's offer was so tempting. The chance to get away sounded like pure heaven. But then she thought about the key. About Charlie's medicine cabinet. She shook her head. 'Now Charlie's gone I've got a load of stuff to sort out.'

Jackie sprang to her feet. 'Talking about sorting out you can help me get my feckin' case closed.'

She ushered Daisy into what was once her bedroom. All traces of her youth had been cleared, with the room now transformed into an office that Jackie's husband, Schoolboy, used for his catering business. After that first dreadful night here this room had become her sanctuary, the place where she could shut the door and stare down at Regent's Canal below and sort through her thoughts. Now she stared at Jackie's bulging leopard print suitcase that lay open on the floor.

'Looks like you're packing to go away for a lifetime,' Daisy said as she hunched down next to the case. Jackie laughed as Daisy rifled through it making decisions about what could stay and what could go.

'Do you really need to be taking this?' Daisy's hand shot in the air. She held up a lime green vibrator. 'Won't this count as a very offensive weapon?'

'Oi.' Jackie gave her a mock stern look. 'Pop Juicy Lucy back like a good little girl. And anyway it's medicinal; I use it to massage my back.'

They both chuckled as they looked fondly at each other. Suddenly Jackie's laughter drained away. 'I never regret the day you became my daughter.'

Daisy froze at the unexpected words. She eased to her feet and faced her adoptive mum.

'Not even after what I did in this room?' She regretted the words as soon as she saw the blood drain from Jackie's face. But she pressed on. 'Or when I went clean off the rails and then up the platform back when I was sixteen?'

'It's only natural that you should've wanted to find out about your mum. Any kid would want to.' She ran one hand down Daisy's left arm 'Do you still think about her?'

Daisy thought for a few seconds. Shrugged. 'Sometimes. Not as much as I did in the past. But it would be great to meet her, if nothing else to close that chapter on my life. It's kind of sad to think that if she passed me on the street I wouldn't even recognise her. But then again, my dad always said I was better off without her.'

'Never in a million years did I think I'd agree with something your old man said, and I know I shouldn't say this, but something here,' Jackie's hand dropped from Daisy's arm and covered her own heart, 'tells me you're better off not knowing about your mum.' Jackie had always had good instincts about people. 'Look, I know you can look out for yourself, but I'm still your old girl, so if you need anything while I'm away please give Misty a bell, OK? That's why I asked you to come to see me, cos I want to make sure you're alright when I'm away.'

Daisy smiled as she thought about Miss Misty McKenzie, drag queen extraordinaire. She always found it hard to pin down exactly what was Misty's relationship to Jackie and her surrogate aunts but the best way she could describe it was that Misty was like their big sister. How they'd all met she didn't know, but together they owned the trendy Shim-Sham-Shimmy club located in London's docklands.

Jackie pointed her finger at her. 'I mean it Daisy.'

Daisy nodded. But in her mind she decided that she wouldn't need to contact Misty. Nothing major was going to happen in only two weeks was it?

Stella watched one of her newest girls getting half-strangled on the CCTV screen. She sat alone in her private office on the top floor of the brothel. Everyone did a double take when they saw her office. Most people expected either flock wallpaper, paintings with women posing in their birthday suits and dildo-shaped furniture or a cold, minimalist, business-like space, with a U-shaped desk, with two chairs, neutral coloured carpet and not much else. What people got was a trip to another age. A roughly made wooden desk, brick walls, a real log fire and windows covered with white curtains printed with brightly coloured flowers. The door was bright yellow with the words *Calam and Stella* painted in black fancy print. Pride of place, behind her desk, high on the wall, went to the large framed poster of the movie *Calamity Jane*. Doris Day posed, whip in hand, decked out, from head to toe, in classic cowboy gear, her name in bold, red print beside her under the tagline: 'YIPPEEEEE! IT'S THE BIG BONANZA IN MUSICAL EXTRAVAGANZA!'

She had CCTV everywhere in the brothel, which she watched from her private office on the top floor of the house. Of course, her punters didn't know that, most crept in wearing hats and with their collars up. If they'd known they were the amateur turn in Stella's home movies they'd have probably stayed at home with a mucky book and a hanky, the dirty bastards. Her place might not be in Park Lane or some other swanky part of town like some brothels, but she had a reputation for running a clean and discreet show.

She charged a minimum of a grand for a whole night with one of her girls and the only people who could cater to that weren't your usual Joe but men with money to burn in their pockets. Politicians, entrepreneurs, lonely businessmen in a strange city, whose auditors didn't ask any questions about their expenses. If you had the money, Stella had the tricks. There wasn't much that she didn't cater for. Only thing she didn't do was anything to do with kids. Never kids, not inside her four walls.

The young man fucking the girl senseless with his hands around her throat was a rising star in the city, the eldest son of a prominent family. Of course he'd given a false name when he'd first come here, called himself Ted or some other bogus shit, but Stella had made it her business to find out who he really was. Knowing the names of the people you did business with could always come in useful. And the tapes she kept on all of them made sure that the cops never came knocking at her door. She noticed her girl's hand moving closer to the panic button she'd had put in every room. Stella had learnt the hard way that good boys from good families were always the worst. Her first pimp had been one of those – swore he loved her, but beat her sideways every time he claimed she hadn't bought in enough cash. Eventually he'd sliced off her nipple in a rage one night. The last night she'd ever worked for him. The night she'd realised that, unless you were your own boss, the cards life dealt her would be forever stacked against her.

The girl's hand slipped away from the panic button as bogus Ted collapsed against her. As Stella eased back in her chair thoughts of another punter came into her mind. Or former punter she corrected. Charlie. Poor, dead, sod. She shook her head as memories of him flooded her mind the same time there was a knock at the door. It opened to reveal Tatiana wearing a red silk dressing gown. Without being told the other woman took a seat on the sofa, which was covered in the same bright fabric as the curtains, by the window. Stella joined her. Held out her right hand. The other woman took it and ran her fingers across the deep lines on Stella's palm as the silence drifted inside the room. Then she spoke, giving Stella her fortune. Stella had been having her palm read since she was a teenager. She had always been curious, sometimes desperate to find out what the future held for her. She'd been doing it for so long that it was a habit she couldn't break even if she wanted to.

Tatiana kept her intense, dark eyes glued to Stella's palm. 'I see two women. Both dark . . .' Stella drifted with the younger woman's hypnotic words. Ten minutes later Tatiana's hands began to smoothly move up Stella's arms. Stella eased back into the softness of the sofa. The other woman's hands moved to her stomach, and up to her breasts. Stella closed her eyes as her boobs were caressed and stroked. She had learnt in life that you took what you wanted and fuck everyone else. If they didn't get it, that was their problem. Stella sank into the magic of the prostitute's touch when the door crashed open. Her eyes rejoined the world. A distressed and panting Molly, the pint-sized receptionist, stood in the doorway.

'It's the cops. They're raiding the place.'

'You're making a big mistake, fellas,' Stella stormed as she was jostled down the stairs by a uniformed cop.

Stella was pissed off. Her place was never raided. Some of her clients were people with influence and that meant a blind eye was turned to the goings on at her place. She'd also been given to understand by a person in a position to know that the police had more important fish to fry, like the influx of Turkish and Kurdish gangsters into their patch, than high-street knocking shops. Providing they didn't make any trouble for the law-abiding locals, that was, and Stella King didn't make any trouble for them at all, she ran a very tight ship.

And now it looked like she might have to share some of her tapes with interested parties to get her wheels turning again. She reached downstairs, where shamefaced customers were having their details taken and near-naked women stood backed against the walls. She noticed one of the female cops talking to one of the women who had recently arrived from the Ukraine. Shit, this wasn't good. One of the cops approached Stella. Big, uniformed, with acne on his face. His sharp eyes settled on her.

'Officer, this is a respectable hotel,' Stella said with all the dignified outrage she could muster. 'What the residents get up to is their business.'

'Really? I must be Batman then – what with you being the Joker an' all. Some of these ladies are claiming you brought them to this country illegally and then forced them to work as prostitutes. Would you care to comment on that?'

'I ain't saying nuthin' until I clap eyes on my brief. He plays golf with your superiors you know . . .'

The officer just scoffed and swung around. 'Let the rest of them go,' he shouted. Then he turned back to Stella. Grabbed her arm. Marched her outside without speaking inside.

'What's going on?' Stella demanded as they approached a police van.

She'd never heard of a raid without the Bill taking everyone down the nick. Why were they just taking her? The policeman didn't answer her. Instead he opened the van and strong-armed her inside. The door banged shut behind her. The darkness cloaked her as the van sped off. The ride went on for five minutes. Ten. Fifteen. Wherever she was being taken to she knew it wasn't the nearest nick because it was a five-minute journey from the brothel. What was going on here? A few minutes later the van jerked to a halt. She heard the passenger's and driver's doors slam shut. Heard footsteps coming closer on the ground outside. The footsteps stopped outside the back of the van. A key rattled in the lock. The doors were thrust open. Revealed the people who stood outside. Heart beating like the clappers, she stared at the faces of two men. Men she'd hoped never to see again in her life.

Ten

Jim Clarke and Courtney Johnson.

'How's business, Stella?' Johnson said.

'Twenty years ago we agreed never to cross paths again,' she spat back, tensing on the seat.

'That was then. This is now. Circumstances change,' Clarke answered.

'Look boys, what's the deal here? You running a bit short? You need a loan?' Stella mocked. 'Just tell me what you want and let me go so I don't have to see your ugly mugs ever again.'

Stella backed up violently into a corner at their next move. Johnson got inside the van and Clarke followed. Clarke shut the door and then both men sat down. Stella stared at them in the semi-darkness.

Her voice broke the silence. 'What's happened to my girls?'

'Nothing,' Johnson answered. 'They're still at your place. A mate from the local nick owed me a favour. I told him that you were blackmailing my brother-in-law and was threatening to tell my sister all about it tomorrow. He was more than happy to give me some space to have a little chat with you so that we can put things right.'

'You could ruin my business.'

Clarke said, 'That doesn't need to happen if you're helpful.'

'See, *we've* got a bit of a problem,' Johnson said. 'It seems our little secret might not be a secret for much longer.'

Stella drew in a sharp breath. She didn't want to be reminded about that night all those years ago. She ran her hands up and down her arms as she said, 'That isn't possible unless the other person involved is running their mouth. And there ain't no way in hell they're doing that.'

Johnson crossed his ankles as he spoke. 'We found out that there might be some evidence still around—'

'What evidence?' Stella reared forward.

'Shut up and listen,' Clarke bit out.

She eased back down as Johnson carried on with his tale. 'It seems that a lawyer might have been holding on to some things all these years.'

'What lawyer?'

'Someone called Charlie Hopkirk . . .'

'Charlie?' The name flew out of Stella in shock.

'You knew him?' Clarke asked.

'We went back years. But we ain't here to chat about a family reunion, so tell me the rest.'

'All you need to know is we think he kept it in a safe-deposit box in a bank. We need to get it before Charlie's widow gets her hands on it after the reading of his will.'

Stella shrugged. 'And what's that gotta do with me?'

'You're going to organise your crew to go and get it.'

'No. Fucking. Way.' Stella shook her head with each word. 'I ain't doing no blag. I'm a respectable businesswoman now.'

Clarke shoved his face into her space. 'Is that a fact? Living off immoral earnings? Trafficking? Distributing drugs? All I've got to do, Stella, is pick up my mobile and you'll be running your respectable business via a smuggled phone from Holloway. But I'm sure the governor will find you some light work running business classes for his "clients", as I believe the inmates are known these days.'

Stella ran her fingertips across her painted red lips. She knew she was backed into a corner. 'OK. Say I do this bank job? What happens to me after?'

'You deliver the deposit box, then we'll lose any evidence, drop any charges and we can get back to our careers. Don't forget you're neck-high in this crap just as much as we are. We go down and you'll be there, plummeting right beside us.'

Stella knew they were right. If anyone ever found out about this she'd be going down for life.

'So which bank are we talking about?'

'That we don't know yet. But we do know who's sorting through Hopkirk's gear in his office and who might've stumbled across the info we need.'

Johnson stopped talking as both he and Clarke looked harder at Stella.

'Well, fucking spit it out. I ain't got all bloody night.' She stared Johnson straight in the eye. 'Who?'

'Someone you know.' Johnson left his words hanging in the air as if he was enjoying her discomfort. 'Daisy Sullivan.'

Stella's face twisted into a mask of dismay. She shook her head. 'No. No. No. I'm not dragging Daisy into this . . .'

'Too late, she's already in it.'

'She don't know nothing about me—'

'What happened between you and that scumbag Frankie Sullivan ain't none of our business,' Johnson cut in. 'But this is the plan, Mommy dearest. You're going to introduce yourself to your little girl and find out what she knows. Make her understand that she doesn't have a choice.'

Stella sat, tense, on the piano stool in the Meet 'n' Greet room in the brothel. It was the same piano that the Russian prostitute – Elena, yeah, that was her name – would give Tommy his lessons. She'd loved hearing that piano fill the house as the girls went about their business upstairs.

The place was dead quiet now. When she'd got back it had taken an effort to calm all the girls down, but she'd done it. Made sure they understood that the cops weren't going to pay a repeat visit. Well, that was as long as she played ball with Clarke and Johnson.

Fuck.

She didn't want to do this. Robbing banks was for seventies revivalists. But she was gonna have to do it. She didn't have a choice. And Daisy? How the heck was she going to handle that? Just waltz into the girl's life and say 'I'm your . . .'

Stella pushed herself off the stool when the door stormed open. Billy and Tommy. Billy looked frantic, his muscular chest panting with pent-up energy, while Tommy was moving like he was on the point of bursting the seams on his flash leather coat. 'I heard what happened,' Billy said, his lined face a storm of aggressive emotions. 'I should've been here.'

'Look.' Stella held up her palm trying to bring some calm to the room. 'It's all sorted out.'

When the men had quietened down she picked up her words. 'You both need to sit down. There's something I need to tell you.'

So she told them the only thing she decided they needed to know for now – they didn't need to know about the bank job quite yet – that she had another daughter called Daisy. That Daisy was also Frankie Sullivan's daughter. Tommy whistled at that, Billy remained silent.

'The problem is that she's has got something that belongs to me,' Stella explained. 'I need to get it. She works for a law firm called Curtis and Hopkirk–'

Before she could finish Billy slammed to his feet and twisted away from them. Stella's face creased when she heard him mutter, 'Shit.'

'Billy, you alright?' He didn't answer, so she persisted. 'Do you know this law outfit, is that it?'

Silence. Then he finally turned back around. His face was emotionless. 'Nah. Still pissed I should've been here when the Bill turned up mob-handed.'

'Say that name of the firm again.' Tommy cut in abruptly standing up.

'Curtis and Hopkirk.'

'You sure?'

Stella nodded, giving her son a confused look.

Tommy shot his mum a full grin. 'I think I know just the person who might be able to help us with that.'

* * *

The four-year-old girl knelt on the floor, playing with her teddy bear. She sang 'Ring-a, ring o', roses' softly to herself as she swung her teddy around. She wiped away the tears on her cheek. Something funny had happened to her upstairs, which had made her cry. But now she was with teddy and everything was alright. The room was large with a pale, blue carpet, a red sofa, a bar and light green walls. She played in her favourite corner. The one next to the piano. Abruptly she stopped singing when she heard the voices. Big people's voices. Men and women. Coming from upstairs.

'Oh my God. Oh my God.'

'Fucking calm down . . .'

Daisy shot up from her pillow as she screamed into the darkness. She covered her mouth with quivering fingers to hold back the next scream. Eyes wide she stared blindly around the dark bedroom. Her arms clutched tight around her middle trying to desperately still the trembling movement of her body. The cool air settled over her sweating face. She hadn't had the dream since she stopped taking the antidepressant pills years ago. She had no idea who the little girl was, where the house was, in fact she knew sod all about it.

Her hands fell from her mouth as she bowed her head and her hair flopped forwards and shrouded her face. The hungry noise of her gulping in streams of air sounded ragged in the room. Gradually her breathing slowed. Calmed down. Got back to normal. She threw the covers back and swung her legs over the side of the bed. Hung onto the edge of the bed for a few seconds before she got up. She moved slowly towards the dressing table. She stared at her face for a few seconds before she opened the top drawer. And there they sat – her bottle of happy pills. If she took one, just one, mind you, she might be able to shift the stress she was feeling and sleep. But in sleep the dream might come again. Shit. She rubbed the back of her hand against her sweaty forehead, itching to just reach down and take them. It would only be one. Her hand dropped from her head. Moved forward. Just one. Her hand was almost upon the bottle when her eye caught sight of the key she'd found at Charlie's on the top of the dressing table where she'd placed it earlier. She slammed the drawer shut and instead picked up the key. Well there wasn't going to be any sleep for her now. She might as well go to the office and find out if the key fit Charlie's cabinet.

Angel moaned as she hit a premier league orgasm in her new lover's lap on top of the piano. If she'd realised that pianos could be sooo much fun she might've continued taking those lessons her mother had forced on her when she was seven years old.

Angel pushed her limp hair out of her face as she gazed, dazed, at the man holding her. He hadn't even bothered to take his clothes off, which she loved. The rough, the tough, they were the ones who always knew how she liked her lovin'.

'We need to have a chat, babe,' Tommy said, then roughly pushed her off him.

He jumped down and as he seated himself on the piano stool she gathered her clothes and flung them on. She didn't like the serious set of his face. She hoped he wasn't getting all happy-ever-after on her. She eased down and stood before Tommy as she jammed her feet into her heels.

'Honey I hope—' she started, laying her palms lightly on his shoulders. But she never finished because in the blink of an eye he'd pushed her into the piano.

'What are you doing?' Her words were as furious as the movements of her hands as she tried to dislodge him. Her left shoe skidded off her foot.

He grabbed her hair and slammed her head into the piano. She let out a cry of pain as the room rocked around her. His fingers dug into her jaw as he lifted her head to face him.

'You want some more? That's fine. You don't, you'll shut your mouth and listen to me.'

Angel had represented enough criminals to know the ones that would go straight and the ones who were beyond reform; the way Tommy was looking at her told her he was beyond redemption.

'You know a chick called Daisy Sullivan?'

Angel nodded. 'She's my friend.'

'I want you to find out what she knows about Charlie Hopkirk.'

Daisy? Charlie? What the hell was going on here? 'I don't know what you're talking about,' she stammered.

He grinned at her. Slammed her head back into the piano. If he hadn't been holding her she would have fallen down. Before she had time to recover he dragged her by the hair and marched her across the room. He shoved her face above the low-level glass table in the right hand corner. She gasped when she saw what lay on it. Photos of her and him in what looked like the proof pages of a sex manual. And if that wasn't damning enough there were scattered shots of her partaking in coke, the sort of grainy photos you saw in exposes of minor celebs in the Sunday papers.

His words were chilling. 'I'm sure you wouldn't want all them nice lawyers at your firm to see what kind of character they're really working with. You know, your hobbies and pastimes and that, hanging out with the criminal classes.'

She was afraid to ask the next question. 'What do you mean criminal?'

'Don't play me for a dick, darlin'. You knew I was never on the right side of the law when you batted your sweet eyelashes in the courthouse.'

She shook, frightened because he was right. Sure, she had assumed he had most probably seen the inside of a cell more than once in his life, but that he was a big-time crim, never.

'I heard that your father is someone everyone respects. Now wouldn't it be a shame if I made you upload these pix on to your Facebook page and then we emailed all his friends. Or is it Twitter these days? I find it hard to keep up. And I've got a number for the Sundays. They love all this stuff, don't they? They'll have to blank out the really naughty bits but readers will get the picture – know what I mean?'

Tears gathered in Angel's eyes. 'What do you want me to do?'

Tommy King grinned. 'Has this Daisy bird said anything to you?'

Her eyes flickered away from him as she shook her head, hair pelting into her face. Tommy jacked her head up. 'Don't lie to me, bitch.'

'She said that Randal Curtis, the other senior partner, told her to let him know if she found anything unusual in Charlie's things.'

'Like what?' The pressure of his hands tightened.

'I don't know,' she yelled.

He shoved his face almost on top of her face, his breath hot on her skin. 'You better be telling me it all, little girl.'

She was too frightened to even nod back.

The grim expression on Tommy's face deepened. 'We ain't too far from Holborn, so there's no time like the present. I want you to get your sweet little arse to that office now.'

He grabbed her hair. Yanked her head back, and kissed her ever so softly on her bruised mouth.

Eleven

Daisy arrived at Curtis and Hopkirk just minutes before one in the morning. The lights shone throughout the building, making it stand out bright and beautiful in the dark night. The street was quiet and deserted, except for a couple rushing towards a cab on High Holborn. There was always a security guard in place twenty-four hours a day to accommodate the lawyers who sometimes had to work late at night, including Daisy. She'd been doing it so often lately that she knew the night guard well.

She pressed her face against the glass door and smiled when she saw Sean, the security guard, sitting at the desk. He smiled, not surprised to see her, and made his way to the main door. His keys rattled as he unlocked the door.

'Another late night, Miss Sullivan?' Sean said as he widened the door for her to step inside. Sean was a big-hearted Irish man with a shock of white hair and a growing stomach that had a love affair with his wife's home cooking.

Daisy smiled back at him. 'Is there anyone else around?'

'I don't know. I've just got on my shift.'

Daisy hoped that there was no one else here. She didn't need any distractions, just wanted to see if the key fit the cabinet. And if it did? And what if was inside could destroy Charlie's reputation?

She left Sean, took the lift and was soon on the second floor. She yawned as she made her way to Charlie's office. Trust her to start feeling tired now. She tried to shake the sleep from her eyes as she opened the office door. Switched on the light. It was exactly as she'd left it, neat and tidy but with evidence of Charlie's life here making way for the new partner. A wave of emotion settled in her gut. It finally hit her that she was never going to see her mentor again. Another male figure who'd come and gone in her life. Well, at least she still had Jerome. She shut the door, shook off her grim thoughts and quickly made her way to the bathroom. Just as she reached for the handle she heard it.

Bang.

A door inside the bathroom slammed shut.

She froze, her hand hovering over the handle. She heard another bang. Without another thought Daisy wrenched the door open.

'Angel,' Daisy uttered, completely shocked.

What shocked her was not just the fact that Angel was inside Charlie's bathroom, but that her friend looked a total mess. Her hair flew in all directions as if she'd shoved her hand into it one too many times and her mascara streaked her face as if she'd been crying.

As Daisy took a step inside Angel moved back, her hand rubbing frantically below her throat.

'What are you doing here?' Daisy asked gently.

Angel pushed a trembling hand through her hair. 'Um . . . Um . . .' she stammered, breaking eye contact with Daisy. 'I was looking for some papers that Charlie has. Without them I'm going to lose my case.' And then she burst into tears.

Daisy shot forward and enveloped her friend into a tight embrace. Daisy was shocked by the tremors that rippled through Angel's body.

'I don't know what to do. I don't know what to do. I don't know what to do,' Angel chanted over and over until her voice sank once again into gut-wrenching sobs.

This was so unlike Angel that Daisy wondered if she'd been doing gear. She'd lost documents about a case a couple of times before and never reacted like this. Strange how popular Charlie had become all of a sudden now he was dead, Daisy mused. First Randal Curtis told her to let him know if she found anything inter-esting; then Jerome said that Charlie might have something that would help his class-action case; and now Angel looked like it was the end of her life because Charlie had her documents.

Suddenly Angel wrenched herself out of Daisy's arms. She shook her hair back. 'I'm fine. Completely OK.' But her voice sounded as tight as a violin string. She twisted around and grabbed her bag near the sink.

'Angel.' Daisy moved towards her, concerned about the state of her friend. But before she could reach her Angel swung around. 'I'll see you tomorrow.' And with that, head down, she pushed past Daisy and was gone.

Dazed, Daisy watched the empty space for a few seconds. What the hell had just happened in here? Earlier that day at the funeral Angel had whispered that she had a hot date with the new guy in her life. Daisy rubbed her hand over her face. She was too tired to figure it out. She'd see Angel tomorrow and help her find her documents. She pulled the key out of her pocket and moved towards the cabinet.

The key didn't fit. She rattled it anxiously and it became stuck. By turning it very slowly, she managed to get it back out again. She held the key up to the light. It had seen better days, it was marked and chipped but she knew it was the one. It had to be the one. She took some hand cream out of her bag and rubbed some over the key. Then, very carefully, she put it back into the lock, turning it gently one way and then the other until finally it caught the latch and the door creaked open.

Inside were two shelves. None of the usual bottles and boxes found in a typical medicine cabinet. Certainly not the illicit drugs she thought Charlie might have locked away. Instead, sitting pretty, on its own, on the top shelf was a large, beige A4 envelope.

Puzzlement rippled over her face as her hand felt what was inside. Flat, long, rectangular. She put her hand in the envelope and drew out three sheets of A4 paper.

Daisy plonked herself down in Charlie's swing chair. Switched on the desk lamp. She held the stapled sheets of A4 paper in her hand. Scanned the information on the top sheet. Relaxed back in the chair when she realised that what she was reading were the details of a safe-deposit box in Charlie's name. Her gaze flipped back up to the top of the paper. To the address of the bank where the box was held:

K&I International Bank
Canary Wharf Square
Isle of Dogs

So Charlie had a deposit box, nothing strange about that. But why would he keep the papers locked away and hidden in a medicine cabinet? She flicked to the next page. Details of ownership. Charlie's name and signature. She looked lower down the page. That's when her world rocked. At the bottom a single name was scrawled in black pen.

Frankie Sullivan.

Angel watched, hidden in a corner of the second floor, as Daisy bolted out of Charlie's office. The distressed look on her friend's face told her something was wrong. Daisy hustled into the lift. Angel eased from behind her hiding place and gave it five minutes, enough time for Daisy to be well away from the building.

She pulled out her mobile. 'Sean,' she addressed the reception downstairs. 'I wonder if you can come up here for a minute. I seem to have locked myself in the Ladies.'

She punched off and ran for the stairs. When she reached the reception it was empty, as she knew it would be because she'd just sent Sean upstairs. She ran into a room directly behind the reception desk. She stared at the surveillance equipment, which included a divided screen so that the security guard could observe each floor. She rushed forward when she saw the machine tape-recording all the images. She pressed eject. Shoved the tape under her jacket and raced to the exit.

Angel waited nervously near her silver Porsche on the roof of the four-storey car park. She'd called Tommy after belting out of Curtis and Hopkirk and he had asked her to meet him there. She shivered in the cool night air; this wasn't an end of town she usually came to. All she wanted to do was hand over the tape and then pretend she'd never met him. Daisy had always said that her love of men would get her into trouble one of these . . .

She whirled around when she heard a footstep next to her. Her hand tightened on the tape as her petrified gaze found Tommy inches away from her. He wore a thigh-length leather jacket and stood tall and mean in the night shadows. Her breath tightened in her throat.

'So what you got for me?'

She thrust the tape at him as if it were a disease. 'Daisy was in Charlie's office—'

'Doing what?' His question was hard as he took the tape.

'I don't know. But whatever she was doing is on that tape. It's the security tape.'

Tommy smiled as he shoved the tape into his pocket. He looked up at her. 'You done good, girl.'

Angel took one, then two steps away from him. A crooked smile flashed onto his mouth. 'Where you going in such a hurry babe?' He spread his arms wide. 'I think my girl deserves a treat.'

Angel swallowed as she hesitated. The she cautiously moved forward, one slow step at a time. His arms engulfed her. Pulled her tight. He dropped his mouth close to her ear. 'There's no need for my girl to feel frightened of Tommy.'

Frankie Sullivan. Frankie Sullivan. Frankie bloody Sullivan.

Daisy paced up and down inside her lounge as she saw her dad's name over and over again on Charlie's safe-deposit box papers, which she held in her hand. She had always thought her dad's lawyer had been Bell Dream, Anna's girlfriend. How the heck was her dad, a gangster, connected to Charlie, a lawyer and family man? She knew whatever Charlie's deposit box held about Frankie wouldn't be good. Frankie might have been the best father in the world to her, but to most of the world he was a psychotic bastard who let nothing and no one stand in his way. Her dad hadn't broadcast his work in the house, but as she'd got older she'd heard the stories about him. Like that time she was in the loo at school and heard a group of girls on the other side of the door, who weren't aware she was in there, whisper scandalously about how Frankie Sullivan had put one of the other dads in hospital with both legs broken and smashed ribs because he hadn't paid back money he'd owed to him on time.

Daisy stopped pacing as a horrifying thought slammed into her. What if something inside that box linked Frankie to her? Made Randal Curtis realise that she was Frankie Sullivan's daughter? The sweat deepened on her skin as she saw all her plans for her career and Jerome blowing in the wind. All her dreams about having her own family disappearing in the dust. Another thought slammed into her. What if it connected Charlie to something unsavoury and ruined his reputation? She couldn't let that happen to Charlie. Happen to the man who had become like a second father to her in the last two years.

Deflated she finally stopped pacing. Her head thumped like crazy and she felt as stressed as she'd done the first night she'd come to live with Jackie. She couldn't go on like this. She needed to figure a way out of this mess for Charlie.

She hurried to her bedroom, hand still tight on the safe-deposit box papers. She stopped in front of her dressing table. Placed the papers down. Pulled out the drawer. Drew out her happy pills. Just one, that's all she needed. Just to see her straight. Just to get her to think. She dropped a single, small white pill into her palm and hesitated, remembering how messed up her mind sometimes got after taking one. Not to mention all that stuff in the papers and on the Internet about the dangers this drug was supposed to pose to a user's mental health. Those stories about breakdowns, hallucinations and suicides. Websites for 'victims' of the drug, questions in parliament, petitions to get it banned. But she was only going to do it this once. Wasn't she? Besides the tabs didn't always make her go gaga. Sometimes they made her come over all calm, really relaxed, back in control of her life. And that's why she kept a bottle close at hand. It made her feel better knowing that they were there.

She popped the pill. Swallowed. Held on tight to the dressing table. Then she thought, 'what the fuck, I need this' and took one more. Closed her eyes. Stayed like that for God knows how many minutes. Her breathing eventually evened out. Slowed down. Her heart returned to its normal pace. She sighed. That was it, they were doing their magic. Untwisting her tangled nerves, setting her heartbeat back to its regular pace. The images in her mind were still running a bit too fast, but she knew that would sort itself out. She stayed like that for some time, knowing she needed to give the medication the time to work. Finally she re-opened her eyes. And froze at what was reflected back at her in the mirror, swimming in her mind, like a mist in human form. There on her bed, with a half-smoked fag hanging from his lips, sat the last person she'd ever expected to see again. Her dad. Frankie Sullivan.

Twelve

Everything around Daisy disappeared. The furniture. The walls. The very ground beneath her feet. The only thing that existed was her dad.

He eased the cigarette from his mouth and gave her a bitter-sweet smile. Then he started to sing, their song, The Mamas and Papas' 'Dedicated To The One I Love'.

His voice was husky and soft, taking her back on a journey of her childhood – summer days in Southend on Sea; afternoons spent at the matinee show at the pictures; dancing together, once a month on a Friday, at the Hammersmith Palais. She'd loved those Fridays. Loved dancing. Safe and secure in her dad's arms, laughing and smiling, looking forward to the other great things she knew that they would do together in the future. Suddenly his voice stopped. Daisy couldn't look away.

'Hello, gel.' He pulled a lug from his ciggie. Let out the smoke slowly. 'Who would've ever figured that a girl of mine would go over to the bright side? Not that your ol' dad ain't pleased, of course I am. What father wouldn't be?' The smile dropped from his face as his expression set into one resembling the coldest piece of marble. 'Don't spoil it all by coming over to my side. In both senses of the word.'

Abruptly she crashed into the dressing table, sending its contents – perfume bottles, jewellery box, pills – banging and rolling across its surface. With shaking hands she steadied the dressing table. Flicked her terrified gaze to the mirror.

He was gone. She twisted desperately around. No smoke. No sign of anyone else. The furniture was back. And the walls. And, thank God, the ground beneath her feet. She hadn't ever told Jackie, hadn't ever told anyone, not even the doctor or therapist, that when she took the pills sometimes she'd start seeing her dad. Because as terrifying as it was, at least she had the chance to see him.

She covered her face with her trembling hands, wanting to cry. But she didn't. What a bastard of a day. First burying Charlie and now seeing her dead dad. She quickly righted the items on the dressing table. Placed the spilt pills one by one back in their bottle. That was it, she wasn't ever taking them again.

Her hand fell on the safe-deposit box papers, reminding her of what she had to do. *'Don't spoil it all by coming over to my side.'*

She dismissed the warning words from her mind. She had to get that box before someone discovered how Charlie was mixed up with the illegal activities of her dad. And she had no doubt they would be illegal because why else would Charlie keep them in a deposit box? But how was she going to get a safe-deposit box securely locked away in a bank?

Stella, Billy and Tommy looked at the fuzzy black-and-white images of Daisy on the TV screen. Watched her come out of another room in the office. Watched as she sat down and then take some papers out of a large envelope. Watched as she covered her mouth in horror. Watched as she bolted for the door.

'You done good, Tommy,' Stella said, raising her head to look at him. 'But how did you get this? And so quickly?'

Tommy eased back away from his mum's desk in her private room on the top floor of the brothel. 'I ain't thick am I? I know people . . .'

Stella sighed. Everything lately with her son was a competition. If she did something he had to go one better. Mind you, she couldn't fault him this time.

'I hope you ain't done nothing stupid.'

For a millisecond Tommy averted his gaze from her. The piano tattoo on his neck moved as a vein throbbed in his neck. Then he was back to his cocky self, gazing straight into her face. 'Course I ain't. My contact knows the score.'

'So what happens next?' Billy asked. His gaze kept moving strangely back to the screen to stare at Daisy.

Instead of answering Stella pulled out her mobile, dialled and waited. 'It's me . . .' she said into the phone. 'I know it's late, but don't forget you came to me not the other way around. I've got someone on the inside of this law firm who's given me a security tape—' She gritted her teeth at what the other person was saying. 'Listen, you dick, she's found something . . .' A fuming Stella shot to her feet. 'I dunno what. But whatever it is made her run from the room like she'd grabbed an old dear's purse.' She nodded a couple of times, then cut the call.

She looked back at the two men, their gazes pinned squarely on her. Finally she spoke. 'It's been twenty years.'

'You what?' Tommy threw out looking at his mum as if she were crazy.

'Twenty years since I've seen my daughter. And on Monday that's all about to change.'

Johnson stared at the mobile in his hand. He looked across the bed at his wife. Thank God she was still sleeping and didn't hear him talking to Stella. He eased out of the bed and walked, in his jim-jams, into the hallway. He made the call quickly.

'You were right, it is Daisy Sullivan. That's the good news. The bad is she might have found something.'

The person on the other end of the line said, 'Get Clarke to follow Daisy's every move, every day until I say otherwise.'

'You sure you want it to be Clarke and not me?'

'Is there something I need to know?'

Johnson hesitated. Then said, 'I'm worried about him. Keeps going on about what a great copper he used to before . . . Well you know . . . His life went downhill after that night back in ninety.'

'I'm fully aware of that. But remember we made a choice. A choice about what is right and what is wrong. Clarke will be fine. While he's following Daisy Sullivan I want *you* to be on Stella King's tail. Never, ever, underestimate Stella King.'

Thirteen

Misty McKenzie wasn't wearing her face as she walked towards the Shim-Sham-Shimmy Club in Wapping, it was only 7.05 in the morning after all. She shielded her make-up-free features behind a burgundy scarf and a slanted hat that she called her raspberry beret because of its colour and her love of Prince's song. Misty had started life as the youngest brother in the once notorious McKenzie underworld crew, but now he was a she and had become one of London's best-known drag queen bees, if not, as she would have you believe, the reigning monarch. Misty could be downright stroppy or an absolute doll. This morning she was definitely in stroppy mode because her hay fever was playing up something chronic. That's why she'd decided to get out of bed and get to the club early before anyone else showed their face. No one had bloody well be there because she hated anyone seeing her without her face on.

She walked past the warehouse conversion that Daisy lived in, which was a hop, skip and jump away from the club. She gazed idly up at the building as two people hustled past her on their way to Wapping tube station, wondering if everything was OK with the younger woman. Jackie had asked her to keep an eagle eye on Daisy while she was away. Jackie always worried about Daisy, and although she never said it, Misty suspected she worried that Daisy would turn into a carbon copy of her old man. Misty chuckled; Daisy was the most respectable out of all of them. She'd built a career for herself on the right arm of the law and had a terrific boyfriend on her other arm. Mind you, Misty had not always felt like that. She remembered the horrified words she'd said to Jackie when she found out who Jackie had taken into her home.

'*You take in Frankie Sullivan's little girl and you better be prepared for what's going to land on your doorstep one day, wrapped in a black bow – trouble.*'

But Daisy had proved her wrong. Except for that first night when Daisy had stayed at Jackie's, she had been the model of the perfect daughter. Maybe she should pop in, say hello. She thought for a minute as the sun broke through up above. Shook her head. Leave the poor cow alone, she must need a mega-snooze session after the sad business of Charlie's funeral.

Her heels clicked rapidly against the pavement as she walked towards the club. The Shim-Sham-Shimmy Club was one of London's legendary nightspots. It sat nestled, a long rectangular two-storey building, in a prime position overlooking the Thames. Misty co-owned it with Jackie, Anna, Ollie and Roxy. She knew that people whispered about where they'd got the cash to renovate the disused building into a swanky nightspot, but none of the rumours ever came close to the truth. Even Daisy didn't know the story and they'd all agreed it would stay that way, because if they told her they'd also have to confess how they'd been mixed up in Frankie Sullivan's life. And death.

Misty entered the club and sniffed. Shit, this hay fever was really knocking her for six. She walked quickly through the narrow reception and into the main room. She kicked off her new four-inch lilac heels and headed for the lipstick red stools at the bar. She sat and immediately twirled her pinched toes. Left foot, right foot. She shut her eyes. That felt sooo divine. Suddenly her head rocked in a violent sneeze. Bloody hay fever was doing her head in. She searched in her Burberry jacket pocket for her packet of antihistamine tablets and pulled out the first thing she found. Shit. She stared at the small long vial in her hand: Midnight Blue, one of the newest drugs doing the round in town, which she'd taken off one of the club's punters last night. The club had a strict no gear in here policy. She was about to shove the vial back in her pocket when she heard it. A noise, coming from somewhere upstairs. She twirled the stool around, her sharp grey eyes shooting up the steel spiral staircase that led to her office. The sound came again. Bollocks, there was someone in her office. Couldn't be the cleaner because it was too early. Couldn't be the girls because they were all chillin' out in sunny Spain.

Misty twisted her lips as she straightened her back, her hand tightened on the vial of Midnight Blue. Whoever it was wasn't going to believe what hit them once she got her manicured fingers on them. She eased off the stool. Headed to the other side of the bar. Picked up the first bottle she came across. Krug rosé champagne. On her turquoise-painted tiptoes she headed towards the stairs, holding the bottle of fizz in the way when she'd been a number one baseball bat wielding handy Andy in her family's outfit.

She took the steps two at a time, pushing her six-three frame forward. Reached the top. The white door was partially opened. She stopped for a few seconds, just to listen. Heard the noise again. The slam of a door inside. She hoisted the bottle higher as she eased quietly forward. Slipped her body inside. She spotted them immediately. Smaller than her, wearing black jeans, black jacket and black hair that fanned to their shoulder. The intruder trium-phantly whispered 'Sorted' as Misty took another step forward. She kicked her foot back. The door slammed dramatically behind her. The other person twisted around as Misty brandished the bottle, one-handed, over her head . . .

Daisy stared back at the one person she'd hoped not to see. Miss Misty. Daisy never called her plain Misty like her adoptive mum and aunts. This woman was the head of the family, the bossette, and Daisy had never felt comfortable just calling her Misty. So she called her Miss Misty, like most other people, out of respect.

Daisy clutched her black shoulder bag close to her side as she stared at the older woman in shock. Misty met her stare with suspi-cion, making Daisy feel like she was in front of a one-woman firing squad.

'Miss Misty,' was all Daisy could say.

'Miss Daisy,' Misty threw back. The wariness grew in her grey eyes. 'A bit early for you to come a-calling?' Misty's eyes darted around the room as if looking for something that explained Daisy's presence. Her gaze landed back on Daisy. She carefully placed the champagne bottle and vial of Midnight Blue on the desk.

'I couldn't sleep,' Daisy finally said. 'Went for a walk and somehow ended up here.'

Daisy had often come to the club with Jackie when she was younger. Daisy had loved the excitement, the noise, the chit-chat inside the club. And Misty had adored having her here.

'I suppose you're going to tell me that you're sleepwalking. Well, click your heels three times, girl, because it's time to wake up.' Misty peered anxiously at her. 'You ain't in a bit of bovver?'

Daisy vigorously shook her head as her hand tightened on her bag. 'Since Charlie's death I'm finding it hard to sleep.'

Misty rushed forward. 'Oh, you poor darling.' She wrapped Daisy into a huge, comfy hug. 'You wanna have some of that Midnight Blue on the table.' Daisy's gaze flicked to the side and settled on the vial on the table. 'I hear it can knock people out in minutes if they take enough. That's a joke by the way. I don't want to see you take stuff like that just to get a good night's kip.' Daisy looked up at the older woman. 'It ain't easy dealing with a loved one's passing.' Misty's voice dipped low. 'But then you know all about that.'

Daisy knew she was referring to her dad's death. Her heart beat faster as it always did when she thought about being fifteen and standing over her dad's coffin. Throwing a handful of dirt as the chill wind blew over her. No, it wasn't easy and it didn't get easier as time went past.

Suddenly Misty sneezed violently. She pushed Daisy away as she held a finger under her nose. 'Hay fever is murdering me.' She popped a heart-warming smile on to her face. 'Why don't I make us a brew?' Her eyes twinkled. 'With a little slug of gin in it to brighten up the day.'

Daisy couldn't help but smile back. 'No. I've got to go. Got a busy day at work.'

Misty tilted her head at her. 'You work too hard, you do. I know you want to prove that you're the best, but you've got to know when to kick off your heels and just shut the door on the world for a couple of hours.'

Daisy ran a hand wearily through her hair. Misty caught her arm as it fell from her hair. Her fingers touched Daisy's bracelet. Daisy sucked in her breath. It was an unspoken rule that no one ever touched her there. Never spoke about that night when she was fifteen. Never reminded her about what a foolish thing she'd done. She tried to wrench her arm away, but Misty wouldn't let go. Instead Misty spoke softly. 'Jackie and my other girls might not have figured out why you work so bloody hard, but I have. Jackie's gave you a home, gave you back a sense of family. But you want your own family and the only way you can do that is to work your cotton socks off.' A faraway look settled in Misty's eyes as she sighed. 'I know how that feels. When I decided to let the world know that I was Misty not Michael, I was shitting myself. Thought I was going to lose the only family I ever had. But you know what I realised?' The twinkle glimmered back in her eyes. 'Family ain't just your blood, the people you sat around the box watching *EastEnders* with. Your family are the people who look out for you, who love and hug you, who call you a silly cow when you need putting in your place, who don't ask questions you don't want them to.'

Silence fell around them as they stared at each other. The sun touched the river and swam into the room. 'But you know what,' Misty broke the silence. 'I'm a nosey bitch, so I'm going to ask a question maybe you don't want me to. What's on your mind, Daisy? Why are you really here?'

The question took Daisy by complete surprise. She thought she'd been playing it quite cool and that the other woman would never guess that her mind was in meltdown about Charlie's safe-deposit box. But then, someone was offering her the chance to unburden herself, and she was going to take it. 'What would you do if you—?' The ring of the phone on the desk stopped her words.

Misty swore as she marched towards the desk and checked the

caller ID on the phone. 'Sorry, I've really got to take this call. I've been trying to get hold of this supplier for ages – they're going to get a mouthful from me if they don't get that order sorted.'

As Misty picked up the phone Daisy headed for the door. 'Stay put,' Misty ordered, but Daisy was already opening the door.

'We'll chat later.' Daisy blew Misty a kiss and was gone.

Misty kept one ear on the telephone conversation as she watched Daisy quickly cross the dance floor below. Something was on that girl's mind. She'd been too nervous, like a cat that had just had its tail trodden on. If there was one thing that Misty could sniff out it was when trouble was brewing.

'If it ain't here by the end of the day, mate,' Misty shot into the phone, 'The Shim-Sham-Shimmy will be taking its business elsewhere.' She cut the call and hugged the phone to her chest. Something was going on with Daisy; maybe she should contact Jackie. Mind made up she swung around and made her way to her desk. Trawled through the top drawer looking for the contact number of Roxy's villa in Spain.

She plonked herself down as she dialled. The line connected. The other phone rang once. Twice. She slammed the phone down. No, she decided, she was being a silly old moo. Daisy had never done anything stupid in her life. Well, not since she'd done that crazy thing on the first night she'd been with Jackie. She was a good girl and a bloody hard worker and, if what Misty heard was true, was going to be one of the best lawyers in town one day. If Daisy was in any trouble she'd come and tell ole Misty? Wouldn't she?

Misty put the phone aside. Started to put on her face. As she ran her flame red lipstick across her lips the words she'd told Jackie all those years ago kept going around and around in her mind: She remembered the horrified words she'd said to Jackie when she found out who Jackie had taken into her home.

'*You take in Frankie Sullivan's little girl and you better be prepared for what's going to land on your doorstep one day wrapped in a black ribbon – trouble.*'

*   *   *

After leaving the club Daisy went straight to Curtis and Hopkirk's. She knew what she had to do if she was going to get her hands on Charlie's safe-deposit box. Quickly she shut the door of Charlie's office and sat at the computer. Turned the machine on. She was asked to put in Charlie's password, and she frantically tried a few combinations of numbers and letters until something clicked in her brain. Of course. She typed in 'jennifer', Charlie's daughter's name, and the screen changed to the main desktop display. As her hand moved towards the mouse she heard a door slam somewhere outside. Her hand hovered over the mouse as she twisted her head towards the door. Shit. Someone else was at work. She knew she had to move quickly because she couldn't afford for anyone to find out what she was really doing in Charlie's office. Her heartbeat increased as she flicked her gaze back to the computer. She moved the mouse until the cursor shifted across the screen. Clicked onto a folder. Clicked once again when she was inside. She scrolled down the long list of files. Shit, she didn't know which one it was. She heard a door outside open. Her hand stopped moving. She stopped moving. Footsteps sounded outside in the corridor. Got closer to the door. Her breathing pumped loudly as she waited. The foot-steps reached the door. *Please, keep moving. Please keep moving.*

The footsteps walked past. A wave of relief swept over her. She settled the arrow back over the first file. Clicked inside. Checked the contents. *Shit.* It didn't contain what she was after. She went to the second file. The third. The fourth. The fifth.

Her hands punched high into the air as her mouth formed a silent, triumphant 'Yessss!' when she found the document she was searching for.

Quickly she copied and pasted the information on to a new document and began to type. Five minutes later she looked at her handiwork. Half the job was done. She searched back through the files. Kept clicking until she found what she was after. Charlie's electronic signature. She clicked, dragged and pasted it onto the bottom of the document. She scanned the page quickly to ensure the alterations she had made were all in place. She found the print icon on the Toolbar and pressed. She got up and walked quickly to the printer on the other side of the room. A minute later she had the papers in her shaking hand. Read them. As she moved towards her bag she heard the footsteps again. Shock made her immobile. The footsteps grew closer. She dived for her bag. Picked it up. Opened her bag the same time the door of the office opened.

Daisy let out a huge pent-up breath as she stared at Sean, the security guard from downstairs. He stood in the doorway, an apologetic look on his face.

'Yes?' Her voice was impatient. She didn't need to be held up, not bloody now.

'Wasn't sure if you were in yet, Miss Sullivan.' His tone was quiet, his accent Irish. 'There was a delivery for you. The guys who brought it have left it in your office. I hope that was alright for me to tell them to do that?'

So that was all the noise she'd been hearing outside. 'Yeah, sure.' She waved her hand dismissively at him and turned back to the computer.

'Huge crate it was . . .'

She ignored him. He got the message and closed the door. Immediately she reached for her bag. Checked inside. Gazed at the safe-deposit security papers and the other document she had just printed. She slung the bag over her shoulder as she stood up and marched for the door. She opened it and stepped slap-bang into Randal Curtis. The impact jolted her back into Charlie's office. Randal's hands shot out to steady her.

'You're in early this morning,' he said once she had her balance back under control. Two men, in beige overalls and baseball caps were wheeling a large trolley past them towards the lift.

She stared nervously at the wrinkles around his questioning eyes. Her fingers rubbed against her left bracelet. 'Just getting some bits and pieces ready.'

'So, have you finished packing Charlie's belongings?'

Her fingers trailed to the straps of her bag. 'They'll be ready for his wife to collect by the end of the day.'

He pulled the lapels of his jacket together and spoke to her in the voice he used to wow the jury during closing statements. 'Nothing interesting then? For me, I mean?'

If only he knew, she thought. 'Just the usual stuff you'd expect to find. Charlie was a straight-down-the-line kind of man.'

'Of course he was.' He looked at her for a few seconds. 'Good work, Sullivan. You're the kind of person I would consider for partner in the future.'

If he had said this to her last week she'd be jumping for pure joy, but not today. 'Mr Curtis, I was wondering if I could take a few hours this afternoon just to sort some bits and pieces out?'

He nodded at her and was gone. She collapsed back against the wall. A few seconds later she hitched herself up and marched towards her office. She kept moving as she flung the door open. She stopped mid-stride and took an immediate step back when she saw a large wooden crate in the middle of the room. The security guard hadn't been kidding when he told her it was huge. The crate was tall rather than wide. She stepped towards it, giving it a puzzled look because she hadn't ordered anything. Then a huge smile beamed across her face. It must be from Jerome. Every now and again he liked surprising her with pressies, which she loved. Looking at the size of this one he'd outdone himself this time. It was a few inches shorter than she was, so she stood on a chair, and began to eagerly remove the lid. She placed it on the floor and shot back up to peer inside. The top was stuffed full of crumpled newspaper with strands of something that reminded her of tousled blond hair peeping from the middle. She couldn't even begin to think what type of present this was. She leant down and swept the newspaper to one side. Pushed her fingers into the hair-like mass. Tipped it sideways. She gasped, covering her mouth in horror when she realised what it was. Who it was. Angel. Her friend's sightless eyes stared back at her. Daisy's gaze skidded downwards and stopped when she saw the line of dried blood on the neck. Angel's throat had been cut.

Fourteen

Daisy covered her mouth with horror as she stared at . . . at . . . at . . . Her hand pressed harder against her mouth. She felt her tummy move. Shit, she was going to be sick. Her cheeks bellowed to the size of mini balloons as she dry heaved. As she stared at the dead body of her best friend.

She might not be dead, Daisy reasoned crazily. She might just be . . . hurt. Daisy's trembling hands fluttered away from her face. She could barely look at her friend, whose grey face had lost its artificially tanned look. She leant forward, moving her hand cautiously towards the body. Her bracelet jangled as she reached towards the pulse in Angel's neck. She avoided looking at the deep cut below. She found her pulse. Froze. She didn't need a doctor, the coldness of the skin told Daisy all she needed to know. Angel was dead.

A few tears spilt down her cheek as her hand moved away. She got off the chair and eased backwards. Towards her desk. Reached towards the phone. Punched in 999. But before a voice could ask which service she required, she slammed down the phone as a terrible thought came to her. What if the police came and asked her what she was doing in the office so early? What if they found the documents in her bag? She shuffled back from the desk as panic took hold of her and leant against the wall. Shit, what was she going to do? Without knowing she was doing it, her hand dived into the pocket of her business jacket. Found her bottle of happy pills. She had meant to throw them away but somehow she found herself putting them in her pocket earlier, before she left for the Shim-Sham-Shimmy. Mind still moving at a mile a minute she unscrewed the lid. Tipped the bottle to her mouth. Closed her eyes as soon as she felt one of the pills fall on her tongue. Swallowed, hard. She stood traumatised, fixed in position, still trying to figure out what to do. She gave the medication time to work, but just taking them had a placebo effect. Her breathing slowed down. Her nerves settled back. Her blue eyes flashed open. She knew what she had to do. She was going to move the body. Get it out of her office.

'That's not clever is it? You're my kid, aren't you? Think about what you're doing . . .'

Startled she swung her gaze in the direction of the voice. Frankie Sullivan's voice. And there he stood, as casual as they come, leaning on the wall on the other side of the door. He was decked out in black jeans, a plain polo shirt with the collar turned up and his golden hair was tousled as if he'd just woken up.

He popped off the wall. Sauntered towards her. From the deep colour of his eyes she could see that he was furious with her. 'You can't move a body. Look at the size of you.'

'But Dad, the cops might think I had something to do with it.'

He pushed his palms flat onto his hipbones. 'And why the bollocks would they think that? Unless you're hiding something, of course.'

Daisy's clamped the bag closer to her body using her upper arm and elbow. 'Dad, tell me what to do?' she pleaded.

Frankie didn't answer her. Instead he moved closer to the body in the crate. Tilted his head, making his hair flop over his face, as he peered hard at the now dead Angel. 'The first firm I ever really joined was when I was your age when I died, fifteen years old. I was a general dogsbody, run-around-kid, kept my mouth zipped and did what I was told. My first job was to help this geezer move the body of this woman.' Daisy sucked in her breath, but he didn't look around. 'Don't know what the poor cow did but they fucked her over so bad you couldn't see her face no more. Fuck, that was the first time I ever saw someone who was brown bread. So I helped shift her and you wanna know what I found out?' Now he cocked his head back at her. 'A dead body is one of the heaviest things to move. I developed muscles moving her I can tell you. So the first reason you can't do it is cos you couldn't carry it anyway. And number two, the cops won't think you done it.'

'I found the body didn't I? I'll be in the frame.'

He turned back to the body. 'She's been dead too long. She was killed when you were still in bed.' He peered deeper. 'And look at this.' His finger waved above the cut on Angel's throat. 'This was a professional hit. Severed her windpipe quick and clean. You're not a professional killer are you? They'll know that.' He studied the dead body. 'You know what we've got here don't ya?' He turned his eyes back on her. She shook her head. 'A horse's head.'

'A what?'

'Remember that scene in *The Godfather* where the bloke wakes up to find the head of his favourite horse on the pillow next to him? That was a warning. This is your warning, girl. That's why she's been dumped in your office. Someone's trying to tell you something.'

She stared at the body even more confused now. A warning of what? No one else knew about Charlie's deposit box.

'You need to watch your back,' Frankie gave his own warning as he straightened up.

But before she could respond the door handle started to move. She sprang off the wall. The handle kept turning.

'What do I do?' She looked beseechingly at her dad. The door started opening.

'What any other female would do in this situation.'

As the person at the door pushed inside the room, Daisy let out a blood-chilling scream.

Daisy burrowed her distraught face deeper into Jerome's neck. They sat at the desk in Randal Curtis's office. Shock was still pulsing in her from finding Angel. Charlie was dead and now so was Angel.

'Feeling better?'

Daisy lifted her head. 'How could anyone do that to Angel?'

Jerome rubbed the pad of his finger gently over her beauty spot. 'Just tell the police everything you know.'

Daisy's eyes darkened. 'But I don't know anything.' She shrugged her shoulders. 'The security guard told me a large package had been delivered to my office and the next thing I know I'm looking at Angel's . . .' Her voice ceased up. All she could do was numbly shake her head. 'Where's my bag?' She anxiously looked around.

'I've got it.' Jerome picked it up from the floor and passed it to her. She held it tight to her tummy as she checked her watch.

'You got somewhere to be?'

Daisy dipped her head so he couldn't see her eyes. 'Yeah. You know what it's like, appointments coming out of my ears.'

Jerome placed his arms around her again as he said, 'Don't worry about those – the police will be here soon to interview you.'

She nodded just as the door opened. Daisy and Jerome pulled away from each other. A rumpled and stressed Randal Curtis strode in. Behind him was another man that Daisy couldn't quite make out. Randal stepped to the side revealing the other man. Tall, finely suited and black.

'Hello again, Miss Sullivan,' Curtis said. 'This is Detective Inspector Johnson.'

'You murdered her didn't you?'

Johnson felt like punching the wall he stood against outside the law firm. And if Stella King had been there he would have beaten on her as well. Instead he accused her furiously on his mobile. He'd just finished taking a statement from a dazed Daisy Sullivan. For all the good that had done, she'd been too shocked after discovering her friend's body.

'What the fuck are you on about?'

'The girl at the law firm. The one who works with Daisy Sullivan.'

'Sorry mate, you're going to have to give me a bigger clue than that,' she responded sarcastically.

Johnson fought for control with his anger. 'You told me you got the security tape from someone inside the firm and my guess is that someone was this Evangeline Spencer-Smith who is currently in Daisy Sullivan's office with her head nearly hanging off her shoulders.'

'You're shitting me ain't ya?' He heard the shock in her voice. But he was having none of it.

'Listen up, bitch, I don't want to play with you anymore than you want to play with me. I'm giving the orders and you're taking them, get it? So from now on, keep the stiff count down.'

'I'll get it sorted out.'

'She's a bit sparked out about her friend's death, but things are already getting out of hand, so make sure she knows that Mummy's back in town soon.'

'Don't worry,' Stella said softly. 'By Monday afternoon she's going to be wrapped up in my loving embrace.'

'You sure you don't want me to come in?' Jerome asked.

They were outside her apartment in Wapping. He looked at her with such tender concern Daisy almost cried. The interview with Detective Inspector Johnson had been gruelling, one question after another after another until she wasn't even sure she would have been able to tell him her name if he'd asked her. As she fought with her emotions she ran her fingers lightly down Jerome's cheek. 'I'll be fine. Oh no.' She let out a weary sigh as her eyes skidded down her arm and caught the time on her watch.

'Forget the rest of your appointments today.'

She bit into her lip. 'Sure,' she replied rapidly. 'I just need to lie down for a while.'

He pushed his head back to get a good look at her face. 'Anyone would think that you're trying to get rid of me.'

'No,' she almost shouted. 'No,' she continued more calmly. 'I just need to relax.'

'Right, I'm coming in and tucking you up in bed.'

Although she protested he wouldn't hear any of it and hustled her into her flat. A few minutes later a fully clothed Daisy lay on the top of her bed with Jerome beside her.

He kissed her sweetly on the lips. 'You fancy bangers and mash, just give me a shout.'

*   *   *

Jerome eased silently off the bed as he gazed down at Daisy. She was fast asleep. In some respects they were like chalk and cheese but in others they fitted so well together. He'd fallen in love with her the first time he'd seen her. Sounded naff but it was as simple as that. And next week, at his parents' cocktail party, he had a surprise waiting for her. He left her sound asleep and quietly closed the door as he went out of her apartment.

Ten minutes later he was at another door. Knocked. The person who opened the door said, 'Does she know you're here?'

'No. When I left she was dead to the world . . .'

Fifteen

Two days later, on Monday morning, Ricky Smart ducked his large frame slightly as he stepped out of the gates of Belmarsh Prison. His smooth, brown face breathed in his first shot of free air. He whistled Billy Joel's 'Movin' Out' as he rummaged in the blue carrier bag that held his belongings until he found his gold stud earring. He fixed it into the lobe of his left ear. Took out a fag and puffed, wishing it was a spliff instead. He slung the bag over his shoulder and started moving casually away from Her Majesty's pleasure. He hadn't reached the end of the road when he heard the purring of a car moving towards him from behind. He twisted around, smoke still in his mouth. A huge monster set of wheels, a sleek black SUV with smoky tinted windows. The car stopped beside him. The driver's window didn't ease down, instead one of the back doors sprang open. His body tensed the same way he'd learnt to do growing up on East London's streets. When a strange car glides beside you and opens its doors you better be ready that the greeting you get doesn't come courtesy of the nozzle of a gun.

He relaxed when he saw no shooter and pushed the smoke from his lips at what he did see inside. A woman. Stark bollocks naked. Slim, bleached blond top and below, seductively swaying to the old-style piano music tinkling inside and reclining against the puffed-up leather seats. He caught her eyes. Everyday blue, her pupils wide, riding high on either coke or crystal. She gave him a come-hither smile as she parted her legs slightly. He nodded but didn't smile back.

His head swung to the front of the car as the driver's window finally eased down. He walked over and peered inside. A white guy kitted out in a black designer suit wearing shades. He didn't need to be told who it was: Tommy King.

'What you waiting for, Ricky?' Tommy said, grinning revealing a set of crooked, but gleaming white teeth. 'Jump in the back and get stuck in.'

Ricky drew the last puff from his ciggie. Flicked the butt into the air. He reminded himself that this was Tommy King and he should keep a respectful tone to his voice. But on the other hand, he didn't want Tommy to think he was talking to a wuss. 'My mum always told me never to speak to strangers.'

The other man grinned. 'Tommy King's the name. I hear you're looking for work.'

'What man in my situation ain't? But I like to be self-employed, it's less trouble.'

'It's all about connections these days, Ricky Boy. The high street can't compete with the superstore – know what I mean? Small time means no time these days, so do yourself a favour.'

Ricky stared hard at Tommy and then got down to business. 'So what's on offer?'

Tommy's smile grew stronger. 'Plenty of time to chat later. Why don't you slip into the back and enjoy one of the perks of the Tommy King organisation?'

Ricky walked casually towards the back of the car. Jumped in. The woman's cheap perfume swam over him, pushing him back into memories of another woman who'd worn a similar scent. Remembered the last time she'd kissed him on the cheek when he was thirteen years old, before she went to entertain her clients. His thoughts hardened as he remembered the photo in his pocket. He ignored the woman beside him as he closed the door. Tommy juiced the engine and soon Ricky was moving from one chapter in his life towards another.

Without speaking to him the woman next to Ricky flipped out a compartment in the armrest between them. Ricky's eyebrows rose when he saw a mini Aladdin's cave of hardcore drugs – coke, smack, crystal, crack and two joints rolled up and ready to go. The woman's slim hand settled onto his crotch. He gazed at it as she started caressing him. He laid his hand over hers. He didn't look up to see her smile. The smile was soon wiped from her face as he eased her hand away.

Ricky sat back as his hand dipped inside his jacket pocket. His hand smoothed over the photo. Over the face of his sister, Jenna. Tommy King didn't know it yet but he was taking Ricky to the one woman who could answer questions about Jenna's disappearance twenty years ago.

An hour later, a blonde woman entered the K&I International Bank in the business district of Canary Wharf. It was twenty minutes after midday. She was dressed in an all black ensemble of a formal skirt suit and low level heels, and wore just a touch of gloss on her lips. She clutched her shoulder bag close to her side and hid her eyes behind Jackie O-style shades as she walked briskly past the security guard inside the entrance. The foyer was large, decorated in soft red and white and was surprisingly quiet. A young woman, wearing a navy, conservative suit, cream blouse and a jackpot-winning smile eagerly came towards the newcomer.

'Hi, my name's Teresa,' she stated in her I'm-your-new-best-friend voice. 'Can I help you?'

The woman didn't smile back. Instead she said, 'I've come about a safe-deposit box. It belongs to Charlie Hopkirk.' She extended her hand. 'My name's Jennifer. I'm his daughter.'

Sixteen

Ricky didn't like the turning Tommy's car took. It shot into a part of East London where he'd flexed his muscles as a street hood in his younger days. Dark alleys, stained cobble streets, grim lock-ups and even grimmer lives. Most people didn't come here unless they were forced to. His body tensed.

The car did a swift turn, which made Ricky breathe easier as they hit a stretch of road that resembled civilisation: some shops, a cab office and a few people milling about. The car stopped abruptly outside an amusement arcade. Tommy turned to face Ricky and threw something at him. Instinctively Ricky's hands came up. Caught what was lobbed his way. He looked. His breathing stilled in his throat. A gun. A semi-automatic pistol.

'I've seen your CV but you still need to do an interview,' Tommy said.

He followed his words through by stepping out of the car. Ricky followed him, leaving the woman next to him behind with a sulky look on her face. He thrust the shooter into his waistband. Once they entered the building Ricky realised that this was no amusement arcade. It was a players' club, its membership strictly reserved for gangsters. The décor was deep red, the lighting dim. There were tables, sofas, armchairs and fruit machines, while drinks – and anything else – were served at the long, chrome bar. The day might just be beginning outside, but in here it still could have been the dead of night. The clientele mainly stood around in their suits and designer clobber, no doubt bragging and laughing about rivals they'd sorted out, weapons they carried and jobs they might or might not ever do. Tommy approached a table where four men were deep into a game of poker with a bottle of whisky.

As if sensing his approach one of the men lifted his head up. He was younger than Tommy, but not by much; thin, with a pock-marked face, gelled dirty-blond hair and a gleam in his eye that said he thought he was king of the world.

He tilted his head to the side and threw Tommy a fuck you stare. 'Look who it is, fellas?' He plastered a cocky grin onto his chops. 'Tommy King. Thought you were only seen about town hiding behind your mum's skirt.' One of the men at the table laughed wildly. The other two didn't. Joke about Stella King in public and you were asking for trouble. Around them the room fell silent.

Tommy glared back at the man as if he were looking at doggie do under his shoe. 'I caught one of your girls dealing shit in my place. I've told you before, Johnny Digby, to stay off of my patch.'

The men's posse at the table shifted from relaxed to high alert.

'Whoever's been whispering in your ear has fingered the wrong bloke. Couldn't have been me, I've been too busy with my lawyer, lovely girl, who just got me off a charge.' He dismissed Tommy with a contemptuous look. Stared back at the cards in his hands. 'Come on fellas, let's get back on with—'

'You ain't speaking to your bitch brief now, sonny,' Ricky butted in, stepping forward, his imposing height casting a vast shadow across the table. 'Mr King told you to do something, nice and polite, so why don't you give him a nice, polite nod of the head.'

Johnny raised his head and stared at Ricky. Decided he was another piece of worthless shit. 'Is Mummy busy? Is that why you've brought your boyfriend instead?' He let out a hoot of a laugh rocking back on his chair.

Ricky leapt forward. Grabbed the back of Johnny's head mid-laugh. Smashed his face onto the table. 'When Mr King asks a scrote like you a question . . .' He jerked the man's head back up. There was blood pouring from his crushed nose. He slammed his head back on the table. ' . . . you open up that lying gob of yours.'

He raised his head again. Banged it back onto the table. 'And you tell him what he wants to hear.'

Ricky anticipated what happened next. The other two men lunged at him from the table. Ricky grabbed a leg of Johnny's chair and whipped it from under him. The largest of the men was almost upon him. Ricky lifted the chair and swung it in one movement so it crashed into the big guy's face, caving in his nose and cheek and sending him reeling backwards, spilling blood everywhere. The other guy seized Ricky by the windpipe in both hands, pushing him down on the table. The table collapsed under their weight. The man squeezed so hard Ricky could feel the life being wrung out of him. With his vision swimming Ricky's hand searched on the ground. Found the bottle that had rolled off the table and smashed it into the side of his opponent's head. Ricky's face splattered with sticky liquid, a mixture of blood and Jack Daniels.

Ricky staggered, breathing hard, to his feet. The others in the room were fixed in their positions. No one came forward. It wasn't their fight. Tommy stood there, arms folded, which didn't surprise Ricky. This was Tommy's little test to see where he fit into his crew. Ricky heard a moan. Turned to find the source. Johnny was lying on the floor, coming to, and Ricky had a little surprise for him. Ricky kicked the remnants of the table aside giving everyone an open view of what he was about to do next.

He stood over the younger man, lying twisted on the floor. 'Like I said, when Mr King asks a question he expects to be answered.' He pulled out his shooter. The whole room gasped and he didn't need to look to know that included Tommy. Aimed at the man's thigh. Pulled the trigger. The man screamed as the bullet tore into his leg. Without a flicker of emotion Ricky shifted the gun higher and plugged another cap into his shoulder. 'And that one's for Mr King's mum. If I were you I'd take the first bus out of here before she finds out that you've been running your mouth about her.'

'Time to go,' Tommy said.

Both men turned, moving past the silent crowd. As they reached the door Tommy shoved a wad of notes into the bouncer's pocket. 'Sorry about the damage. And tell him my mum says hello.' The bouncer paled. Just mentioning his mum's name would make sure that no one came calling on Tommy for compensation for the damage.

Once they were back in the car Ricky asked, 'Ready to tell me where I fit into your organisation, Mr King?'

'A mad cunt like you is only gonna be in one place – right by my side.'

Tommy's mobile started ringing. He pulled it out, listened. 'You what?' he yelled. He cut the call. Looked at the woman in the back seat. 'Alright, darlin', your taxi ride's over. Now fuck off.'

The woman reared up. 'But I haven't got any clothes . . .'

'That's alright. The sun's shining. Now get outta the fucking motor.' Whoever Tommy had just spoken to on the blower had really poked his ribs. The woman slipped her shoes on and got out of the car buttoning her coat. Tommy threw the car keys at Ricky. 'Get me to Bow now. There's some business I gotta sort out. And this time I'll do the fist-work myself.'

'This is Jennifer Hopkirk,' Teresa, the bank employee introduced her, voice still cheerful, to a male colleague who sat at his desk.

They stood in another room, which was rectangular and the size of a school assembly hall with polished floors, large clock on the wall and people working at desks on the edge of the room. A security guard stood posted just inside the door.

The man at his desk shot to his feet and introduced himself with a handshake. 'I'm Adam.' He was lanky, with a welcoming smile that highlighted his wholesome boy-next-door looks.

She took his hand. 'I need to talk to you about my father's safe-deposit box.'

He waved his hand at the chair on the other side of his desk. Once seated he clasped his long fingers together and said, 'I'm afraid it's the bank's policy not discuss any client's account unless you happen to be that client.'

She sagged in the chair as she ran her finger under her sunglasses as if she were wiping a tear away. 'My father recently . . .' She paused as if she found the words hard to say. 'Recently passed away.'

The happy-go-lucky attitude fell from Adam. 'I'm so terribly sorry to hear that. Please accept my condolences.'

She nodded and sniffed. 'I apologise for the sunglasses. I haven't stopped crying since I heard. It was such a shock.' She shook her head as her hand dived into her bag. She pulled out a hankie and dabbed it under the glasses.

He leant over and whispered, 'Please, take your time.'

'I was clearing his things away when I found this.' Again she dug into her bag. She placed a handful of papers in front of him on the table. He scrutinised the papers. Then turned to the computer on the desk and began to type away. Suddenly he started tutting as he continued to look at the screen. He pressed the space bar and at the same time shook his head. He shot the woman sitting opposite him an anxious look.

'Is there a problem?' she asked.

'No, no, madam.' He turned back to the screen.

Her fingers played with the clasp of her bag as she twisted towards the entrance the same time a security guard came into the room. The guard kept moving. In her direction. She twisted back towards Adam. He darted another anxious look her way. Her hand tightened on her bag as the security guard kept moving towards her. He pulled out his walkie-talkie. Her unpolished nails sank into the soft leather material of her bag.

'Sorry about that.' Hearing Adam's voice she swung back to face him. The security guard was almost upon her as he spoke into his walkie-talkie. He drew level to her. And walked right past.

'Miss Hopkirk, are you OK?' Adam asked enquiringly. 'Can I get you some water?'

The blonde shook her head. 'It's just the strain of Daddy's death has been immense.'

He shot her a sympathetic look. 'And making you wait so long I'm sure hasn't helped. Sorry about that but we seem to have some gremlins in the computer system today, which means everything is taking twice as long.' He paused so that he could fully face her. 'Our records show that the document you've given me is an authentic copy of your father's safe-deposit box form, but I'm afraid I still can't release anything to you.'

She pushed inside her bag again and pulled out another clutch of papers. 'And I found these as well.' Her hand shook as she passed them to him.

He quickly scanned the contents. 'It says that your father has given you power of attorney over his deposit box.' His gaze rested on the spot where Charlie Hopkirk's flourished signature lay. He raised his head to look at her. 'Have you got any ID?'

She shook her head, sniffing as if she was about to cry. 'I didn't realise I'd need any. Daddy's unexpected death . . .' She let her sad words hang in the air.

He looked at her for a few seconds, eyes flickering. Then made his decision. 'I understand. Let me see what I can do. Because you haven't got any ID I will need to ask my manager if I can proceed. I'm sure you understand . . .'

'Of course.' She leant forward and covered his hand with her own and mouthed thank you.

He blushed at her intimate gesture. Clearing his throat he got up and walked towards a woman sitting at the desk nearest the door. He leant down and spoke to her and slipped the paperwork onto her desk. The woman raised her head and made direct eye contact with Jennifer Hopkirk. The woman gave her a hard assessing look. The kind of look that said that this woman took her job way too seriously.

Finally Adam's manager looked away. The woman picked up the phone on her desk, moving her lisp tersely as she spoke. She ended the call. Spoke to Adam. Passed him the paperwork. He was soon striding back towards Jennifer.

'My manager knew your father and apparently he often talked about you. So she's willing to let you have access to the deposit box.'

She stood up. 'I can't thank you enough.' She held out her hand and took the papers that he gave her. Startled she looked up at him. 'The power of attorney papers are not here.'

'My manager insisted on hanging onto them until we've finished.'

The woman at the desk peered at Adam and Charlie Hopkirk's daughter as they made their way to the exit. She turned her attention back to the papers. She drummed her fingers against the desk as she reread them. Her fingers stopped moving. She turned to her computer and started tapping away at her keyboard, her eyes glued to the computer screen.

'I'm gonna be a couple of hours,' Tommy said as he drew up outside a high rise in Bow. The type of tower block that looked like it hadn't seen a lick of paint since it had been built. He took out his wallet and threw some cash at Ricky. 'Get yourself down to Canary Wharf and buy yourself some decent clobber. I've got an office dress code. Get with it . . .' He chucked the keys at Ricky. 'Back here in a couple of hours, OK?'

As Tommy eased out of the car, a loud skidding noise tore up the air outside. Suddenly the car jumped forward. Ricky ended up flat on the backseat and Tommy half on and off the driver's seat.

'What the fuck?' Tommy growled as he leapt out of the car the same time as Ricky. They both turned to find another car had banged into their motor from behind. A medium-sized man got out of the other car. He had the type of clothes and face that blended into a crowd. He looked nervous as Tommy stormed over to him. But he never made it because Ricky grabbed his arm.

'Leave this to me, Mr King. You go and make your visit and I'll sort it out.'

Tommy shook his arm free. Sent the shaken-up man beside the other car a lethal look. 'Make sure he understands whose motor he's pranged,' he hissed. He turned and moved away. Then stopped and twisted back to Ricky. 'I hate all that mister shit. Just call me Tommo.'

Ricky nodded as he walked away. Ricky stormed towards the other man. Before the man could open his mouth Ricky grabbed him by the collar and slammed him into his car.

'Me and you need to have a chat.' He twisted his mouth, but said nothing for a few seconds. Then whispered, 'Has he gone?'

The man he held looked over his shoulder and nodded and rubbed his forehead. 'Ease up, Ricky, you don't need to be that good.'

Ricky loosened his grip. 'Never mind your head – I'm in. Did you bring it?'

The other man nodded.

'Good. I've got a couple of hours so follow me to Canary Wharf and you can give it to me then. Plus I'll give you the full SP on what I've heard from Mad Tommo so far.'

'I don't mean to rush you,' the blonde walking next to Adam said as they moved down a flight of stairs 'But I've got to go and look at some headstones . . .' Her words ended on a croak followed by a sniff.

Adam wanted to put his arms around her, but that was against bank policy. Never get emotionally involved with a client. But he felt bad leaving her in this distressed state. He stopped abruptly, startling her. 'I've got the number of a really good grief counsellor . . .'

'Thanks, but I've got that all sorted out,' she cut in, her words falling rapidly in the space between them.

'I know exactly how you're feeling. My dog died last year and—'

'Please.' His mouth snapped into place, startled by her hard tone. 'Just show me the deposit box.'

Feeling slightly peeved at her manner Adam escorted her along a narrow corridor, towards a large door. He pulled out a bundle of keys. Unlocked the door. Adam noticed the sweat beading the woman's forehead as her hand pressed her hair into place at the back of her head. He pushed the door back. Another corridor leading to another door.

'You don't believe in taking any chances here,' she said, as glanced down the corridor.

'Only the best security at the K&I bank,' he informed her proudly.

They moved down the corridor, the click of her heels echoing loudly as she quickened her pace. They reached the door. He opened it revealing a six-foot plus security guard waiting on the other side. The woman next to him missed her step and stumbled.

Adam's manager looked closely at the computer screen. She raised her head and signalled with her hand for a colleague at a neigh-bouring desk to join her. The other bank employee quickly did her bidding. He leant over her shoulder as he too looked at the computer screen. They looked at each other. Her colleague shook his head. She grimly twisted her mouth. She picked up the power of attorney papers and briskly made her way towards the exit. She paused in front of the security guard who waited against the wall. Spoke to him. When she exited the room he followed her.

The security guard and Adam nodded at each other.

'Finally here,' Adam said as they moved past the security guard and approached yet another door. He opened the door to reveal a room. The same shape as the room upstairs but much smaller, with plain-coloured walls, containing only a single desk with two chairs positioned in the middle.

Adam gestured to one of the chairs. 'Please take a seat.'

She followed his instruction and watched him walk towards a door set in the right-hand wall. He opened it and disappeared into another room.

Adam's supervisor stepped off the final stair. Walked briskly down the corridor with the security guard still behind her. She opened the first door and stepped inside. The security guard kept pace with her.

Adam reappeared in the room carrying a steel box, the size of a vanity case. He placed it in front of Jennifer Hopkirk. She ran the tip of her tongue over her bottom lip as she stared hard at it. Her gaze flipped up as he held out a small key to her, which she eagerly took.

'I'll be waiting outside,' he quietly informed her, his voice echoing in the almost empty room.

She slotted the key into the lock.

Adam's manager and the security guard reached the other guard stationed next to the entrance of the second door. She barely looked at him as she pressed onwards towards the door leading to the room that connected to the room containing the safe-deposit boxes. As soon as she was through the last door she saw Adam leaning against the wall outside of the room. He sprang forward when he saw her.

'Mrs Ahmed . . . ?' He questioned, clearly surprised to see her.

Without acknowledging him she past by and swept into the room. She watched Jennifer Hopkirk swing around to her, her hand on the key slotted into the lock of the deposit box and her other hand around the top of her bag.

Mrs Ahmed shifted the power of attorney papers into her other hand. 'I'm afraid I can't let you have access to the box.'

Jennifer Hopkirk shot to her feet, her hand grabbing her bag. 'Is there a problem?'

Mrs Ahmed moved towards her as she held the power of attorney papers with both hands. 'I'm afraid there is.'

The blonde stared at Mrs Ahmed. Then at the guard stationed at the door. Back to Adam's manager. At the papers in the older woman's hands.

'The papers should all be in order.'

'I'm afraid that our computer system is down and means we're not going to be able to release the box today.' She handed the power of attorney documents back over. 'But if you come back tomorrow, with your ID this time, we should be able to assist you.'

'That's a shame but I understand. Thank you for your time.'

She pushed past the security guard and calmly walked behind an apologetic Adam who escorted her back upstairs, where she bade him a crisp goodbye. The blonde crossed the reception. Walked out of the bank. She clutched her bag tight to her side as she quickly walked away. She carried on moving, the sun lashing heat on her back until she found the underground car park. Her walk length-ened into a stride as she moved past the cars until she found the one she was after. A red sports car. She tore off the blond wig revealing her own black hair knotted at the back. Whipped off the sunglasses revealing her stunning eyes. Bright and blue.

Seventeen

'What the fuck are you doing back here?' Tommy said as he swept into the one-bedroom flat on the sixth floor of the tower block in Bow.

Jo-Jo, his younger sister by two years, stared back at him with her arms folded across her chest. They'd kept contact with each other since she'd been thrown out of the house, speaking on the phone every week. Tommy knew that if his mum ever found out she would likely give him the full Stella King treatment

He should shake her repeatedly for coming back, but instead he rushed forward and swept her off her feet into an all-round hug. She squeezed him back fiercely. She was so small, like a delicate doll that needed constant looking after. They'd been through so much as kids. Stuff they'd never told their mum. Stuff that had shaped the course of their adult lives. The only person that Tommy had ever cared about was his baby sister Jo-Jo.

'You're taking a chance, aren't you?' But he followed his words by sweeping her off her feet into another hug. He eased her back to the ground, but kept his hands tight on her shoulder. 'She's gonna kill you if she finds out that you're back.'

Jo-Jo shrugged herself free from his grip. 'Two years is a long time.' She let out a nervous laugh. 'She must've forgotten all about it for now.'

'Forgotten? Are you off your head? Mum doesn't forget anything; it's the secret of her success.'

'It's a free country, I can go where I want.' And with those defiant words she headed into the living room.

Her brother followed her, his eyes skimming over the almost empty room. 'How can you stay in this dump anyway?'

'The tenants I've been letting it to have let the place go a bit . . .'

'Want me to find 'em and sort 'em out?' She knew he would do it if she gave him the nod. He'd always been there for her, not like that bitch of a mum of theirs. No, she'd been too busy building up an empire to notice what happened to her kids every time they were left with the sitter she got to look after them. Jo-Jo snapped her thoughts away from the memories because if she carried on thinking about them she'd go crazy.

'So you clean?'

'Told you I was off the gear months ago. That's one part of my life I won't be going back to.'

'You can't stay around here because she'll find you.'

'I know.'

Something about her reply worried him. 'You ain't thinking of going to see her? Are you sure you're off the stuff?'

She looked down at the thin carpet for a while. Then lifted her caramel eyes and gave him a bright smile. 'Let me make you a brew.' She twisted around, but he clamped his hand over her arm stopping her. 'Don't do it. Don't go and see her.'

Her features flattened into a bleak expression. Then she plastered the smile back on her face. 'Only thing I'm doing at the mo is making a nice cup of tea.' She pulled her arm free and glided out of the room and into the small kitchen. She breathed a sigh of relief when he didn't follow her. She popped the kettle on. Rummaged in the cutlery drawer. Pulled out a small knife. She waited for the kettle to boil. Then she poured scalding water over the knife's sharp blade. She sat on the solitary plastic chair by the window. She rolled up the right leg of her jeans. Stared at the criss-cross of horizontal scars that covered her lower leg. She bent over looking for a patch of clean skin. Without another thought she flicked the knife against her leg. A single line of blood bubbled to the surface. She leant back and closed her eyes feeling a great rush of relief. Now she could think. As the blood dripped down her leg she thought of the one reason she'd come back. To claim her mother's love. And God help anyone who got in her way.

Daisy leant on her car in the underground car park as she let out a huge sigh and momentarily shut her blue eyes. She scratched her head. The bloody wig had been as itchy as hell. That, she decided, had been one of the scariest experiences of her life. No, the second most frightening, as her mind winged back to the horror of Angel's slashed body in her office. Her finger rubbed furiously at the concealer and powder she'd used to disguise her beauty spot as she recalled how she'd plotted and planned over the weekend exactly how she was going to get try to get Charlie's deposit box. The plan had all hinged on her resemblance to Charlie's daughter. But Jennifer had blond hair while hers was black. She'd racked her brains last night thinking of a way forward. She could dye her hair? No, if she turned blond it wouldn't be a disguise anymore. Next option had to be a wig. But where the bloody hell would she get a wig that quickly from? Her mind had raced a mile a minute as she'd tried to sort that one out. Then bingo: she realised who had more wigs than a high court judge – Misty. So she'd gone to the club early and used her key to get inside. Sprinted up to Misty's office and checked through the cupboard where she knew Misty kept an emergency supply of clothes and accessories. She'd almost yelled out a triumphant 'Yessss!' when she'd seen the shelf with its display of wigs. Hairpieces in all colours and styles. She'd pulled down a buttermilk one with its punchy bob cut. As she'd slipped into her bag that's when Misty had barged in on her. That had been touch and go because she didn't like lying to Misty, even for a good cause.

But she'd got away with it and had got on to the next step of her plan. Forging power of attorney documents. Getting the documents was easy, they were on the law firm's general computer system. Getting Charlie's signature had been trickier. That is until she'd remembered that each lawyer had a copy of their electronic signature in their personal computer. Finding Charlie's hadn't been a problem, but the appearance of the security guard when she was stuffing the documents in her bag had shaken her up. And then running into Randal Curtis outside Charlie's office . . . Disguise and documents in place she'd been ready to rock 'n' roll towards the bank.

That was until the biggest bombshell of the day – Angel's body. That had shaken her up so badly that she didn't think she was going to be able to go through with it. Throughout the whole weekend all she could see in her dreams was Angel's dead body. She'd woken up every time shaken and confused. But on Sunday evening she'd gathered her nerves. She had to find out what was in that safe-deposit box for Charlie's sake. For her own. So she'd put in an early morning appearance at work, slipped out, then gone home, popped on her disguise and went to the bank where she'd played the grieving daughter to Oscar-winning level. She'd had the deposit box in her hand. Had held its key. Had . . .

She jacked backward, out of her thoughts, and squealed as an arm locked around her throat snapping her neck back.

'Just give me the bag and you won't get hurt.' The voice was gruff, male and hot against her ear. The stench of booze hit her nostrils, choking her already panicking airways.

She began to slip the strap of her bag from her shoulder. His body softened as he reached for it. That's when she made her move. She arched her body forward. Smoothly shoved her right hand between their bodies. Jabbed her fingers backwards into his eyes but didn't connect properly so he in was pain and shock rather than actually blinded. He yelped and his grip loosened on her neck. She drew her jaw back, lowered her mouth and sank her teeth into his forearm. He screamed as his arm fell away. Daisy jack-knifed away from him in a single step. She twisted around to find his fist shooting straight for her. Jumped back but wasn't quick enough. His fist caught her on her right breast. She slumped forward in pain. His hand grabbed the bag that hung loosely from her arm. But she locked her elbow up and wouldn't let go. With a yell she raised her fist and stepped forward with her whole weight behind her move. She caught him a stinging jab on his jaw. As he tottered backwards she raised her right leg. Pivoting on her supporting leg she dealt a powerful roundhouse kick to his side. He staggered and crumpled, limping backwards, propped against a wall, a few yards away.

It was only then that she clocked he was wearing a balaclava. This was wrong, all wrong. She knew street thieves, they have a go and if it doesn't work out, they run, there'll always be someone else coming down the road minutes later. And street thieves didn't announce their intentions through their head gear. But her friend wasn't running anywhere. He pushed his hand into his jacket pocket where he gripped something tightly.

'OK, show's over – now give me the bag.'

But she didn't hear his words because she was paralysed by what was in his hand. A wicked-looking kitchen knife.

When Ricky Smart spotted the man and woman he knew he was walking into trouble. He stopped in his tracks as he made his way to Tommy's car, which he had parked in an underground car park. He waited in the shadows. Kept watching. Suddenly the woman took a step back. The man stepped forward. That's when Ricky noticed two things at the same time. Number one, the man wore a balaclava. Number two, the man was brandishing a blade at the woman. Ricky tensed as he suddenly realised what he might be witnessing. A mugging? Attempted murder? Whatever it was he knew he had to make a decision what to do. Fast.

The man lunged towards the woman making Ricky's decision for him.

'Bitch, you wanna see the sunlight shining in your life again you'd better slide that bag towards me.'

Daisy remained transfixed by the knife. She couldn't move. Wasn't even sure if she was breathing. Wasn't even sure if this was real. Then she heard her breathing, rough and raw against the air.

'Now!' he yelled, taking a threatening step towards her.

She did what he asked her. Threw him the bag. She flicked her head up towards the man. That's when she saw him. A powerfully built black man standing behind her attacker.

Her attacker must have read the surprise in her eyes because he abruptly turned around. But he was too late. The man behind him let loose with a powerful chop to the side of his neck. Daisy scrambled back as her attacker staggered to the side. The newcomer flicked his right foot out in one of the best ninety-degree kicks Daisy had ever seen in her life. His kick caught the other man's hand, blasting the knife into high heaven. Her attacker gave the knife once last look, then spun around and ran for the exit.

The other man turned immediately to Daisy and walked towards her.

'You alright?' he asked, stretching his hand out towards her. She heard his voice for the first time. Deep, cockney, with a hint of Caribbean street style, very masculine. Friend or foe? She wasn't taking any chances. He took another step towards her, stretching out a hand. Before she knew what she was doing she'd grabbed his outstretched hand, twisted it around, kicked him behind a knee and flipped him onto his back.

Daisy jammed her thin, sharp heel onto his heaving chest, holding him down.

'Is this how you treat all your new friends?' Ricky asked between panting breaths, his face screwed up in pain.

Daisy took immediate offence at his cocky manner. Despite his pain he gave her a cheeky grin that *so* made her want to slap his face. 'Who are you? What are you doing here?'

'I'm just a guy, out for a walk. That's not a crime is it?'

'I don't know. It might be. What sort of guy are you and what sort of walk are you on?'

His cockiness grew. 'It's been eighteen months and ten days.'

'What?' she threw back, confused.

'Since I was given an eyeful of what a woman hides up her skirt.'

Daisy spluttered as she realised where his dark eyes were resting.

He moved with a speed that took her by complete surprise. He grabbed her leg and flipped her onto her back. She let out a loud groan as a powerhouse of pain shot throughout her body. Before she could take her next breath he was over her. Now he was the one looking down and she looking up. She breathed harshly as she stared at him and for the first time realised that he was a looker and a half. Smooth, dark skin and flirty, take-me-to-bed-now eyes. This was a man who played hard well past midnight. They stared at each other, both breathing heavily. Then he shot out a punchy little laugh. Moved back and stood up. Daisy scrambled to her feet, groaning as pain rippled inside her.

'Are you OK?' he asked.

She glared at him. 'Sure,' she answered sarcastically. 'I feel on top of the world after someone tries to mug me.'

Ricky tilted his head, surprise creeping across his face. 'So you think he was just trying to mug you?'

'Of course. What else could it be?'

He straightened his head. 'It's just that I've never seen a mugger wearing a balaclava. It's a bit too dressy for your usual hit and run street robbery.'

'You sound like an expert.'

The expression on his face became closed. 'You wouldn't believe the type of things I know darling.'

Yeah, and I don't want to find out, Daisy thought. She needed to get out of here quickly.

'Thanks for being my knight in shining armour, but I've got to go.'

His cocky grin shot back onto his face. 'Name's Ricky.'

'Da—' She blushed remembering the part she was playing. 'Jennifer. I really must go.'

She strode towards her car. As she opened the door she heard him say behind her, 'Ain't you forgetting something, Jennifer?' She turned and her breath caught. In one hand he held her wig and in the other her bag. *Shit*. How could she have left the evidence lying around? She briskly closed the space between them and took the items from him.

'One more thing, Jennifer.'

Irritated she looked at him. 'What?'

'Well, since I've seen you from "below" I might as well do this as well.'

Before she could respond he cupped her face in his large hands and lowered his lips. He gave her one of the most earth-shattering kisses she'd ever had in her life. He didn't use his tongue; he didn't need to with lips like his. Smooth and warm and moving with pure magic. Suddenly it hit her what she was allowing him to do. Allowing herself to do. An image of Jerome flashed through her mind. She stamped on his foot.

'Ouch, girlfriend,' he said with mock hurt clouding his mischievous eyes. 'That ain't the way to respond to a free gift.'

With a huff she twirled away and stomped back to her car with his laughter sounding out behind her. She jumped into the sports car. Checked her rear-view mirror. All signs of her kiss-nabbing knight were gone. She should be furiously scrubbing his mark from her, but instead ran her tongue over her lips. She chucked the wig on the passenger seat. Dropped the bag into her lap. Opened it and pulled out her bracelets. Pushed them back into place over her wrists. As she pushed the key into the ignition her mobile went off. What now?

She grabbed it from her bag.

'Yes?'

It was Charlie's PA 'I wouldn't disturb you because of what happened to Angel, but you need to get back here now.'

'Look, I'll be just a while . . .'

'You've got a visitor.'

'Tell them to make an appointment.'

'She says she's your mother.'

Eighteen

'She got away,' Clarke panted into the mobile.

He clutched his side as he leant heavily back in the seat of his motor a few minutes run away from the underground car park. Pain radiated from the four corners of his body. He was well out of shape for this type of run around. He'd been trailing Daisy Sullivan every step of the way. When she went to the club in Wapping; when she went to work; when she left tarted up in a blond wig; when she'd entered the bank.

'How did that happen?' Johnson's tone was disgusted.

'She was a bit tasty with her fists plus she had help.'

'Help from who?'

Clarke shook his head. 'Dunno. Boyfriend maybe? Big black guy with a pair of feet on him. Funny thing is I know I've seen him somewhere before.'

'Yeah? Look him up in our rogue's gallery sometime. Did she get anything from the bank?'

'She came out with exactly what she went in with. Mind you, I never saw what was in her bag, so she might have got the stuff from Hopkirk's box. What do we do next?'

'Nothing. We leave the rest up to Stella King.'

Ten minutes later Ricky was back outside the tower block he'd dropped Tommy at in Bow. His new boss was already waiting for him.

'I thought I told you to kit yourself up?' Tommy said as he eased into the back seat, happy to let Ricky drive.

Ricky checked him out in the rear-view mirror. Watched as Tommy dropped some white powder onto the back of his hand. Sniffed. Leant his head back against the leather seat as he closed his eyes.

'I had to see my grandmother on the Island,' he lied, using the local nickname for the Isle of Dogs. It wouldn't do for Tommy to know what he'd been really up to.

Tommy's eyes snapped open as he let out a loud laugh. 'My mum's gonna love you. She loves anyone who takes care of their dear ma and granny.'

'Where to, boss?'

The fun slipped from Tommy's face. 'We need to go to my lock-up to pick up a van.' He caught Ricky's gaze in the rear-view mirror. Caught the unasked question in his eyes. 'My mum needs us to do a job.'

Something must have gone wrong.

The thought beat urgently inside Daisy's brain as she walked briskly towards Charlie's PA's desk. She had changed quickly in a lightning visit back at her home, dropping her bag there and picking up a different one, and was now back to being Daisy Sullivan, highflying lawyer. Why would Jackie be back when she was meant to be on holiday? Why wouldn't she have called her? Daisy prayed that no one had been hurt. That something terrible hadn't happened to one of Jackie's kids.

'Is she in my office?' Daisy asked in a rush.

'No.' The other woman twisted her lips. 'I couldn't put her in there because . . . you know.'

Yes, Daisy knew. Her office was most probably still being treated as a crime scene after Angel's death.

'I put her in Charlie's office.' The other woman gave her a smile. 'She looks a lot like you. Tall and that beauty spot just above her lip.'

That stopped Daisy in her tracks. Tall? Beauty spot? Jackie was as small as a five-pence piece and the only thing she had directly above her lip was a nose. Daisy stared at the PA with a dazed expression as her finger self-consciously touched her own beauty spot.

'Are you sure she said she was my mother?' Daisy got a confident nod in return.

As she strode towards Charlie's office a strange, trembling feeling washed over her.

'She says she's your mother.'

Charlie's PA's words hit her again and again and again with every step that she took.

Her mother?

She shook her head slowly. The terrible feeling turned to dread.

No it couldn't be. No way . . .

The PA was right. The woman inside the office was tall. She stood with her back to Daisy, silhouetted by the light coming in from the window. She wore maroon stilettos and a leopard-skin fur coat that reached midway down her thighs. Her hair was pale and fluffed out and back.

'Can I help you?' Something held Daisy in the doorway. Dread? Panic? Fear? She wasn't sure, but she was not taking another step until this woman turned around.

She didn't have to wait long. Almost in slo-mo, the woman turned herself to face Daisy. Her breath caught in her throat as stared at just one thing on the woman's face. Not her heavy make-up, not her expertly plucked eyebrows, not her expression, which was half friendly, half closed. But at the beauty spot that was a replica of her own. Daisy's hand gripped the doorframe. Suddenly the woman's face slashed into a blinding smile. She held out her arms wide. And in a throaty, husky, cockney voice she said, 'Ain't you gonna give your ol' mum a hug?'

Daisy had always imagined the day she would meet her mum. She'd find her living in some pretty suburban house just outside of London. She'd go up the door. Press the bell. Anxiously wait on the doorstep. When the door opened it would reveal a woman, with a lovely smile. And when Daisy said the magic words, 'I'm your daughter,' her mother would fling her arms around her and start crying. Start telling her how she'd never wanted to give her up and had longed for the day she would see her again. And in return Daisy would sob back, 'Mum, Mum, oh, how I've missed you.' They'd cling and cry softly together. Speak aloud the plans they had to make up for lost time and dream up a future together.

Then the words that her dad always said to her when she asked about her mum came crashing back to her: *'Believe me Daisy baby. You'll never be old enough to know about your old girl.'*

Instead of a hug Daisy calmly closed the door behind her. The woman claiming to be her mum dropped her hands back to her side. Daisy kept her distance as her fingers stroked her left bracelet. 'What do you want?' Her voice tight, filled with so much cold resentment that the words almost froze in her throat. How could this woman, who looked like a stolen million dollars, have the nerve to come looking for her now? Have the nerve to have turned her back on her daughter so easily?

'You've still got Frankie's eyes.' Now the woman moved. Took one step closer, smiling at her all the way. 'My little girl has grown up to be a real stunner.'

Daisy folded her arms tight across her middle. 'I don't remember your name.'

'Stella. Stella King.' She took another step. 'Course me and Frankie never tied the knot so you're a King as well.'

Daisy repeated her earlier question. 'What do you want?'

'Look.' Stella waved a gold-ringed hand in the air. 'I know how you're feeling, babe. Pissed off. Angry—'

'You don't have a clue how I'm feeling.' Daisy's words were hard. 'How would you know what it feels like to have your mother turn her back on you when you're only five years old?'

Stella's deep voice dropped even lower. 'You don't understand Daze . . .'

Daze. Daisy flinched at the shortening of her name. 'You're right. I don't.' For the first time Daisy stepped forward. 'And maybe too many years have passed for me to give a flying f—' She sucked the word back, remembering this woman claimed she was her mum, 'toss about wanting to.'

With a snap of her head Stella threw her hair off her shoulders. She drew the strap of her bag securely over her shoulder. 'This was a mistake, alright.' Her features were tight. 'I should never have come here.' And with that she rushed past Daisy towards the door.

Daisy heart rate jumped as she watched Stella's hand reached for the door handle. That was her mum and she was getting ready to once again bolt out of her life. Daisy could feel her heartache starting all over again.

'Please don't go,' rushed out of her mouth before she could take the words back.

Stella froze. 'Please,' Daisy pleaded.

Stella's hand fell away and she turned. She sent Daisy a soft smile. 'You won't regret this, Daze.'

'I've missed you like hell, baby.'

Daisy winced at the words. They sat in a small café around the corner from the law office on Chancery Lane. The place was bustling with city workers looking for a quiet spot to take a breather from the daily grind of life. A latte and a mug of tea lay on the round white table between them. They'd already been here for a good ten minutes, with Stella firing eager questions at her.

How did you end up as a lawyer?

Have you got a boyfriend?

Where do you live?

Daisy looked at Stella; she so wanted to believe her words. But there were so many questions in the way. 'I went to live with Dad when I was five and I'm now twenty-six. That's just over twenty years, why leave it so long?'

Stella eased back in her chair and flicked her hair back with both her hands. 'I'll be straight up with you, Daisy. Neither Frankie nor me lived on the right side of the law. He went down for a four stretch, so I had to look after you the best way that I could. It ain't easy for a woman on her own. Then when he came out he said that he didn't want you living with me no more.'

Daisy tilted her head looking puzzled. 'But why would he say that?'

Stella leant across the table, her expression grim. 'You lived with me in a brothel.'

Daisy reared back in shock. 'We lived where?'

'Like I said.' Stella waved her hands in a carefree gesture. 'Times were hard for a woman like me. I had to put bread in our mouths and that meant finding work—'

'You mean,' Daisy stammered, butting in. 'You were a . . .' She swallowed. 'Sex worker?'

Stella threw her head back and laughed. 'Sex worker, eh? At least Frankie bought you up to have some manners.' Her laughter stopped abruptly. 'You want the truth, so here it is. I was a prostitute, a tom, on the game, call me what you like, but I was also a mum who was gonna make sure her kid was never kitted out in gear from the charity shop. I grew up in the gutter and there was no way I was gonna make you cut your teeth there as well.'

'But surely—'

'You wanted the truth, my girl. I could sit here and spin you a line about being a poor, innocent girl selling flowers in Covent Garden, but that ain't how it was.' She placed her manicured fingers over Daisy's cold hand. 'I love you and it don't matter what I've done in this life, I always will.'

But the life the other woman was placing before Daisy did matter. She snatched her hand back. Folded both her hands nervously in her lap. 'If you felt so strongly about me why did you turn your back?'

Stella eased back. 'I wanted to see you, but Frankie wasn't having none of it. Said as long as I was on the game the door was shut squarely in my face.'

Daisy's urgent words pushed her forward. 'Why didn't you come and get me once he died?'

'I had problems of my own going on and it didn't seem right to drag you into them. Plus I was a married woman, with two more kids to feed. So I waited and waited. Then the other day someone is telling me about how this solicitor called Charlie Hopkirk had gone to join the majority and that he had this really smart girl called Daisy Sullivan working for him. So I put two and two together and here we are now.'

Daisy ran two of her fingers across her bottom lip, her mind still in a daze. Was she really sitting across from her mum? 'This has all been such a shock. I'm going to need time . . .'

'Ah, but that's the problem Daisy, we don't have time.' For the first time Daisy saw a flare of solid steel enter the other woman's eyes.

'What are you talking about?'

'Like I just said, you worked for Charlie Hopkirk, didn't you?'

'You know I did,' Daisy answered, confused.

'Me and good ol' Charlie go back years. He was my first ever brief.' She leant forward. Her voice lowered as if she were telling a secret. 'Charlie was a favourite among my girls.'

Daisy let out a shuddering gasp as she realised what Stella was implying. That Charlie visited a . . . Daisy shook her head. No way. Not Charlie. Not her mentor. He was a family man. The man she'd placed way up high on a pedestal.

'I can see that you're shocked at the idea that Charlie liked a bit of illicit tickle. His sort are my best customers, you need to have a fair bit of poke to afford my prices.'

'I don't believe you . . .'

'Everyone's got secrets dear. And Charlie's got hold of one of mine. See, he's got something that belongs to me and you're the only one who can help me get it.'

Daisy's face sank. 'Is that what this is about?' Her voice was loud. People at the other tables turned to look at her. 'You never came here to see *me* . . .'

'Keep your voice down and don't get your M&S drawers in a twist,' Stella's voice was totally controlled. 'Let's just say I'm killing two birds with one stone.'

Killing. That's exactly what Daisy felt this woman doing – killing her.

Daisy half rose out of her seat.

'Sit back down.'

But Daisy just straightened to her full height.

'Sit down, Daze – or do you want to explain away your family history to all those nobs you knock about with these days? Your old mum, a "sex worker"?' Stella said softly. 'And I bet they don't know about good ol' Frankie. That's not a good career move is it? A big-time criminal on your birth certificate? Surely there's rules against gangster's kids being lawyers, ain't there?'

'I am not ashamed of who my dad was,' Daisy hissed.

'Maybe not. But how are you going to feel if I waltz back into your office and start telling your la-di-da friends my life story?'

Daisy wavered at the harsh realities thrown at her. She'd worked too long to let anyone spoil her future. She eased back down.

'See? That wasn't hard was it? Now, the thing is Charlie's got a safe-deposit box,' Stella swiftly started. 'And I know you know where it is. Because a little bird saw you take something from Charlie's office late last night.' Her voice hardened. 'I need that box.'

It took Daisy two seconds to remember she was also Frankie Sullivan's daughter. She lied like she'd never lied before. 'I don't know what you're talking about.' Daisy stared Stella straight back in the face.

Stella shoved her angry face across the table. 'Please, Daisy. Let's not spoil things – you know what happens to kids who tell fibs don't you? They get a smack. A big smack.'

'I don't know what you're talking about, but I tell you what I do know, I don't ever want to clap eyes on you ever again.' She grabbed her handbag off the back of the chair.

'All you've gotta do is give me the details,' Stella ground out as Daisy stood up.

Daisy flung the strap of her handbag defiantly on to her shoulder. She stared at the woman she'd waited years to meet.

'You might be my mum, God help me, but you can sod off.'

She twisted around and marched towards the door and was soon disappearing into grey, moody, afternoon light.

*   *   *

Daisy walked quickly as tears streamed down her face. Her gut tight-ened with tearful rage as she thought about the woman she'd just left behind. That was her mum? That evil witch? The woman she'd waited practically her whole life to meet? The sick shot up from her tummy. She covered her mouth. Quickly ran into a side street. Bent over and threw up. This couldn't be happening. This was a total nightmare. What was she going to do? She needed help. Now.

She straightened up and wiped her mouth with the back of her trembling hand. She pulled out her phone. Scrolled through the contacts list. Found Jackie's number. Made the call. Pressed the phone to her ear. It rang. And rang. And rang. Where the hell was Jackie? In her shock she had forgotten that her adoptive mum was on holiday.

'Bollocks,' she let out as she cut the call and slammed the phone against her chest. Her mind whirled as she thought about who else she could call. Jerome? That thought made her feel even more sick. What would she say to him? 'Oh, by the way, my dad was a gangster and my mum was a tart.' Jerome was a definite no-goer.

Who else? Who else? Who else?

She leant on the wall and breathed easier as a name suddenly pinged on in her mind like a light bulb

Misty. Of course.

Misty would know what to do. Her finger ran down her contact list as she quickly moved back into the main street. The rush of a speeding engine sounded somewhere behind her. She took no notice as she found Misty's number. Just as she was about to press it two arms like steel bands grabbed her around the waist. A hand clamped over her mouth pushing back her scream. The arms around her pressed painfully against her ribcage and lifted her off the ground. Legs kicking in front of her she was shoved face down inside a van. The door slammed as she scrambled on to her front. Terrified she watched as a young man crouched in front of her. He had a piano tattooed on the side of his neck. He smiled like he was about to coo to a baby in a pram.

'Hello there, sweetheart. I'm your kid brother, Tommy.'

Then his fist shot out and landed on her jaw.

Nineteen

Daisy slowly woke up to complete darkness. She couldn't see a thing. No shadows. No lights. Nothing. Didn't know where she was. She groaned, as pain suddenly burned across the lower half of her face. The right side of her face felt like she'd smashed her head into a wall. She tasted the metallic flavour of blood inside her mouth. Her body tensed as the previous events ran through her mind like a mad movie. The van. The man with the tattoo. The punch. She tried to shout for help, but something large and round, like a ball, was jammed into her mouth holding her tongue back. That's when she realised why she couldn't see. There was a hood over her head.

And the way her hair fell inside the hood and the sagging of her clothes and the pressure of blood in her head told her she was hanging upside down. She tried to move her legs, but they were secured, with something that felt like metal, maybe chains, to something else, perhaps a beam in the ceiling. Desperately she tried to move her hands, but they were wrenched behind her back by something cold, hard and round. Handcuffs.

'She's awake.'

It was a male voice. Not too far away, but not close either. She cringed as footsteps beat against the floor. Then she heard a squeaky cranking noise. Her body jolted as she started to move downwards. She wriggled her body in her desperation to get away. Someone laughed. For him at least the day had turned out OK. The blood rushed to her face as her body continued to move down. And down. And down. Her head smashed into a wall of freezing water.

The water clung with the heaviness of an ice-cold block against her face. The soaking hood clung, like a new skin, against her ears, her nose, her mouth. Shit, she couldn't breathe. In panic she screamed, but the ball inside her mouth muffled her noise. The pressure of the water grew. The hood grew tighter. She tried to kick her legs, but the muscles only tightened and twitched. Tried to move her arms, but they bunched and bounced behind her. She gulped hard, fighting for a new supply of oxygen to fill her lungs. But there was none. No relief. Tears sprang to her eyes because she knew she was going to die. How long she was under she didn't know but she could feel death clinging to her like the hood itself. Her body started shaking as her vision blurred.

Suddenly she was pulled up and out. Desperately she tried to draw in new waves of oxygen through her nose.

'Had enough?'

She trembled as she heard the voice. Throaty. Husky. Her mum. Stella King. No way. Her mum wouldn't do this to her? Try to murder her? Even the evil woman who'd paid her a visit must have her limits.

'All you've gotta do, my girl, is hand over what you found out about the deposit box.'

She wouldn't do it. But then she thought back to the water. To the sensation of losing her grip on life. Losing touch with reality. Losing everything she'd ever dreamed of. She made her decision.

Rapidly she nodded as more tears began to fall.

'See? That wasn't hard was it? Do you think I like doing this?' Stella whispered huskily.

But instead of being taken down she plummeted downwards again. This time she let out a muffled animal scream as she hit the water. She coughed as she shifted her head from side to side trying to get away from the hood. From the ball in her mouth. She wheezed as the hood and water tightened their grip around her nostrils. She fought for as long as she could. Then the other darkness came as she started to lose her grip on consciousness. As her eyelids fluttered down she was hauled back out.

'That was just a reminder, not to forget.'

The soaking hood was pulled from her dripping head. The ball gag unfastened at the back. She drew in air like a newborn babe. She squinted sharply as the electric light broke against her eyes. The first thing she saw was an elaborate claw bath, filled with clear cold water, underneath her. She ran her gaze over the rest of the room. She thought she'd be somewhere dark and dank, the type of place where gangsters took their victims to be tortured in the movies. But it wasn't. The walls were white with a hint of lilac. On the wall opposite was a huge Moroccan-style mirror with alcoves that housed unlit candles on either side of it. The floor around the bath was stripped wooden boards painted white. Where the hell was she?

Suddenly she felt big hands circle her ankles. Heard a clicking noise. One of her legs sprang free. She dangled one legged in the air. An arm cupped her back as her other leg was released. Before she could fall strong arms curved around her. She coughed as she pushed the wet strands of her hair from her face to look at who held her. She did a double take when she realised who had her in his arms.

Her saviour from earlier on in the day.

Ricky.

'Meet the family, Daze. Family is important to people like us.'

Daisy, who had been placed in a chair by Ricky, lifted her pale, freezing face at her mum's words and stared at the other occupants of the room. Unlike her they were all standing. The tattooed man, the man claiming to be her brother, who had punched her lights out just after he introduced himself as Tommy. Another man, older, more muscular and beefy. They made eye contact. He was the first to look swiftly away. Her gaze darted onto Ricky, whose eyes had looked fiercely at her as he'd placed her in the chair as if warning her to say nothing about their earlier encounter. She'd kept her mouth well and truly shut. And, of course, her loving mother.

Stella King moved towards her, her strong face set into a grim, deadly mask. Daisy cringed back in her chair as the other woman stopped in front of her.

'That one over there,' she pointed towards Tommy, 'is your younger brother, Tommy. He loves playing the piano when he's not breaking people's necks; I'm afraid he doesn't do requests.' Tommy smiled at Daisy as his hand went inside his black leather jacket. He pulled out a large blade and waved it in greeting at her as if it were his hand. Daisy sharply looked away.

'The man next to him is Billy, my right-hand man.' Stella's face glowed with a wide smile. 'The sweetest bloke in the world. You wouldn't believe it but he helps the lads at this boxing club. But what you got to understand is that his take on life was slightly altered after he did a ten-year stretch for killing his old man at the age of twelve. His old man throttled his mum to death. Now that's what I like, a man who is loyal to a woman.'

Daisy and Billy made eye contact, as they did earlier and again they looked swiftly away.

Her eyes swung around to Ricky. 'And this is . . . actually, who are you?'

Ricky leant relaxed, arms folded against the wall. He grinned back at Stella. 'I'm a dark, handsome stranger, Mrs King, the sort who steals the hearts of the maturer kind of woman.'

Stella giggled like a teenager. 'Saucy sod . . .'

'Excuse me, Mum,' Tommy warned. 'He's on my payroll, not yours. It was me that recruited him, not you. He's fresh out of Belmarsh and I'm not paying him to play boy meets girl. Certainly not with my ol' dear anyway.'

'Knock it off, kid,' Billy warned the same time he took a menacing step towards Tommy.

Daisy watched the family ping pong, stunned out of her head. Was this really her long lost family? Murderers? Jailbirds? *East-Enders* meets *One Flew Over The Cuckoo's Nest*?

'OK, that's enough,' Stella said calmly. 'You know the rule, Tommy boy, no one comes into this outfit without my say-so.'

Tommy puffed up his chest. 'Well, *I* say-so.' The tension tightened in the air. 'Anyway all I need to know about Ricky is he's handy with a shooter and defending my back without me having to ask.'

Stella hitched her head back. 'He ain't proved dick to me.'

'If it's dick you're after, Mrs King . . .' Ricky cut in softly.

Stella pierced him with her silver gaze. Then laughed.

'Where am I?' Daisy croaked, speaking for the first time.

Stella turned her attention back to Daisy. 'The Deadwood Hotel, Finsbury Park, it's one of my palaces of varieties. You wouldn't believe it but some men pay a load of money to be hung upside down and shoved head first into a bath of water. Near-death experiences really give some men the horn.'

'You mean this is a knocking shop?' Daisy squirmed on her chair as if there was something nasty on the seat.

Tommy let out a booming, bouncing laugh. Stella's eyes blazed, not at him, but at Daisy.

She grabbed Daisy's upper arm, half dragged her out of the chair and spat, 'Don't play Lady Muck with me, Daze. Bad-mouthing your own flesh and blood? That's not nice is it? Besides, everyone is recycling these days and that's all my girls do, recycle their bodies.'

Daisy rapidly nodded, seeing that the woman above her didn't care for having her profession dissed. Stella shoved Daisy back in the chair. Stepped back, her right hand rubbing absently over her left breast. 'Don't upset me, Daze. I'm a traditionalist, people like me still bury people like you under concrete foundations. And there's a load of scope for that with the Olympic village being built up in Stratford and all. You could bury the contents of an entire graveyard up there and no one would notice.'

An image of being buried alive in concrete swept Daisy's mind. A chill ran over her already cold body. She crossed her arms over her middle as she watched the anger slowly seep from her mother's eyes.

'Now, where is it?'

Daisy knew what *it* was, the safe-deposit papers. 'Back at my place.'

'Go and get it and bring it back here.' Stella turned swiftly around. Pointed at Ricky. 'I want you to go with her. Take one of my motors parked around . . .'

But before she could finish another voice cut in from the doorway, 'Is this a private party?'

Stella snarled loudly at the newcomer in the doorway and growled, 'It's not a private party but I don't think it's your kind of do, sweetheart – it's a soft drinks only affair, if you know what I mean.'

Jo-Jo King waltzed into the room, with tiny birdlike steps that fit her petite frame. Tommy shot off the wall, but Jo-Jo ignored him. She carried on walking towards her deeply unhappy mum. 'Now is that any way to greet your daughter, Mummy dearest?' She tipped up on tiptoes and planted a tiny kiss on her mother's reddening cheek. 'You told me not to darken your door again until I was clean. Well, I'm pleased to announce that I'm sparkling. Wanna check?' She rolled back the sleeve of her blouse to display her bare arm. 'You won't find a fresh track mark on me.' Her arm fell limply to her side. 'Mind you, I still like a slug of something every now and—'

'Want me to get rid of her?' Billy punched in, pushing himself towards the two women.

'Oh dear, Mum, I see that plan to improve the quality of your staff didn't work out,' Jo-Jo sneered as she twisted to face Billy. 'Go for a walk, Lurch, this is a family thing.'

The tension between Jo-Jo and Billy sizzled.

'Go and wait upstairs,' Stella ordered.

Jo-Jo ignored the command as she finally noticed Daisy. She gave Daisy the quick once-over, as a strand of the purple streak in her hair flopped on to her forehead. 'Who's she? One of your new girls?'

'No she's . . .' Tommy answered. His mum shouted 'No!' at him, but his mouth continued to run on. ' . . . Mum's other little girl.'

'Mum's what?'

'Your sister. Half sister. She's Mum's kid . . .'

There was a pregnant pause as Jo-Jo stared at Daisy in shock. She twisted around to her mum and broke the silence with words filled with accusation and betrayal. 'You never told me you had another kid. Another daughter?'

'Like I said, do one upstairs.'

Tommy stepped forward and addressed Daisy. 'Give mum what she wants and then turn your back for ever. See, our mother has a way of fucking up the lives of her kids.'

Billy rushed forward and grabbed Jo-Jo's arm. As he dragged her towards the door she began cursing and screaming abuse. Her voice faded up the staircase as Stella switched her gaze back to Daisy. Folded her arms.

'You've got less than two hours to be back here with Charlie's stuff.'

Twenty

'Here's a grand. Now piss off.'

Jo-Jo looked at the loose notes her mum slung on the desk. They were in Stella's private room on the top floor. Her mum stood with her hands on her hips in front of the *Calamity Jane* poster.

Jo-Jo stared back defiantly with her arms crossed tight over her clenching stomach. 'Don't want to know me now you've got another daughter.'

Stella's lips curled as she watched her youngest child with disgust. 'How could you have done what you did?'

The trouble from two years ago sprang dead centre between them. 'It was the gear, Mum,' Jo-Jo pleaded. 'You know what it's like, it sent me crazy. I didn't know what I was doing.'

'*What?*' Stella exploded back. 'Nicking from me so you could shoot up was alright, was it? Plus you didn't know you were copping a feel with my fella? Do you have any idea how I felt coming into this room and finding you with your legs wrapped around him in my chair?'

Sometimes Jo-Jo thought that was the problem, not that her mum had caught her going at it with her latest bit of arm candy but that they'd been doing it in her chair. A chair that had once belonged to her dad, the late, infamous Stevie King. The chair had been her dad's throne and catching Jo-Jo humping someone on it had sent her mum ballistic. Stella had beaten and kicked her black and blue and would have continued if Billy hadn't pulled a screaming Stella off.

'I'm a changed person, Mum,' Jo-Jo continued quietly. 'I know it was wrong to sleep with Mitch and take your cash . . .'

'You're trouble, Josephine-Joanne. You have been since the day you refused to take milk from my breast. And all that trouble at school when you were young . . .'

Jo-Jo's face crumpled. 'I missed you, Mum.'

Stella almost softened. She so wished Jo-Jo would be the type of daughter she wanted – trustworthy, keen to learn the family business, thinking about bringing a couple of grandkids into the fold. But Stella wouldn't allow herself to be soft. She twisted her mouth. 'Yeah?' Stella sneered back because she knew all her wishful thinking was a fool's dream. 'Well, I miss the sunshine in the winter, but you know what? I've got used to it not coming out for most of the year. So take the money and get that skinny, sorry arse of yours out of here. Go and blow it on blow like you did with the rest of the cash you've had – and nicked – out of me over the years.'

Jo-Jo took a half step forward. 'I don't want your money—'

Stella screamed, 'I haven't got anything else, I only do money, I haven't got anything else to give.'

'Yes you have,' Jo-Jo yelled back. 'I just want—'

'What?' Stella flung her arms out.

Your love.

But the words never passed Jo-Jo's lips. Instead she straightened up. Turned and left.

The youth of today, Stella thought, as she headed for the door leading to a smaller room. Stella closed the door and leant heavily against it. This was her private sanctuary. Her hand found the light switch and flicked it on. The light shone against the photos stuck on the wall. Photos of her and Frankie. Her gaze did a grand sweep of the pictures as she tried to capture the life they had once lived together. Frankie and her celebrating her twenty-first; at Walthamstow Dogs hugging and kissing after a huge win; on the night before he went down for a four-year stretch; Frankie on his own in his coffin the night before he was laid to rest. She sniffed back the tears as her gaze remained on that photo. And she remembered another night: 20 July 1990. The night their lives had changed for ever. The night she'd lost both his love and Daisy for good. The night that had now come back to haunt her. She looked at her hands remembering the blood that had stained them.

As soon as she got back to her car, Jo-Jo made a deep cut in her right thigh with the razor blade she kept in her purse for exactly that purpose. The release of blood made her breathing much easier. She slashed another cut. And another, until she was back in complete control. Why hadn't she just told her mum about what happened when she'd left her and Tommy with the babysitter all those years ago? *You know why,* Jo-Jo told herself, *because you're afraid she won't believe you.* Her face twisted as the tears began to fall. Tommy had found peace playing that bloody piano, whereas she'd hunted peace in drugs, sex, booze, eventually doing anything that would hurt her mum. And now her mum had another girl she could give all her love to. Well that just wasn't gonna happen, Jo-Jo vowed.

'So, who *are* you exactly?' Daisy asked Ricky.

They had been on the road for a good thirty minutes before she popped the question. The dimming lights of the city whizzed past her as she shivered in her damp clothes.

Ricky gave her a quick sideways look, then plastered his gaze back on the road ahead. 'I could ask you the same question.' He paused dramatically. 'Jennifer.'

She blushed as she remembered the lie she'd told him when they had first met. 'I'm whoever you want me to be,' she answered. His comeback froze her in her seat.

'Frankie Sullivan, one of London's more memorable and intelligent naughty boys. Had an empire that stretched from east to west, north to south, and some say abroad as well. Died at the age of forty-three, inside a church of all places. And he wasn't there lighting a candle, you can be sure of that. Not many people know this, but he had a daughter. Fifteen years old when they boxed Frank up. Her name's Daisy and it sounds like she didn't know much about her mum until today.'

Flustered, she said, 'You sound like a detective inspector: Nosey Parker of the Yard.'

He laughed at that, but said nothing else. The car left the Limehouse Link Tunnel and was soon sweeping into Wapping. As the car took Wapping High Street Daisy shoved her hand into her pocket. Pulled out her bottle of pills. She could feel his eyes on her, but she didn't care, she was as stressed as hell. Needed to calm her nerves down. She popped a pill, leant back against the headrest and swallowed.

'This it?'

She nodded, slightly dazed as she gazed up at the building in front of her. Ricky started to cut the engine, but she stopped him. 'We can't park here.' At his questioning look she dug into her bag with shaking fingers and pulled out her keys.

'Back up to the gate.'

Once in front of the large twin iron gates she wound her window down and leant outside. Pressed the fob key against the security pad and the gates started to open. He drove the car down the ramp into the brightly lit underground car park and swung the car into the first empty space he came across.

'Let's go.'

They got out of the car. She walked towards a lift with steel doors and he followed beside her. She pressed the button to call the lift and waited in the cool air.

As they waited she looked up at him and asked, 'You never did tell me who you are.'

He kept his face towards the lift. 'A bloke who's just finished eighteen months admiring the walls of a cell and has just found employment without the assistance of the job centre.'

'Since you gave me chapter and verse on my dad tell me about the Kings.'

Now he did look at her and a shadow shrouded his face. 'They're lower than a dachshund's privates, even the underworld think they're over the top.' Suddenly he turned the conversation. 'Why did you get attacked this morning?'

She shrugged her shoulders. 'Must be my turn to be awarded the punch bag of the day prize.'

He persisted, voice ever so light. 'Did it have anything to do with this stuff from the bank that Stella King's after?'

The lift arrived. Opened. She played dumb and didn't answer him.

He got in after her and they rode up in silence. The lift opened into a brightly lit, spacious reception hall. Nothing fancy, just clean and the only smell was of people who had a lot of poke in their pocket. Behind the desk sat the suited concierge, a man in his mid-fifties, with a face that said retirement couldn't come a day too soon.

'Miss Sullivan,' the man said with a smile, getting to his feet. He threw the newspaper down on the horseracing page. His smile died as he caught sight of Ricky.

'Everything alright, Miss Sullivan?' He gave Ricky a stiff once-over. His expression read, *'We don't usually see your kind in here.'*

Silence passed between the three of them. *This is your chance, Daisy*, she thought. *Just tell him and you'll be safe.* She opened her mouth the same time Ricky thrust his arm into the crook of her arm. He pulled her tightly against his side. Smiled at the man.

'You won't believe this, but I'm Daisy's long-lost brother. We ain't seen each other for yonks. Ain't that right, sweetheart?' He increased the pressure of his arm.

'Yes,' she ground out, knowing he had her fixed into place with nowhere to run. 'Thanks for the concern, James, but we've got lots of catching up to do.'

The man still didn't move. Just swept his eyes from her to Ricky. 'But you're white and he's . . .'

'Black?' Ricky supplied. 'Same dad, different mums.' He gave Daisy an affectionate look. 'I used to fence the sweets she stole from Woolworth's.'

Blushing furiously at his last comment Daisy nodded her head slightly at the shocked concierge and pulled Rick towards the lift.

Ricky whispered, 'Don't think I didn't see that little brain of yours ticking away. Don't get any ideas. Me and you are locked together like a pair of star-crossed lovers. So don't spoil things . . .'

Once away from the view of the concierge she wrenched free of his arm and pressed the button. The lift was a much more upmarket model than the one they had recently left, larger with its mock-gold sheen gleaming from a recent polish. It opened immediately. They stepped inside. Once again she pressed a button. Ricky whistled when he saw which floor.

'You must be on some killer wages to be slumming it in the penthouse.'

Daisy didn't answer him. Instead she kept her eyes on the closing doors as the hallucinations created by the drugs started to dig deeper in her mind.

'Come on, Daisy.'

She heard his voice before she saw him. Frankie stood on the other side of the closing lift door. He looked fresh, alive in his summer three-quarter shorts, pale blue and white polo shirt and hair so vibrant it looked like the sun was setting in it. But she noticed none of that. She only saw the hand that he held out to her.

'You can do it. It's all about timing . . .'

The doors kept closing.

She kept looking at his hand.

The gap between the doors was getting smaller.

'Come on, baby.'

Her heart galloped inside her chest.

'Come to Daddy.'

She leapt forward through the small gap between the closing doors. She landed outside as the doors banged shut.

She heard her late father snigger,

'Easy.'

Twenty-one

'Fuck,' Ricky cursed.

Now he knew she didn't live in the penthouse suit. She'd pressed the top floor to make sure he was stuck inside the lift giving her as much time as possible to make her escape. He frantically pressed the ground floor button. But the lift kept moving up. He kicked the door in frustration.

Her dad was gone, back to wherever it was he came from. Now she was on her own. Daisy knew she couldn't run. Well, not yet anyway. If she did James the concierge would get suspicious. Instead she swiftly walked, heels clicking madly against the floor, across the main reception area. She saw James lift his head. Quick as a flash he stood up.

'Miss Sullivan?' he questioned in alarm.

She gave him a blinding smile, but kept moving. 'I forgot something in the car.'

She didn't wait to hear his response. Soon she stood outside the lift, heart beating like crazy. She turned her head to look over her shoulder as if she expected to see Ricky standing there. But there was no one. She twisted back to face the lift.

Come on, come on. Come on.

Rocking on his heels, anger blowing out of his nostrils, Ricky watched as the lift opened at the penthouse suite.

Lights on, definitely no one at home. He punched the button

for the ground floor. Nothing happened. He punched it again. No movement. He punched it three times on the trot. The doors started to close.

Daisy's breathing rattled in her chest as she waited. But the lift still didn't come. She heard footsteps. Held her breath as she twisted around. She let it out when she saw a man in a business suit, who she recognised as one of the building's other residents. But what if it had been Ricky? What if . . . ?

She ran towards the emergency exit doors.

4
3

Ricky watched the red light of the lift indicating the floors. When he got hold of her he was going to . . .

2
1

And he would get her. And when he did he was going to make Daisy Sullivan realise that he wasn't a man to fuck around with.

G

The doors eased open. Ricky flew out. He marched across the reception ignoring the man at the desk who called out, 'Young man . . .'

He knew where to find her. He bypassed the lift and punched open the emergency exit doors.

Daisy ran through the brilliantly lit underworld of the car park. Rummaged in her bag as she finally spotted her red sports car. She pulled her keys out as she increased her speed from easy run to sprint. Her thumb pressed against the fob for the automatic lock. The car responded with its familiar high-pitched noise. She breathed in as much air as she could as she reached the car. Pulled the driver's door open. Instead of jumping into the seat she wriggled herself, on her knees, to the floor. She leant towards the passenger side of the car. Flicked back the carpet. She let out a huge sigh when she saw that they were still there – the safe deposit documents.

She propelled her body backwards onto the driver's seat. Stared at the papers in her hand. She needed to destroy them before Stella managed to get her hands on them, but she also needed to keep a copy. How the heck was she going to do that? She thought and thought and thought, but nothing came to her.

Shit.

'You're thinking too much like a good girl and not a criminal.'

The sound of the voice made her jump. She swung her head around to face the back of the car and there in the back seat, reclining as if he had all the time in the world, was her dad.

He shuffled forward, his blue eyes blazing. 'What would the daughter of a gangster do?'

'I don't know,' she yelled back.

'Think about it. You can't keep all that information in your head, but have you got anything on you that can?'

She didn't have time for riddles. 'What do you mean what have I got on me? I've only got my clothes.' She patted her hand down the side of her clothes to illustrate her words. That's when she felt it, in her pocket. Her phone. Of course. She whipped it out. Twisted back around. Lay the papers on the passenger seat. Fiddled with the touch screen of her phone until she found the camera icon. She held the phone high over the papers, in the portrait position, and pressed down. Snap: she had a copy of the first page. Snap. Snap. She took copies of the remaining pages. She scrolled back through the photos. Smiled roughly when she saw the perfect images.

'Thanks, Dad,' she said, quickly turning back around. But the back seat was empty. He was gone; he was as come-and-go in death as he had been in life.

She shoved the phone back into her pocket. Picked up the papers. She engaged the car's cigarette lighter and set fire to them. *Got you, Stella*, she thought triumphantly. Her heart lurched when she saw a swift shadow from the corner of her eye. She swung her head towards the passenger's side. She screamed when she saw something black moving towards the passenger window. The bottom of a large shoe and accompanying leg. The shoe crashed into the window, shattering glass. She ducked as glass splintered into the air and on to her. She let out another scream when a hand grabbed her hair. She was yanked across broken glass towards the passenger side of the car. She raised her head when she felt something wet and sticky fall onto the side of her head. The first thing she saw was the arm that belonged to the hand that was tangled in her hair was dripping with blood. She shifted her gaze higher to find a face imprinted with a furious expression tearing into her.

Ricky.

He snarled, 'You might have big balls, lady, but mine are massive, so get the fuck out of the motor.'

Twenty-two

Tommy got as far as his car, after leaving his mum's brothel, when he was hauled backwards by his shirt. He twirled around, lost his footing and ending up crashed on his back on the ground. Before he could right himself a booted foot landed a hefty blow to his stomach. He groaned as he rocked half up, hands going protectively to his midriff. Another blow landed against his shoulder blade forcing him back down again. He squeezed his eyes against the hot pain.

He reopened his eyes and gazed up, his mouth falling open in surprise. Over him stood his mum and her bully-boy Billy.

'What the fuck is going on?' he grunted.

His mum crossed her arms over her chest. 'You tell me, Tommy.' She spoke through her teeth. 'Yesterday you said you could help me out, you knew someone inside this law firm. I told you to watch your step . . .'

Tommy knew where she was going. 'Mum . . .' But his pleading ended in a half squeak, half groan when Billy kicked his hip. 'Shut up and listen to your mum,' the older man warned.

'When you came back with the tape I can't tell you how proud I was of you.' She lifted the side of her mouth in scorn, making the beauty spot above her mouth appear as if it were jumping for freedom. 'But I ain't so proud of you anymore cos someone's been giving me grief about the present you left in my girl Daisy's office.'

Billy kicked the other cheek of his backside. Stella got down and looked deep into her son's face. 'Plod are just waiting for us to make the wrong move because of what you did to that director's daughter three years ago. They're like that. It's all very personal for them. Can't imagine why . . .'

Tommy nodded. She smiled at him. Tenderly touched the side of his face. 'That's my boy. One more shit move out of you and you won't need to worry about the coppers because I'll take you out of action myself.'

Ricky winced in pain as Daisy stuck the tweezers into his hand. They were sitting in the main room of her apartment as she pulled out the tiny splinters of glass embedded in his skin. The deep brown of his skin posed a striking contrast to the pale painted walls.

'Oooooh, matron,' Ricky said in a mock Kenneth Williams 'Carry On' voice.

She tutted at his cheekiness. 'That'll teach you to go breaking and entering. Crime doesn't pay.' He winced again as she eased out the final tiny shard.

'I've got a job to do here and you ain't making it any easier. Although I've always believed in mixing business with pleasure.'

Daisy didn't answer him. Instead she picked up the tube of antiseptic cream next to her and squeezed some onto her finger. She rubbed the cream, in small circles, over the cuts on his hand, her bracelet bobbing against her skin.

'Mmm.' Ricky inhaled as he closed his eyes. 'That feels real good, babe.'

Flustered, Daisy snapped her fingers away from his flesh. 'Right, that should do the trick.'

Ricky opened his eyes and stared at her. 'How about you kiss it better?'

'In your dreams,' Daisy growled as she stepped back.

The room shook with Ricky's outrageous laughter as he got to his feet.

'Mrs King ain't gonna be happy that you torched those papers.'

When she didn't answer he carried on with a rough shake of his head. 'The Kings ain't people you want to muck around with.

You're peanuts to them, family or not. They'd skin their own granny for a kilo of coke.' The warning in his jet-black eyes deepened. 'People say that Tommy was involved in the death of a high-up's daughter a few years ago. You know how much effort the police put in to a case like that. And he's still on the streets, so you can see how it is.'

Daisy shivered at hearing that last piece of information. 'Don't worry about me, I can take care of Stella King. I'm going to change into some new clothes.' He took a step towards her. She put her hands up. 'Don't worry, I'd need an axe or a parachute to bail out of here. And I haven't got either.' Disregarding her words he followed her into the bedroom. The room had white-walls, with a low level bed made for two, which had fluffed up pillows that matched the colours of her eyes, built-in wardrobe and a dressing table nestled next to a single white chair.

Her eyes blazed with fury at him for invading her private space. She whipped her jacket and top off. Kicked off her skirt.

'This your fella?'

She turned to him in her matching turquoise and black Betty Boop patterned bra and panties. Ricky was holding the framed picture of Jerome she kept on the dressing table. Her heart quickened. She didn't want Jerome anywhere near this mess. 'No, it's my granddad. Worn well, hasn't he?'

He peered closer. 'He looks posh. I would never have figured Frankie Sullivan's daughter stepping out with a Hooray Henry.'

She was about to let loose with another comment when she noticed him looking at her as if he'd never seen her before. Then she realised that she was standing before him practically starkers, with only underwear and a pair of heels for cover. Blushing, she crossed her arms over her boobs and strode towards the built-in wardrobe. Feeling his eyes still burning through her she quickly shoved on a pair of jeans, T-shirt and top. She kicked off her shoes and put on some trainers. She unwound her damp hair. Still flustered she turned back around. They stared at each other.

'I like your hair like that.' His voice was soft and low.

'What?' Daisy self-consciously touched her hair.

'Loose.' They stared at each other again for a few seconds too long.

'Daisy?' A male voice called from somewhere in another part of the flat.

Ricky kicked the bedroom door shut. Turned the lock. Turned back to Daisy. He grabbed her arm and dragged her towards him. And whispered, 'Did you call someone?'

'No. It's Jerome.'

'Daisy?' This time Jerome's voice was more insistent. And closer.

Ricky pulled back from Daisy and opened the flap of his jeans jacket. She gasped when she saw the handle of a gun peeping from the top of his waistband. 'Tell pretty boy to take a hike.'

She headed for the door. Undid the lock. Closed it behind her and moved across the lounge the same time Jerome entered it. He was still dressed in his business suit and had a harassed expression planted on his face.

She walked up to him and planted a gentle kiss on his mouth. 'I didn't know you were coming over tonight.'

'I wasn't going to,' he replied, as he got comfy on the sofa. 'But I just wanted to make sure that my girl was doing OK.' He leant over and took her in his arms. 'How are you feeling now about Angel's death?'

It was horrible to admit it, but her friend's death was the least of her worries. Meeting Stella had made her worry about her own demise, especially now that she had burnt the papers. She leant into his warmth. Maybe she should just tell him what was going on. No, she couldn't do that, not with Stella's hired hand in the bedroom tooled up to the teeth.

'Shattered,' she finally answered. 'Still can't believe both Charlie and Angel are gone.'

'Have the police got any more information about her death?'

'I don't know. There can't be a funeral until they've done a full post mortem, which must be really hard on her folks.'

'Do you want some company?' He looked over at the bedroom.

'No.' She sounded very sure about that. Seeing the look of alarm on his face at the force of her response she softened her tone. 'Charlie's and Angel's deaths have hit me really hard. Randal's agreed to let me have next week off, you know, just to get myself sorted out. I was surprised but Randal doesn't seem to mind me not being around for some reason.'

He gave her another deep kiss. Then they pulled apart. 'Don't forget that it's my parents' cocktail party on Wednesday.' There was a gleam in his hazel eyes.

'What are you up to?' she teased.

'Never you mind.'

'I wouldn't miss meeting your parents for the world.' She kissed him on the lips. From the corner of her eye she caught the bloody tissues she'd used to clean Ricky's cuts lying on the arm of the sofa. Shit. She grabbed Jerome's arm, pulled him up and whisked him to the door. 'I'm off to Spain for a couple of days,' Jerome said as they hit the hallway. 'To see if I can find Maxwell Henley . . .'

'Who?' Daisy's voice was distracted as she looked over her shoulder making sure that the bedroom door was still shut.

'Am I so handsome you don't hear what I say? The class-action case, remember? There's rumours that he may now live in Spain. I haven't managed to get hold of him, but I've got a contact who is going to help me track him down. If I can . . .'

'I'm really sorry,' Daisy cut in. 'But I really need to put my head down.'

Jerome gave her one last kiss and was gone. As soon as the door shut she leant heavily on the wall.

'Very touching.'

She kicked off the wall at hearing Ricky's voice. Headed for the TV where the *Calamity Jane* video box lay. She'd never upgraded it to a DVD because the video version was the one she'd watched with her dad. It bought back such lovely memories of them cuddled on the sofa watching it together. She picked it up the same time Ricky scoffed, 'I don't think your mum has got time for films.'

'It's the movie *Calamity Jane*. I used to watch it with my dad.' She placed the video box back onto the TV.

He shook his head in disbelief. 'Not even Doris Day with her Colt 45s is going to be able to stop Mrs King from taking you apart when she finds out what you've done with those papers.'

Twenty-three

Ricky was right. Stella went postal.

'What do you mean you ain't got it?'

Daisy remained calm as Hurricane Stella hit land. They were upstairs in what Daisy could only assume was Stella's private office in the brothel. Tommy sat on a piano stool and Billy and Ricky were positioned on either side of the door. Daisy sat in the seat opposite her raging mother at the desk, occasionally looking up at the large framed poster of *Calamity Jane*. Fancy her and her mum liking the same movie. And the room was decorated exactly the same as her own front room in the style of Calamity Jane's cabin.

'I burnt them,' Daisy answered brazenly.

Before anyone could say another word Tommy stormed off the piano stool, across the room and kicked the legs of the chair Daisy sat on. She landed on her back, the breath whooshing out of her body. Before she could move Tommy was over her with a knife at her throat. 'Want me to finish her?'

Before Stella could answer Daisy screamed, 'If I gave you the information how do I know you weren't planning to kill me?'

'I'm your . . .' Stella stumbled over what she was going to say, '. . . mum for God's sake.'

Daisy looked up to find the tall image of Stella standing over her. Tommy increased the pressure of the blade. Daisy's fighting instincts kicked in. Tommy didn't realise it but she'd already judged him to be a crap fighter. He was more a classic brawler with so many defences open it would be easy for her to take him down. All she had to do was kick him in the nuts, or maybe double jab him in the eyes, or catapult him so far in the air that when he landed he wouldn't be able to tell his arse from his elbow. But she suppressed her fighting instincts. It wouldn't do for Stella to find out she could stand on her own two feet.

'You just tried to drown me,' she finally shot back.

'If I'd wanted to top you, you wouldn't be lying on your back now giving me a load of lip. How do I know you didn't get anything when you went into the bank today?'

That shook Daisy up. Stella smiled. 'You've been followed every step of the way, my girl.'

'So you were the one who sent that man after me today?' Daisy croaked.

Stella moved away from Daisy and stared up at the *Calamity Jane* poster on the wall. 'Me and you used to watch this when you were little.' She gazed at Daisy as if it were just the two of them in the room. Suddenly Stella grinned. 'You loved that bit where she gets to Chicago and starts singing about the Windy City. And when she sang the word pretty and made it sound like "purty" you always joined in.' Abruptly the smile disappeared. 'Now why don't you be "nice and purty" and tell me what the number of the deposit box is?'

'Can't do that.' Daisy continued with the lie she'd rehearsed earlier on. 'You see, Charlie was having an affair. He kept a woman nicely tucked away in a house he bought for her. The deeds to the property are in the deposit box. I promised him that if anything ever happened to him I wouldn't let his wife find out about the affair. That's why I went into the bank today to try and get the deeds. I made a promise and I want to keep it.'

Tommy growled. She felt a slither of blood trickle down her skin as the knife nicked lightly into her neck. But she held firm. She knew she was the one holding all the cards. 'The only way you're going to find out which safe-deposit box belongs to Charlie is with me by your side.'

Billy took a step forward. Ricky pulled himself off the wall.

Tommy gazed at her showing the disbelief the others were all feeling.

'What do you mean?' Stella asked.

Daisy swallowed. 'Whatever you're planning to do to get Charlie's deposit box, you're going to have to take me with you.'

Daisy rubbed her throat. The only damage Tommy had done was a scratch. After Daisy's outrageous demand the room had grown quiet. Stella had looked at her as if she'd never really seen her before. Eventually Stella had called Tommy off and told Daisy to sit her backside down.

'You're playing a dangerous game, my girl.' Stella was back in Stevie King's chair behind her desk.

'Maybe.' Daisy tried to make her voice sound like she was in court, trying to talk round a judge. 'But at least this way I'll still be alive and get those property deeds before Charlie's wife finds them.'

'You're Frankie's kid alright, I don't need a DNA test to see that.' Daisy didn't reply so Stella carried on. 'Perhaps we can cut a deal here but let me tell you how it is. Number one, I give the orders and you follow them. Number two, you'll be stopping here until the job's over.'

'What job?' It was Ricky who spoke. Everyone looked at him. Realising the hired help weren't meant to ask questions Ricky added, 'No disrespect intended, Mrs King.'

'Yeah, what job?' Tommy echoed. He rubbed the piano tattoo on his neck.

'You'll find out tomorrow morning.'

'I can't stay here,' Daisy said.

'You got a problem with houses of ill repute?' Stella sneered. 'Shame because the only way you're in is if I have you tucked up right under my nose.' Stella dismissed Daisy as she looked over at Ricky. 'I'm appointing you as her personal bodyguard which means you stay with her twenty-four seven.'

Daisy looked at Ricky. Then back at Stella. Her mother couldn't mean . . . Daisy shot to her feet. 'No way am I sharing a room with him.'

* * *

Five minutes later Daisy realised that it wasn't only the room she was sharing with Ricky but the bed as well. The room they entered froze every muscle and movement in her body. It was classic little girl pink, with a teddy still propped inside the cover of the double bed, furniture in colours a child would just adore and a dressing table that every little princess dreamed of. But what caught her eye was the framed photo of Frankie Sullivan smiling by the seaside, on the table by the bed. God how she needed her dad right now to help her figure her way out of this mess.

'I'm glad to see you remember it,' Stella said in the room.

Daisy finally moved into what had once been her bedroom as a young child. Funny she didn't remember much before the age of seven, but this room had always stayed with her.

'I always knew you'd be back.' Stella smiled. Daisy tensed. She always worried when Stella smiled. 'So I kept it ready just for you. Still got the same double bed you picked out yourself.' Stella moved towards the door. 'No pillow fights, you two.' And with that she closed the door behind her.

'Let's get one thing straight,' Daisy shot at Ricky immediately. 'You stick to your side of the bed and I'll stick to mine.'

'What? You don't want me to roll over and whisper sweet nothings in your ear?' His reply was offhand as his eyes roamed around the room as if he was looking for something.

'What are you doing?' Daisy asked as she plonked herself on the left corner of the bed.

Ricky shot his gaze back at her. 'I'm wondering why you never gave Mrs King what she wanted and then caught a bus back to Poshville?' He held up his hand as her mouth opened, halting her reply. 'And don't give me no crap about this Charlie geezer having some bit of skirt cos I ain't buying it.'

She snapped her mouth shut. Screw him, she didn't owe him an explanation. She ignored him and lay down on the bed. Tucked her body into a ball and faced the wall. She'd lost all track of time and hadn't realised that the day had moved into the night. She pulled her phone out of her pocket. Immediately went to her saved photos. And stared at the safe-deposit box document images.

Box number 41.

While Daisy turned her back on him on the bed Ricky checked inside his carrier bag and looked down at the item his contact had given him in Canary Wharf.

Stella watched the black-and-white images of Daisy and Ricky on the screen transmitted by the security camera in their room. She listened intently to their chit-chat because she knew that Daisy was up to something. Did Daisy really think she believed that cock-and-bull patter about needing to be present at the job because there was evidence that Charlie was pushing his post through another woman's letterbox? She suspected the only naughties he ever indulged in were the pay-as-you-screw variety she provided. No, Daisy was up to something alright and Stella was keen to find out what it was. She turned away from the screen when she heard the door open and softly close on the other side of the room. Billy.

She turned back to watch the screen. 'That girl's playing me for a complete tit. I should've made it my business to keep an eye on her all these years but I didn't so I want you to find out everything about her. Who gets into her knickers; who took her in after Frankie went south; does she like watching *Snow White* or shoving it up her snout? Everything.' She lifted her head to look at him. 'And while you're at it check out Tommy's new gun-for-hire as well.'

Almost half an hour later Ricky was in the bog. The one on the second floor, with the three cubicles and mirrors from wall to ceiling. He could've used the en suite in his and Daisy's room but she might have heard what he was up to. Mind you, he needed to be quick because Stella had ordered him to be with Daisy every second of the day. In his experience he knew that loos were usually the only places that didn't have CCTV. He sat on the toilet seat as he quietly spoke into his mobile phone.

'They're planning something. A job.'

'What type of job?' The man on the other end of the line was the person who'd rammed his car into Tommy's SUV.

'Stella needs to get a deposit box. It's inside a bank. Belonged to a lawyer called Charlie Hopkirk. That's all I have for now. You figure it out.'

'You mean a bank job?'

'Can't say for certain . . .' He stopped when he heard the main door open. A set of feet, no, two sets of feet, one in heels.

'Sh,' he whispered into the phone.

He heard the cubicle door furthest away from him open.

'Now put your head inside the toilet, slave,' a woman ordered.

'Yes, mistress,' a timid male voice replied.

Great, Ricky thought. He had to choose the loo where a dominatrix was earning her fee making some poor john suffer. 'Now what does every slave deserve when he's naughty?' she bit out.

'A good spanking, mistress.' The male voice had risen to heaven-high excitement.

Yes, mistress, no, mistress, three bags full, mistress. It was like being married, Ricky thought as he rolled his eyes. Then he heard a whooshing sound tear through the air. 'Ouch. More, mistress,' the punter begged.

'Talk later,' he whispered. Cut the line and crept out of the loo with the sounds of sexual pleasure ringing in his ears.

'We're gonna do a bank job this Friday.'

Stella's bold statement jolted the occupants in her office the next morning. Billy. Tommy, at his usual spot on the piano stool. Ricky. And, of course, Daisy. No way, Daisy thought. No way could she get involved in a robbery. *You put yourself in the shit, girl*, she chided herself, *and now you can't run away.*

Stella carried on talking. 'That means we've got three days only, so pay attention. And of course whatever I say in this room stays in this room.'

Appalled at what she was hearing, Daisy finally shot to her feet. 'No, I can't get involved in this . . . .'

Stella cut over her with scorn. 'You had your chance to back away yesterday, girl, and you never took it. You're the one who said you wanted to be involved—'

'But you never said anything about a robbery!'

'What did you think was going to happen?' Stella stared at her as if she had two heads. 'That I'd switch my phaser to stun and ask Spock to beam it up?'

Daisy slowly sat back down. Stella was right, she should have figured out where this was all going. Damn, damn, damn.

'What bank?' Tommy asked as he leant forward on the piano stool.

Stella pinned Daisy with her gaze. 'That's where our lovely Daisy comes in. She's the only one with details of the box. And we know which bank it is, Daisy, don't we?' Stella continued smugly. 'Because a mate of mine followed you to the K&I International Bank in Canary Wharf.' Daisy knew there was no point denying it, so she nodded.

Stella continued. 'Now we know the bank all we've got to do is plan how to get in there and take it.'

'Not to mention grabbing all the other gear they've left lying around,' Tommy added.

Stella glared at him. 'This isn't a cash job, son, it's far more important than that. We focus on getting in there and getting the box.'

'Are you nuts? They'll have millions in there!' Tommy gazed at his mum as if she really was on Star Trek's payroll. 'You're expecting me to go in there, get some box just because someone is holding something over your head? Fuck that. You get your box, I'm getting rich.'

'Sit down and shut up.' Billy's voice was hard and furious.

Tommy ignored him. 'We're going into a bank and coming out empty-handed? That's like going into a knocking shop and having a J Arthur. I mean, for fuck's sake.'

'I'm the one running this show,' Stella hissed. Then she looked at everyone in turn. 'You got that? Me. Stella King. Get that in your heads right now. That includes you, Tommy boy. Even if you spot the bloody crown jewels in there you leave them alone, do you understand?'

Tommy stared at her defiantly for a few more seconds, blowing off steam.

'Does anyone else want to tread on my tail before I go on?' Her question was greeted by a nervous silence. 'We've got to find out as much as we can about the bank. What time it opens; what time it shuts; how many people work there; what security systems it has; how many security guards there are; who's the head honcho.'

'Why don't we just go in, tooled up with masks, frighten the bastards and take it?' Tommy's hands twitched on his thighs as if he was already mob-handed in the bank, issuing threats.

'You disappoint me, kid, you really do,' Stella shook her head. 'Once we know what kind of bank we're dealing with, then we can decide the best way to do it.'

'Stella's right,' Billy backed her up. 'We need to figure out the quickest way to get in and out with the least mess.'

Ricky finally spoke. 'So if we ain't going to blast our way in, what are we going to do?'

'First we need to get someone on the inside to find out as much about the bank as they can.' Stella scanned the faces in the room. 'Someone who looks like they belong to that world. Respectable. Someone who ain't gonna lift any eyebrows. Someone like . . .' She fixed her gaze on Daisy.

Suddenly Tommy swung around to the piano and started playing. 'Has Anybody Seen My Gal?' he sang.

'Someone slam the lid on his fingers, he plays piano the way he plans bank raids.' his mum growled. Tommy hit a deep note that sent a sound of doom around the room.

'It can't be me.' Daisy's head moved rapidly from side-to-side. 'I've already been in so they know what I look like.'

'Not if you wore a disguise they wouldn't.' Stella peered hard at her. 'You must've done that the last time you went into the bank?' The blush that crept across Daisy's face was all the answer Stella needed to her question. 'I want you and Ricky to pretend to be a couple looking to open a safe-deposit account.'

Daisy looked wide-eyed at Ricky. No way did he look remotely respectable. Mind you if she shot off her mouth about it she might be stuck with Tommy. She kept her thoughts to herself.

Stella shoved a mobile phone at Daisy across the desk. 'Get the bank on the blower and make an appointment to see the manager today.'

'I don't have the number . . .' Daisy stopped, remembering her own phone. She pulled it out. Touched the Internet icon.

'What is she fucking doing?' Tommy yelled.

Daisy answered him, but kept her gaze squarely on the phone. 'Finding the bank's details and telephone number . . . Here we go.' She took a deep breath. Got up and pulled the other mobile off the table. Looked at the number on her own phone's screen as she tapped the number into the other mobile. 'Hello. My name's . . .' She hadn't thought of a name. 'Mrs Michael Saviour-Jones. Good day to you as well.' She pasted a fake smile to her lips. 'My husband and I would like to arrange an appointment with the bank manager today because we're very interested in possibly opening a variety of accounts, including a safe-deposit account.' She stopped and listened to the reply. 'You can't fit me in today? Don't worry, we'll take our business elsewhere.' She caught the disbelieving look on Stella's face. Ignored it. 'Thanks for your . . . What? You can fit us in. Great.' She waited. Smiled. 'Two o'clock it is. Thank you so much for your time.'

'You were taking a bit of a chance,' Stella said as Daisy handed the phone back to her.

'Not really. None of the banks these days are in a financial position where they can afford to be turning away business, especially from someone with a double-barrelled name. So what do Ricky and I do next?'

'Listen carefully, because this is what I want you both to do today . . .'

As Stella carried on talking she threw the mobile at Tommy. He caught it. Dropped it on the floor. And ground it to pieces beneath his heel, destroying the evidence that could link them to the bank.

Twenty-four

Jerome let out a quiet wolf whistle when he saw the villa in Spain. Maxwell Henley obviously had more money tucked away than you would expect a council leader to make. The villa was huge, put together with large white and tan stones and a typical Spanish tiled roof with impressive palm trees shading it from the sun. Jerome wiped the sweat from his forehead as the sun beat down on him. He approached the door. Knocked. Fiddled with the lapels of his jacket as he waited. No response. He left the front door and moved around the side. Stopped at a black rail fence. Through the bars he could see a well-kept garden and a big swimming pool. In the pool a woman was floating on her back, enjoying the water and the sun at the same time. He pushed the gate and stepped inside.

As he got nearer the pool the woman raised her head. She was a looker, with straight black hair, deep, brown eyes and deeply tanned skin.

'This is private property,' she called out. A London voice, which surprised him because he'd assumed she was Spanish. Jerome pulled his shades off. Took a few steps closer. 'I'm looking for the owner of the house.'

'You're looking at her.'

'So you're Mrs Maxwell Henley?'

'Who?' Abruptly she jumped out of the pool, showing off a great body covered by a very revealing turquoise bikini. Wrapped a large pink towel around herself. She moved towards him. Her hand came up to shade the sun from her eyes.

'I was told that I could find a Maxwell Henley here.'

She shook her head making wet strands of her hair cling to the side of her face and throat. 'Never heard of him.' She didn't take those deep eyes of hers off him.

'But I checked the property deeds and they're registered in the name of Maxwell Henley.'

She pushed her fingers into her wet hair moving it off the side of her face. 'This is Spain where the paperwork doesn't always get done properly. But like I said this is my place.'

'I'm a lawyer from England and it's imperative that I find him.'

'Real sorry, mate.' Her London accent grew stronger. 'Can't help you.'

'But I was told that he lived here,' he persisted.

Her hand clutched the corner of the towel. 'Maybe he did, but when we purchased the house we weren't told who the former owner was.' She wrapped her arms around her middle as if she were cold despite the heat from the sun. 'I'm sorry but I'm going to have to ask you to leave.'

With a huge wave of disappointment he nodded and left. Damn. He knew he didn't have a hope in hell's chance of winning this class-action abuse case if he didn't track Maxwell Henley down.

The woman watched from the gate as the lawyer from England got into his hire car. As soon as the car drove off she rushed into the house. The Moroccan-styled blue and red floor tiles were cool and slippery against her wet feet as she made her way into the office at the far end of the hallway. Once inside the room she headed for the phone. Hand trembling, she picked it up. Made her call.

'What the heck's going on? Someone from England has just been here asking about Maxwell.'

Tommy was back to being fucked off with his mum again. As he walked towards his club, he thought of the meeting he'd left half an hour ago. Who did she think she was, mouthing off at him like that in front of the others like he was some skivvy? Telling him what he could and couldn't do? Whoever heard of doing a blag and not taking the bankroll?

'Need a ride?'

He turned sharply at the voice that had interrupted his furious thoughts. Jo-Jo. Sitting behind the wheel of her car, soft-top down, wearing a pair of Jackie O shades even though the sun had disappeared hours ago. She eased the car to a halt. Leant over and opened the passenger door. *Why not?* he told himself. He hopped in.

She revved the engine and said, 'Why do I get the impression my brother's not a happy bunny today?'

Instead of answering he pulled out a square silver compact. Flipped the lid up. On one side was a small mirror and on the other a rolled up note. He pulled a stash of coke from his top pocket. Shook some onto the mirror. Cut it. Picked up the note and was soon in junkie heaven.

'Wanna cut?' he offered.

'I've told you I'm over that. So what's the matter?'

He pinched his nostrils and laid his head back on the headrest. 'I've gotta keep this . . .' he pointed to his mouth, ' . . . zipped.'

She took a smooth turn as her words became softer. 'Come on, you can tell me anything. We've been holding each other's secrets since I was eight, yeah?'

Eight years old. He knew what she was talking about and didn't want his thoughts going back to the days of the babysitter. And why the fuck shouldn't he tell her? His mum didn't own him.

'Mum's planning a job'

'Yeah?' His sister kept her voice light, her eyes on the road.

'A bank job.'

'Thought that was the type of stuff Dad used to do, not Mum.'

'Well she's changed her MO because she needs to get her mitts on something stashed in a deposit box.'

She gave him a quick sideways look. 'Always nice to have a bit more poke in your pocket.'

He sat up, shoulders rigid. 'See, that's what got me all over mad. We ain't allowed to touch the money.'

'Are you for real?'

Seeing he now had an ally he quickly took her through the

events at the meeting. Jo-Jo stiffened when she heard Daisy's name. Her hands tightened around the wheel. So Mum could ask her new daughter to join the club but not her? Out with the old and in with the new.

'What you gonna do about it?'

Tommy slumped back in the seat. 'No one goes against Mum. You know that better than anyone.'

'You gonna let her get away with talking to you like that?' He said nothing. 'Bet she made you look like a grade A pussy.' Still he didn't respond. But that didn't stop her turning the screw some more. 'A bank's got money and if you're gonna hit it you take the money too. Only a fucking fool would leave it behind.' His erratic breathing filled the car. 'How much do you reckon that bank's got down in the vault? It'll make Brink's-Mat look like shoplifting.'

She bought the car to a sudden halt. They'd reached his club. Finally she looked at him. 'You take that money and you'll finally be out of living in Mum's shadow. That's what she's worried about. Tommy, that you'll become the top fucking geezer.'

He got out of the car without saying a word.

'Pull yourself together, you're shaking like a woman on death row.'

Ricky's hand touched Daisy's shoulder as they sat in the car. He was right, she was trembling like her bones were in meltdown. She couldn't believe that she'd agreed to take part in a bank job. Become a bank robber. A criminal just like her dad. But only she knew why she'd made herself a player and she had no alternative but to play the game to the end.

She pulled herself straight, making Ricky's hand fall away. Looked him in the eye. 'I'm fine.'

'Whatever you say, babe.'

'Don't call me that,' she snapped.

Ricky looked at her intently as he pushed his head to the side. 'You know what I can't figure out? What's made a law abiding girl like you go all Bonnie and Clyde?'

'And what's a man like you, who's just got out of E-Wing, doing getting involved with the Kings instead of trying to make something of himself?'

He laughed, short and hard. 'If you've ever walked the streets of London, babe, you'd realise that there ain't many straight routes. I don't know what you're hiding, but you ain't telling your new-found mummy a straight story.'

'The story's simple. I made a promise to Charlie and that's what I'm going to do.'

'Yeah, whatever. Sure, you're Frankie Sullivan's daughter, but something tells me you broke that tie a long time ago. So why reconnect now after all these years? You're Daisy Sullivan, up-and-coming lawyer, posh boy on her arm, posh in-laws just around the corner. You know what I think?' He straightened his head as his eyes bored into her. 'I think there's something in that deposit box you desperately want to get your hands on and it's got nothing to do with Charlie Hopkirk. You've already tried to get into that bank once and now Stella's giving you another opportunity to get your hands on it.'

'Everyone's Inspector Morse these days, aren't they?'

'I'm right though, ain't I?'

'Yes and London's a tropical paradise.'

His face was dead serious. 'You sup with the devil and the only after dinner drink you get is pure poison.'

'You've been sitting at their table longer than me and you're still here.'

Deciding that he couldn't argue with someone who'd already made up her mind he moved the conversation along. Back to the job they had to do. 'Let's go and pick up some new clobber to play the loving couple in the bank.'

Ricky gave Daisy a slow once-over that made her feel like he was peeling off her new clothes one layer at a time.

'So, what do you think?' she asked as an unwanted heat crept up her body as she stood in front of him in the bustling clothes store on Oxford Street. She had no right to be blushing like some silly teenage girl looking at her first date because she already had a man she loved; and she *did* love him. She wore a fitted black number with a lace trim that fell just below her knees and a black no-nonsense jacket. The type of clothing she hoped would make her forgettable when they met the bank manager later today.

Ricky said nothing. Instead he tilted his head to the left and deepened the look he gave her. Shit, she could feel her nipples going into autopilot, moulding into the material of the dress. Quickly she grabbed the edge of the jacket over her chest and said, with a huge dollop of irritation, 'I take it that it looks OK?'

Ricky straightened his head. 'You'll do.'

Flustered, Daisy swiftly turned around and re-entered the changing room. As soon as she was safely back inside the cubicle she slumped against the wall. She closed her eyes, her heart beating to the rhythm of a race it ran on its own. She flattened her palms against her breasts and muttered, 'Down, girls,' desperately trying to get her nipples back under control. Herself under control. She didn't like the way that Ricky made her feel. Only one man had the right to do that to her. The man she was hoping to have a family with. She was going to be mummy and Jerome was going to be daddy and there was no room for these hot feelings she had every time Ricky looked her way. Dismissing Ricky from her mind she got dressed.

Ten minutes later they were on the escalator to the menswear department, her new purchases in a large bag in her hand. They reached the floor and took in the clothes around them.

'I think you need to get a suit, black, of course,' she told Ricky. 'And a tie. Formal shirt as well.'

'You still mad at me?' His question took her by surprise. She stared up at him and could've slapped his face when she saw the know-it-all grin playing across his lips.

'I don't know what you're talking about. We've got a job to do so let's do it.'

'So you ain't mad that your raspberry ripples went on high alert when I looked at you in your new threads?'

A deep heat of embarrassment stained her. As she opened her mouth to give him a tongue lashing a body bumped into her at the top of the escalator. Only then did she realise that she was standing at the edge of the escalator blocking the way. She fell forward slightly as an arm snaked around her to steady her.

'Sorry, sweetheart,' the other person apologised as she righted herself. She looked up and said, 'Don't worry about . . .' Her words dried up when she saw who she was talking to.

Jo-Jo entered her mum's private office knowing she should have taken a tin hat. No doubt about it, her mum was going to go ballistic when she saw her again. Stella's head was lowered as she read something on her desk. Jo-Jo quietly closed the door behind her.

'Hi, Mum.'

Stella froze. Didn't raise her head. Jo-Jo didn't have to see her mum's face to know she was re-shaping it into a very nasty expression. After a beat Stella slowly raised her head. She levelled her deadly grey eyes on her daughter.

'You tired of living?'

'Mum I–'

But Stella never let her finish. 'Don't make me get up because if I do it means you're going to be lying down.' She paused. 'Permanently.'

Jo-Jo ignored the threat and moved towards the desk. 'I've got something I think you should know.'

Stella crossed her arms, which was never a good sign. 'I'm gonna count to three. One . . .'

'Tommy told me all . . .'

'Two . . .'

'. . . about the bank job.'

'He what?' Stella rose to her feet. Jo-Jo inched closer. 'I know all about the safe-deposit box. About Daisy . . .'

'That boy is going to wish he'd never been born.' Stella stormed towards the door, hair flip-flapping at her shoulders.

'And do you know what else he said?' Stella stopped at her daughter's words, hand midway to the door handle. 'You made him look like a total tosser because you won't let him take the money in the bank.'

Stella's hand dropped. She turned back around. 'Oh, did he now? That boy needs a lesson in family manners. Quite a sharp one.'

Jo-Jo moved to stand nearer to her mother, but not too close because she knew when Stella was in one of her moods she was liable to lash out at the nearest thing to her.

'I've got a better idea. Why don't you let me stick around and I can report back everything he says to you.'

Stella reared back, folding her arms across her chest. 'Oh, I get it. This is your way of trying to get the name King back on your birth certificate.'

'I know I owe you, Mum, and it makes sense. You can't afford for Tommy to fuck up this job.'

Stella looked at her youngest child and thought for a while. As much as she didn't want to admit it, Jo-Jo made sense. If Tommy was stepping out of line she needed someone on his back. She made up her mind. Without warning, she raised her hand and slapped Jo-Jo sharply twice across the face. Jo-Jo gasped as pain shot through her. She felt a trickle of blood seep from the corner of her mouth. She held her hand across her mouth as she raised her head.

'Now you're back that's just to remind you that there's only one queen bitch in this house.'

Daisy knew she was in deep shit. Miss Misty was the last person she wanted to bump into on a day like this. The older woman was decked out in casual clothes – jeans and hooded top. The only things that stood out were her lime green heels and the surprise on her face.

'Daisy?' Misty raised her finely plucked eyebrow. 'Fancy meeting you here.'

Daisy recovered quickly. Settled a welcoming expression on her face. 'I could say the same for you. I didn't think the menswear department was your style.'

Misty let out a throaty laugh. 'I've still got me meat and two veg between my legs, you know.' Then she clocked Ricky. Her eyes squinted as she stared at him, making Daisy swallow convulsively.

Misty folded her arms across her chest. Looked back at Daisy, her eyebrow shooting higher. 'So who's your friend?' The tone she used made it very clear she didn't like what she was seeing.

Daisy's brain went into overdrive. Quick. Quick. Think. Think. Who could she say Ricky was? But before she could answer Misty stepped closer to Ricky and peered at his face, her eyebrow dropping and wrinkling with concern. 'Don't I know you?'

Ricky straightened his shoulders and gave Misty a who-cares look. 'Not unless you've spent the last couple of years inside Belmarsh prison.'

Daisy could have socked him one right there on the spot. If there was anything guaranteed to arouse Misty's suspicions it was discovering that Daisy was hanging out with a former jailbird. But, surprisingly Misty took no notice of his words. Instead she took another step closer to him. Peered harder at his features. 'I never forget a face.' Suddenly Daisy noticed the worried look that covered Ricky's face. 'Got it,' Misty whispered. 'Bloody hell, you're Jenna Smart's little brother. Ricardo, that's it.'

Ricky's face lost its smooth, brown glow.

'You might not remember me but Jenna would bring you to a club I once performed at. The Groove Palace, remember, it was around the corner from Stepney Green station.'

'I remember,' Ricky whispered in a tone that said he didn't want to.

'I heard what happened. That she took off one day. Did she ever come back?'

Ricky just shook his head as if the words were too hard to say.

'I told her she was better off working the streets than getting involved with a nut job like Stella King.'

'You know Stella King?' Daisy's eyes widened in surprise.

'Everyone knows her.' Misty's hands waved around. 'She's got a mouth as big as from here to Southend. Drugs, prostitution, nicking the bibs off babies, she's been involved in the lot.' Misty's hands fell to her side as she peered suspiciously at Daisy. 'How do *you* know her?'

'I don't, really,' Daisy quickly denied. 'I heard one of the other lawyers talking about her, that's all.'

Misty pointed a finger at her. 'You keep it that way, sweetheart. Stella and that psycho son and doped-up daughter of hers are bad news. What I still don't get is what you two are doing here and how you two lovebirds know each other?'

Ricky quickly glanced at Daisy. Her gaze back at him said, *'You better get us outta this.'* Ricky pinned his eyes back on Misty. 'Miss Sullivan is my brief. Unfortunately I got into a slight bit of bovver.'

Misty balled her fists onto her hips. 'First time I've heard of a jailbird playing dressing up with their lawyer. Besides, I thought I heard on the grapevine that Jenna's brother had gone straight. That his grandma's really proud of him.'

'You heard wrong,' Ricky quickly cut in. He turned to Daisy. 'I'll get myself sorted out, Miss Sullivan. Don't forget we need to get my statement together by two o'clock.'

Then he was gone, weaving his way towards the suits.

'Daisy, what's going on here?' Misty held up her hands before the younger woman could answer. 'And don't bullshit me.'

Daisy took a deep breath. 'OK, this is the truth.' She crossed her fingers behind her back. 'Ricky is going up before the judge tomorrow, but he hasn't been long out of prison so he doesn't have any decent clothes. I'm just trying to help a client out.'

Misty peered hard at Daisy as if trying to read between her words. 'Be careful. You don't want to get personally involved with his kind of people.'

'So what's the story on his sister?' Daisy swiftly changed the subject.

'Well, she disappeared years ago. That's all I know.'

'I need to go.' Daisy pushed herself onto her toes, flung her arms around Misty and gave her a huge smacker on the lips.

Misty ran her thumb gently down Daisy's cheek. 'You take care of yourself. And if you need me, give me a bell.'

As Daisy strode away, bag flapping by her side, Misty kept watching her. First time she'd heard of some crim playing dress up with their lawyer. She didn't like this one bit. She pulled out her phone. Cursed when all she got was an answerphone.

'Jackie, sweetheart, it's me. Sorry to drag you away from your sex and sangria, but you need to get back here pretty pronto. Daisy's in trouble.'

Twenty-five

'You never said anything about your sister working for Stella.'

Daisy looked at Ricky as they sat in a quiet café, in a court off Dean Street in Soho, her statement placed squarely on the teak table between them. Daisy sensed Ricky's foul mood as soon as they met up just outside the clothes store. She suspected that the strained expression on his face, as if the blood was slowly draining away from his heart, had something to do with Misty mentioning his sister. So she'd pretended that she was tired and needed a quick pick-me-up drink. And now, here they were, sitting opposite each other, with her playing the role of chief prosecutor.

His dark eyes flashed at her. 'And I never told you that Belmarsh was a bit short on nightlife. No big deal, right?' He pulled out a spliff, then remembered where he was and shoved it back into his pocket. 'And if you know what's good for you, you won't mention it to Mrs King either.'

'Sounds like I'm not the only one with secrets.'

The silence hung between them as the waiter arranged their refreshments in front of them.

'Can I get you anything else?'

They both answered the waiter together. 'Bangers and mash.'

They each shot the other an amused look. The waiter quietly told them it wasn't on the menu and left. Ricky looked at her with a cheek-popping grin. 'I wouldn't have taken you for a bangers-and-mash type of gal.'

She smiled back. 'And being black I wouldn't have taken *you* for a bangers-and-mash type of guy. Rice and peas, shouldn't it be?'

'My sister used to make it for me.'

'My dad used to make mine.'

A tingling intimacy flowed across the table.

He fired at her, his whole face sparkling. 'Bet you can't beat my best ever, ever in the world, mash potato recipe. My sister taught me it.' He leant forward, jacking both his elbows on the table. 'Potato, sweet potato, one of them ones with the orange flesh inside, butter, milk and a little bit of coconut milk and Bob's your uncle, girl, your mouth will come alive.'

She leant forward, shaking her head as her smile grew. 'No way. You can't touch my dad's recipe. Red potatoes, a hint of garlic, butter, condensed milk and cream. Always mash it while it's still on the cooker. Bob's *your* uncle, your mouth will simply die.'

They looked at each other and started laughing. His hand settled next to hers on the table. Suddenly he grabbed her arm and pulled it towards him. 'Why do you always rub your fingers over your bracelets?'

She tried to yank her arm back but he was already using his other hand to unfasten the chunky gold bracelet. In dismay she watched as it fell onto the table revealing the one thing she never showed anyone – the ugly scar that ran across her wrist like the set of a thin, sad mouth on an even sadder face. An overwhelming wave of shame pulsed in her body at the idea of someone else looking at it. At the memory of what she'd done. Before she could make a move or say a word he pulled her wrist closer to him as he stretched across the table. He raised her wrist and kissed the scar.

Jerome grinned as if he were enjoying the best day of his life as he stepped out of the jeweller's. The jewellery shop wasn't your usual high-street outfit, but an exclusive business in Soho that his family had used for years. He'd come straight from the airport to London's West End. He whistled as he moved along with the crowd outside, the lukewarm sunshine beating down on his back, even though he felt such disappointment at not finding Maxwell Henley in Spain. He couldn't wait to see Daisy. Couldn't wait to see her face when he gave it to her. He laughed out loud, pushing his head high, which made a few people look at him as if he was out on day release from the nearest psychiatric hospital. But what did he care? He had the girl he'd been dreaming about all his life. As he passed a café window he did a double take. Froze. He stared hard, not believing what his eyes were telling him. There was Daisy – his Daisy – sitting at a table with some tall, good-looking guy who had his . . . No, Jerome told himself, he couldn't be seeing straight because it looked like the man was kissing her wrist. Shit, damn, he was. Jealousy, hot and quick, gripped Jerome.

Sweat beading against his forehead he moved quickly to the side, deciding what to do. First reaction was to storm in there and demand what the hell was going on. He shook his head. No, he wasn't going to do that because the one thing a McMillan never did was make a scene in public. Dirty washing should always stay inside the home. No, he'd talk to her later. He was sure it was all innocent. The guy might be one of her clients he reasoned. His Daisy was a straight-down-the-line kind of girl, one of the many things he adored about her.

He opened the small bag he was carrying. Took out the purple, velvet box. Flipped it open. Stared at the gold ring with sapphires that matched the colour of Daisy's eyes. The ring he was going to present to her at his parents' cocktail party this Wednesday when he asked her to marry him.

Daisy sucked in a sharp breath at the feel of Ricky's lips against the reminder of what had once been one of the most painful times in her life. He raised his head and stared at her. Maybe it was the compassion she saw in his eyes, maybe it was because she knew he'd lost his sister, maybe it was because she finally wanted to share the pain.

So she told him, in a quiet, faraway voice. 'After my dad died I was heartbroken. I wanted to be with him.' Her free hand pressed underneath the pulse in her throat. 'So I slit my wrists.'

Every word she spoke cut into her throat so deeply she was

forced to remember the pain. She remembered thinking, dazed out of her mind, she should have cut the left one first not the right because she was right handed. She'd laid down, fifteen years old and wanted to die. And almost had except Jackie and her husband Schoolboy had found her. She'd never had a woman weep over her before the way Jackie had. And that's why she loved Jackie so much, because she'd saved her life in more ways than one.

'When Jenna disappeared,' Ricky spoke softly still holding her wrist, making her heart-wrenching memories fade, 'I went crazy. Started hanging out with ghetto rats on the street. Getting into bovver with the cops. Bunking off school. I didn't realise it at the time but I was slowly cutting my own throat. We all deal with the bad times in our own way.'

Finally he let her arm go. Quickly she refastened her bracelet. 'This is between me and you.'

'Bangers-and-mash honour,' he replied, giving her an aye-aye captain salute.

He flicked his gaze at the diamond-shaped clock on the wall. 'We need to get that clobber on or we're going to miss our appointment with the bank manager.'

'OK.'

'You're playing the little lady of the house and I'm the one who wears the pants with the big wallet. Agreed?' She gave him another nod. 'You still got that high-tech phone of yours?'

'Yeah. Why?'

'Our job is to check out details. How many security guards, how many cameras, and if we get down to the vault with the deposit boxes what it all looks like. I want you to use the video camera facility on your phone to capture as much of it as possible.'

Stella and Jo-Jo entered Preston Parking Services in Bethnal Green. It was located under the railway bridge in an area simply known as The Arches. The whiz of the steam cleaning machines from the premises next door sounded harshly in the background. The room was large, with its old Victorian-bricked walls painted over in white. It was decked out as an office, not the type of around and caught the eyes of a few mechanics outside one of the garages who were cleaning two black cabs.

Stella took a menacing step forward. Voice stone cold quiet. 'If you are ever going to make something of yourself in our line of work, which I doubt, you need to keep an eye on your temper. Because a temper can make you say and do things that are best left unsaid and undone and that can have very unfortunate consequences. Ask around here. People will tell you.' His jittery gaze shifted to Jo-Jo. 'I hear you've got kids yourself? A boy and a girl, I believe? Of course, no genuine East Ender is going to hurt a kid are they? But that's only up to a point. You know what I mean?'

He swallowed. Twisted around and got back in his motor with his thug close behind. Stella watched him drive away with the same speed with which he'd arrived.

'Dad would've never let a slag like him talk to him like that,' Jo-Jo said.

'Don't worry about Ray-Ray Digby. After the job we'll remind him who's got what in their trousers around here.'

Daisy made the final adjustments to her handbag as she sat with Ricky in the car parked across from the bank.

'Is it sorted?' Ricky asked looking at her handbag.

They'd had to think of a way to video inside the bank without anyone noticing. Ricky had come up with the suggestion. Cut a hole the size of her phone in her handbag, and then secure the phone with tape around the hole inside the bag. This would create an ordinary looking shiny black panel that would be found in many handbags and they hoped that most people wouldn't look twice at it.

'I know this is going to be hard for you to do,' Ricky started slowly.

'You don't say,' she cut in sarcastically. 'I do this type of thing every day of the week.'

'I don't mean that.' She looked at him puzzled. 'I mean your bracelets.' His gaze slid to her wrists. 'You're going to have to take them off, just like I've taken my earring out.'

place you'd expect to find in a stretch of road that was known for its garages. The room contained three desks, with people going through paperwork.

'Mrs King.' One of the people at the desks stood up.

Stella nodded at the man who walked towards her. Mickey Preston. He was in his late fifties, with a body that had once been packed tight with muscles, but now was more lean and trim with a bald head he shaved once a month. If you needed a car in a hurry, Mickey was your man. When he reached her he shook her hand and nodded at Jo-Jo.

Stella got straight down to business. 'I need two motors. Something low key. Something the cops wouldn't follow even if it had a black bloke at the wheel.'

'Do they have to be fast?'

She considered his question. Normally they would, of course, but she wasn't so sure this time. After the robbery the law would be looking for something a bit nifty, not something an East German wouldn't be seen dead in. She shook her head at him.

'Let me show you what I've got.' They followed him to the back of the building, where there was a wall to floor sturdy double door. He took out a key and unlocked the padlock. Pushed and opened up into a yard that was filled with cars. Jags, limousines, Morris Minors, you name it Mickey had it and if he didn't he knew a man who did. Ten years ago he'd expanded his steam-cleaning operation next door to include a wheel clamping service. If someone wanted their towed car back there was an eighty quid a day charge for holding it. But this was the East End and a lot of people didn't come and collect their cars for one reason or another. 'I think I've got just what you're after,' Mickey said as he continued to walk.

They followed him, weaving through the vehicles, until they came to two Minis. Both black. Stella moved forward checking over the cars. She looked back at Mickey with a lopsided smile. 'I want the windows changed to something private and then have them delivered to my place in Finsbury Park later today. Put it on my slate, I'm good for it, you know that.'

Without another word she turned and started walking away.

Jo-Jo hurried along beside her. Now all Stella needed to do was organise the final thing she would need for the robbery. Some serious hardware from the firearms department.

Mickey pulled out his mobile as he watched Mrs King and her daughter disappear into the main building. 'Alright, mate? I hear you've been asking about Stella King . . .'

Twenty-six

As soon as Stella and Jo-Jo emerged outside a black Jag stormed up. It skated to a stop a few inches from them. A man in his thirties, with spiked gelled hair, a silver earring in his left ea and a face like an undertaker got out of the car and shot towar Stella. He was followed closely by a huge man, wearing shad and an expression that could spook the bravest, who st keeping guard by the car. Stella gazed at the man who swagg towards her. 'I want a word with you, missus. Your fuckin is out of control.'

Calmly she eyed him up. Knew who he was. 'What do yo Ray-Ray?' Ray-Ray was the head of the Digby crew, a mi End outfit who were all mouth but not much trousers, that's how Stella saw it.

'You need to keep that boy of yours under mann wasn't sure if it was the steam machine she could hear coming out of the silly sod's ears. 'He came into one with one of his goons and shot my younger brother i

Stella made maximum eye contact. 'I brought my he doesn't go round shooting people; at least not in joints you run.'

Ray-Ray screwed up his face and stabbed 'Tommy's been chucking his weight around eve that city director's dau–' His words fell away. H knowing he'd crossed a line. He'd told the truth was never a good idea with the likes of Stella.

Daisy instantly retreated hard into her seat and shook her head.

Ricky leant towards her. 'We can't afford for them to remember anything about us. Nothing distinctive.'

She knew he was right. But she'd never been in public without her bracelets on, except for the time in the bank yesterday. No one was ever allowed to see her scars. Her secret. Her shame. Without a word Ricky reached for her hand. She didn't resist him as he first took off one bracelet and then the other. He placed them gently in his pocket as she shivered with vulnerability. She pulled the cuffs of the sleeves of her jacket over her wrists.

'Put the camera on,' Ricky ordered.

She did what he asked.

They got out of the car. Daisy in her black dress, jacket, hair hanging loosely down and face covered in fake tan from a bottle they'd bought in the cosmetics department; Ricky in his new ebony suit and thick-framed designer glasses. The greying clouds above looked as rocky as Daisy felt. She took a deep breath. They crossed the road and made their way up the steps. Halfway there Ricky grabbed her hand.

'What are you doing?' Daisy's steps faltered with the feel of Ricky's flesh against her own.

'We wouldn't want the bank manager to think we weren't in love.'

Daisy tried to remove her hand, but Ricky tightened his grip as he kept moving forward. Resigned, Daisy moved with him. They reached the entrance. Stepped inside.

Daisy barely remembered the reception area from her first visit, she'd been too wound up to notice. She quickly looked around and sighed with relief when she didn't see any of the bank employees she'd spoken with yesterday. Even the receptionist was different. They approached the reception desk. The woman behind the desk was about Daisy's age and had sparkling big black eyes. She beamed at them. 'Can I help you?'

Ricky answered in a voice that held no trace of a street-wise London accent. 'We've got an appointment to see Mr Miah. It's Mr and Mrs Saviour-Jones.' Ricky turned and looped his arm around

Daisy's waist. He drew her close as he gave her a gooey we're-in-love smile. 'We've actually just got back from our honeymoon.'

The woman let out an 'ah' then reached for the phone. As she talked Daisy drew Ricky slightly aside and sharply whispered, 'Don't overdo the loved-up routine.'

Daisy let out a gasp as Ricky pulled her sharply into him. What he did next nearly blew the stockings off her feet. He lowered his lips and kissed her. Her first instinct was to resist. But she couldn't do that because that would wreck their plan straight away. So she took the kiss as she silently thought of all the ways she could get even with him later for taking such a liberty. But her thoughts of retribution died away as the movement of his lips spread warmth through her whole body. A feeling she'd never experienced with Jerome.

Abruptly Ricky raised his head and hooked his arm around her body so that her side was tucked into his. He eased the side of her head into his shoulder and whispered, 'There are two cameras, one on the right and one straight up ahead. We've gotta make sure no camera gets a good look at us. We kiss, we cuddle, keep our heads down and play with our hair so our hands mask our face. Got it?

He started kissing her again, this time spinning her around. Suddenly she understood what he was trying to do, get all-round footage of the reception area on the camera. 'Excuse me.' The receptionist's voice made them twist around. They let go of each other. 'Mr Miah's PA will be down shortly. Can I get you anything to drink? Tea? Coffee?'

Daisy played with her hair, masking half her face while she shook her head. The heat rose in her cheeks as she thought about the bank's cameras watching her.

A few minutes later a smartly suited young woman took them in the lift upstairs. They got out on the top floor. Daisy kept her head down as they moved along a brightly painted white corridor. She noticed that Ricky kept flicking his head up and she realised that he was counting how many security cameras he could see. Two mounted high in separate corners at the end of the corridor. The woman ahead of them opened a door that led into a large carpeted area with a desk and soft sofa to one side. She approached another door. Opened it. A small and slight Asian man, reaching the end of his forties, with thinning black hair and a take-life-easy face that could tempt the Devil himself to get into savings and pensions, stood up behind the desk

'Mr Miah, Mr and Mrs Saviour-Jones are here for their appointment.'

Daisy took a huge breath as she stepped inside.

Mr Miah was a typical bank manager – he got down to business straight away. 'Will you be considering a sizable investment?' He almost rubbed his hands together with glee.

Ricky answered. 'It will be very sizable indeed. My father recently passed on, leaving me a substantial sum. My accountant wanted to handle negotiations with the banks but I'm a hands-on guy and I wanted to visit any potential investment houses myself. You can tell a lot from the reception you get. Take you, for example,' Ricky smiled, piling on the charm. 'I can see you're a solid and reliable type, not the sort of chap who treats his clients' money like chips on a roulette table.'

Mr Miah puffed out his chest at the compliment. 'Let me take you through some of our investment portfolios . . .'

For the next fifteen minutes his words swam around Daisy. As the minutes ticked by she became increasingly tense. She'd put her handbag, with the mobile phone camera on the desk closely facing a framed photo of a smiling woman and two, beaming small children.

'Do any of those options appeal to you?' Mr Miah's voice drew Daisy to look at his face.

'They sound very attractive,' Ricky replied, smiling. 'Why don't you give us some material to take away and we'll get back to you.'

Mr Miah smiled liked the cat that got the cream as he replied, 'Of course.'

Ricky shuffled closer in his chair as if he were about to tell a secret. 'My father also left me some family heirlooms, jewellery and other valuable pieces that I don't want to leave inside the house. Thanks to our hug-a-thug government London has criminals everywhere these days.'

'We can take care of that for you as well. We have a safe-deposit box facility that can be yours for a very reasonable fee.'

'These pieces have been in my family for a very long time, so I'm sure you can understand my anxiety about making sure they are housed under the tightest security.'

Miah nodded his head. 'Our facility is second to none. Why don't I give you a quick tour downstairs and you can go away and consider your options?'

Now Ricky smiled too, it seemed there was cream for everyone, 'Excellent idea.'

They all stood up. Ricky put his arm around Daisy's waist. As the bank manager made his way around the desk a knock sounded at the door. The door opened revealing Mr Miah's PA.

'Sorry to interrupt but it's the police.'

Ricky and Daisy stopped as if glued to the floor. Rick's fingers bit into Daisy's waist. She was glad of his arm holding her because she knew if it wasn't she'd have collapsed onto the floor. *This can't be happening. This cannot be happening,* her mind screamed. An image of herself being hauled off in handcuffs blasted through her mind. Another of Randal Curtis standing by her side while the judge screamed guilty of attempted robbery. She'd be lucky to see the light of day after ten years. Her legs wobbled.

'Keep calm and leave it to me,' Ricky whispered as he pressed as light kiss below her ear.

'I'm sorry about this,' Mr Miah said as he looked at them apologetically. He shuffled past his PA and stepped outside, leaving the door partially open. Daisy saw a plain-clothes man and woman waiting by the PA's desk.

'They must be here on other business so just stay calm,' Ricky said as they both watched the manager talk to the police.

Calm? Calm? Had Ricky lost whatever marbles he had left? There they were, checking out the bank, with the cops a few feet away and he wanted her to stay calm.

'We've got to get out of here,' she hissed.

'No, we haven't. Just stay cool . . .' His words stopped as Mr Miah and the police suddenly looked their way. 'Shit,' Ricky muttered under his breath.

Mr Miah started to walk back towards them, with the police following behind. Daisy started to shake as they got closer. Ricky's arms tightened around her. The trio were almost inside the doorway. Daisy's head swung wildly towards the window as she wondered what would happen to her body if she leapt from three storeys up. The police stopped just inside the door. Mr Miah kept moving. He reached Daisy and Ricky. Looked at them. Passed them as he made his way to his desk. He opened a drawer and took out some papers. Ricky smiled at the police while Daisy avoided their eyes. Mr Miah strode past them as he approached the police. He left the room with them.

'Told you it would be alright. Stay by my side, girl, and you'll be fine.'

'I'm going to be sick,' Daisy groaned.

'You ain't got time for chucking up cos we ain't finished what we came here to do.'

A few seconds later Miah returned. Alone.

'Sorry about that. We had a false alarm yesterday and the police were just checking that everything's still alright.' He smiled at Ricky. 'And that's why your investments will be safe with us. We have an alarm system that's connected to both the local police station and our own private security firm.'

Miah was proud of his advert and clasped his hands together. 'Right, shall we go to the most secure part of the building, where we keep the safe-deposit boxes?'

Both Daisy and Ricky kept a tally of the number of security guards they came across as they made their way downstairs. One by the main door. Another by the reception. Another was posted at the top of the steps that lead downstairs. Three. He gave Mr Miah a short nod as they walked past him. They reached the ground floor. She kept her handbag low so that the security guards they passed

wouldn't notice it. Just like yesterday there was a guard posted at
a door at the end. Daisy pressed the camera off. The guard caught
her hand movement. Gazed into her face. She pulled out a stick of
lipstick. He looked away.

'Mr Miah,' the guard said stepping aside.

Mr Miah shoved a smaller key in the lock. Turned. Opened the
door. They moved inside.

'As you can see,' the bank manager started proudly. 'Our security
system is pretty tight. No one can get in here without the keys and
if they did they'd have to get past our security guards. You won't
find this level of security at other banks.'

'Very impressive,' Ricky agreed.

'Now this is the room,' Miah waved his hands around, 'where
customers can comfortably check their boxes. As you will see there
are no cameras to allow our customers total privacy.' He moved
towards the door. 'And here is the vault where we store the deposit
boxes.'

Ricky moved forward but Miah's next words stopped him. 'I'm
sorry, but for security purposes only bank employees are allowed
inside.'

Twenty-seven

Ricky held Daisy's head as she threw up near the car. She'd never thrown up so much in life like she had since her mum had re-entered her life. Tears stained her face as the waves of sick rolled out of her. As soon as they'd left the bank the tension inside her had shot up and she knew she was not going to be able to hold it back. Shaking, she pulled in huge gulps of cold air as the sickness finally stopped.

'You OK?'

Daisy eased up but was too embarrassed to look Ricky in the eye. Instead she folded her arms over her chest and kept her head low. Finally she gazed up at Ricky and nodded.

'You don't have to do this, you know.'

'You don't understand,' she flung back at him passionately. 'I can't . . .' She shook her head realising she must not tell him the truth. 'I don't have a choice.' Her last words were flat.

'Is this something to do with your dad?'

'No, of course it isn't.' Her denial was quick. Much too quick.

His hard gaze roamed over her, but he didn't challenge her. Instead he said, 'We need to get out of here to tell Mrs King the good news and the bad.'

'What's she doing back here?' was Billy's first question as he stepped inside Stella's office.

He stared daggers at Jo-Jo as she sat with her feet curled under her on a chair, next to the TV, which was on low.

Stella knew that the relationship between Billy and her daughter had always been like two cats scrapping in the night. She leant forward in her chair. 'I've had a change of heart, I'm an old softie at heart, Billy, you know that. A right puddin',' was her simple response.

'You haven't told her about . . . ?'

'She knows the lot, she's family.'

Billy swung his furious gaze onto Jo-Jo. 'I don't trust her. She's—'

'Fuck off granddad,' Jo-Jo spat.

Stella stood up and slammed her fists against the desk. The phone rattled as the desk shook. 'I know you don't like each other and that's just how it is. But until we've done this robbery we play happy families. Get it? I want you –' she pointed at Jo-Jo, 'to keep the filth off your tongue. And you –' her finger flicked to Billy, 'need to understand that whatever happens she'll always be my daughter. You know what Stevie liked about you? You never asked any questions. So let's keep it that way.'

Billy's face looked humble as he heard the name of his former boss. Stevie King had been the only one willing to give him a job after leaving prison and for that Billy had been on his side one hundred per cent.

'We need to chat,' Billy looked over at Jo-Jo. 'Privately.'

Jo-Jo shrugged her shoulders as she uncurled her legs. 'Don't worry, I know when I'm not wanted.' She moved across the room and stopped when she reached Billy. 'You know what you need? One of mum's girls to suck you off and lighten your attitude.'

Stella shook her head as she watched her daughter leave. Having Jo-Jo back in the fold wasn't going to be easy. Jo-Jo opened the door. But instead of stepping out she stepped abruptly back. 'What's that?'

Stella gazed at what Jo-Jo was looking at. The writing on the bright yellow door. She'd got someone in yesterday to change the writing from Calam and Stella to:

Daisy and Stella

'What's her name doing on the door?' Jo-Jo stared daggers at the writing.

'Shut the door on your way out,' Stella answered impatiently.

The door slammed.

Stella re-took her seat. Billy sat opposite her. 'I've checked out the girl. After Frankie died, she was taken in by a woman called Jackie Jarvis. I'm sure you heard the rumours like the other people at the time saying that this Jackie woman was behind Frankie's death, which makes no sense to me because he drew up legal documents saying she was to look after his kid if he ever died. Daisy's got a boyfriend, a Jerome McMillan, who's a well-known lawyer and comes from an upmarket family. Can't find a speck of dirt on her.' He shook his head. 'She's a respectable and upstanding member of the community. Not someone anyone's gonna think is Stella King's daughter.' He half turned his face away from her. 'Plus someone told me she did a young lad a good turn the other day in court. Got him off a serious assault charge.'

He carried on talking but Stella's eyes were glued to the TV, which showed a news report about the ongoing class-action trial bought by adults who'd once lived in a care home. The lawyer representing the adults was talking. His name was written along the bottom of the news report. Jerome McMillan.

'That her bit of posh?' Stella asked Billy, pointing at the screen.

He turned to face the TV screen. 'It's the right name and the right description. Floppy-haired rich kid who fancies himself as the attorney general one day.'

The news item changed to show the female newsreader reporting about the announcement of the new police commissioner of the Metropolitan police on Thursday at a gala dinner at City Hall, which sat on the banks of the Thames near Tower Bridge. A large photo of a serious looking Barbara Benton, in uniform and all her stripes, was in the background.

Suddenly Stella swiped the remote control off the desk and snapped the TV off.

'I know I'm meant to be a man who don't ask questions, but how come you never kept tabs on Daisy as she was growing up?'

Stella was silent for a while, then said, 'If there's one thing I've learnt about your past is when you walk away you should *never* look back. And that's how it had to be for me and Daisy.' She shook her head sadly. 'Besides, she was better off without me being anywhere near her life. What about Tommy's new man?'

Billy whistled. 'If you were looking for a new member of the crew you couldn't have chosen better. Grew up on the Stafford Cripps Estate in Whitechapel. Sounds like he was in and out of trouble before he finished wearing nappies. His dad did a bunk when he was four and his mum died when he was nine. His sister and granny bought him up. No one's quite sure what he did when he was nineteen but he was certainly running hot. That's when he disappeared, some say to Jamaica to get away from the heat. Reappeared in this fair city two and half years ago and went down almost as soon as he stepped off the plane for an eighteen-month stretch, which he did in Belmarsh.'

He stopped looking at Stella's face. Finally she spoke. 'You trust him?'

'Only person I ever trusted was Stevie.' He could see the hurt look on her face that he hadn't included her as well. 'You can't trust no one, Stella. Even your own flesh and blood.'

Before he could say anything else the door opened. Daisy and Ricky entered the room. 'Mrs King, you got a computer?' Ricky asked.

They all watched the moving images, which were a bit hazy, on the computer screen. Daisy had hooked up her phone to the computer using a USB cable that Molly the receptionist downstairs had provided. The image of the reception area spanned on the screen.

'Here and here,' Ricky pointed at the screen, 'are the security cameras. You can't see them on the screen but there are two more near the door.' His finger moved right as the images changed. 'That's the guard who is always posted at the entrance. As you can see most of the guards are young and fit and carry comms.'

'You see any weapons?' Billy asked.

'No.' Ricky looked at him. Then swiftly turned back to the screen. 'The other side of the reception leads to a room where most of the bank's business takes place.'

'He's right,' Daisy chipped in. 'That's where I was taken to talk about Charlie's box the first time I went to the bank.'

'Anything else we need to know about it?' Stella asked.

'No.' Daisy shrugged. 'It just seems to be where they do most of the paperwork.'

They were silent for a while, all absorbed by the action on the screen. The image suddenly became lopsided. Stella turned to Daisy and said, 'Hmm, thing is, Daze, I'd stick to defending Joe Public in court if I was you, you're no Quentin Tarantino, dear.'

They all smiled, relieving some of the pent-up tension. Ricky started moving through the images again. 'This is the floor that leads to the manager, Mr Abdul Miah's office. See right there.' His voice jumped as his finger moved to the top right-hand corner. 'Two more cameras. But you'll notice now . . .' He strung his words out as they waited for the image to change. 'Inside Miah's office there are no cameras.'

The camera panned around capturing the bookshelves lined with files; the large single window; the desk, which had the usual telephone, ruffled paperwork and in-tray. The on-screen imaged wobbled as the camera moved into a close up of the framed photograph of a woman in her thirties wearing a beautiful red head scarf, with a black beaded fringe and two children, a girl and a boy. The boy was about eight years old and the girl several years younger.

They carried on watching, their interest becoming more intense as the film showed the foot of the stairs leading to the basement corridor. Ricky's voice piped back on. 'There's a guard posted at the top of the stairs. The deposit boxes are kept in a vault in the basement. As you'll see there are three locked doors to get through before you reach the deposit boxes.'

They watched for two minutes as the camera took them along the narrow corridor. 'And this,' Ricky again pointed out, 'is the room that takes you to the vault. Seems there's a security guard posted outside the door, but the room is private and has no cameras.'

They watched the images inside the room. Ricky eased back up onto his chair. 'And that's all folks.'

A dissatisfied Stella looked back at him. 'What about inside the vault?'

Daisy and Ricky looked at each other. They knew that Stella was going to be pissed at this one. Daisy delivered the news. 'He wouldn't let us in. Bank employees only, for security reasons.'

Tommy spoke for the first time and as usual his words only made a tense situation worse. 'I'd have got in there, no problem.'

'And how would have you done that?' Daisy threw back. 'Used that legendary Tommy King charm?'

Tommy's hands balled into fists. 'You'll see some of my charm soon enough if you keep rubbing me up the wrong way.'

'Tommy . . .' his mother warned.

He tightened his lips together, but everyone could plainly see that the words he couldn't say were flipping around his mind.

'What about the security system?' Billy asked.

Daisy and Ricky once again looked at each other. They'd agreed not to tell the others about the police because it might cause more tension than it was worth. Daisy was the first to look away. 'It's got an alarm system that's hooked up to both the local nick and the bank's own private security firm.'

'That ain't good,' Tommy blew out, flopping back in his seat. 'Unless one of us is a security expert how the fuck are we meant to get in?'

'Plus we'd need Harry Houdini to get through all those locks in the basement. Mind you, doing a bank is never an easy thing,' Billy added.

Daisy caught Billy's eyes. He quickly looked away. The tension inside the room grew tight as everyone threw themselves back into their own thoughts.

'We ain't got no alternative now, Mum,' Tommy said shattering the silence. 'We're gonna have to do this the old-fashioned way. The way Dad would've done it.' Every eye turned to him as he carried on. 'We go in there mob-handed and do the "hit the decks, mutherfuckers" routine and get them to take us to the stash downstairs.' He looked scornfully at Daisy and Ricky. 'All this hidden camera malarkey from James Bond and his girlfriend here, I mean, give me a break . . .'

Stella calmly looked at him. 'Shut. Up.' She turned to Daisy. 'Play the section back inside the manager's office.'

Daisy leant over the desk and rewound the footage. Pressed play. As everyone again turned their attention back to the screen Stella asked, 'What did you say the name of the manager was again?'

Ricky responded. 'Abdul Miah. In his late forties. Pretty cool and confident customer.'

'Pause it,' Stella told Daisy.

Daisy froze the image on the screen.

'That's how we're gonna do it.'

They all looked at the screen. An image of Miah's desk.

'I don't get it,' Tommy said confused.

'We'll take his family hostage, of course.'

They all twisted around and looked back at the screen. But not at his desk. But at the framed picture of a smiling woman and her two children.

Twenty-eight

Daisy shot to her feet. She wanted out of this madhouse now. 'No way, they're just kids, we're not kidnapping kids.'

Stella smiled. 'Good point. Kids are difficult to shoot when they're running around.'

Daisy shook her head vehemently. 'I don't want any part of this . . .'

'You're already in too deep.' Stella stood up and walked around the desk towards her. She stopped in front of Daisy. 'You had your chance to give me those papers and return to that upstanding, Lady Muck life of yours. But no, you had to play the big I Am. Well here you are and let me tell you this much, my girl.' Stella moved her neck forward and got deep into Daisy's face. 'The only way you're leaving here is in a pine box that's only going one place: six feet under.'

Daisy swallowed convulsively at the thought of her death. At the thought of what Stella might do to Miah's family. 'You won't hurt them?'

Stella stepped back and addressed everyone in the room. 'We're not animals, are we? But we need to make this Miah geezer understand that if he doesn't play ball his family will pay the price. Ricky and Daisy, tomorrow I want you two to be outside the bank just before it shuts and follow him. Find out where he lives.'

Before anyone could speak, Daisy's phone, still attached to the computer started to ring.

Everyone froze. She looked at Stella. The other woman gave her the nod. Daisy reached for the phone.

'Hello.'

The blood drained back from her face as she recognised the voice. She listened and nodded. 'Fine. I'll be there.'

She clicked off and looked worriedly at the others.

Stella asked the question. 'Who was that?'

'Charlie's wife. She said that his will has been read.' She swallowed watching Stella's face with worried eyes. 'She wants to see me tomorrow morning.'

'Daisy?'

Daisy barely heard her name called after her as she made her way to her temporary home on the floor below. Her nerves crackled like dynamite ready to explode. How could her life have come to this? Bank robberies? Hostage taking? What next – murder?

'Daisy?'

This time she heard, and turned around to find a smiling Jo-Jo approaching her. Instantly she froze. She hadn't liked Stella's daughter – she wasn't going to call her sister, no way – the first time she'd seen her and didn't like her much more now.

Jo-Jo stopped in front of her, letting her smile broaden as her purple fringe flopped onto her forehead. 'We haven't really introduced ourselves to each other. I'm–'

'Yeah I know,' Daisy butted in. 'Jo-Jo, my kid sister. No disrespect but I'm not doing the huggy thing right now.'

The smile fell from the smaller woman's face, making her look like a child that had just grazed its knee. 'I'm sorry about what happened when we first met. I don't usually behave like that, it's just me and Mum have got a few things to iron out.' She pushed a sheepish grin on her face and stuck her tiny hand out. 'No hard feelings. Let's be mates.'

Before Daisy could reply a door at the bottom of the steps flew open. Two woman spilt out. Half naked, going at it like their tongues were inside a boxing ring.

'You're just jealous of my talents,' one spat at the other.

The other ran her eyes up and down the other contemptuously. 'Well, I ain't jealous of your tits.'

That was it. The women lunged for each other. Jo-Jo shouted out, 'Oi, ladies.' They both stopped and looked up at her. 'You know the rules. No rowing inside the house. You wouldn't want me to tell Mum now would you?'

At the mention of Stella both women gazed at Jo-Jo with fear. They took themselves back inside the room and slammed the door. Daisy could only stare with her mouth wide open.

Jo-Jo turned back to Daisy. 'See we all fall out sometimes. But in the end we make up again.' She stuck her hand out once again. Daisy studied it for a moment, not sure what to do. Reluctantly she took the offered sign of peace. As soon as she touched Jo-Jo's hand, the other woman tightened her grip on Daisy's hand and pulled her close. She whispered, 'Anytime you want out of this shit you just let me know. It ain't easy sleeping at night knowing you're gonna wake up the next morning and traumatise a mum and her little kids.'

She let go of Daisy's hand and started to skip, whistling down the stairs. Suddenly Tommy burst from his mother's office, pushed past Daisy and shouted at his younger sister. 'I want a word with you.' He grabbed her by the arm and dragged a protesting Jo-Jo down the stairs.

What a total madhouse, Daisy thought. She shivered as she thought about the other woman's words. She did want out of this shit and yeah, it weren't going to be easy putting her head down on a pillow at night knowing what she had to do. Her nerves were shot to hell. She dug into her bag hunting her bottle of pills. She hoped she might get to see her dad. But before she got there she felt a presence beside her. She turned swiftly to find a tense Billy standing next to her. She was reminded instantly of her description of him being like a mountain the first time she'd seen him. And the first time she'd met him hadn't been in Stella's brothel. She straightened. Looked him in the eye. This time he maintained eye contact with her, unlike the other times he'd looked at her inside the brothel.

'Miss Sullivan.'

'Mr Doyle.'

'I believe it's time for me to honour that favour I promised you in court.'

*   *   *

Tommy had taken his sister outside and in a rage, shoved Jo-Jo into the brothel's hard brick wall at the back of the building.

The traffic buzzed in the foreground as the summer air kicked around them.

He pointed his long finger into her face. 'You fucking well had better not have told Mum what I said to you.'

She settled her innocent eyes on him. 'Course I didn't. What do you take me for?'

His finger remained in her face. 'Then how did you manage to worm your way back into her good graces?'

'She gave me a bell, didn't she?' Jo-Jo flicked her eyes away from him. 'Said she was sorry and wanted me to come back.'

He grabbed the front of her top and slammed her once more into the wall. 'You were doing alright till then. Mum said sorry? Yeah and Beckham plays snooker.'

'She did,' Jo-Jo shot fiercely back. 'She said she loved me.' Tears gathered in her eyes. 'Said she'd missed me. Wanted me to come back home where I belonged.'

Her brother's hair flew wildly around his face as the wind tossed around him. He stared hard at his sister. Then let her go. 'If I find out you've so much as said one word . . .'

She placed her tiny finger on his lips. 'Sh. It's still only between me and you.' Her voice dropped low. 'I'm on your side, remember? Why don't we go inside and you can play me a tune on the piano? You're dead good at that, it's very soothing . . .'

She looped her hand in his. They made their way to the meet 'n' greet room where the first piano he'd ever played was. Jo-Jo's other hand twisted into a fist and her fingers jumped inside her palm. Her nails gouged into her skin. She desperately needed to find a solitary place so she could cut herself.

It was too risky to talk inside the brothel, so Daisy and Billy had slipped outside, and met in his car. She'd been shocked the day Stella tried to drown her to find one of the men in the room had been the same man she'd met in court the day she'd found out about Charlie's death. The big tough guy who helped the boys at the gym. Helped the boy who she'd defended and got off the ABH charge and then introduced himself to her. And he'd promised her anytime she needed a favour she was to look him up.

'Don't think I'm happy about this. But needs must,' Daisy said brazenly. A lawyer got used to plea-bargaining in the tightest of situations.

'I think you'll like what I'm offering.' With that he shoved his hand into the inside pocket of his jacket. Pulled something small out. Laid it in her lap. She looked down to find a gun. Compact pistol. Her breath caught in her throat.

She reached for the gun, but before she could pick it up his large, rough hand slammed over hers.

'Only one rule.' She looked up at him. 'You never use it against Stella. If you do I'm going to come gunning for you.' He released her hand. Leant over her. Popped the passenger door open. She got out as she shoved the gun down the back of her pants.

The four-year-old girl knelt on the floor, playing with her teddy bear. She sang 'Ring-a, ring o', roses' softly to herself as she swung her teddy around. She wiped away the tears on her cheek. Something funny had happened to her upstairs, which had made her cry. But now she was with teddy and everything was alright. The room was large with a pale, blue carpet, a red sofa, a bar and pastel green walls. She played in her favourite corner. The one next to the piano. Abruptly she stopped singing when she heard the voices. Big people's voices. Men and women. Coming from upstairs.

'Oh my God. Oh my God.'

'Fucking calm down.'

'What we're gonna do?'

'Shut up.'

She knew that voice. That was her mum. She pressed two fingers against her lips as she stared at the door. As she angled her head, something from above dripped onto her forehead. Her fingers moved from her lips to touch her forehead. She ran her fingertips into what had fallen onto her skin. It felt wet. Sticky. She looked at her fingers. It was horrid and deep red.

The blood fell on the girl, then on the bear. The girl screamed and ran out of the room. Up the stairs. Into the first room she came to. And what she saw . . .

Daisy bolted upright, breathing so hard she thought her chest was going to cave in. She didn't open her eyes. That's when she felt the arms around her and she started to fight. Her arms and legs thrashed out. *They weren't going to take her. They weren't going to take her. They weren't . . .* The air cracked as someone slapped her across the face. She stopped and slumped forward. The arms tightened around her.

'Daisy?' She opened her eyes at the sound of the male voice.

Ricky. Holding her secure in his arms. She rested her cheek against his shoulder.

'You're alright, babe. You're alright.' His hand ran in soft, soothing motions across her back as her breathing calmed down.

He held her for a few minutes, just rocking her. Finally she pulled herself out of his arms. 'Sorry about that. Just a bad dream.' She couldn't meet his eyes. Felt like a complete idiot.

His hand reached out and cupped her jaw. He pulled her head up, so that she could no longer avoid his troubled gaze. 'You don't have to feel embarrassed in front of me.' His voice fell softly into the room. 'We all get them you know. Fucked up dreams.'

The beat of her heart jumped up and she knew it had nothing to do with her nightmare. 'I think we should pop the light on.'

Instead of answering his head started moving towards her. Oh my God, she thought, he's going to kiss me. And she knew she wanted him to. But what about Jerome? Her gaze fixed onto his full lips. She couldn't drag her eyes away. His lips got closer. And closer. She shut her eyes ready for his kiss. But instead of her mouth his lips brushed her ear. And whispered, 'Mrs King has got a camera in here.'

Her eyes snapped open. 'What?' She hitched her head back and stared full at him.

'Sh. She must have cameras in all of the rooms the customers use. So anything we talk about we do it outside.'

A wave of disappointment hit her, not because her mum was spying on her, but because he hadn't followed through with the kiss. She threw her disappointment off and leant over the bed to pick up her bag from the floor. She dug inside. Took a pill.

'Saw you take one of those in the car. Didn't take you for a pill popper.' His surprised eyes dug into her.

'Just something to help me sleep.' Her reply was rough. 'Thanks again.'

She lay back down and turned towards the wall. The bed moved as Ricky shifted back to his side of the bed. The pills swung into action and eased her nerves. Her eyes settled on the framed photo of her dad at Southend. She remembered that day. They'd built sandcastles, dipped their toes in the sea, sank back and relaxed in the summer sun. Carefree days a million miles away from the dangerous jam she now found herself in. Suddenly Frankie winked at her from the picture. She snuggled deeper into the bed as she smiled back at him. He grinned and then started to softly sing, in that smoke filled voice of his, their song – 'Dedicated To the One I Love'. She closed her eyes as he serenaded her to sleep, just as he used to do when she was little. Her breathing gentled as his voice faded and she fell into a trouble free slumber.

2.33 am

Ricky eased quietly out of bed as soon as he knew Daisy was asleep. The brothel was quiet and the only sound was a car rushing by. In the dark he pulled on a T-shirt, tracksuit bottoms and his trainers. Walking lightly, but quickly, he made his way to the door. Slowly he eased it open. Stepped outside.

Twenty-nine

Ricky walked through the chilled air and down the stairs. He reached the next landing. Through the dark he moved towards Stella's office. The one room he knew she didn't monitor with a security camera. He pressed his ear against the door. No sounds. He reached for the handle. Turned. The door was locked. He pulled out a pair of steel tweezers from his back pocket. He leant down and inserted the tweezers into the top of the keyhole. Gently he pushed it forward and pressed up until he felt the pins in the lock. Pressing against each pin one at a time, he pressed them all the way up. He applied more pressure until he heard a click as the upper pin fell back onto the lock's inner cylinder. He used the tweezers to lightly turn the cylinder anticlockwise and then clockwise. The lock sprang back from the doorframe.

Quickly he turned the handle. It opened.

Stella's car stopped outside the brothel. She'd just been to sort out some argy bargy at one of her other houses in New Cross, South London. One of the girls had OD'd on some smack. Stupid cow. She'd considered dumping the body, but that wasn't how she liked to treat her ladies. Instead she'd organised for one of the girl's family to pick her up and stuffed a grand in his top pocket to make sure he kept his gob shut about where the body had been found.

She tilted her head and looked up at her reflection in the rear-view mirror. Shit, she looked like . . . shit. Her foundation powder had worn off revealing the tiny wrinkles around her eyes and mouth.

Her lipstick was long gone. She reached for her make-up in her handbag. It wouldn't do for anyone to see Stella King looking like some tired, beat-up old dog. No, in the life she'd chosen appearance was everything. She patted her powder puff over her face. Ran some cherry lipstick across her mouth. As she creased her lips together she gazed back up at herself in the mirror. She tilted her head left, then right. She smiled, happy with what gazed back at her.

She got out of the car. She was halfway across the driveway when she heard the rush of a car engine coming from her left. She twisted to see a car speeding towards her. Its headlights blinded her for a few seconds. It was coming with such a speed she knew she wouldn't have a chance to get out of the way. She reached inside her coat pocket. The glare from her eyes disappeared the same time she gripped and raised her gun. The car was almost upon her. She pointed the gun straight at the car's windscreen. The wind battered her face as her hand curved around the trigger. The car screeched to a halt inches in front of her. She kept the gun aimed, but didn't fire. Her accelerated breathing shook in the air.

The right side passenger door sprang open. Slowly she lowered the gun. She looked at the two faces in the front of the car and knew she had no choice but to get in.

Ricky started with the desk. He figured it would be the most likely place that Stella would keep her secrets. He counted four drawers. He tried to pull out the drawers. Locked. So he did the magic with his tweezers again and less than a minute later the first drawer was open. Mostly paperwork. He pulled out his torch. Flicked it on. Ran his gaze quickly over each paper as he shone the small, intense light on it. A few minutes later he scanned the last piece of paper. Shook his head. Nothing. He replaced the paper, careful to make sure it was in the same order as before.

He did the same to the next drawer. Piles of loose cash this time. Hundred-pound notes. He whistled. He still flicked through just in case there was something at the bottom. The next drawer drew a blank. The last drawer revealed something that made him stop. A navy blue notebook, all on its lonesome.

He flicked through the pages with a finger and thumb. Names. All male. And the type of sex acts they liked to indulge in. Bondage, feet, nappies, twosome, threesome, pain. A hell of a lot of them liked pain. A name caught his eye. A major-league politician. He wasn't surprised. Then more names started to jump out. More politicians. High-profile city faces at the top of their game. A couple of clergymen. Celebs. A few cops. He smiled at that. He took out his mobile. Got the camera ready. Took snapshots of each page. As he turned the final page something fell out and floated onto the desk. He looked at it. A torn piece of paper. He picked it up. It was blank. Turned it over. A photo of a big man, with dyed black slick back hair, grinning displaying a gold side tooth and wearing a sharp blue suit. Ricky ID'd the man instantly. Stevie 'Crazy' King, Stella's long departed husband. Stevie King's hand was outstretched as if he were shaking someone's hand. Ricky could not see who the other person was because they had been torn out of the picture. Ricky's gaze darted to the far left corner of the picture and froze. There in the background, at a table, sat a man and a woman. He didn't know who the man was but he knew the woman. His sister, Jenna. His heartbeat so fast he thought he was about to keel over. Her hair was styled around her chin, a cut she had had done a few weeks before she'd disappeared. But who was the man with her? He racked his brain. No, he hadn't seen the dude before in his life. He wanted to take the picture, but knew he couldn't. Instead he posed it on the table and took a snap of it with his phone camera.

He rubbed his finger lovingly over Jenna's face, then placed the photo back in the book. He put the book back in the drawer making sure he angled it the same way he'd found it. He turned his attention to the rest of the room. Checked cupboards, under cushions, inside lampshades. He took a breath as he looked around some more. Two adjoining rooms. One led to the bathroom. The other led he knew not where. He approached the second room. Turned the handle. Locked. He got the lock open in no time. Stepped inside. Shone his torch. What he found made him draw in his breath sharply.

*   *   *

'You could've fucking well killed me.'

Stella glared at Johnson and Clarke as she sat in the back of the car.

'Just having a little bit of fun,' Clarke replied chuckling.

'Yeah, but what if your flippin' foot had slipped and I was a goner? What do you think your guvnor's gonna say when they find out the reason I can't pull off the job is because you two fuckers just wanted to have a little bit of fun?'

That wiped the smile off Clarke's face. Any mention of the other party involved in this mess always had that effect.

'If this is just your idea of fun and games I'm out of here.' She reached for the door handle. But Johnson's voice stopped her. 'You're going to need this.'

He flung an A4 manila envelope at her. She opened it. Pulled out a folded piece of paper almost the same size as the envelope. She unfolded it. A blueprint. Then she realised it was a plan of the bank.

'Ain't you gonna thank us?' Clarke said with mock sweetness.

She glared back at him. Who the fuck did this washed-up cop think he was talking to? Some teenage tom grateful for the few quid he'd stuffed in her palm after giving him a hand job?

She tried to keep her simmering anger down as she looked at Johnson and said, 'This will come in very handy.'

Stupid fuckers. Neither of the men spotted that she was lying through her teeth. Having decided to take the bank manager's family hostage she didn't need plans of the bank. But she kept her mouth shut about her plans. She'd learnt years ago that the only way you stayed in the game was to keep one step ahead of all the other players.

'I'll be in touch,' was all she said. Then she got out of the car.

She looked up at the house and made her way to her office.

Ricky stared up at the shrine to Frankie Sullivan. Pictures of him laughing; smooching; playing the gangster. Never in a million years would he have clocked Stella as the devoted type. One look at the way she treated her kids told him that. But this gave him a new insight into the woman he'd come to hate. A woman who maybe had a heart? No, he pushed that thought to the side. She was the woman who had been involved in his sister's disappearance, and perhaps her murder? He moved deeper into the room the same time he heard a noise. He froze. Held his breath. He punched the torch off. Heard another sound. A footstep.

He waited in the dark, as the footsteps got closer. They stopped outside the door. On tiptoes he moved to the side of the door. Flattened his body against the wall. The door handle turned. He raised the torch up high. The door slowly opened. The person eased inside. Ricky's hand whipped out. As the person began to turn he jumped forward, his hand snaking around their head. His hand curved around and clamped over their mouth. He jammed them into his body, the same time the torch in his hand came swiftly down. The same time he realised who he held captive.

Daisy let out a sharp groan as something heavy glanced off her arm. Her yelp of pain was muffled by the hand over her mouth.

'What the fuck are you doing here?' Ricky whispered harshly in her ear.

His hand dropped from her mouth as he stepped back. And cursed. She twisted around and glared at him in the dark as she rubbed her arm.

'You could've broken my arm,' she accused.

'You and your arm would be nice and safe if you were tucked up in bed.'

They threw furious looks at each other. Daisy was the first to speak. 'I heard you leave the room, so I followed you.'

'I'm meant to be watching you twenty-four seven, not the other way around.'

'So what are you doing sneaking around Stella's house of horrors?'

'Stretching my legs and getting some fresh air.'

'I don't—' Her words abruptly stopped. She peered closer at the wall. 'What's that?' She pointed to one of the pictures, but without the flashlight on it was still too dark for her to make it out.

'We need to get out of here.' He didn't wait for her to reply instead moved towards the door. But she didn't follow him. Instead she moved closer to the wall. Before he could say or do anything her hand whipped out towards the picture. Pulled it down. Raised it close to her face.

'Dad,' she let out softly. She caressed Frankie Sullivan's frozen face with a shaking fingertip. 'This is a picture of—'

'Frankie Sullivan. I know.'

'But what . . . ?' she began. He didn't let her finish. Instead he turned his flashlight on to the wall lighting up the other pictures. She gasped with complete disbelief.

'What are all these pictures of my dad doing here?'

'They ain't just pictures of your dad, they're of Mrs King as well.'

And not one of her, she realised.

'Maybe she did love him after all. Then why didn't she love me?'

Suddenly Ricky placed a finger across his lips.

She gave him a puzzled look. The main door of the office was flung open. They froze. Footsteps. High heels. Clack, clack, clack. Neither of them dared move a muscle. The footsteps got closer. And closer. They moved past the room they were in. The door to the adjoining room was opened. Something banged onto the floor. Then silence. Daisy stared up at Ricky. A muscle ticked away in his cheek as he gazed back at her. Clack, clack, clack. The other person was back on the move. The door to the adjoining room banged shut. Clack, clack, clack. The main door shut. Daisy let out a long breath, but Ricky placed his finger against his lip again in warning. She didn't move. They waited for one minute. Two. Then Ricky moved towards the door. Slowly opened it. Peeped outside.

'We're alright,' he announced as he moved into the main room. Daisy quickly followed him. Startled, she watched as he headed for the adjoining room.

'What are you doing?' she whispered.

But he didn't answer. Just opened the door. Moved inside. She followed. Inside the room were the monitors for the camera that kept an eagle eye on the comings and goings inside the brothel. She scanned the screens and stopped on the one that showed Stella in the hallway downstairs with her mobile against her face.

'We should go,' she whispered frantically to Ricky.

But once again he didn't answer. Instead he reached for a button. Turned it. Stella's voice filled the air as she spoke on the phone . . .

'You wanna get your two poodles to stop trying to piss up my leg.'

'How did you get this number?' replied a voice, someone that Stella hadn't spoken to for years.

'The same way I get everything: by waving a wad of cash in someone's face. It's very effective'

The other voice grew low and tight. 'Don't mess with me, Stella, because I could really hurt you.'

'You want me to tell your daughter the truth and see the hurt written across her face?'

There was a gasp at the other end. 'Now you listen . . .'

'No, I think it's time for you to listen. Don't threaten me, because I'm holding the one thing that could blow your world and I ain't only chatting about the insides of Charlie's safe-deposit box. Push me and you're going right over the edge as well. The cliff's wide enough for all of us.' Silence greeted her words. 'Keep Clarke and Johnson well back from the action. The way they're going at it they might as well have a megaphone broadcasting what happened on the twentieth of July back in ninety . . .'

'Never, ever, mention that time on the phone.'

Stella held back her words because she knew the other person was right.

'Take care of Daisy, won't you?' Stella wasn't surprised by what the other person said.

'Of course I will. She's my daughter, ain't she.'

They watched as Stella cut the call and waltzed out of the front door.

It was Daisy who spoke first. 'Who do you think she was talking to?'

'Dunno. Real bitch we couldn't hear the other person, but whoever it was has got a daughter.'

'A daughter who is going to get hurt if she finds out the truth. What truth?'

Ricky finally pushed himself off the wall as he let out a weary sigh. But he didn't speak, so Daisy carried on throwing out her questions. 'And who are Clarke and Johnson?' Her skin wrinkled across her forehead as she thought. 'Those names sound familiar . . .'

Ricky's whole attention fixed completely on her. 'How familiar?'

Daisy bit into her bottom lip as she thought. Finally she shook her head. 'I can't remember. Maybe it was a case I did once. And what happened back in July 1990?'

This time Ricky looked away from her. He wasn't about to tell her it was the same month his sister had disappeared.

'This bank job is starting to sound like a lot more than it looks.'

Finally Ricky spoke. 'I'm paid to keep my beak out of everyone's business. You wanna take a leaf out of my book and stop behaving as if you're in the courtroom.'

Daisy ignored his advice. 'Stella is not doing this bank job on her own. She's working with someone who has a daughter and who has two associates called Clarke and Johnson. And this all might be connected to a day in July 1990.'

'We need to get out of here,' was Ricky's only response. 'Don't forget we've got to be up bright and early cos you need to suss out if Charlie Hopkirk's widow knows anything from the will and then we need to find out where Mr Bank Manager lives.'

As they crept back downstairs the information Daisy had just learnt began to shift through her head. She couldn't figure it all out, but she did know that her dad was involved in it up to his neck. Why else would Charlie have kept information about Frankie Sullivan in a safe-deposit box?

'You want me to tell your daughter the truth and see the hurt written across her face?'

That was the line from Stella's conversation that played in her mind before she found sleep that night. She knew two other people connected to this who had daughters – Charlie's widow and Randal Curtis.

Then there was Clarke and Johnson. Where had she heard those names before?

Thirty

The next morning, a bright but breezy Wednesday two days before the robbery, Charlie's daughter opened the front door of her parents' house.

'Hi, Daisy,' Jennifer Hopkirk greeted her, reminding Daisy immediately of her impersonation of the other woman at the bank. Daisy nervously looked behind her towards the car that Ricky was sitting in on the opposite side of the road.

'Come on in,' Jennifer said ushering her inside. 'Mummy's in the lounge.'

As Daisy followed her all she could think about was what she would say if Mrs Hopkirk asked after the deposit box. She knew she would lie of course, but would Charlie's wife believe her? She entered the light, airy room, with its view of the pretty garden in the back, to find Charlie's wife sitting straight and regal in one of the floral armchairs. Daisy nervously walked across the soft carpet as the other woman stood up.

'I'm so pleased you could come.' A warm smile lit up her face. 'Please,' she waved at the other longer sofa. 'Take a seat.'

As Daisy eased herself down, Mrs Hopkirk retook her seat. 'Can I get you some tea? Coffee?'

'No thanks, Mrs Hopkirk . . .'

'Priscilla, please,' the other woman cut in, folding her fine hands in her lap. Although Daisy had met Charlie's wife many times and had been welcomed into their home on numerous occasions she'd never felt comfortable calling the other woman by her first name. Maybe it was a respect thing, she just wasn't sure.

Priscilla's fingers tapped against each other like a nervous tick. 'My Charlie was really proud of you. He always said that you're going to make one of the best lawyers the firm's ever had.'

Daisy smiled. Then it disappeared when she thought what Charlie would say if he could see how her life was turning out now.

Priscilla scooted to the edge of her seat. 'I hope you don't mind me asking to see you.'

'Of course not. If there's anything I can do.'

The older woman ran her tongue over her lips as her deeply mascaraed eyelashes fluttered. The tapping of her fingers grew quicker. 'Yesterday we read Charlie's will and he said that he had a safe-deposit box. But I've looked high and low and can't find any information about it.'

Daisy's throat ran dry as she gulped. Shit. She quickly looked down at her hands.

'I know you've been sorting through his belongings at work and just wondered if you came across anything.'

'No.' Daisy lifted her head and rapidly shook it. 'No. I'm really sorry I can't help you.'

'I just thought maybe . . .' Suddenly Priscilla's hands balled into fists in her lap. 'I know Charlie trusted you so I know this information won't go any further.' She wet her lips with her tongue. 'I think Charlie may have been, let's just say, looking after some things for one of his clients. One of his more infamous criminal clients, if you understand what I mean.'

Frankie. The name blasted through Daisy's mind. 'What makes you think that?'

The other woman waved her delicate hand in the air. 'Just things he said over the years.' Her voice shook with her next words. 'I've just got a funny feeling that whoever broke into the house when we were all at the funeral was looking for something. Maybe something to do with this deposit box. And I'm terrified that if I'm right they'll be back.'

Priscilla covered her mouth with her hand and sobbed. Daisy

flew across the room to her. Knelt down and put her arms around the shaking woman. 'No one's going to hurt you.' She rubbed her hand over Priscilla's back. 'Besides, Barbara Benton swore it was a random burglary. Some scumbag saw us leave for the funeral and took their chance. Don't worry about this deposit box. I'm sure the papers are at work. When I return to work in a few days I'll find them for you.'

Priscilla looked at her through tearful eyes. 'Charlie was right; you're a girl in a million.'

Daisy smiled reassuringly, feeling like a complete fraud. What if this devastated woman was right and the burglary had something to do with the deposit box? There was so much about what she'd gotten herself into that she didn't know about.

She eased to her feet slowly. 'Really sorry but I've got to go.

'I wish I could help, but . . .' She left her words hanging in the air.

'You take care,' the older woman said. 'But if you find anything do let me know.'

A wave of guilt swept Daisy at the soft anxiety in the words. She nodded and left. Once she was outside she sucked in a cool stream of air. She started to make her way to the car but halted when she heard her phone ping. She pulled it out. Text message.

```
c u at mum and dad's tonight.
I'll meet u there.
ILU x
```

Damn. She'd completely forgotten about Jerome's parents' cocktail party. There was no way she could not go. It was too important to her. She wasn't sure how she was going to do it but somehow she was going to have to give Ricky the slip later on and get there. She had the address. If she missed this opportunity to meet his parents it might never come her way again.

She texted back.

```
I'll be there
LU2 x
```

By hook or by crook she was going to make it to that cocktail party tonight.

Priscilla Hopkirk waited a half a minute after Daisy had gone, then headed for the phone.

'She's just left.'

'What did she say?'

'That she knew nothing about it.' She wiped a stray tear from her face. 'What are we going to do now?'

Daisy lied to Ricky when she sat back next to him in the car.

'So what did the lawyer's old lady want?' He sucked on a half spliff.

'Nothing really.' Daisy shook her hair back. 'I think she was missing Charlie and wanted a talk about him to someone who knew him. It's hard letting someone you love go.' She tried to keep her eyes steady on his face as she spoke, but couldn't do it. She dipped her head and stared at her lap. The scent of cannabis floated down on her as she felt him inch closer. She almost jumped when his finger tucked under her chin. He tipped her head up. Now she had no alternative but to stare in his eyes.

His voice was soft and steady. 'What you've got to understand about me, babe, is that I've taken the kind of road in life where I've met every sort of human being. Murderers, thieves, kiddie fiddlers.' He paused and then whispered, 'Fibbers.'

She gulped and tried to move her head. But he wouldn't let her go. 'And those big blue eyes of yours are saying porkie pies and whoppers. So why don't you tell me what she really wanted?'

'Make your mind up – are you playing Al Capone or Jeremy Paxman?'

'I can turn my hand to both as necessary, I'm very flexible. A week ago we would've passed each other on the street, you going one way and me going another. But that ain't where we're at anymore. You're walking on my side of the street now. My world. A place your little pretty head is all confused over because you can't figure it out. And let's face it: you need someone looking after your back and there's only one person at the top of the queue with a sign that reads "this way back to respectability" – me.'

She finally managed to hitch her head away from him. 'You work for the Kings, so anything I tell you, gets passed up the line.'

'Not necessarily. We've all got our secrets. Look at you for example – I'm sure you've got plenty. And anyway, I don't work for Stella, I'm freelance. Of course I'm always willing to go into partnership with others but that's up to you.'

She folded her arms. 'You're forgetting, I work with men like you professionally. I know what you're like. How can I trust you, a man who's been under lock and key for some things while no doubt getting away with plenty of others?'

Indecision covered his face. Then, with a sigh, he dug deep into the inside pocket of his leather jacket. He held out a small photo to her. It showed the laughing face of a mixed-race girl in her late teens with loose corkscrew black hair and a smile that any man would be grateful to see greeting him at the front door after a hard day's work.

When he started talking Daisy was surprised by the soft tone of his voice. 'This is my sister Jenna. Well, half-sister. Same dad, different mums. Most people where we lived looked down their noses at her and you wanna know why?' Daisy said nothing. Her teeth twisted into her bottom lip. 'Cos she was a pro. A Tom. A whore.' The words were filled with pain. 'But you know what? I didn't care what she did cos she was the best sister a boy could have. She did what she had to do to put bread on the table. Then one night when I was thirteen, she tucked me into bed and never came back.' Daisy knew exactly how he felt, because she'd felt the same after her dad died. 'I never stopped looking for her. In clubs, among the girls walking the street corners. Then I found out that she worked for Stella King. That was the last place she was seen on the twentieth of July, 1990.'

Daisy froze to her seat. 'That's the date Stella mentioned when she talked about the deposit box on the phone yesterday.'

He nodded. 'My gut is telling me that whatever is in that deposit box is gonna tell me what happened to my sister.' He quickly placed the photo back in his pocket as if it were too precious to let the world see for too long. He turned back to her. 'I don't know what your reasons for wanting to be involved in this crap are and hey, I don't care, but I'm in this as deep as you. If finally finding out what happened to my sister means hooking up with you, then that's how it is.'

Now it was her turn for indecision to do a lap of her face. She unfolded her arms and ran her palms nervously along her thighs. 'Stella can't know about this, alright?' Ricky nodded. 'Charlie's wife knows about the deposit box, but she doesn't know what bank it's in. She wanted to know if I'd found anything about it. Plus she thinks it might have something to do with the burglary at her home on the day of Charlie's funeral.'

'What did she look like when she was telling you all of this?'

'Scared out of her wits, but also sort of nervous. Like she's another person with secrets.'

'Like a woman with a daughter who might get hurt if she finds out about those secrets?' Ricky put into words what Daisy wouldn't say. She didn't want to believe that Stella had been talking to Priscilla Hopkirk on the phone last night. But it all fit. Priscilla had a daughter, Priscilla knew about Charlie's deposit box . . .

'You think she's the other person involved in this?' Ricky cut into her thoughts.

'I don't know.' She shook her head. 'I just don't know.'

'Whatever the situation we need to get that box before she does and we need to get back to get ready to follow the bank manager to find out where he lives . . .' The ring of his mobile cut off his words. He flipped the phone out. 'Yeah?' He tutted and sighed. 'Look, sweetheart, I've told you it's all over . . . And spare me the blubbing, I'm not that kind of boy.' He looked at Daisy and lifted a finger and mouthed one minute.

He jumped out of the car.

Ricky turned his back on the car. Walked a few paces away. The tone of his voice changed.

'The Kings are planning to hit the bank on Friday. I want you to find out everything you can about Priscilla Hopkirk, Charlie Hopkirk's widow . . . Daisy Sullivan?' He listened. 'Don't worry about her. She isn't going to be any trouble at all.'

Stella stared out of the brothel's top floor window as she watched Daisy and Ricky drive off. Her instructions to them had been clear. This ain't TV, just follow the bank manager and find out where he lives. They'd bloody well better not screw this up. If they did she would make sure that dying wasn't going to be easy for either of them.

'Mum, come and run your eye over this.'

At hearing Jo-Jo's command she turned away from the window. She'd forgotten that her daughter was there. And sometimes wished she could forget that she was there for the remainder of her life. She still had this awful feeling that letting Jo-Jo back into her life was going to be one of the biggest mistakes she'd ever made. But looking at her youngest child's wide, innocent doe-like eyes reminded her of the young woman she would've liked her daughter to have been.

She approached Jo-Jo who sat at the computer on her desk. She was gazing intently at the screen.

'Shopping are ya?' Stella said flippantly. 'Found a bit of designer tat you want? I suppose you want me to put my hands in my pocket so you can pay for it?'

Jo-Jo tilted her head sideways to face her mum. She wore one of those smiles that, frankly, Stella found creepy. 'I think you're gonna wanna pay *me*, Mum, when you check out what I've found.'

Curiosity pushed Stella to the computer. She looked over Jo-Jo's shoulder at the screen. Disbelief caused the skin on her well-powdered forehead to crease as she read. Stunned, she looked sideways at her daughter, who wore a mouth splitting grin. 'Told you, Mum, you wouldn't regret taking me back.'

From what Stella had just read on the Internet she couldn't argue with Jo-Jo. Maybe her youngest kid wasn't such a waste of space after all. She straightened up. 'We're going for a ride.'

Thirty-one

6.15 p.m.

Abdul Miah whistled Abba's 'Money, Money, Money' as he stepped out of the bank, carrying an everyday rucksack on his back. He never noticed the two people wearing baseball caps and hoodies watching his every move from a car.

Rick and Daisy gave him a minute head start before Ricky revved the car into motion. Just as he got ready to press forward he suddenly switched the engine off.

'What you doing?' Daisy asked, eyes wide.

'He ain't going to a car, he's going to the tube.'

'What are we going to do?'

'We'll have to bloody follow him on foot.'

The rush hour was still in full swing as they kept a discreet pace behind their target as he briskly walked across the huge concrete park that led to one of London's busiest underground stations. They followed him into the entrance, which was covered by a huge glass canopy, and down the long escalator. When they reached the bottom they saw the last thing they were expecting to see: the police.

'Shit,' Ricky spat as he ground to a halt.

Up ahead stood six uniformed cops, one who was holding a large dog on a leash. They stood next to a metal frame, eyeing the commuters as they streamed past.

'What's going on?' Daisy's voice was fretful and nervous.

He grabbed her arm and propelled her to the side. 'It'll be a stop and search for knives.'

'So what, we're not carrying are we?' She looked up at him. 'Are we?'

'No.' he answered. 'But you can bet your life I fit their profile for a quick frisk. I knew I should have whited-up before I went out playing tag.' His hand moved inside his pocket. 'I gotta get rid of this.' He pulled out a small block of black cannabis resin. 'If we're delayed we might lose him. You go up ahead, get the tickets and keep an eye on him.' He popped the resin in his mouth. Chewed. Screwed his face into a very unpleasant expression. Swallowed. 'What you still doing here?' he hissed.

'But won't they stop me as well?'

'Nice white girl like you?' he scoffed. 'Yeah, you well fit the profile, don't you?'

And with those last words she left him and nervously made her way in the direction of the police stop. She slapped a smile on her face as she got nearer. She reached the police and kept moving. Two of the cops eyed her up, but no one stopped her. Quickly she looked down and found their target moving down the stairs towards platform 1. She looked back and saw Ricky making his way towards the cops. And prayed that he wasn't stopped. She headed for the ticket machine and punched the top selection. Purchased two tickets. She twisted back around and groaned when she saw the cops stop Ricky in his tracks.

'Would you mind coming this way please, sir.' The policeman stepped back as he indicated for Ricky to go through the metal detector.

Knowing there was little he could do about it Ricky stepped through it. The metal detector pinged. With a flourish Ricky opened his jacket. 'It's my belt.'

Ignoring his information the policeman insisted, 'This way please sir.'

Ricky moved to the side. Two cops approached him. 'If you could stretch your arms out.'

With a sigh Ricky spread his legs and arms. One of the cops ran his hands under Ricky's arms. Ricky caught Daisy from the corner of his eyes. She held up a single finger and he knew she meant that their target was on platform 1. As the cop ran his arms over his arms Ricky looked up and caught the display board.

1 STRATFORD 2 MINS

If he didn't get out of here soon they would lose him. Irritated he looked at the cop as he leant down. Annoyance got the better of him and although he knew he shouldn't do it he began to mouth off. 'Any chance you could speed this up boys? Only in my line of work, time is money – drugs don't deal themselves you know.'

The police took no notice of his sarcasm; they'd heard it all before. Ricky continued his rant. 'Cos that's what us black folks do, you know? When we're not holding them wild all-night parties, of course.'

The police said nothing. As the cop ran his hands down Ricky's legs he caught Daisy in the distance shaking her head and waving her hands in the air at him and mouthing 'Shut up.' He took a deep breath. She was right. As the cop's hands ran down the outside of his legs he said, 'Sorry, guys, I know you're only doing your job.'

The cop didn't acknowledge his comment, just kept on with the search. Ricky glanced furiously at the screen.

1 STRATFORD 1 MIN

They weren't going to make it.

'Thank you, sir.' The policeman straightened up.

As Ricky went to move forward the cop held up his hand holding Ricky back. What the fuck now? He took out a leaflet and handed it to Ricky.

'This is to explain why we stopped you. If you have any questions please contact . . .'

Ricky didn't hear his last words. He watched the train pull in, saw the pushing and shoving when its doors opened, the doors closing, before finally he watched it slowly pulling away.

They'd lost him.

'I can assure you sir that we are not stopping men from particular ethnic groups, but all males who fit our profile in the eighteen-to-thirty age bracket. And . . .'

'Yeah, thanks boys. Keep making London safer . . .'

The police finally let him go. He walked briskly towards Daisy.

'What were you doing?' she blasted at him.

'Save it. We've missed the train.'

'No we haven't. That was platform two.'

Before she could finish a male voice on the loudspeaker announced, 'The next train to Stratford is approaching platform one.'

'Come on let's go.'

They rushed towards platform 1. Hung back as they looked down at the people-packed platform. 'Where is he?'

'I tried to keep an eye on him but I lost him in the crowd.'

They took the steps two at a time. They hit the platform, the same time the train rolled in.

'You look that way.'

Daisy followed Ricky's order, desperately scanning the people and faces on the left side of the platform. The crowd started shuffling forward, each person trying to get into pole position to board the train. Her eyes darted left, right, back, forward. She couldn't see him. The train stopped.

'Can't see him,' she shot back at Ricky who was on tiptoes scanning the crowd.

The train's doors opened. The crowd surged forward. Someone knocked Daisy in the side almost toppling her over.

'There he is.' Daisy followed Ricky's gaze and saw their target boarding the train three carriages ahead of them.

'Get on,' he whispered urgently.

They jumped onto the carriage facing them.

'This is what we're going to do,' Ricky whispered as the train took off. Suddenly he blinked his eyes rapidly and shook his head.

Concerned, Daisy whispered back, 'You OK?'

He shook his head some more. 'Just the weed doing its thing.'
She'd completely forgotten about his eating the cannabis. He waved
his hand. 'Forget that. We're gonna make our way down to the far
doors, OK?'

She nodded. They weaved their way through the jammed block
full of people reading novels and newspapers, staring blankly into
space, or lost in the world of music from their ipods – basically
doing what Londoners did best, pretending they were on a desert
island. They kept going until they were stopped by a mum holding
a pushchair in one hand and a toddler in the other. Ricky tried to
ease past, earning a tut of irritation from the woman as she pulled
the pushchair out of the way. Ricky nodded his thanks, but the
woman just threw back a lethal look. Finally they reached the end
door and stopped under a Metropolitan police poster advertising
for community support officers. As the train rocked and rolled to
the next station they stood by a couple of women engaged in a
chit-chat.

'. . . Can you believe it, when the starter arrived instead of
waiting for mine to come he just tucked in. By the time mine had
arrived he'd not only finished but had time to wipe his mouth. A
second date, well I don't think so . . . .'

Daisy let the conversation go over her head as she watched
Ricky. He looked composed as if he did this type of stuff every day
of the week. She, on the other hand, was a lawyer for God's sake,
so why the heck was she following someone on the tube system?
The train rolled into the next station. Shuddered to a stop.

Ricky stuck his head out watching the passengers from the other
carriages get off. Their target wasn't among them.

'Quick.'

He jumped onto the platform. In a blur Daisy followed him
not sure what they were doing. He rushed forward and jumped
onto the next carriage. But Daisy was too slow. The doors began
to close. She looked at Ricky's disappearing figure in disbelief.
Breathing heavily she rushed forward, but she knew she'd never
get in the gap. She wasn't that skinny. Suddenly Ricky's hands
gripped the doors. He groaned. Managed to hold the doors back.

But the gap was still too small. But Ricky didn't let go. He wasn't leaving without her. Abruptly the doors jerked back. He let go. She jumped on.

Daisy pushed her hand over her forehead as most of the eyes in the carriage glued to her.

The driver's voice came on. 'Can I remind passengers that obstructing the doors is dangerous and causes delays.' As if his words opened a floodgate a few of the passengers sent her dirty looks. She tucked her head down too embarrassed to meet their gazes. But Ricky defiantly threw back a few 'What's your fucking problem' stares of his own.

He pulled Daisy towards him as the train resumed its journey. 'Stay close.'

'What do you think I was trying to do?' Her words were furious but quiet. 'If you'd told me what we were doing I would have followed you.'

Ricky gave her a cheeky grin. 'Even into the Gents?'

She gritted her teeth. This wasn't a time for joking. This time she took the lead as they made their way to the end door.

They kept up the carriage jumping until they reached their target's carriage. They spotted him immediately at the far end, his head deep inside one of the *Evening Standard*. Ricky and Daisy caught each other's eyes with relief. Daisy leant back against the door.

The train rolled into Stratford station.

Ricky whispered, 'If you lose me next time I'm gonna have to go it alone, got it?'

Stratford station was heaving. The station had been transformed from what some said was a shabby junction whose only purpose was to take you Up West in quick time to one that was now a major gateway just waiting for the 2012 Olympics to roll along.

Daisy and Ricky kept a respectable distance as they tailed Miah through the station. When he turned they turned. When he went up they went up. When he went down they went down. It was Daisy who finally realised where he was going – the Central Line.

They followed him up the stairs to the eastbound platform. The crowds were still thick even though it was almost seven. The platform was at ground level. The sky was fierce as night took hold.

They shuffled closer to Miah and watched as he folded the newspaper under his arm, then pulled something out of his pocket. His mobile.

'I'm nearly home, love. A few delays . . .' A huge smile flashed on to his face. 'Sure, I'll pop into a shop. Bye, love.'

Daisy winced as she heard him talking. Hearing him speak to his wife it finally dawned on her what they were going to do. Take this man's wife and maybe his kids hostage. A week earlier she would have been nodding in agreement at an outraged caller on a phone-in demanding the rope for people who hurt women and children. Now she was one of those people with the noose around their neck. Ricky caught her thoughts.

'Don't do it.'

Daisy stiffened in the cold as she tilted her head to her partner in crime. 'Do what?'

'Turn him into a husband and father. It will only make you feel worse.'

She didn't try to deny her thoughts. 'I can't feel any worse than I already do.'

'Believe me it could be much worse. At least they don't want to pour petrol on him and threaten to set him alight. That happens.'

The Epping train pulled up. Miah moved forward. Got on. They got on using the next door. They jammed themselves into a corner as they continued to secretly watch Miah.

Passengers got on and off as the train whizzed on, the crush of people jamming Daisy and Ricky into a corner near the red emergency stop lever. Their target remained in place as the train rolled into station after station.

Leyton.

Leytonstone.

Snaresbrook.

The thickness of the crowd almost obscured their view of Miah. The train pulled into South Woodford station. No movement from

Miah as the doors opened. Daisy eased back taking a few much needed deep breaths.

'Keep focused, he's on the move.'

Ricky's words made Daisy look alarmed through the crowd to see Miah approaching the open doors. Miah was off the train before they could shove through the crowd. The doors banged shut.

'What we going to do?' Daisy whispered frantically as the train started to move.

Ricky rubbed the back of his hand against his mouth. 'Throw yourself on me. Make it look like an accident.'

'What?'

'Just do it.'

She threw herself against Ricky, throwing him against the doors. She realised what he was about to do when she saw his hand move. Her body acted as a shield so that no one else saw. One of his hands snaked around Daisy's waist and held her tight. His other hand whipped up. Grabbed the emergency stop lever. Pulled. The train wheels screeched as the train slammed to an abrupt halt. Someone screamed as the force of the unexpected stop flung people on top of each other. A child's cry ripped through the air.

People started muttering as they righted themselves. The doors jerked open. They wasted no time in pushing their way through. They hit the platform. Miah was long gone.

'Keep your head down and keep moving.'

As they moved towards the stairs they heard the train driver announce that the emergency lever had been pulled and the train would remain stationary until the reason for this was discovered. They ran up the escalator and Ricky vaulted the ticket barrier to save time. Daisy fumbled in her pocket for her ticket. Ricky rolled his eyes.

'Jump the barrier, you posh bint. This is Essex, not Chelsea . . .'

She climbed onto the barrier and Ricky leant over, picked her up by her waist and put her down on the right side. The Underground employee who'd drawn the 'stop the fare-dodgers' short straw sprang into action.

'Oi.'

Ricky twisted around and confronted the irate man. He set his features into his most mean face. 'Leave it, mate, you don't earn enough money to take a beating for an Oyster card.'

The man moved out of their way. He knew Ricky was right.

They ran. Kept up their pace until the station was far in the distance. The rain licked them in the face as they kept motoring forward. Ricky checked behind and slowed down as he realised that no one was following them. Daisy leant heavily on him gulping in much needed air.

He grabbed her below both elbows and pulled her straight. 'We haven't got time for this, we need to find him.'

'How are we going to do that? He's long gone.'

'Let's just walk around.'

They walked along the main road as the rain became intense and people started to run for cover. The noise of traffic whined beside them.

'Ricky, this is a dead loss,' Daisy pleaded. She was about to continue when she saw a figure exiting a shop. A man carrying a rucksack. Same height, same clothes.

'There he is. Of course he told his wife he'd pick something up, it must've been some extra shopping.'

They kept their heads down as they followed him along the breadth of the road. Suddenly he made a left turn into a tree-lined street. A nice street. The type of street where the milkman still delivered milk and postmen didn't have to worry about junkies stealing their post for the giros. Cars were parked outside modest, well-kept houses. They carried on walking as they watched him. He stopped outside the fifth house on the left. Walked up the driveway, where there was a car parked outside. He moved to the front door and opened it. Stepped inside.

A car horn blasted making them both jump. They turned and saw the car of the person they were least expecting to see.

Thirty-two

Stella King.

Both Ricky and Daisy looked at the other woman as she sat in the passenger seat of her car. Daisy wore a stunned expression, while Ricky's look was halfway between guarded and boiling mad. She just gave them a cocky look back.

In the front seat sat a preening Jo-Jo. 'Hello, lover boy and sister dearest.'

Stella ordered, 'Get in the car and I'll tell you all about it.'

Once inside the warmth of the back seats Ricky said, 'Has this been some kind of test?' He was pissed. Really pissed. 'Sending us spinning around town cos you wanted to see if we were up for the job?'

Jo-Jo started to giggle. Stella slammed her with a withering stare. 'Knock it off, shortie, before I stick you over the rear-view mirror.' She turned back to Ricky and Daisy. 'After you were long gone Jo-Jo came to see me. She checked out Miah on the Internet and found out that he is the head of the local gardening society. It had his contact details, including his address.'

Jo-Jo slowly turned so that she faced them. Her features were smug. 'Now if you two were up for the job you would've known to do that. His details were even in the phone book.'

'So why didn't you get us on the blower?' Ricky persisted.

'Don't get your boxers in a twist, lover boy. We tried both your mobiles but with no luck.'

'We were underground, on the tube.' Daisy joined the furious ping-pong conversation.

'Well we're all here now,' Stella cut in slashing back any words the others were ready to say. 'So we know where he lives. His wife arrived back just before seven. After that a woman left who I think must be their babysitter. I want you two to stay here for a couple more hours, just to make sure we haven't missed anything.' She threw the car keys at Ricky. 'And make sure you both come straight back.'

Without another word Stella and Jo-Jo got out of the car and disappeared into the dark, evening light.

Ricky and Daisy were soon in the front of the car, eyes pinned to the house, a disgruntled silence between them. Neither of them said a word, not until Daisy heard Ricky moan, that was. She turned to find his face contorted in pain and his hand clutching his stomach.

Both shocked and concerned she swiftly let out, 'What's the matter?'

For a few seconds he didn't answer, the pain rippling deep into his face. 'I don't recommend eating dope on an empty tummy. I should have had some chips with it.'

She remembered the cannabis he'd swallowed just before going through the police check. 'Do you need to go to the hospital?'

'Oh yeah. And when I explain what's caused my symptoms, they'll call the cops. And we really need to see them, don't we?'

He lurched for the car door handle. Opened it. Leant outside and puffed and sucked in fresh air After a few minutes he drew himself back inside, gulping harshly, his forehead streaming with sweat.

Daisy kept her body close to his, the worry imprinted on her face. 'I'm taking you to the hospital.'

'No,' he replied weakly, looking at her. 'I'm alright. I just need to chill for a few minutes.' She gave him the time he needed, then asked, 'If your sister bought you up to be a good guy how did you end up on the bad side of the law?'

Ricky sang the first line from Sam Cooke's 'A Change Is Gonna Come' about being born in a tent by the river. Seeing the puzzlement on her face he continued, 'Not a Sam Cooke fan then – "A Change Is Gonna Come"?'

Next he did something that made her stiffen. He ignited the engine.

'What you doing?'

'We're heading back.'

She spluttered, 'But we can't. The house. Stella.'

'Fuck Stella . . .'

'But what if . . . ?'

'The Easter bunny comes hopping out of the door?' He laughed softly making Daisy wonder how stoned he actually was. 'All Mr Bank manager and his missus are gonna do is slip their slippers on and have an easy family night in. It's not like you've got anywhere else to go tonight now is it?'

'No I haven't, but you're in no state to drive.'

They swapped seats. As she drove away from the bank manager's house Ricky flipped the radio on. The doomed beat of Seal's 'Killer' boomed around them.

Suddenly Ricky shot up straight in his seat. 'This ain't the way back . . .'

'I know.' Daisy kept her grim blue eyes on the road.

'What are you up to?'

'Let's just say there's a few people I need to visit.'

Ricky had done loads of crazy things in his life but climbing over the gates into a darkened graveyard was a first.

'Come on,' Daisy urged, already climbing over the brick wall at the back end of the cemetery. Ricky shook his head but followed. They both landed next to a large tree with a wind chime ringing sweetly in the night breeze.

'Perhaps you can explain, seeing as we're not actually dead yet,' Ricky stared sarcastically. 'What we are doing here?'

'Visiting,' was her simple response before she charged forward.

Humming Michael Jackson's 'Thriller', Ricky followed. They twisted and turned through the graves. Finally they stopped beside a grave with a black headstone, gold writing.

'I envy you,' he said suddenly with a soft gentleness.

Strange thing to say, Daisy thought. 'Why?'

'At least you were able to lay your dad to rest. I've never had that with Jenna. That's why this is important to me. I need to lay her to rest.'

She thought about what happened when she took her pills. 'Even when they're dead they don't necessarily rest.'

They stood in silence for a while. Then she said, 'That's my Gran next door.' Ricky took a step to the right and looked. Onyx headstone, gold writing.

MILLICENT 'MILLIE' SULLIVAN

An oval photograph was in the right-hand corner. The dark obscured most of the features of the woman, so Ricky leant forward and peered harder.

'My dad hated her. I never knew why.' She shrugged her shoulders. 'But he'd always take me to visit her grave. Insisted we clean it every time we came.'

Ricky caught the lower half of the woman's face in the photo. She was smiling. His head rocked back in confusion. He was sure he'd seen that smile before. He looked sideways at Daisy. No, he hadn't seen it on her. He carelessly shrugged his shoulders. A million people must have that smile.

Ricky's thoughts slid sideways as his mobile went off. He walked away leaving Daisy some privacy with her dad.

The man on the other end of the line immediately said, 'Tell me my eyes are lying and that wasn't Frankie Sullivan's daughter I saw you with?'

'Stop worrying. Daisy's just a background player in all of this.'

'Don't tell me you're developing the horn for this girl.'

Ricky was needled, 'Never mind no girl. What you need to know is that the job is on for Friday.'

'What's happening tomorrow?'

'I assume that Stella King's is getting her troops and gear into place.'

'You're definite that it's all going down on Friday?'

'Of course. If it weren't, I would know about it. Wouldn't I?'

Jo-Jo was pleased with herself, so she gave herself a little treat. She cut herself three times across her lower leg. She sat on the ledge of her bath in her flat as the blood eased down her pale skin. For the first time in years she'd seen the love her mum had once had for her start to grow back in her eyes. That's all she had to do was make Stella think she was useful. That she couldn't live without her. That she couldn't do this bank job without her. Mummy's little girl was going to become the centre of her life.

She picked up the quarter bottle of gin next to her and drank hungrily from it. As the booze and adrenalin pumped through her a fist pounded against the front door. She sprang up, disorientated. She wasn't expecting anyone. Quickly she cleaned the blood from her leg. Wrapped her long dressing gown over her naked body. The pounding started again.

'Keep your drawers on.'

She curled her lips when she saw who was on the other side of the door.

Billy. In his hand he held a small holdall bag.

He muscled inside without saying a word. She twisted around, ready to blast him with her tongue, but he slung the bag at her feet. 'There's a hundred grand there. I want you to take it and clear out for good.'

The latest scars on her legs started to itch as the fury exploded from her mouth. 'Who the fucking hell do you think you are? Coming into *my* gaff and telling me what I should be doing with *my* life.'

He took a step towards her and sneered, 'We all know what you are and I ain't letting you come into your mum's life to hurt her again. Or anyone else.'

Suddenly she grew very calm and walked ever so slowly towards him. 'What you worried about, Billy boy?' Her question was soft. 'Worried that Mummy's gonna find out that it weren't just her fella I was screwing all those years ago?'

His Adam's apple bobbed as he swallowed convulsively. 'Now you listen here . . .'

'Did you come back for some more, Billy?' she continued, her voice even softer. 'You been missing getting your mitts on these?' She pulled the top of her dressing gown apart revealing her small breasts.

Strain tightened on his face as he stepped back as if her words had ignited a wall of flames in front of him. 'Just take the money . . .'

But she kept advancing. 'It ain't me who wants to do the taking, now is it?'

He tried to dodge her by trying to walk around her, but she flung herself at him. Wrapped her thin arms around his waist. Ground her breasts against his back. 'I like a bloke who knows what he likes.'

As swift as her whispered words left her he half twisted his body and lifted her off her feet. He slammed her into the wall. She breathed heavily as she looked at him and knew that he was either going to punch her lights out or fuck her until she couldn't stand up.

He hoisted her up and wrapped her legs around him before she could muster another thought. Was shoving himself force-fully inside her, grunting and groaning like a man at the gates of heaven. As he came heavily into her she whispered, 'You know who should be head of Mum's empire? Should be you, Billy. Something might happen to Mum during this job. You gonna let a dimwit like Tommy rule the roost? He'd spoil everything for everyone. He hasn't got it. Not like you have. Everyone says so.'

He flung her away from him. Pulled up his zip. 'Take the money,' he spat out. Then was gone.

She lay crouched on the floor where he'd pushed her. After a few seconds she smiled up at the closed door. Heaved herself to her feet. Ignored the bag of money. Ambled towards the bathroom to cut herself again. Five minutes later she headed for her bedroom. Sat on the single bed and popped up the lid of the laptop she'd been using earlier. An Amy Winehouse screen saver stared back at her. She pressed the toolbar and activated the website she'd been looking at earlier.

Jim Clarke was stone cold sober for the first time in twenty years. He sat alone, in the sitting room of his semi in East Ham. Sat on the rumpled blue settee that he'd often fall asleep on because he was just too pissed to make it to his bedroom upstairs. He stared at the framed photograph in his hand. His graduation picture from Hendon. The wrinkles around his eyes and mouth crinkled as he admired his young self, all pristine and neat, back in the days when he vowed to be the best cop on the beat. Back in the days when he believed there was a clear line between right and wrong. Back in the days before that night twenty years ago. His smile disappeared as his lips trembled.

For twenty years he'd been using the booze to run away from the guilt. But he was tired of running. Tired of the drink. Tired of the guilt. His fingers clutched the photo as he switched his gaze and looked at what he held in his other hand. A gun. He gazed at the idealistic man in the photo one last time.

The tall man walked into Daisy's apartment block. He had a determined face, sharp suit and shoulder-length chestnut hair that kicked up with each purposeful step he took. He strode past the concierge as if he didn't exist. Something about the man held an air of violence that kept the concierge welded to his seat. The concierge might be paid to man the reception hall but his wages didn't cover putting his life on the line for nobody.

The man knew exactly where he was going. Took the lift. Got out on the right floor. Reached Daisy's door. There was no need to break in because he had a key. He let himself in. Moved inside. Quietly closed the door. He gave the entrance hall a quick once-over. Strode into the main room. Scanned around. His gaze stopped when he saw a tissue on the armrest of the single sofa. He picked it up. Sucked in his breath when he realised what was on it. Dried blood.

His gaze swept around looking for more blood. Signs of a struggle. When he found none he walked into the bedroom. The first thing that caught his attention was that the wardrobe door was open, but other than that everything else looked normal.

He stepped back into the main room. He walked towards the TV and looked down at the *Calamity Jane* video box on top of it. Pulled out his mobile. 'It's me. She's gone. I found blood in the sitting room.' He paused as the other person spoke. 'When can you get here?' He listened. 'Tomorrow morning? Let's hope that's not too late. As soon as you get in, we go and find her.' He stopped as the other person interrupted him. 'I know who she's with alright.' He paused as his tongue wet his lips. 'You ain't gonna like this. She's hooked up with Stella King.'

Thirty-three

As soon as they left the cemetery and got back to the car Daisy's phone went off. Ricky twisted the ignition as Daisy stared at the caller ID on the screen of her mobile. Shock rippled through her. Jerome. Shit, she was meant to be at his parents' party. How the heck could she have forgotten?

She pushed the phone urgently to her face.

'Jerome, sweetheart . . .'

His interruption was angry. 'Where the hell were you?'

'I'm really sorry . . .' She could feel Ricky's eyes burning into her.

'You made me look like a real fool. I bought a ring. I was going to ask you to marry me.'

Daisy sucked in her breath. 'Marry me?'

'Yeah. Stupid me. I was hoping to announce our engagement before Mummy and Daddy go on holiday early tomorrow.'

She couldn't tell him the truth. 'An emergency came up . . .'

'Like another man maybe?'

'Jerome,' she pleaded down the phone, but the line was already dead. 'Fuck. Fuck. Fuck.' She held the phone to her chest and started to sob.

She only realised that Ricky had pulled the car to a stop in a side street when she felt his arms go around her.

'Posh boy giving you a hard time?'

She raised her tear-streaked face to him. 'It's me who's giving him the run around. I was meant to meet his parents for the first time tonight. His mum and dad are really important people. I totally forgot. Why am I making a mess of my whole life?'

Ricky soothed his hand over her hair. 'You know what my sister would have said? It just weren't meant to be.'

Her expression turned from upset to furious in a heartbeat. 'What are you saying? That a girl like me doesn't deserve a slice of the happiness pie?'

His hand slid to cup her neck. 'No, I ain't. But tell me if I've got this wrong? This Jerome geezer was your entry into a world that you never thought in a million years you would get your foot in. You were finally gonna leave the trash that comes with being Frankie Sullivan's daughter behind. I bet your fella don't even know who your old man is?' He knew from her expression that he'd hit that one right on the nail. 'Is that what you're gonna do for the rest of your days, Daisy? Pretend you ain't who you are?'

Her hands lashed out so quickly he never saw them coming. She smacked him across the face with such fury that his head rocked back. She did it again. And again. Ricky let her, not moving a muscle to defend himself. As she went in for the kill a fourth time she suddenly sagged on to him and started to cry like she was a kid all over again.

His arms tightened around her trembling body. 'You've been angry for a long, long time. Why did Frankie Sullivan have to be your old man? Why couldn't your mum have been the apple-pie-scented woman next door?' He placed a gentle kiss on the top of her head.

She eased her head back and stared up at him, her blue eyes damp and lost. They just stared at each other for a few seconds. Then his hands cupped her face. His lowered his lips and softly touched them to her quivering mouth. He deepened the kiss. She opened her mouth. As their tongues tangled her hands shot down and fumbled with the zip on his jeans. He urgently pulled down her tracksuit bottoms. Ten seconds later they were deep into the wildest sex Daisy had ever had in her life. They clung together as they reached a shattering climax. And then, as soon as it was over,

Ricky swore viciously. 'We shouldn't have done that. No way was that meant to happen'

Surprised, she stared at him. Wasn't that her line? She was the one with the boyfriend. She gazed at him, miffed that he was already regretting what for her had been a moment full of fireworks and extreme pleasure.

'Don't worry about it. It didn't mean anything,' she replied between pants as she pushed him off.

His cocky grin blasted across his face. 'I know. Ain't no way proper little Miss Daisy wants to be seen with a jailbird on her arm.' He looked at her as she righted her clothes. 'What I meant was I didn't mean that to happen because I wasn't packing any protection. Are we OK?'

Daisy sucked in her breath. Of course. Shit. She wasn't on the pill as it made her feel really bad, so she and Jerome were always careful. A baby? She didn't need that kind of complication. She shook her head. No, they'd only done it once, it just wouldn't happen. Would it?

Ricky's grin broadened. 'Little Miss Daisy holding a little version of Ricky, now wouldn't that be something.'

She almost lunged for him, but didn't. Instead she used her tongue as a weapon instead. 'Why don't you put your deflating dick away and get us back to the house of the rising sun.'

Johnson cursed inwardly as he approached Clarke's house. He'd called that fat fuck a million and one times with no response. When he got him he was going to beat him sober and slap into him that they still had a job to do. Two more days and the job would be over and he could get on with his life and never have to set eyes on his former partner again. He banged on the blue front door and yelled, 'Clarke, it's me, open up.'

He tapped the heel of his Italian shoe impatiently against the concrete doorstep. No response. He knocked again. Waited. No response. He shifted to the window at the side. Curtain closed, but lights on. He gave his head a savage shake. Clarke must be out like a pop star with a royalty cheque. He sidled back to the door. Looked around checking there was no one in sight. He tore off his jacket. Rolled it around his arm. Smashed the side of his covered hand into the glass on the door. The glass shattered into the hallway. He pushed his hand further in, to the side. Found the lock. With a single twist opened it. He pulled his arm back and opened the door.

His head reared back at the stale smell that greeted him. He hadn't realised that things had got this bad for Clarke. He shut the door and briskly walked towards the room where the lights were on. The door was partially opened. He pushed it with his foot. His whole body jerked back at the sight that greeted him. Clarke was slumped back on the sofa, but he wasn't drunk. Blood and his brains were splattered against the wall behind the huge bullet wound inside Clarke's mouth. In his lap lay the gun he'd used on himself.

In a daze Johnson stepped forward, shaking his head all the time. 'You stupid bastard. You stupid . . .' Howls, mixed with tears, erupted from his mouth.

He bowed his head and rubbed his hand against his forehead. This was all getting out of hand. He knew that Clarke hadn't been up for the job. He should've insisted that Clarke stay out of this, that he didn't have it in him anymore. He sucked in a deep breath. Pulled himself together. Took out his phone.

'Clarke's dead.'

'What?'

'He's eaten his own bullet. I warned you that he was acting funny. That this was pushing him over the edge.'

'OK, that's bad but you need to calm down and think straight. This isn't anyone's fault.'

'So what do I do now?'

'Does anyone else know about this?'

'No.'

'OK then, call the police and report it but don't give a name. No prints, you know the drill. Then you're going to have to do the rest of the job on your own.'

He nodded, but defiantly asked, 'You still think what we did twenty years ago was right?'

Thirty-four

Eight hours later, dead on five, on Thursday morning, one day before the planned robbery, Stella King barged into Ricky and Daisy's room where they were fast asleep. She held a bundle of clothing in her hands. Ricky was the first to wake up and shoot up straight in his bed. He pushed the duvet back revealing his bare chest and boxer shorts. Stella ignored him and moved over to Daisy, who was just waking up. She shook Daisy roughly. 'Rise and shine, sleeping beauty.'

Rubbing the sleep from her eyes Daisy asked, her voice all drowsy, 'What's going on?'

'We're doing it now.'

'What?' This time it was Ricky who asked the question.

Stella strode back to the middle of the room so that she could see the both of them. Calmly, as if she was telling them they were going for a stroll around the park she said the words that shocked them both to their feet.

'The bank job.'

'Hold on a minute, Mrs King,' Ricky shot back. 'The job's all planned for tomorrow.'

'Change of plan, handsome. It's been my way to keep everyone guessing and keeping everyone guessing is the secret of my success.' She threw what was in her hand on the floor at her feet. 'Get yourselves kitted out with this lot and be downstairs in twenty minutes.'

Without another word she twirled around and opened the door and almost bumped into one of her working girls, Tatiana. The other woman nodded and briskly moved on as Stella closed the door.

'Did I just hear what I think I heard?' Daisy's voice was clogged with confusion.

'Sounds like your mum has been keeping us all in the dark.' He moved to stare at what Stella had left on the floor. Crouched down, inspecting the clothing. Tracksuit bottoms. Hooded jackets. Gloves. All black. Daisy bent down beside him and urgently whispered, 'But we haven't had time to make plans about the deposit box.'

'I know. We're just gonna have to play this one as we go along. Now we need to get ready.' He grabbed the larger clothes and stood back up. He moved to his bed and took out his carrier bag that he'd come out of prison with. 'I'm getting ready first.' Without waiting for her response he headed for the bathroom. Shut the door.

Ricky leant on the door and pulled out his mobile. He stared at it. Knew what he should do. His instructions were clear – if there were any changes he was to give them a heads up immediately. But if he did that he might not be able to get the box. Might miss the chance forever to find out about his sister. But he had a job to do. He swore. Stared back at the phone. Made his decision. Punched in the number. Put the phone to his ear. Shit, he couldn't hear a dial tone. He pulled the phone away from his face and checked the front of the phone. No bloody signal. Shit, shit, shit. Quickly he tapped in a text message.

The job's going down now

He pressed send and prayed that the message got where it was going.

He shoved the mobile back in his pocket. Reached inside his bag for the one item he would need for the bank job.

Daisy popped a pill as she nervously waited for Ricky to come out of the bathroom. She sat heavily on the bed. Couldn't believe that it was finally happening. That she was about to take part in a bank raid. Fucking hell. Was she really going to do this? Then Charlie's smiling face swam into her mind reminding her why she was doing it. Charlie had always been there for her and this was her chance to be there for him, to make sure that his reputation remained whiter than white. If Stella ever found out exactly what her plans were . . .

Suddenly the mattress sagged beside her and she didn't need to look to know it was her dad. But she did look and saw him sitting there his face as serious as the tailor-made suit he wore.

'You know what the number one mistake bank robbers make is?' She stared at him mesmerised by his words. 'After they leave the bank they run. Stupid move, cos when the cops check CCTV or are coming down the street full steam they don't have to look far to know who done it.'

She didn't let him finish, her desperation pushing her words out. 'I'm scared, Dad.'

Frankie shoved his hand through his blond hair. 'I told you to walk away but you wouldn't listen. Ain't no way you're gonna get out of this now. Believe me, I know, Stella.'

Suddenly she became very angry. 'I wouldn't be in this shit if it weren't for you, Dad. I can't have a decent life with your shadow hanging over me all the time.'

Sadness gripped his face. 'Remember baby, don't run,' was his simple response. Then he was gone.

She wanted to cry, but instead shoved herself to her feet. Despite her dad's advice she felt like running. She got dressed quickly before Ricky came back. Then she leant over the bed. Pulled back her pillow. Picked up the compact pistol Billy had given her.

The working girl-cum-palm reader Tatiana sneaked out of the brothel, clutching her belongings, via the back entrance. As her heels click-clacked quickly towards the main road she wondered how a woman with Stella King's brains could have not realised that the only way to tell the future was to use your eyes and ears. Just like she'd been doing watching and listening at doors gathering all the information she could on the bank job. She made a right turn. Briskly walked across the road and made a left. She spotted the car straight away.

The driver's window rolled down revealing a slim, black man. She didn't know his name, but knew enough about the colour of money he offered her.

'What's going on?'

She leant down and stretched her hand out. 'Cash first.'

His hand moved with a speed she never saw coming and flew out of the car. His fingers gripped her around the throat and dragged her towards him. 'You don't get nothin' until you tell us what we want to know, you tart.'

'They are going out now to do it,' she choked out.

He let go of her neck and she staggered back. He held a bulging envelope towards her. Immediately she forgot about her pain and took it. She walked quickly away. Towards the new life she hoped the ten grand would help her start. There was no way she could go back to the brothel because she knew that if Stella King ever found there was only one thing waiting for her – and it wasn't ten grand.

Johnson pulled out his phone as he watched the tom walk away. 'Sounds like Stella is trying to pull a fast one. She's doing the job now not tomorrow.' He stopped and listened. His face grew grim at what he heard.

'Just make sure that whatever's inside that deposit box stays gone for ever.'

5.23 a.m.

'I want each of you to take a shooter.'

They were all gathered around the piano in the meet 'n' greet room downstairs. This was the first time Daisy had been inside the room. As soon as she'd stepped through the door a shiver went straight through her as her gaze hit the piano. Like she'd been in here before. She shoved the unsettling feeling off as she checked out the others. Like her they were decked out in the same gear, all in black. They stood around the gleaming piano looking at the assortment of guns that lay on top of it.

Semis.

Pump-action rifles.

Revolvers.

Shot guns.

Daisy felt sick when she saw the weapons. Of course she'd seen guns before and knew how to use one well, thanks to her dad. But she wasn't going to admit that to Stella. She needed as many surprises up her sleeve as she could if her plan was going to work.

'I don't know which one to take,' she stammered.

It was Jo-Jo who offered her the advice she didn't really need. 'You don't want one of them big bastards.' Jo-Jo waved her hands over the shotguns. 'You want one of these.' She picked up a smaller gun. 'Double action pistol. That'll put anyone down if you point it straight.'

'Thanks for your input, dear,' Stella said sarcastically. She turned to Daisy. 'You won't need one darling.'

Daisy said nothing. Just caught Billy's quick look. He was the only one who knew that she was packing the heat he'd given her yesterday. He raised his eyebrow. She knew it was a warning that if she used the gun against Stella she was a dead girl.

The others took their guns.

Only Tommy made no move to get one.

'Get the rest of that gear off,' he told Jo-Jo. She gathered the remaining guns and placed them back into the bag on the other side of the room. While she did that Tommy opened the lid of the piano. Inside lay a Remington pump-action shotgun. He pulled it out, his face filled with pride. 'I never go on any job without Dad's shooter.' The gun had belonged to Stevie King and had been the first shooter Stevie had used on his first post office raid as a green criminal making his mark on the world at the age of seventeen.

'Right, I want you lot to listen up. We've got two getaway motors as you know. Jo-Jo's gonna be in one parked a bit of a distance from the bank and Billy's gonna be stationed in one a few minutes from the bank. Me, Daisy and Ricky are going to get in the one with Billy and Tommy—' Stella addressed them with a Glock balanced in her hand.

'No, Mum,' Jo-Jo cut in. 'You get in the one with me.'

Stella flashed her steel eyes at her daughter. 'I'm giving the orders here.'

'But, Mum, two women in a motor are less likely to get stopped by the Bill.'

Stella chewed over her daughter's words. 'Yeah, maybe you're right.' She nodded. 'Yeah, that's how we're gonna play it. This is how the rest of it's gonna go down . . .'

Thirty-five

7.34 a.m.

A heavy mist covered Kersley Crescent, masking what lay below. The residents were waking up, getting ready to start another day. And the residents at number 12 had no idea that that day was going to be the start of one they would never forget.

Stella's crew waited in two cars. Jo-Jo was in one, on her own, at the end of the street, while the others were packed in the car just in front of her. Ricky and Billy were up front, Stella and Tommy in the back with Daisy sandwiched between them. The tinted windows made sure that no one could see inside, but they could spy on the world around them.

'We all know what we're doing?' Stella asked, as she eyed each one of them in turn.

Daisy's face was pasty-white. Stella leant over and pinched Daisy's right cheek. Then her left. 'That's put the colour back into your cheeks. Don't forget to act normal.'

Normal? Was she off her head? None of this was normal. Daisy gulped. Swallowed. Then nodded back. She pulled the brim of her baseball cap tighter over her face. Zipped up her jacket until the top rested over her mouth. She reached for the door handle and stepped outside. Head down she walked briskly towards the house. The mist settled on her already chilled face as her nerves kicked in. Her heart beat like crazy as she finally stood outside number 12. The curtains were still drawn, the house still not woken up. She tried to shake her nerves off as she walked up to the front door.

She pressed the bell. A child's laughter shook inside the house. Then she heard footsteps. A woman opened the door. She was shorter than Daisy by at least four inches, aged about forty, with thick black hair tied behind her back, copper-coloured skin, with lines around her mouth that showed she liked to laugh a lot. But she wasn't laughing at Daisy, instead she hung onto the door frame with a puzzled expression on her face. 'Yes?' Her voice was pure South London.

'Mrs Robertson?' Daisy asked polite and quietly.

'Mrs who?' The woman's hand tightened on the edge of the door making Daisy notice for the first time that she had beautifully manicured fingernails painted in a classic red shade.

'Robertson. Isn't this the Robertson residence?'

'I'm sorry you've got the wrong house.'

'Really sorry to have troubled you.'

Daisy turned away the same time the door slammed. She took long, rushed steps back to the car. Jumped inside. Everyone looked at her expectantly.

'They're up and about. A woman opened the door, who I think is definitely his wife. She looked more pissed off than suspicious that someone was at her door so early.'

'We've got them where we want them,' Stella said. 'So all we've gotta do now is go and get them.' She gave Billy and Ricky a grim look. 'You've got ten minutes. Then we drive the car around the front of the house.'

A dog howled from the back of one of the houses. Both men slipped on their balaclavas. Stepped outside.

1

2

3

4

The minutes passed like the blows of a hammer. The tension inside the car was high. No one spoke. Stella tapped the side of the steering wheel. Tommy fingered the trigger of his shotgun. And Daisy? Well, she just sat there like a statue.

5

6

7

8

The waiting was eating away at Daisy. She fiddled inside her pocket and found a packet of chewing gum. She popped one into her mouth with shaking fingers.

'Get rid of it,' Stella growled. Daisy caught the older woman's eyes watching her in the rear-view mirror.

'What?'

'The fucking gum.' She swung around to face Daisy. 'Wanna know one of the ways they caught the Great Train Robbers? The story goes that one of 'em got all soppy and gave the cat at the farm they were hiding in some milk in a saucer.' Still seeing Daisy's puzzled expression. 'Left his bloody fingerprints all over the dish. Your DNA is gonna be all over that gum and we can't afford for you to chuck it in the house.' She held out her palm. Daisy took the gum from her mouth and rested it in Stella's hand. Stella shoved it in the ashtray. Then she flicked her wrist up and checked her watch.

'OK. Let's do it.'

It took the car less than ten seconds to get to the house. Daisy's heart pumped so violently she thought it was going to pop out of her chest. They all looked up at the house, but nothing happened. They waited.

11

12

And waited.

13

14

Tommy's voice broke the silence, finger still on the trigger. 'Where the fuck are they?'

'Hold your horses and stay calm.'

'Calm?' he bellowed back at his mum. 'Something must've gone wrong. I told you, you should've let me do it instead of that old tosser you keep by your side twenty-four seven.'

Stella's face grew red at his unflattering reference to Billy. 'Shut it.'

But he wouldn't let it go. 'Something's wrong. We need to get outta here. Now.'

'Tommy . . .' But she never finished talking because her son suddenly leant over her trying to grab the steering wheel. His sudden attack took Stella by surprise. She fell against the door. His hands made it to the steering wheel. Stella lurched up pushing her hands against his chest. He fell back. He reared up, but stopped dead still when he realised that Stella had her Glock pointing straight in his face.

'Don't think because you're my boy I won't pull the trigger. Now ease back, settle down and keep that –' she pointed at his mouth, '– shut.'

Their breathing was the only thing that could be heard in the heavy silence. Stella turned to Daisy, the gun still in her hand. 'Go back up to the house. Knock on the door and check out what's happening.'

Daisy leant urgently forward. 'But what am I going to say?'

Stella lost her rag. 'Some lawyer you are. Use your imagination. That's what you lawyers are all good at, making up stories. You've got less than a minute.'

Daisy fumbled with the door handle. Jumped out. Tiny drops of rain spat in her face. She tried to pull the baseball cap deeper down her face but it wouldn't budge another inch. Her legs trembled as she walked across the street. Up the driveway. Towards the door. She looked up at the upstairs windows and saw a movement. A small body. One of the kids. She wiped the thin sheen of sweat from around her mouth. Pressed the doorbell.

'Coming,' a voice called. The voice was calm. Too calm if there were intruders in the house.

The door jerked open. But abruptly stopped because this time the chain was on. The same woman peered at her. Because of the chain Daisy could only see a slice of her face. The woman's expression was suspicious now.

'You again?'

'I'm really desperate to find the Robertsons . . .'

The woman cut in. 'Don't think I don't know what you're up to.' Daisy's face became pale. 'We've had lots of you junkies knocking on the door telling some sob story to get money. Now sod off or I'll call the police.'

The door slammed in Daisy's face. Daisy quickly turned and rushed back to the car.

'This time she *was* suspicious.'

'I told you we need to get out of here.'

Stella ignored Tommy. 'What did the place look like?'

'Same as before. If they're inside there somewhere they must be the invisible men. And the woman said . . .' Daisy held back.

'Spit it out.'

'That she's gonna call the cops if I come back.'

'I told you so. Right, that's it, Mum, we're leaving.'

'No.'

'She's most probably on the blower to the Bill right now.'

'Then we're better get inside the house before Mrs Bank Manager does anything stupid.' Stella checked the chamber of her gun. 'Balaclavas on. You both follow me and do what I say . . .'

'But, Mum—'

'I mean it, Tommy.'

His swearing tore up the tense air, but he did what she said and put his balaclava on. Daisy did the same with shaking hands. They shoved their hoods over their heads. Stella was the first to get out of the car. Daisy and Tommy followed. Heads down, with quick steps they walked briskly to the house. The rain was pelting in a mad, rhythmless dance. 'Tommy,' Stella commanded.

He knew what she wanted. He positioned himself in front of the door. Raised his leg. Flung his foot back ready to kick the door in. But before his foot could connect the door was flung open.

A breathless Billy ushered them inside. He panted heavily behind his balaclava. The hallway was deserted, an unnatural silence hanging over its few furnishings, the heart-shaped wall mirror, the lattice-engraved panel that covered the radiator and a long coat rail filled with a jumble of coats.

The door slammed, shutting the world out. Tommy immediately shoved Billy against the door. He grabbed the front of the older man's jacket and got right into his face. 'What took you so fucking long?' His spit hit Billy with each word.

'There was a dog on the other side of the fence. A big mother. As soon as he saw us he starts growling like he'd seen his dinner. There was no way we were gonna get in without him either attacking us or waking the whole bloody street. So I chucked him a couple of my sleeping pills. Gobbled them up like it was the bone of the week. Then we just had to wait for them to work. Took a good ten minutes. Once he was out cold we were up and in.'

'We were sitting out there like total pricks.'

Tommy finally let Billy go. Billy straightened his clothes. 'They're in the front room.'

They walked to the room. Stepped inside. No one took any notice of its homely set up, with family pictures littered around the walls, a reproduction fireplace, an elaborately patterned rug covering the deep blue carpet and plasma screen TV tucked neatly into a corner. All they saw were the people inside. A terrified woman sat with her arms around two children. A boy and a girl. The little girl's body shook as she sobbed quietly into the woman's side. The boy clung tight to his mum's hand as he stared at them with tear-filled eyes. The man of the house, Abdul Miah, was across the room propped in a chair. Bruised and bleeding from a cut above his right eye and the side of his mouth. His hands were bound and there was metallic silver tape over his mouth. And sitting calmly in a chair was Ricky Smart. With a gun pointed at the boy's head.

'Me and Mr Miah need to have a little chat.'

Stella's voice was calm. Billy briskly walked over to Miah and pulled the tape from his mouth. The man gasped huge lugs of air into his lungs.

Stella took a few, unhurried steps towards the bound bank manager. Her voice was polite. 'I'm real sorry to disturb you so early in the morning but I need to ask you a little favour.'

'Please let my wife and children go,' he pleaded.

'I'm going to let them go, dear, but I need you do me a favour first.'

'Please don't hurt them.'

Stella widened the stance of her legs. 'That's up to you, Mr Miah. If we're all sensible, nothing bad is going to happen. You just need to help me out.'

The little girl's sobs rose to an hysterical level.

'Want me to shut her up?' Tommy took a menacing step towards the girl. He drew the shotgun from its hiding place against his legs. Pointed it at the terrified girl.

Miah's wife grabbed both children's heads and slammed them protectively into her body.

'That's alright.' Stella's answer was soft. 'Excuse my colleague, Mr Miah, but I'm afraid there's a touch of insanity in his family. That's why you need to do exactly what I say or who knows what nutty boy here might do.'

The man rapidly shook his head. Stella moved forward and perched herself down next to the girl. The woman tensed as any mother in this situation would. Stella's hand came out and touched the girl's hair. The small girl tried to burrow deeper into her mother, but Stella didn't remove her hand. Instead she caressed the girl's hair as she spoke.

'They're God's gift, ain't they, kids?' Her stroking deepened. 'All any parent wants to do is see their young 'uns grow up. I hear it hurts like crazy to have to bury your own child. So this is how it's gonna go, Mr Miah.' Her hand dropped from the child's head and she turned to fully face him. 'You're gonna help us get into your bank. You're gonna go to work as usual. I'm gonna give you a list of instructions so listen carefully.' Stella paused, watching his face. 'Number one, your first instruction is to send an email around telling everyone they need to be out of the building by five because your private security company is going to be doing a check of the alarm system. Number two, let the security people in the bank know that all cameras are to be turned off by half past four in order to help with the security check.' She looked hard at him. 'Are you with me so far?' He nodded. She carried on. 'Number three, you're to tell your secretary that you've got some people coming from the private security company for an appointment for four forty-five. For the rest of the day you stay calm, go about your usual business. Three things, that's all you've gotta do. I want you to repeat back what I've just told you.'

Through his bleeding lips he quickly recited what she'd just told him. 'Good man. When it's four forty-five we're gonna arrive at the bank. You're gonna take us to your office where we will stay until everyone exits the building at five. Once everyone's gone you're gonna take us down to the safety deposit boxes. You get it open for us and we take what we need. Once that's all done and dusted, we'll be out of your hair. Then you can have your loving family back.'

She stood up. Walked slowly towards him. Stopped in front of him. He looked up at her, the blood drying on his face. 'I'm not going to repeat myself so listen up.' She crouched down. 'If you make one stupid move, like get on the blower to the Bill, the next time you see your family they're gonna be . . .' she looked over at Tommy. Laughing he pulled out a wicked-looking knife from his inside pocket. 'In pieces. I'm gonna chop your little girl in the hallway, so she's the first thing you see when you get back home. And your wife, well, she'll be a little surprise for you upstairs on your bed. That would be so unnecessary and we really don't want that to happen.' Miah's skin became paler at Stella's chilling words.

'Do we understand each other?' He nodded like the weight of the world was pressing down on top of his head.

Suddenly the boy shot to his feet. His knees rubbed together as he moved his legs awkwardly, crying. 'I need to go for a number one.'

Stella took some pity on him. She'd seen that look before. Knew what it felt like to be young and terrified of what was waiting around the corner. Hadn't she wet herself enough times each time her mum bought a new man to her bedroom before she was thirteen years old. She swallowed a wave of sick. A tough woman like her should've got a handle on those memories years ago. But she hadn't.

She turned to Daisy. 'Go with him.'

* * *

Go on, Daisy, this is your chance to leg-it and not look back. Forget about your plan and hightail it outta here.

The words terrorised Daisy's head as she led the kid out of the room. The full horror of what she was involved in had played out before her in a suburban sitting room. Crying children, guns and a knife. If she'd known what robbing a bank really involved she would have never got involved in any of this. Would she? Even to save her respectable life?

The boy's sniffles dragged her thoughts to the present. He wiped his eyes as he made his way to the staircase. She lightly touched his shoulder with a hand. He froze. Gently she squeezed. 'You're going to be just fine. OK?'

He sucked in his bottom lip as he gazed at her with deep, chocolate eyes.

'Let's get you sorted out.' Daisy grinned at him. Then realised that he couldn't see it because of the balaclava. What must she look like to this kid? One of the baddies out of one of the computer games she was sure he played. He moved up the stairs with her following him. They reached the top. He looked over his shoulder at her, with a look in his eye that said his brain was on the go. They moved along the narrow landing. He darted a look back at her. Then twisted back around and looked straight ahead. His eyes fixed onto the wall where there was a button, which she assumed was a light switch. As she lifted her foot into the next step, the boy suddenly sprinted ahead of her. She lunged for him, but was too late. He reached the end of the landing. Leapt up and banged his palm against the button on the wall. A deafening, high-pitched, electronic wailing filled the house.

Thirty-six

The boy cringed in the corner as Daisy stared at him dumbstruck. Yells and shouts boomed from downstairs. Daisy ran towards the alarm button the same time footsteps sounded in the hall underneath. She pressed her hand against the button as footsteps took the stairs two at a time. But the noise wouldn't stop. She pressed it again. And again. But it wouldn't stop.

'What the fuck's going on?'

She twisted around to find Tommy and Ricky standing behind her both with their shooters aimed high ready to go. Daisy's hands fluttered in front of her. 'I couldn't stop him. He just ran and hit this button.'

'You total twat.' Tommy barrelled forward and before Daisy could stop him he'd delivered a stinging slap to the side of her face. She rocked back on her heels and hit the wall. Dazed, she looked back up to see his fist coming her way. She held up her hands in a defence move. But his fist never connected. Ricky had grabbed his arm and held it in a vice grip. 'You don't put your hands on her. Ever. You get me?'

Tommy stared back at him with fury bubbling from all the pores in his body. 'No one touches me and lives to tell the story.'

Ricky eyeballed him back 'You wanna slug it out I'll meet you in the playground anytime. But for now you're gonna have to put your fists away because we need to stop this racket before God knows who comes to the door.' He let go of Tommy's arm. Stepped back.

Ricky tried punching the button with the side of his fist, but the alarm wouldn't go off. Tommy twisted around and looked at the terrified boy. He lunged for him and dragged him towards him by his collar. With one hand he lifted the boy up and slammed him into the wall. The boy cried out as the air was knocked from his body. Tommy shoved the barrel of his gun into his small face. 'You've got three seconds to tell me how it stops.'

The boy swung his head from side to side. 'I dunno. I dunno.'

'1 . . .' the boy carried on shaking his head. '2 . . .' Now he screamed out for his mum. '3.' Tommy's finger curved around the trigger.

Bang. A shot rang across the landing.

They stood in silence. Stared at Ricky, who held his smoking gun. He stared at the huge hole in the wall he'd made where the alarm button had once been. The gunshot had blown a deep hole in the wall, finally silencing the alarm.

A woman's heaving sobs floated up from downstairs. Tommy was the first to make a move. He dropped the boy to his feet, but didn't let him go. He dragged him behind him. He cried as Tommy carried him like a bag of rubbish down the stairs. Ricky moved to stand in front of Daisy, who was still shaking and dizzy against the wall.

His hand came out to touch the balaclava on her cheek. 'You alright, babe?'

She took in a couple of shattered breaths as she nodded. She pulled herself straight. Off the wall. Without speaking they moved down the stairs. The sight they found in the front room made them both halt in the doorway. Daisy gasped. Tommy held the tiny girl off her feet, his arm locked around her. His gun big and dangerous pressed against her temple. Stella's hand was wrapped around Miah's wife's mouth. The woman's blouse had been ripped open. Her left breast bulged outside of her bra. Stella held Tommy's knife under her nipple.

'Who's connected to the alarm?'

Stella's voice managed somehow to be soft and hard at the same time. The woman in front of her trembled. Miah opened his mouth, but shut it quickly when Stella growled, 'I'm asking her not you.'

The woman's eyes were piled high with fear. Stella pushed the blade higher. The woman sucked in her breath as it cut a thin line into her skin. A red line of blood appeared.

'The police,' she finally answered.

'Oh great,' Tommy rubbed his face, 'let's get out of here.'

Unfazed, Stella calmly carried on. 'How long will it take for them to get here?'

'Five, ten minutes, I would think, we've had false alarms before . . . I don't know.'

'We've gotta get out of here.' Tommy's tone was frantic. His legs moved from side to side, his gun still at the girl's head.

'She could be lying,' Ricky calmly put in, taking a step into the room.

'I'm not,' Miah's wife threw back desperately. 'The bank had it installed just case anyone tried to do what you're doing today.'

Tommy dropped the girl, who immediately scrambled for safety in a corner. He began to frantically pace, waving his gun in the air. His swearing and cursing tore up the air.

'Cool it,' Stella called out.

But he wasn't listening to her. 'I told you we should've skipped out when we were in the car, I was right as usual but no one listens do they?'

'Skipped out?' Now it was Billy's turn to join in, escalating the tension.

'Well, what were we meant to do when you two monkeys didn't get it done in ten minutes?'

'Shut up the lot of you,' Stella's voice struck with the power of the blade she was holding. The situation was fast descending into one of chaos and if she didn't pull it back the whole operation was going to go tits up and she couldn't afford for that to happen.

'Listen up because this is what we're gonna—' But she never finished because the phone in the hallway started ringing.

Stella flung the woman away from her. Pointed the knife at the bank manager.

'Answer it.'

He sprang out of his chair. His feet were unsteady as he moved towards the door, his hands still bound. Tommy's gun was aimed at him every step of the way. Stella kept pace with Miah as he reached the door. He stepped out into the corridor. Found the phone on the table underneath the oval mirror. Stella picked it up and held the receiver to his mouth.

'Hello?'

The blood drained from his face in response to whoever it was on the other side. He looked at Stella and mouthed, 'The police.'

She whispered in his ear, 'You know what to say.'

'Everything's alright at home. One of my kids accidentally touched it,' Miah let out a nervous laugh. 'You know these kids, as soon as you tell them not to do something they want to do it . . . so sorry for wasting your time.'

Stella whipped the receiver away from him and replaced it on its cradle. She shoved him back towards the main room. He stumbled back towards his seat.

'Right we're all back on track now.'

'I don't like what he said to them,' Billy said.

'Whatcha mean?'

'He said "everything's alright at home". That's a strange way of speaking if you ask me. Say it was code for something else. If they put an alarm in here because they're worried that this kind of stuff will happen they will have worked out a code that only him and they know.'

'I'm telling the truth,' Miah yelled, his voice clogged with unshed tears. 'There's no way I would endanger the lives of my wife and children.'

'Let's hope so, Mr Bank Manager,' Stella spat. 'Because if the cops come calling all they're gonna find is a fucking bloodbath.' She marched across the room to where the girl was being comforted securely in her mother's lap. Grabbed the little girl, with one hand and dragged her crying away from her mother. Stella sat down. Pulled the hysterical girl onto her lap. She soothed the girl's hair. 'Hey, there's no need to cry. Everything's gonna be alright.' Then she pulled her gun out of her pocket. Held it loosely in her hand.

'What now?' Ricky asked.

Stella let her gaze take in everyone in the room. Only the ticking of the clock could be heard.

'We wait.'

Ten minutes came and went and no one came to the door. Fifteen minutes. Twenty.

'Looks like you were right,' Stella told the bank manager. She let the girl off her lap. The girl rushed over to her mother.

'If I don't leave soon I'm going to be late,' Miah said softly. 'And I'm never late. People are going to know that there's something wrong.'

Less than ten minutes later Miah waited nervously, with his rucksack on his back, by the front door.

'Make sure everything gets done,' Stella reminded him tersely.

He nervously nodded. She turned from him and called out, 'Bring the woman out here.'

They appeared in the hallway. The woman's blouse was smeared with blood over the area Stella had cut her. Tommy prodded her forward using the gun he held in her back. Stella smiled at her. 'Just thought you might wanna kiss your hubbie goodbye. I'm soft like that.'

The woman threw herself at her husband. They embraced strongly. Kissed deeply. Reluctantly Mrs Miah stepped back with tears streaming down her face.

'Nice. Let's keep it that way. Identifying your dearly departed down the morgue when they pull that sheet back can really put a crimp on your day.'

Miah swallowed once. Opened the door. And was gone.

Stella watched his progress as she peeped behind the curtain of the front room window. She let the curtain fall back when he was out of view.

'You trust him?' Billy asked as he came to stand behind her.

Stella raised an eyebrow. 'This from the man who told me not to trust anyone?' A tiny smile flickered across Billy's lips. Without waiting for his response Stella pinned her eyes straight onto Miah's terrified wife.

'I think it's time for a nice family photo,' Stella said with forced sweetness. 'I want you to get over there and sit down with your kids. You in the middle.'

The other woman quickly followed Stella's orders, scrambling out of the chair and rushing towards her kids who were huddled together on the sofa. A tense Tommy, gun in hand, stood behind them. Mrs Miah smiled reassuringly at her children as she eased down between them.

'I want you to put your arms around them.' Mrs Miah pulled the children into her side, her face flicking up at Stella most probably wandering what hideous punishment Stella had in store for her now. Stella pulled out her throw-away mobile phone.

'You,' she called to Tommy. 'I want you to pretend that you're playing the lead in *The Long Good Friday*.' He instinctively knew exactly what his mum wanted. He raised his shotgun up and pointed it at the family on the sofa.

'You can't . . .' Daisy belted out.

'Shut up,' Stella snapped back as she raised her mobile. She turned the phone sideways as her finger found the camera icon. Positioned it at the family and clicked.

'What's hubbie's number?' Mrs Miah quickly shot out the digits across the room.

Stella tapped in the number and sent the photo.

Stella moved towards Billy and whispered, 'I bet Miah's almost shitting himself in the street now when he looks at that photo. He ain't going to bleat to the cops, no way. He loves his family too much. Giving your family that much power is a dangerous thing.' She looked at Billy with a faraway look in her eye as if she were remembering a time in her life when family had been important. 'We want this house to look as normal as possible. This is the kind of street where if the neighbours see the curtains all drawn they'll think something's up. We need to get them upstairs. You,' She pointed at Daisy. 'Open the curtains. Do it quick so that no one can see you.'

Stella turned to Miah's wife. 'You got any plans we need to know about today?'

She shook her head, arms around her children. 'And what about the kids' school?'

'They won't ring up, not on the first day of an absence.'

Tommy levelled his gun at the woman and children. They stood up. He waved the gun towards the door. They quickly followed his instructions. As he reached the doorway handle they heard a key turn in the front door. The front door opened.

Tommy dragged the woman backwards. Kicked the door shut. Slammed the barrel into her face. The front door shut.

'Who the fuck has got another key to the house?'

The woman's eyes bulged wide as the barrel of the gun became the only thing she was in her life. Her mouth flapped open, but no words came out.

'It might be the husband coming back,' Ricky whispered.

'No that ain't him,' Stella shook her head. 'The footsteps are too light. Is it one of your neighbours?'

Whoever it was burst into song, filling the house with their rendition of one of the latest tunes heading up the pop charts. Female voice, crap singer.

'Maria.' They all looked at the little girl.

The woman covered her mouth as she breathed in hard. Her hand dropped away. 'It's our cleaner. I forgot all about her.'

'Give her the day off you bitch.' Tommy pushed her against the wall. Squeezed his fingers around the corner of her lips, twisting her mouth into a grotesque shape. 'Fucking. Get. Rid. Of. Her.'

The cleaner jumped when she saw the lady of the house. The cleaner was small, with short dark hair and clothes that suggested she was a dedicated follower of Primark.

'Mrs Miah, you give me a fright,' she said, her voice accented with what sounded like Spanish. 'No work today?'

'No.' Mrs Miah's hand clutched nervously at her blouse so that the other woman couldn't see the rip in it. 'In fact I'm not feeling well and wondered if you would mind not doing the cleaning today.'

The cleaner peered closely at Mrs Miah's pale face, then at the hand held tightly against her chest. 'Mrs Miah, you OK?'

'No. No I'm not.' Stella tensed behind the sitting room door. 'Like I said I'm not well and just want some peace and quiet. Look . . .' With her free hand she grabbed her purse that was lying on the side table near the telephone. Opened it and took something out. She shoved it into the hand of the younger woman. 'Here's your money for today.' She grabbed the cleaner's coat and pushed it at her. 'Now, I really must ask you to leave.'

She hustled the woman towards the door. As she frantically opened the door the woman halted. 'If you have flu I look after you. Ginger tea and lots of water. I make you better.'

The tears sprang to Mrs Miah's eyes. 'I wish that was all it took to make it better. Thank you, but I'm really feeling dizzy and need to lie down.'

Finally the cleaner nodded and smiled. Then turned and was gone. Stella rushed towards the front room window. Peered at the cleaner's retreating figure as it disappeared down the street. When she turned back around Mrs Miah was once again inside the room.

'I asked you if you had any arrangements going on today . . .' Stella's voice was quiet, with an edge to it that spelt bad news for the bank manager's wife.

'I forgot.'

'Anything else we need to know about?'

The woman shook her head. Stella steamed towards her and slapped her backhanded across the face. The woman cried out as she rocked backwards. Her children started sobbing.

Stella looked at her with no pity. 'Then explain to me what the cleaner meant when she said you have a job?'

'Leave my mommy alone,' the boy screamed. His little chest puffed high in anger and frustration.

Stella caught the look on Tommy's face and knew what he was remembering. The times when he'd been a young lad and yelling at a few of the punters who she took back to her place and decided to use her as a punch bag. Back then Tommy had been her knight in shining armour. Ready to do anything to protect his mum. Where had that little boy gone?

Tommy moved, bringing Stella back to the present. He touched the boy on the shoulder with a gentleness that Stella hadn't seen him display in years. 'Let's get the kids upstairs,' he told Billy and Ricky.

But before anyone could move Stella turned to Billy. Pulled him aside and whispered, 'Don't forget as soon as five o'clock strikes make sure the wife and kids are tied up securely upstairs. Then get yourself in the motor in position near the bank. And every half hour, on the dot, keep sending Miah pictures of his loved ones as a reminder not to do anything stupid.'

Billy's expression became grim. 'Still think it's risky me just leaving them. What if the wife manages to get away? I should stay here until you send me word that the deed's done.'

'Lock them in a cupboard as well or something. Just make her know that if she tries anything her hubbie is fucked.'

And with that Billy nodded to Tommy and Ricky. They bundled the children out of the room leaving Daisy and Stella alone with Mrs Miah.

'I asked you a question.'

'I'm on leave, so there was no need to mention it.'

Stella ran her gaze over her face looking for a lie. Finally she said, 'Upstairs.'

Thirty-seven

'Your old man would be proud of you.'

Daisy shivered at her mum's words as Stella drove them away from the Miahs' house with Tommy beside his mum. Ricky sat wedged between her and a silent Jo-Jo in the back in the other car that Jo-Jo had sat in while they were in the house. Billy had been left back at the house with the family.

Daisy looked at Stella not sure if she was expecting an answer. Suddenly the anger rose up in Daisy. 'No he wouldn't. He did everything he could to keep me away from this kind of world.' The spite rose inside her. 'You know what he would say to me every time I asked him about my mum – "Believe me Daisy you wouldn't want to know about her."'

Instead of looking offended Stella started to laugh. 'He got that right. Self-centred. Carving her way to the top. Treading on anything that got in her way. Yeah, he got that right Daisy, you wouldn't wanna know about your mum.'

'At least you admit the kind of person you are.'

Stella said nothing. Instead she gazed at Daisy in the mirror with a mixture of what Daisy was sure looked like regret.

Daisy knew she shouldn't say what was on her mind, but she couldn't help herself. 'What happened in July 1990?'

Stella's hands faltered on the steering wheel. The car did a mad swerve in the middle of the road.

'What did you say?' Stella ground out once the car was back under control.

'She didn't say nothin', did you, Daisy?' Ricky punched in.

'I asked you a question.' Stella stormed bringing the car to a mad wheel screeching halt.

'And I am not giving you an answer.'

Stella twisted around to face Daisy. She screwed up her lips as she raised her hand and swung it in an arc towards her daughter. Daisy grabbed it and held on tight. Stella tried to move her hand, but Daisy increased the pressure. Stella winced.

Through gritted teeth Daisy said, 'You wouldn't believe the things that Frankie Sullivan taught me.' She held onto the older woman's hand for a few more seconds. Then let go.

Stella rubbed her hand as she looked at Daisy. 'Whatever you think you know, Daisy, believe me you want to forget it.'

And with that she turned back around, ignited the engine and kept her face straight and concentrated on the road. Daisy caught Ricky's eyes glaring at her. His expression said one thing – you stupid fool.

Suddenly Stella's words filled the car. 'Don't forget the plan after we leave the bank. The rest of you head to Billy's car and I head for the one with Jo-Jo in it. Got that Jo-Jo?'

Her youngest daughter spoke for the first time. 'Sure. Me and you are going to do alright together, Mum.'

'They're still in the knocking shop,' Johnson reported on the mobile.

He sat in his motor across the street from Stella's main brothel. He'd observed Stella and her crew come back a good five hours ago, minus her thug Billy.

'What do you think they're doing?' the voice on the other end of the line asked.

'Can't be sure but I reckon . . .' His voice stopped. He peered hard out of the window. 'Here we go, they're on the move again.'

'You know what to do?'

'Sure. We've got our little surprise all ready for our old friend Mrs King.'

*   *   *

4.45 p.m.

They entered the bank dead on schedule. This time they were suited and booted in sharp, black trouser suits, sunglasses and black, peak-edged caps that concealed their faces and that they hoped made them look like dead ringers from the bank's private security firm. Stella took the lead, a black holdall bag in her hand as they walked past the security guard. Daisy was sandwiched between Ricky and Tommy. Both men had a hand close to their jacket pocket. Close to their guns. Stella moved with an ease and confidence that Daisy didn't feel. Instead she walked with a tension so electric she thought she might burst into flames at any moment. *Cool it girl. Take a breath.*

She pulled a short, sharp shot of air inside. They reached the reception desk. A young woman with the peachiness and enthusiasm of a fresh-faced sixth former looked up at them. She gave them a smile and launched into the 'welcome to the bank' patter. As agreed Stella did all the talking. She leant on the desk as if she came here everyday. Shifted her head to the side and flashed a cool as cucumber grin.

'We've from the private security firm and have got an four-forty-five appointment with Mr Miah.'

The receptionist dipped her head as she scanned the appointment book in front of her. Her head flipped back up. This time there was no smile on her face. 'I'm sorry but I can't see any appointment.'

Daisy tensed behind Stella. She quickly caught Ricky's eyes. Tommy shoved his hand inside his jacket, near the waistband of his trousers.

'You must be mistaken.' Stella's voice was calm and confident. 'Mr Miah knows that we're scheduled to do a full points check on the alarm system today.'

The woman checked the book again. Her head came back up. 'There's nothing here. Are you sure it was for today?'

Daisy saw Tommy's arm start to twitch.

The receptionist waved her hands in a flustered motion. 'Why don't you take a seat and I'll make some enquiries.'

They moved towards the group of chairs near the window with rivers of rain seeping down it.

'This is a set up,' Tommy growled. 'Billy was right, he must've been using code with the police this morning—'

'Cool it . . .' Stella threw back.

'We're sitting here as hot as a lad facing his first fuck and you want me to cool it—'

His words abruptly stopped as they watched the receptionist beckon an older man to her desk. At the same time the security guard by the door moved deeper into the reception hall. The receptionist pointed a finger at them. A police siren screamed from somewhere outside.

Tommy shot to his feet. 'I ain't being taken down without a fight.'

Before anyone could stop him he briskly moved towards the reception desk as his hand shoved inside his waistband.

'Shit,' Stella said. But she remained in her seat.

Tommy reached the desk. The man and woman looked up at him. His hand started coming out of his pocket.

'Gillian?'

They all turned to see Mr Miah emerging from the corner where the lift was placed.

'Oh, Mr Miah,' the receptionist called back. 'I'm so glad to see you. The people from the security company are here, but I couldn't . . .'

'That's fine.' He reached the desk the same time Tommy's hand eased back. 'I will take it from here.'

As soon as the door closed to Miah's office closed Tommy slugged him one in the stomach. Miah toppled over onto his desk, his arm flinging the framed photo of his family on the floor. Tommy jacked his forearm and elbow under his throat.

'What the fuck was that all about downstairs?' Stella demanded.

'You told me to tell my PA about your appointment. You didn't say anything about the receptionist!' Miah croaked.

Tommy jammed his arm deeper into the man's windpipe. Desperate choking noises erupted from Miah's throat.

'I don't fucking believe him,' Tommy spat into the man's face.

'Pack it in. We need to get ready.' Stella's command was soft, but loaded with a tone that said you better follow my instructions or else.

Tommy twisted his mouth to an ugly angle. He removed his arm from Miah's throat. Hauled him to his feet. Marched him to the wall. Grabbed the back of his head and twisted his face to the wall.

'Stay put. And I haven't finished with you yet.'

While he remained immobile against the wall, Stella reached into the holdall bag and threw the items inside at everyone. They quickly undressed and in less than five minutes were back in the clothes they wore earlier when they took Miah's family hostage. Stella, balaclava in place, moved towards Miah. Grabbed the back of his head and twisted him around.

'And just to remind you which page you're on, you might wanna see this.'

Stella held her mobile up. When he saw the screen he covered his mouth with his hand and trembled. A grim photo stared back of his wife and kids bound and gagged inside his bedroom. He lifted his head sharply to look at Stella.

'Believe me, I've done everything you've asked me to do. I wouldn't do anything that might hurt my family.'

'You keep that family photo in mind every time you think about playing the hero.'

He pushed himself off the wall the same time there was a quiet knock at the door. Everyone froze. Looked at the door. Tommy whipped out his gun and pointed it at Miah.

Stella nodded at Miah. He pushed his hand through his hair, flicking back into place the few strands that were plastered to his forehead with sweat and quickly moved to the door. Tommy's gun kept pace with his every step. He let out a funny little cough, then pulled the door back slightly. He let out a sharp breath when he saw who it was. His PA.

'Shall I get some coffees and teas?'

'No. The bank's going to shut soon, so why don't you get off early.'

She smiled broadly. 'Thanks Mr Miah. I'm off to see a musical version of *The Godfather* . . .'

'Yes, yes, yes,' he replied impatiently. 'Just go.' He stopped, realising that his tone was all wrong. He made his tone lighter. 'I'll see you tomorrow.' And without waiting for a response he closed the door in her face.

He turned back nervously to watch the people in his office.

'Good job,' Stella said. 'Now if you keep it like that everything's gonna be sweet. And before you know it you'll be wrapped in your family's loving embrace once again.' She checked her watch.

4.56 p.m.

'Does everyone know that they need to be out of the building by five?' she asked him.

'I sent an email around.'

'And the cameras?'

'All off. I checked myself at four thirty.'

'When everyone's gone how many security guards will be left?'

'Two. They'll be posted in the reception hall.' His tongue came out and wet his lips as if he were too afraid to ask the next thing on his mind. 'What happens next?'

'You let us worry about that.'

Just then a pinging noise sounded. Someone's mobile. Miah hurriedly pulled his from his jacket. Stared at the screen as he bit into his bottom lip and shook his head. Stella moved towards him and pulled the mobile from his trembling hands. Stared grimly at Billy's latest addition to Miah's photo album – a close-up picture of his daughter with tape over her mouth and large, terrified, brown eyes staring into the lens.

The employees of the bank streamed out at five on the dot. Everyone looked as if they were more than happy to grab this extra time to themselves. No one looked back. All except Mr Miah's PA Pamela Walker. As she waited on the Jubilee Line platform she dug into her bag looking for her theatre ticket. She was dead excited about this evening. It was going to be her first date with James. A delicious smile rippled across her face as she thought about finally getting him in the palm of her hand. She'd been chasing him to hell and back for over a year. Now his divorce was through she could have him all to herself. And what things she had planned for him. The smile slipped off her face as she realised that she couldn't find the ticket. Damn. She'd definitely put it in her bag this morning. Where the hell could it be? She shoved a finger into her mouth as she chewed on a nail, her mind going a million miles a second as she thought back over the day. It should be in her bag. That was the only place . . . Her thoughts stopped as she remembered where she'd placed it earlier for safe keeping. Her desk drawer. If she turned up without her ticket she might ruin her date. No, she wasn't prepared to do that. Nothing was going to get in the way of her finally claiming James Rogers as her own. She had no choice. She'd have to go back and get the ticket.

5.17 p.m.

Stella finally spoke, breaking the silence they had all held for so long. 'Ring security downstairs and get one of them to check every floor to make sure no one's left behind.'

'But they won't leave their post in reception,' Miah answered.

'Just do it, mate, we're not playing games here, I'd have thought you'd have noticed that by now.'

He quickly picked up the phone. 'It's Mr Miah. The security firm want to start checking the equipment but they can't do this until everyone has gone, so I want you to do a quick round robin . . . I know you're not meant to leave your post.' Suddenly his tone changed as he plastered a smile onto his face. 'It's Calvin, isn't it? . . . I understand that you've been discussing taking out a loan. Why don't we sit down and talk about that some more tomorrow. In the meantime, just do this little favour for me.' He put the phone down. Looked across at Stella. 'He's going to call me back as soon as it's done.'

The call came twelve minutes later. 'The building's empty.'

Stella stood up. 'OK, then, let's get down to business. Where's these boxes?'

Pamela Walker caught the eye of one of the security guards and tapped against the bank's glass door. The guard quickly came over and opened the door. She moved forward but he stepped in her path.

'Really sorry, Calvin, but I've got to get back upstairs.'

He shook his head. 'Can't let you in. Orders straight down from the boss man himself.'

'Come on. I'll be in and out quickly. I left something behind, something important.'

'I could lose my job over this.'

'No way. You're the best and Mr Miah knows it. Trust me.'

With a resigned sigh he widened the door letting her in. She checked her watch again. Shit, time was moving fast and James wasn't a man who liked to be kept waiting. She ran towards the lift.

Stella shoved the barrel of the gun tight into Miah's back as they entered his PA's office. 'Stay close to me when we get downstairs. Remember – any false moves . . .' She didn't need to finish. She pulled the Glock back and buried it back into her pocket. They walked across the room and reached the door. Miah's hand shot out towards the handle. But before he could reach it the door was flung back from the outside. Startled everyone stopped. Tommy pulled his gun from his pocket.

Pamela stared horrified at the gun pointed at her. She opened her mouth to scream.

Thirty-eight

It was Daisy who made the move. She jumped forward. Slammed her palm over the shocked woman's mouth. With her other hand she gripped the woman's jacket. Dragged her inside the room. With a twist she spun her inside. Miah's PA wobbled on her feet, trying to get her balance. But it was too late. The force of Daisy's move and the shock rocked her backwards and she lost her footing and tumbled onto the floor. Tommy ran towards her. Fell on one knee. Placed the barrel of the gun point blank in her forehead. He placed a single finger against his lips, letting her know that if she opened her mouth it might be the last time she ever did it. Petrified, she let the scream die in her throat.

'What are you doing back here?' Miah yelled at his PA.

She tried to speak but the terror was too great. All that came out were whimpering noises.

'I'll sort the bitch out,' Tommy said. His finger curved around the trigger.

'No.' It was Ricky who spoke this time.

'I give the orders around here, handsome, you know that,' Stella said.

'I know that. But we're losing focus here, which is the box. All we need to do is to keep her quiet long enough to give us time to get this job done.'

Tommy twisted his head to look up at them. 'Focus? You sound like my old social worker. No, my way's better. Take her out and matey-boy here with the family will know we mean business.' He turned his fierce, furious eyes back onto the PA. 'Proper business.'

The atmosphere in the room deepened. Finally Stella turned to Ricky. 'What do you suggest we do?'

'The bag,' he said to Stella.

She passed it to him. He unzipped it. Pulled out a roll of metallic silver tape. He looked at Stella. She sent him a grim nod. He dropped his bag. Quickly headed towards Tommy and the woman. Tommy shot him a nasty look, which Ricky clearly read as saying, 'That's twice I've marked your card and I won't forget.'

Ricky ignored him. Hunched down. Tommy eased the gun back. Stood up. But didn't step away. The woman's chest heaved back and forth with such power that Ricky thought she was going to pass out. He stretched a length of tape from the roll. The sticky, zapping sound it made filled the room. He bit off a length with his teeth. Moved the tape roll over his hand so that it swung over his arm like a huge, chunky, silver bracelet. He gazed into the woman's tear-filled eyes and said, 'I want you to breathe easy. Just like me. In.' He inhaled. She followed what he did. 'Out.' Exhaled. So did she. In. Out. In. Out. On the fourth breath in, without warning, he slapped the tape over her mouth. He leant over. Grabbed her arm. Hauled her to her feet. He moved behind her. Grabbed her hands. Wound a thick wad of tape around them around them. He grabbed her arm and started marching her out of the room.

'Where you taking her?' Tommy called.

'In the bathroom. Then I'm gonna secure her legs so she can't move.' Without waiting for a response he carried on moving her as the tears now rolled bleakly down her cheeks. He reached the private bathroom in Miah's office. Thrust the door open. Pushed her inside. He kicked the door closed behind him. He spun her around and gave her a killer look.

'Do what you're told and nothing's going to happen to you.'

Pamela rapidly nodded. 'Over there,' Ricky said, pointing with his finger next to the sink. 'Lie down.' Quickly she obeyed him. He wound some more tape around the pipe that ran from the sink into the ground. Then he pushed her legs together and wound the end of the tape from the pipe around her ankles. Once he was satisfied that she was secured he rocked back on his heels.

Pulled out his mobile. No messages. Shit. He didn't even know if they'd got his earlier text. The woman watched him as he started to text another message. The door stared opening. Ricky shot to his feet and slipped his hand with the mobile behind his back. Tommy burst into the room.

'What's taking so long?'

Ricky nodded at the woman on the floor. 'She needed calming down. Come on, let's go.'

As soon as the other man turned his back on him, Ricky slipped the mobile back into his pocket. He didn't know what he was going to do if they didn't come.

They took the lift. Tommy had his shooter riding roughshod by his side. Stella stood behind Miah, while Daisy stood tight next to Ricky. Ricky's hand caressed her arm. She looked up at him knowing immediately what his touch meant. She nodded back, letting him know she was alright. Well, as alright as any lawyer turned bank robber could be.

As the doors began to open Stella's words grated in Miah's ear, 'You know what to do.'

Miah smoothed his hand over his hair. Stepped outside. They shifted behind him and took cover around the corner. Miah moved in the direction of the reception. He came into view of the security guards. The men sat playing cards at the reception desk.

One of them laughed, rubbing his hands together. 'That's three Guinnesses you owe me.'

'The game ain't over yet.'

'It is now,' the other one warned in a rush, seeing Miah coming into view. He jumped to his feet.

The other guard leapt up, desperately trying to hide the cards.

'Mr Miah, we're just getting ready to patrol the upper floors.'

Stella turned to Tommy and gave him the nod. Tommy sprang out with his gun aimed in the air. He ran into the reception hall.

Aimed his gun at the guards. The two men stood frozen. Then one tried to leap back behind the reception desk. Tommy shifted his gun. Pulled the trigger. The bullet blasted a hole in the corner of the desk sending splintering wood in the air. The guard froze in his tracks.

'Any more of that and they'll be playing poker at your wake,' Tommy roared. As if to emphasise his words, he aimed the gun into the ceiling and pulled the trigger. Plaster showered down on the other guard.

'Move slowly towards Miah.' Their ragged breathing filled the air as they followed his instruction. They stopped when they reached the bank manager. 'On your knees.'

The men quickly did what they were told.

'It's sorted,' Tommy shouted.

Hearing the signal the others came out of their hiding place and moved into view. Stella moved towards Tommy. Looked at the kneeling men. She gazed back at Tommy. 'Do it.'

He moved swiftly behind both men. He raised his gun and pointed it at the back of the first guard's head.

Tommy smashed the butt of the shotgun into the guard's skull. The man groaned. Then toppled forward, already unconscious when he hit the ground. A small pool of thick blood began to pool next to his head on the ground. Tommy did the same to the other guard. Both men were laid out cold on the floor. Ricky and Daisy knew what to do next. They moved forward. Each took one of the men's legs and dragged them across the hall until they reached the Gents opposite the lift. The blood oozing from the first guard's head left a trail of blood on the floor. Ricky's back barrelled into the door, pushing it open. The air inside the room was much cooler than outside and the faint smell of disinfectant hung in the air. They dumped the men onto the tiled floor. Ricky used the tape, still around his wrist, to bind and gag them. As he'd done with Miah's secretary upstairs he secured their legs to a set of piping.

Ricky stood back up. Took a deep breath. To Daisy's surprise he rolled his balaclava up and over his nose. He pulled her to him. 'We've got to get that box.'

Daisy rolled her balaclava up as well. 'But how?'

'Dunno. Ain't gonna be easy with Tommy playing the cowboy.'

Daisy's hand reached forward and tenderly touched Ricky's jaw line. 'You OK?'

He gave her his trademark cheeky smile that reminded her so much of her dad. 'With you by my side life's always on the sunny side of the street.' A thrill of intense pleasure shivered inside Daisy. He took her fingers that lay across his skin. He moved them up to his lips and gently kissed each fingertip.

'Well, ain't this all Mills and Boon?' They both jumped when they heard Stella's sarcastic voice coming from the doorway. She held onto the doorframe looking none too pleased. Embarrassed, Daisy stepped back from Ricky.

Daisy and Ricky quickly pulled their balaclavas back into place. Ricky shot past Stella out of the room. Daisy followed him. But when she reached the door Stella's grasp on her arm stopped her.

'The likes of him ain't for you.'

Daisy looked back at her defiantly. 'You've got it wrong. I'm more or less engaged.'

'You wanna know how many engaged and married men come through my door every evening? They don't even have the decency to take off their rings when they're screwing my girls. When this is all done you're going back to nanny-land world. And my advice to you my girl is to make sure you leave Ricky in his.'

Before Daisy could answer the sound of gunfire and shouting coming from the reception hall startled them both. Stella drew her Glock as they started to run.

Tommy was laughing like a mad man as he shot out the lens from the camera in the right hand corner of the hall.

'What the fuck are you doing?' Stella screamed as she lowered her gun.

Tommy swivelled around. 'Someone's watching us . . .'

'The cameras are all down. What's the matter with you?'

'I told him to lay off—' Ricky said.

'You seem a bit confused about your role in this outfit. You don't give orders, you take them.'

'Put that down.' Stella pointed her shooter at Miah. 'Take us to the boxes. Now.'

They moved behind him on the staircase, with Stella taking the lead again.

'Hurry it up,' Tommy growled as he prodded Miah in the back. He quickened his pace down the stairs. Hit the bottom. Came to the first door. Took the keys from his pockets.

'Hurry it up.'

Fingers shaking he thrust the key into the lock. Turned. Pushed. The door eased back. Tommy's hand slammed into Miah's back pushing him forward. Miah stumbled, only his hand catching the wall stopped him from falling. The quickening pace of their feet echoed around the empty corridor. The walls felt tomb-tight; the lighting fiercely bright. And the door up ahead looked a thousand miles away instead of a few seconds. Tommy kept twisting looking down the corridor as if he expected to see somebody back there. Miah reached the next door. His hands were quicker this time, unlocking the door with a flourish. He slammed the door back and moved at the same time. But the others stopped noticing the camera pointing straight at them at the end. With an ugly snarl, Tommy immediately targeted his gun at it.

Bang.

Bang.

Bang.

The glass from the camera popped and dived to the floor, splintering into tiny pieces.

They reached the final door. Thick and defiant steel, nobody's friend. Three seconds later the door was opened and they stepped inside.

'It's over there.' Miah pointed to a door on the other side of the room.

He kept moving as he rattled his keys, getting the right one in position. They waited expectantly behind him. Daisy's hands rolled into fretful fists by her side. God, this was it. This was where she got to see if her plan was finally going to work. Her breathing sharpened in her chest as she watched Miah's every move. He pushed the key inside the lock. Her heart started thumping. He turned the key to the right. The sweat dribbled down the middle of her back. The lock clicked. Then his fingers tapped away at the numbers and letters on the silver keypad. His hand touched the handle. She rubbed her hand over the gun stashed inside her waistband. He opened the door. Wide. They rushed inside.

The room they entered was empty except for two doors. Two steel doors.

'Which one?' Stella asked, her gun, raising nervously in the air to point at Miah.

He didn't answer her. Instead he walked briskly towards the door on the left wall. Tapped his fingers quickly on the steel keypad. Stepped to the side. His hands reached out for the steel bars, but before he could touch them Tommy spoke. Tommy's eyes were fixed firmly on the door on the other side of the room. 'What's in there?'

Miah swallowed as he twisted around. 'That's the money vault.'

'Forget it, son,' Stella cut in as if reading his thoughts. 'We're here for one thing only.'

'I ain't said nothin', have I?' Tommy's voice was casual, but it took him a good few seconds to remove his gaze from the door.

Miah swiftly turned back and got on with the job of opening the doors. The bars creaked as he moved them. Everyone stepped closer to him, hemming him in like a human fence. The bars stopped moving. He took a deep breath. Pushed the door open.

'What was that?' Ricky's startled voice ripped through the air. He twisted his body towards the main door. Cocked his head to the side. Everyone froze.

'What?' Stella answered.

They all twisted towards the door. Tommy raised his gun.

'I heard something.'

'Like what?' Stella asked.

'Dunno. Just a movement.'

Stella turned to her son. 'You did lock the doors upstairs?'

'Course I did.'

They remained frozen. Listening.

'I can't hear a thing.'

'There ain't nothin' out there.'

'We do this now.' Stella faced Miah. 'Which key opens the boxes?'

He showed the skeleton key. She swiped the bunch of keys from him.

They turned back to the room. 'Keep him out here.' She bawled in Tommy's direction. She turned to Ricky and Daisy. 'Both of you in here with me.'

Stella took the first step. Entered. She smiled when she saw what faced her. A wall with lockers just like the ones she used at the spa every week.

'Which one is it?' she asked Daisy.

Daisy moved quickly to stand in front of the locked boxes. She scanned her eyes from left to right. Bottom to top. Her gaze slammed onto it. Number 41. 'It's here.'

Stella scrambled towards her. 'Right, we can't make it obvious what we were after. So we're gonna unlock them all. Empty maybe ten of them into Ricky's bag.' She drilled her gaze into both Ricky and Daisy, with a warning. 'But not Charlie's box. You give me that one in my hand. We start with Charlie's box. Ricky.' She chucked the keys at him. He caught them. 'Start with Charlie's and then do the rest. Daisy you hold the bag.'

Ricky and Daisy got immediately down to work. Ricky shoved the key into number 41. Turned the lock. Click. He pulled the steel box out. Looked up at Daisy. What they wanted was finally in Ricky's grasp. This was their chance. Could they take it?

Daisy lowered her head towards him. Whispered, 'We'll never get it past her and Tommy.'

'What are you whispering about?' Stella's voice boomed behind them.

Daisy sprang up. She had to find a lie quickly. She found it. 'Ricky was going to put it on the floor, but I told him to give it straight to you.'

Stella smiled. Moved forward. 'Good girl.' She held her hand towards Ricky. He clutched the box. Ran his tongue nervously over his bottom lip. Then he passed the box to her. Stella shoved it under her right arm.

'Do the other boxes.'

With speed, he jumped up and began to unlock the boxes starting at the top. As he unlocked Daisy moved swiftly in, pulling each box out and emptying their contents into the bag. Once done she discarded the empty boxes on the floor.

She twisted to face Stella. 'We've got about ten.'

Stella looked at Ricky. 'Just pull the rest out and chuck them on the floor and kick them around.'

Hands and legs moving quickly, Ricky followed her instructions. He pulled and threw.

Thud. The first box hit the ground.

Thud, the second box went down.

Clank.

Clank.

Clank.

As he pulled at the next box, he heard Stella's surprised voice pierce the air.

'What you doing?'

Daisy and Ricky twisted around. What they saw startled them as well. Tommy and Miah were slowly moving into the room. Backwards. Their eyes were on something in front of them out of the room. They didn't have to wait long to find out what they were looking at. Two men holding guns rushed into the room. One of them roared, 'Freeze. You're all under arrest.'

Thirty-nine

'Weapons on the floor. Then place your hands in the air.'

Both men were tall and big wearing black flak jackets and chequered patterned baseball caps. No one moved. Then Tommy swore and threw his shotgun onto the floor and then raised his hands. Stella followed. As she raised her arm the box under her arm clattered to the ground.

'And you,' the cop shouted at Daisy.

'I haven't got one.'

The men inched closer to them, their guns steady and high. One of them moved towards the guns on the floor and kicked them to the side.

'I told you we shouldn't have trusted him. That he'd call the Bill,' Tommy stormed at his mother.

Stella looked at Miah, her mouth ugly and twisted. She ran one of the fingers under her throat as if it were a knife.

Miah shook his head, knowing what her action meant. His family were fucked. 'I never called anyone, you have to believe me . . .'

'Keep your hands in the air.' The cop in charge yelled at Stella. She shoved her hand lazily back up. 'You the bank manager?' he continued as he stared at Miah.

Miah nodded, his lips trembling. 'My family are being held hostage,' he croaked.

'Don't worry about them. Just step to the side please sir.'

Miah hustled away from Tommy. 'Face down on the ground, the lot of you.'

They scrambled down, except for Ricky. The cop in charge stomped over to Ricky and yelled, 'I said, get down.'

'I ain't getting down for you or no one, mate, until you show us your warrant card.'

'Are you for real?'

'Your badge.'

The man quickly darted a look at the man next to him. Shuffled his gaze back at Ricky. 'If you're not careful, mate, you're going to be shot "in the confusion".'

Ricky defiantly held his ground. 'It's standard police procedure, you must remember from Hendon, don't you? Let's see something.' Daisy gazed at him, surprised by the tone he used. One she'd never heard him use before. Authoritative. As if he was the one making the arrests. 'Let me take a wild guess here, lads,' he continued. 'If you're officers of the law then I'm the Lord Chief Justice.'

The man suddenly leapt at Ricky and gave a powerful blow to the side of his head with the butt of his gun. Daisy and Stella gasped as Ricky hit the deck. He moaned as he rolled on his back.

'They're not cops,' he mumbled quickly, his voice streaked with pain.

Stella made a desperate leap for her gun. But one of the men pointed his gun. Pulled the trigger.

The bullet blasted into the ground by her feet. The echo shook the room. She froze, half up, half down, her hand out stretched for her gun.

'Leave it out, darlin', I'm a better shot than that usually,' the man who'd fired at her shouted.

She straightened up, breathing harshly.

'On the fucking floor,' the main man hollered, his ill-fitting police voice now pure underworld.

They scrambled down. Lay flat. From her view point Daisy could see Charlie's deposit box lying on its side on the ground.

The man moved towards Miah. Shoved his gun into Miah's face. 'Where's the cash?'

Miah shook his head. 'We don't keep any here . . . .'

The man curved his finger around the trigger. 'Don't try and blag me cocksucker, I've been around too long. We're in a bank aren't we?'

'It's the truth. Most of our money transactions are done via computer. We don't keep large cash deposits here.'

The man's face grew red with rage. 'I'm gonna take your fucking head off . . .'

'I'm telling the truth.' Miah's shout echoed around the room.

'No he ain't.'

Everyone shifted to find out where the voice had come from. From someone lying on the floor. Tommy. Slowly he rose to his feet. With disbelieving eyes Stella stared at her son.

'What's going on?'

He didn't answer. Instead he moved towards the guns kicked to the side. He found his gun. Stevie King's Remington shooter. Picked it up. Moved back to the group. He stepped over his mum and shrugged his shoulders. Stood over her for the first time in his life. Angled the barrel straight down at her head.

'I'm in charge now,' he pumped out, not once taking his eyes off his mum. He carried on, his voice filled with scorn. 'Did you really think I was gonna pull this job and come out with my arse hanging out of my trousers? You should've listened to me from the get-go and none of this would have happened. That money's my winnings and I'm collecting.'

Stella twisted her face in disgust at Tommy as if the gun aimed at her meant fuck all. 'You think you're smarter than me Tommy? You poor deluded sod.'

'Well, we'll find out won't we?' Tommy's voice was tight. His finger twitched on the trigger. 'You weren't meant to find out this had anything to do with me. Miah was meant to tell them where the stash was and then they would scarper. But since he ain't talking I had to tell them instead. If you played it my way you would've left with what you came in here for. I got my dough and you got your poxy box.'

'I'll run you down, you know that—'

'I know.' His response was quiet. 'I'm sure. But that depends on you ever coming out of here again. And I wouldn't rely on that if I were you . . .'

Stella didn't show her shock. But she did open her mouth. Not to ask why, not to beg. Instead she spat a contemptuous gob of spit at his feet. Tommy visibly flinched and paled as if his mum had spat in his eye. He turned to the men. 'The money's in the other vault.' He flicked his blazing eyes at a cringing Miah.

Having already been on the end of Tommy's nutty-boy antics, Miah didn't lie this time. He got the vault open in double quick time. Tommy's two men whistled in appreciation at what they saw.

'Fucking hell, how many bankers' bonuses does this add up to?' one of the men said.

'Hold your noise and bag it up,' Tommy yelled back.

One of the men unzipped his jacket and pulled out a bag. Soon both men were shoving the money into it like kids in a sweet shop, their professionalism blunted by the sums on offer.

'I think it's time we found out what was in that deposit box that's been giving my mum the willies,' Tommy said, with a huge grin on his face. He looked at Miah again. 'Open it.'

Miah yelled back, 'But I don't have . . .'

Tommy pointed his gun at him. Immediately Miah dug into his pocket as he rushed to his feet. Trembling, looking at the scattered boxes on the floor he asked, 'Which one is it?'

Tommy scanned the ground near his mum. Located box number 41. 'That one.'

Miah scrambled over and down. Picked the box up and quickly opened it with the master key he held in his hand. He tipped the lid open. His head reared back in shock.

'It's empty.'

'You what?' Stella screamed as her head came up.

Tommy started laughing maniacally. 'Doesn't sound like I'm the only one pulling a double cross on you today, does it, Mum? You must be losing your touch. Now put that sweet head of yours back down.'

Tommy watched his prisoners intently as his men continued to gather the cash, moving his gun from time to time, so it was covering his mum, then Daisy, then Ricky. Finally he was in control. His mum's day was over and his had finally arrived.

'Get up,' he shouted at Ricky, waving the gun at him.

Both Daisy and Stella tensed at his words. They twisted their heads to gaze at Ricky. But Ricky didn't look at either of them, he just got slowly to his feet. He stared at Tommy with bring-it-on eyes.

'Twice you've pissed on my shoes today, Ricky boy,' Tommy explained, a nasty smile spreading across his face, but never touching his eyes. 'That weren't smart was it? You said you'd meet me in the playground anytime you wanted me to sort this out.' He raised the gun. 'Well here we are.'

Ricky's hooded eyes rested on the gun. 'Feels like two on one to me.'

'I know. Ain't life a bitch?'

He pulled the trigger. The sound of the shot ricocheted across the room. The bullet slammed into Ricky's left arm, twisting him half around.

'Oh my God,' shot out of Daisy's mouth as she watched in horror as the blood gushed from Ricky's arm. She wanted to get up, but knew she couldn't.

Ricky didn't even make a sound. Just let his arm hang limply by his side as he looked defiantly back at the younger man. 'Real tough guy, aren't you?' he said as if he were talking to a naughty schoolboy.

'Not quite. Now this is gonna make me feel top of the world.' He shifted the gun. Straight at Ricky's chest.

'No,' Daisy screamed. But it was too late. Bam. The impact of the bullet twisted Ricky in the air. He staggered back and fell face down. He didn't move again. Daisy let out heaving sobs as she watched the blood spread from his still body. *Ricky couldn't be dead. He couldn't be dead. Not Ricky.*

'You bastard.' Her voice echoed around the room.

Tommy kept his position as he aimed the gun at her. 'You better tuck your head down, bitch, and settle unless you wanna go Ricky-style.'

Daisy knew she couldn't do anything. So she did what he asked, shaking and crying softly.

Tommy swung around to find his two men looking at him as if he had grown another head. 'Get back on with the job!'

They got back on with it until one of them shouted out, 'Look at this.'

Tommy looked. The other man held a diamond necklace in his hand. 'Found this in a box at the back.' He draped the necklace over himself, 'My missus is gonna look great in this . . .'

'What's the matter with you?' Tommy shot back. 'This ain't the *Antiques Road Show*, get it in the fucking bag and stop pissing about.'

Tommy caught his mother's eye. He was ripping her off and he resented the sneer on her face. Tommy looked away from her and started shouting orders to his men to hurry it up. His look away was all Stella needed to make her move. When you're in a tight corner, you'll always get one chance and you have to take it. Her hand darted down and pulled the .22 revolver she kept hidden in an ankle holster for special occasions like this one. It wasn't a big or powerful gun but it did the job and that was enough.

The shot sounded more like an explosion. The guy in the necklace clutched his throat, blood oozing from between his fingers as he began sinking to the floor. Diamonds from the necklace, scattered on the floor like broken glass. Tommy thought at first that the little twat had shot himself by mistake. It was only after another shot blew away part of the second guy's head showering the metal vault's door in a spray of blood and brains like a graffiti artist's paint can that Tommy realised something was up. He swiftly turned his head back around the same time Daisy scrambled away on her bum towards the other side of the room. She shoved herself against the wall next to a discarded deposit box. But Tommy took no notice of her, he only saw his mum. With her gun pointed straight at him. His own was hanging at a useless 45 degrees. His mother looked at him with contempt.

'Two things,' she finally spoke to him, her voice bristling with rage. 'Always remember to frisk prisoners – that's pretty basic, you don't know what they might be carrying. They might have dialled 999 on a mobile in their pocket for all you know. The other is, never take your eyes off anyone in a situation like this. People only need one chance . . .' Calmly she stood up.

'Mum, I weren't really gonna kill you.' His voice wobbled.

'Sh. Sh.' Stella soothed softly. Tommy nodded his head as his Adam's apple bobbed convulsively. 'There's a good boy, Mummy's here.'

He only saw the flash of the gun. He never heard the shot. Then he had the sensation of flying which ended when he landed on the floor. The only pain he felt was the cut on his face where it scraped on one of the scattered diamonds. And then darkness came.

Forty

Daisy's hands came out from under her jacket as she watched the scene with horror. Blood and bodies, one of which was Ricky's. She pushed her hand down the back of her pants and pulled out the pistol. What she was going to do with it she didn't know, but she held it protectively in her lap. Miah sat weeping in a corner with his hands covering his head. Then the sound that he made was joined by someone else softly sobbing. At first Daisy thought it was Tommy. Then she realised it was Stella as she gazed down at her son.

'You stupid boy,' she said between broken sobs. 'Why couldn't you just do what you were told?' Then she aimed the gun at his head and sent two more slugs into him. Daisy cringed against the wall as Stella made her way to the other bodies and pumped more shots into them. Miah let out an animal scream as she made her way to him.

'Please, please,' he pleaded.

'Shut up.' He choked back the noise coming from his throat as he nodded at her. 'We've still got your kids and wife. You wanna see 'em again, just sit around with the stiffs for half an hour and mind your business.' She didn't wait for his response, instead swung around to face a dazed Daisy. 'We're outta here,' she told Daisy, already moving towards the door.

Daisy leapt to her feet, still holding the gun. But instead of moving towards Stella she ran over to Ricky.

'Leave him,' Stella commanded.

Daisy ignored her. She fell to her knees just outside the pool of blood around the left side of his body.

'Daisy, come on.'

But Daisy reached a hand to touch Ricky's hair. She ran her hands through it as a sob escaped her body. 'Ricky,' she mourned.

Daisy heard running and knew that Stella was gone. She didn't look around, instead she stroked Ricky's hair for a few more seconds. Leant over and kissed the back of his cool neck.

Then she heard his voice. Calm. Reassuring. 'Daisy, baby, you need to shift yourself now.'

She looked up to find her dad standing by her side. She hadn't even taken one of her pills and was seeing him. She really was going nuts. She couldn't see his face because he wore a black balaclava. Held a sawn-off shooter in one hand. 'Told you this was gonna be ugly.'

'He wouldn't be dead if it weren't for you. Why did you have to be my dad?' Her anger exploded in the air.

'I'm your old man and always will be. Running away from the inevitable only causes pain. We'll have to finish this chinwag some other time, babe, because in less than a minute . . .' He paused tilting his head to the side. 'The alarm's gonna be screaming blue murder.'

'What alarm?' Her hand tightened on the gun.

'Automatically kicks in forty-five minutes after it's been switched off . . .'

'But Miah never said . . .'

'Sounds like our bank manager was holding an ace up his sleeve all the time.'

now

Forty-one

Daisy stared at Ricky's body.

At the growing pool of blood.

At the compact pistol in her hand.

'*Whatever you do, never run,*' she heard her dad's earlier warning beating once again inside her head.

But she ran. Shot out of the room. Down the corridor. Took the stairs two at a time. Hit ground level. The sweat trickled down her face from the heat. From the fear. Her breathing cut up the air. She looked straight ahead. More blood on the floor. Red, wavy lines this time. She kept up her pace. Dodged the blood. Reached the glass front doors. That's when she stopped. Gulped in a steady stream of uneven air. One . . . two . . . three. Shoved the gun into her pocket. Rolled the balaclava back off her face until it lay under the low hanging hood she wore. She hesitated at the door as his words came back to her:

'*Whatever you do, never run.*'

She took deep breaths. Pushed her head down and the door at the same time. Stepped outside. Into one of London's busiest business districts. The light from the June sun struck her eyes, blinding her. She rapidly blinked, trying to flick the glare from her eyes. Trying to find out if she could make it without being seen. Her vision cleared. And what she saw horrified her. The area in front of her was filled with crowds of people, workers enjoying a drink and chat in the still bright evening light.

'*Whatever you do, never run.*'

A deafening, high-pitched, wailing noise screamed blue murder from the building behind her.

She ran.

Her heartbeat kicked into overdrive. She didn't look left. Didn't look right. Didn't look at the city workers who she knew were now gazing up at the building rocked by the alarm. Didn't look at the people who were staring after her running figure. Didn't look at the people who were now pulling out their mobiles to call the cops.

Sprinted around a corner. Kept motoring forward until a hand snatched her arm swinging her against a hard wall. The air slammed out of her body in a savage whoosh sound.

'Where the hell have you been?' Relief washed over Daisy as she stared at Stella. She opened her mouth to respond but Stella got there before her. 'Get your arse into gear, we need to get to the car.'

Heads down, they bolted towards the waiting car. They kept going until they saw it in the distance. Saw Billy who was waiting for them in the driver's seat. As they got closer the gun nose-dived out of her pocket. Clattered onto the ground. Daisy skidded to a halt. Whirled around.

'Leave it,' Stella yelled as she kept running forward.

But Daisy knew she couldn't do that. She grabbed it. Rammed it back into her pocket as she stood up. Twisted towards the car the same time Stella reached the passenger side. She sprinted towards the car. Billy blocked Stella from her view. A police siren wailed between the city blocks somewhere in the distance. She ran harder. And harder. She was almost there.

Then there was a loud rolling rumble of thunder.

That's all she heard. A terrifying boom tore through the air. The car she'd been running towards exploded outwards and into a fire-ball. Daisy felt the shock go through her body as if she'd touched a live wire. She somersaulted through the air like a circus acrobat. Landed on her back, winded, as parts of car and street lamps came down around her until she was covered in debris and glass. She could feel something seeping down her face. Blood. Through her hazy vision she saw the shattered and twisted remains of the car as red and orange flames belched with smoke high into the air.

Her vision became fainter and fainter. Her mind started to slip. She heard The Mamas And Papas singing 'Dedicated To The One I Love' as her mind slipped further back. Back to two weeks ago. Back to the day her life had changed for ever. Back to a day that had started with a death . . . .

She was jacked back to the present by the grip of hands under her arms. Large hands. Before she could react she was hitched half upright and whoever held her started to drag her along. She could feel the blood trickling down her face and suspected that the flying glass had cut her. The heels of her trainers burned against the ground as she bumped and swayed. Her heart rate racked up. She started coming out of her haze. Her mind began to tick. Who was behind her? Where were they taking her? Instinct cut in. She started to resist. Madly wiggled her captive arms. Dug her trainers into the ground, trying desperately to stall her legs. Suddenly she was flipped around. She looked up. Her mouth tipped open when she saw who it was. Bloody hell, she must be dead.

Ricky. Blood dripped from his arm and there was a hole in his tracksuit top.

Couldn't be. He was dead. She'd seen it with her own blue eyes. Bang. Bang. Tommy had plugged him twice – in the arm and chest. She'd seen the blood leaking his life away on the floor of the bank. He let her go and she rocked back on her feet. Squeezed her eyes shut. Shook her head. It couldn't be Ricky. Couldn't be . . . An unexpected shot of pain tore through the left side of her face. Her palm leapt protectively to her cheek. Her eyes flew wide open. Ricky stood looking at her with concern, his arm halfway in the air. That's when she realised he'd slapped her across the face.

Bloody hell, he was alive alright. Despite the pain she smiled.

His lips were moving with speed, but she couldn't hear a thing. The blast must have taken most of her hearing away. His mouth stopped moving. Before she could think he grabbed one of her arms and heaved her into a fireman's lift over his shoulders. Her world turned upside down. Her body jolted against his as he hightailed it across the street. Her head swung to the side as he took a sharp left. Her eyes fixed on the square slabs of pavement underneath as they bolted down another road. His body skidded to a sudden halt. He eased her to her feet beside a navy blue car. Without speaking he took out something from his pocket. She couldn't see what it was. He bent at the door on the driver's side of the car. Stuck something into the lock. Twisted. Opened the door. He gestured frantically towards her with his hands. She didn't need words to know what to do. She slung herself into the car. While she crawled into the passenger's side he threw himself into the driver's seat. Slammed the door with one hand as his other went to the ignition. He turned the ignition but she couldn't hear the engine. He was talking again. She screwed her face up. Shit, she still couldn't hear him. The car accelerated forward banging her into the dashboard.

They reached the Westferry Circus roundabout and he slammed on the brakes. 'Which way do I go, which way?' His voice was surprisingly quiet but she sighed with relief as she realised she could hear him again.

'Right,' she commanded. Her dad always said that you don't do jobs on the Island, not unless you could swim. The Isle Of Dogs is like a vast roundabout, surrounded on three sides by the Thames and blocked off on the fourth by the West India docks, there were only a couple of roads off it. So he needed to turn right and drive into the East End along one of those roads, otherwise they were stuck on the Island like rats in a trap.

He careered down Westferry Road taking the swerves and the bends while the speed cameras cheerfully flashed away. Overtaking on blind corners, he clipped a cyclist's handlebars with his wing mirror.

'Wanker,' the cyclist screamed.

They took no notice. Kept motoring on.

Ricky shot her a sidelong look. 'You alright babe?'

She nodded, her breathing still racking up a high speed inside her chest. She wiped the blood from her face with the back of her hand. She had various nicks and scratches, but otherwise was unharmed. 'I don't understand? I thought you were halfway to heaven. Or is it hell?'

He grinned, once again glancing at her. 'Takes more than Tommo King to put Ricky Smart down . . .'

'Let me look at your wound.' Her eyes darted to his arm.

'No time for that, babe. How's that cut on your . . .'

'Fuck. Look out!' Daisy cut over him, yelling.

He slammed on the brakes, veering to the left to avoid another car. The other driver honked their horn furiously. Ricky tried to straighten the car, but it was going too fast and hit the corner of the pavement. He swung the car into a neat half turn. The bumper shook and the car dragged something underneath it that sent the stink of burning metal through the air-conditioning as it set off again. Ricky's eyes flicked towards the rear-view mirror.

'Be careful,' Daisy said.

But instead of answering Ricky's eyes flicked back to the rear-view mirror. 'No can do, babe. We're being followed. Guy on a super blackbird motor bike.'

Daisy swung around to stare out of the rear window. A monster of a bike was behind, the driver wearing a mirrored crash helmet that masked the face.

'How do you know?' she asked, twisting back around.

'There's a wire peeping out of his helmet. He's rigged up to a mobile and he pulled over when we almost hit that car. Now he's following us again . . .' Ricky swung the car into a crazy turn. The bike followed.

'Who is it?' She asked, gripping the door handle.

'Dunno. Ain't the cops that's for fucking sure.' He shot her another look. 'I've taken the wrong turning, so how the fuck do I get us out of here?'

Daisy peered through the window, while Ricky kept his eye on the rear-view mirror and the road. 'You should have turned right at the roundabout. If we stay on this road we'll go right round the Island and get off it on the other side. But they may have sealed that road off at the top already. At the bottom of the Island is a foot tunnel that goes under the river to Greenwich, we could dump the car there and escape that way.'

'If they haven't sealed that off too.'

*　　*　　*

'How far is it now?' They were heading towards the foot tunnel.

'The rate this car's going – about ten seconds.' She peered back behind again. The bike was still sitting pretty on their tail.

The car was flashed by a camera. Ricky smiled. 'I think I might just have lost my licence.'

'As a lawyer, I'd say speeding offences aren't your top priority right now, legally speaking.'

The road began to veer to the left and Ricky followed it round, studying his mirror.

'He's gone.'

'The biker?'

'Yeah.'

'We're alright then.'

Ricky paused, 'Maybe.'

Heaving slightly out of the seat she pointed out of the passenger window. 'Island Gardens is just round the corner here, that's where the tunnel is . . .'

'Bollocks,' Ricky screamed over her.

Daisy flicked her head around and stared with utter horror at what she saw. Out of nowhere a black car, with tinted windows, pulled out in front of them.

Daisy crashed sideways into her seat as Ricky's hands moved frantically around the steering wheel. The wheels squealed as the car veered over to the other side of the road to avoid a full-on collision with the other car. But instead of driving forward the other vehicle crossed over in front of them where it stopped at an angle to the road covering both lanes. Ricky slammed on the brakes.

'Brace yourself,' he yelled.

Daisy tucked her head into her body, her arms over her head. She rocked back and forwards as they rammed into the other car.

Silence. Only the noise of steam hissing from their shattered engine could be heard. Daisy lifted her head to find Ricky half flung on her seat. She unfolded her body. Reached out to him. 'We need to get out . . .'

But before she could finish the driver's side of the car was flung open. Two people, dressed in black and wearing hooded tops that were zipped high over their mouths and hung low over their faces. One was tall and the other a good foot shorter. But it wasn't their clothing or heights that Ricky and Daisy stared at. They stared at the pistol and revolver aimed right at their heads.

Keeping his eyes glued on the guns Ricky said, 'Not really been our day, has it?'

Forty-two

The smallest gunman lifted his hand as if he was going to lift up the hood of his top, but the taller one said, in a husky American accent, 'Not yet. It's too dangerous. Our faces might be caught on CCTV. Let's just do this the way we agreed.' He gripped his gun as if he used it every day of the week and ordered, 'Get in the back.'

Ricky was the first to move. As he eased outside the gunmen took a step back, shooters never wavering from their deadly position. Daisy scrambled out. She didn't know what was going on here. She desperately needed to take a pill, to get her dad's advice. But she knew she was going to have to use her own brain this time. Then she remembered – she still had the compact pistol jammed in her pocket. All she had to do was reach down . . .

'No funny stuff,' the smaller gunman said as if reading her mind.

Daisy and Ricky eyed each other as they did what they were told. They got in the back on opposite sides of the car. The taller gunman jumped in the back, shuffling Daisy and Ricky closer together. The other gunman bent in the open doorway, his gun aimed at them. The gunman in the car pulled out a length of rope. Threw it at Daisy.

'Tie his hands. Double knot.'

Quickly Daisy picked up the rope in her lap. Looked at Ricky.

'Now,' the gunman grated through gritted teeth.

Ricky placed his hands together behind his back as he continued to eye the gun. Daisy wound the strong rope around his hands and tied it once. Twice. The gunman shoved Ricky forward by the back of his head. Reached down and tested the strength of his bonds. Nodded his head. Slammed Ricky upright again. Ricky sucked in a sharp tug of air, reminding Daisy that he had a shot wound in his arm. The gunman eased slowly backwards out of the car. He waved his gun once indicating that they should get out. What was going on here? A game of in and out? Ricky used his strength and upper body to get awkwardly out of the car. As Daisy followed him her mind went back to the gun in her trousers. All she had to do was reach behind and . . . A roaring sound tore through the air. Another car zoomed towards them out of nowhere followed by the super blackbird motorbike that had sat on their arse earlier.

They were frogmarched towards the slowing car. Daisy could see two people in the front kitted out in the same gear as the gunmen. Her fear increased. Five guys, no doubt all packing guns, were kidnapping them. And then what? Torture them? Shoot them? That wasn't happening to her. As she moved her hand flicked to her back. Reached under her top. Eased inside her pants.

'Don't even try it, honey bun.' The lethal voice of the smaller gunman froze the movement of her hand. Shit. She pulled her hand back to her front. The gunman walked briskly behind her. Prodded their shooter in her back as their hand reached inside the back of her trousers. Shit. Shit. Shit. Her chance of escape was gone as the gun was whipped out. The gunman shoved it in his pocket. Prodded his gun in her back. She continued to move towards the car. The gunman demanded they stop near the boot of the car. There was a popping sound. The boot of the car flew open.

Daisy's mouth half flipped open as her eyes grew wide. Surely they weren't thinking . . . Her arms were twisted behind her back. She winced as her arms were tightly secured. At the same time one of the other occupants of the car got out. They approached Ricky. With a professional ease they patted him down from head to foot. Shoved the semi-automatic they found in his socks in their pocket. Stood back up. Without warning they shoved him forward, until he stood gazing down into the empty boot.

'On your back.'

With a shake of his head and a sigh, Ricky awkwardly got inside the boot. The space was crammed, making him curl his long legs to the side. The man in black took something from his pocket. Leant over Ricky and stuck a wide strip of black tape over his mouth. He did the same to his eyes.

'On top of your mate,' the smaller gunman ordered Daisy. Heart beating a mile a second she got inside and placed her body over Ricky's. He groaned in pain.

Her breath fanned his face as she whispered, 'I always prefer it on top.' She knew he was smiling from the lift of the skin around his mouth covered in tape. But any pleasure she felt was short-lived as her head was seized back. As one person held her head another thrust tape over her mouth and eyes. She was pushed back hard against Ricky. The door of the boot slammed shut.

The boot was like a tomb. Hard to see and even harder to breathe. As the car jostled them at a steady speed, Ricky occasionally groaned. She felt a sticky warmth seeping into her sleeve, where her body pressed against his arm and knew that he was bleeding again. She couldn't even ask him if he was alright because of her gagged mouth. She felt the muscles of his chest move in an uncomfortable tense and ripple motion as if that part of his body too was causing him pain. She knew that Tommy had shot him in the chest, but all he had to show for it was a hole in his tracksuit top. No blood, no visible injury so, she didn't know what to think anymore . . .

Her thoughts shifted as the car abruptly stopped. A door slammed. No, two doors. Feet briskly took the ground getting louder as they reached the back of the car. She heard a pop sound. The boot flew open. Cool, but blessed air, swam over her and Ricky. Took the new air heavily through her nose. Abruptly hands dragged her out of the car onto her feet. The wind was strong, her world still black. She didn't know where she was but the ground beneath her feet felt solid. But all changed when she was frogmarched forward. The next step she took she almost fell sideways because the ground started to rock, ever so slightly. A hand grabbed her arm. Steadied her. She was propelled forward, taking each step carefully. Whatever she was walking on still rocked. She heard the soft patter of feet in front of her. The next step she took the air felt different, warmer, as if she was inside somewhere. After three more steps the hand on her forced her to stop. A door slammed. She was twisted around. The tape around her mouth whipped off making her wince. She gasped for breath as the tape around her eyes was removed more slowly as if whoever was doing it cared about the pain they might cause her. Her eyes slowly peeled open. She stumbled back at when she saw the five gunmen standing in front of her. She dived into a free fall of shock. They might have guns, but they weren't men.

'I could murder you.'

Daisy stared at Jackie Jarvis, as her adoptive mum's words lit a path of fury towards her. The older woman's small body and cropped red hair stood stiff with tension, her blazing jade eyes and freckles almost popping off her face. And it wasn't only Jackie's anger she had to deal with. On either side of Jackie stood her aunts, Ollie, Roxy, Anna and of course Misty. Their hoods were down and all were shooting her mad-as-hell looks as well.

'Where are we?' Ricky croaked, voice husky and low. He stood next to Daisy, rubbing his chest, then his bleeding arm

She knew exactly where they were. Knew why the ground beneath her had rocked. They were inside the main cabin of Misty's pride and joy, her longboat, *Miss Josephine*. The room was comfy and cosy, with a certain gleam that spoke of being taken care of with loving hands and furniture that some might say should have seen the junkyard years ago but that Misty insisted were full of rich memories. The last Daisy had heard Misty had moored it on the Regent's Canal next to Victoria Park, which stood between the boroughs of Tower Hamlets and Hackney in East London. So she assumed that's where they were now.

Jackie stepped forward, her finger stabbing in the air towards Ricky. 'Keep it zipped, sonny.' Her voice yelled a don't-muck-around with me tone.

But instead of shutting his mouth he spoke. 'Why didn't you just say who you were instead of shoving us in the boot of some car?'

'Not that I owe you an explanation,' Jackie snapped back. 'But we needed to make sure you and Daisy did what you were told. We didn't have time for any arguments.'

'Daisy.' She turned to find her aunt Roxy moving towards her with a cloth dipped in water. 'Clean your face.' Daisy took the cloth and pressed it to her cut cheek. She winced.

'Are you alright?' Jackie asked with the concern of a mother.

'It's just a cut. Nothing too deep. We need to take care of Ricky.' Her gaze ran over his injured arm. 'He's been shot . . .'

'I'm alright,' Ricky said, but his laboured breathing told another story. 'The bullet went straight through.'

Jackie made a scoffing sound. 'He should be thankful someone got there before me and only blasted him in his arm, because if I had a gun pointed at him now the way I'm feeling I'd be tempted to take his bloody head off.' Jackie dismissed Ricky and stabbed her finger back at Daisy. 'Didn't I tell you that if there was any bovver while I was away all you had to do was pick up the blower and let Misty know?' Daisy quickly opened her mouth, but Jackie kept up her rapid-fire words.

'There I am, lying in my bikini with a Sex On The Beach in my hand when Misty lets me know that you're acting all strange like. Well, as soon as Misty mentioned the name of that she-devil Stella King, me and the girls were back here sooner than you could say the words *bank robbery.*'

Her last two words hung in the air with the impact of a nasty smell there was no way of escaping. Daisy winced. What was the point in trying to pull the wool over Jackie's eyes? If there was one person who could smell a rat it was the raging woman in front of her. 'How did you find out?'

Now it was Misty's turn to step forward. For the first time in her life Daisy *really* saw her as a man. 'I might not be the brain of Britain, young lady, but I don't keep it in my trousers either like a lot of men do.' She jammed her hands onto her hips. 'When I caught you in my club I knew something was up.' Daisy's eyes darted guiltily away as a snap shot image of herself kitted out in Misty's blond wig at the bank flashed through her mind. Her gaze flicked back up as the other woman continued to speak. 'I almost called Jackie there and then, but no, I told myself.' Her head shook. 'If there was a problem Daisy would come to me, now wouldn't she? Then I meet you with naughty boy, over there.' She nodded, face twisted in disgust at Ricky. 'Out shopping with your lawyer – my cross-dressing arse. And the way you mentioned Stella King's name I knew something was up.'

'That's when Misty called us,' Ollie joined in, her black face calm. Nothing ever seemed to faze her, it was as if she'd seen it all before.

'First thing I did,' Misty picked up her words, 'was get on the blower to my mate Mickey. If there's anyone who knows what's happening in this town it's him. Told him to keep his ears pinned back if he hears anything to do with Stella King. Then I took a trip to your flat, back to being Michael for a night so no one twigged who I was. Lights on, no one at home, as they say, love. And when I found those tissues with the blood on my heart popped straight outta my chest.' Misty's voice went up a notch. 'Thought something bloody bad had happened to you.' Daisy rubbed her lips together, her guilt growing deeper. 'Then Mickey calls me up and says that Stella has just ordered a couple of motors from him. 'Course she never told him what they were for but Mickey's been in the biz too long not to spot a job when it's coming. Didn't take him long to find out what the job was. And where it was. Tommy's hired guns are known for their loose lips, if not for their brains. If you were mixed up with Stella King there was only one place you could be.' Misty folded her arms across her chest. 'Deadwood Hotel. Otherwise known as Stella King's number one knocking shop and HQ.'

Anna stepped forward, her long, black hair swishing beside her amber-coloured face. 'At first we kept telling ourselves no way would you be involved. Not our little Daisy. But we couldn't take that chance . . .'

'Why didn't you just come and get her at the brothel?' Ricky stormed.

'I'd keep my mouth shut if I were you, you're in a spot of bovver,' Jackie screamed, moving furiously forward. Misty grabbed her arm and held her back.

'What?' Anna scoffed. 'And face Stella's firepower in her own den? No way. We decided to go to The Island and sit it out near the bank. And when we saw you running out of the bank, girl . . .' Anna's words stopped as if she were reliving a horror story. 'We had our set up in place. Two cars and me on a bike. First chance we got we were gonna nab you. Then lover boy there,' she glanced at Ricky, 'got in on the act.'

'And when that car went sky-high,' Roxy joined in, her white face getting paler by the second, 'we thought you were a goner.'

'Don't you get it?' Jackie jumped in, her voice soft. 'I thought I was going to lose you. Just like I nearly did that first night you came to stay with me.'

All of a sudden the tension became too much for Daisy. Tears bubbled in her eyes as she rubbed her right hand against her left bracelet. Awful, sorrowful noises shot from her lips. Her head bent down with the force of the weight of what her life had become. Jackie's safe arms pulled her into a tight embrace.

'You'll always be my girl,' Jackie whispered. 'Always.'

Daisy clung tight, soaking up the warmth of the smaller woman. They stayed like that for a while, with only the sounds of the lapping water outside to be heard. Finally Jackie pulled away. Used the pads of her thumb to wipe the tears from Daisy's cheeks. 'I think it's time you told us exactly how you got hooked up with Stella King.'

'She didn't have much choice,' Ricky threw in. The woman all shot him a collective look that screamed, 'Stay down, boy.'

'Ricky's right. I had to do it,' Daisy confirmed.

'She got something over you?' Misty asked.

Daisy's mouth twisted. 'You could say that.' She pulled in a deep breath. Her voice was small. 'She's my mother.'

Her mum was dead. But Jo-Jo desperately tried to contact her mum for the umpteenth time on her mobile regardless. She paced, backward, forward, inside Stella's office on the top floor of the brothel. No lights were on, leaving the room shrouded in a thick, unsettled darkness. Jo-Jo let out a small cry as the call went to voicemail as it had done before.

'Mum, it's me. Jo-Jo. Please give me a bell. Please . . . just call me.' She hurled the mobile across the room. She didn't want to believe it. Couldn't believe it. Her mum, Stella King, the one person she loved with a total devotion was . . .

No, she wouldn't believe it. Maybe she was wrong. She checked the time on the clock next to the *Calamity Jane* poster. 7 p.m. She rushed towards the telly. Popped it on. The local news was already on and what she saw made her hug her arms tight around herself. The film on the screen showed the devastated wreck of a car, still smoking and belching twisted flames. The police thought it was terrorism to start with but it didn't take them long to discover the bodies in the vault. The image changed to show a male reporter standing on the other side of the road to the K&I Bank.

'Unconfirmed reports say that the body of known criminal Tommy King and the bodies of two other men were discovered in the vault of K&I Bank. They are believed to have been shot. The bank manager and his family, who are believed to have been taken hostage in their home, are being treated for shock. The car that exploded on the street outside the bank is believed to have been connected to the robbery as witnesses report seeing two people running from the bank towards the car. Police sources are believed to be speculating that they may have been known criminal figures Billy Doyle and Stella King. Three people were reported to have also been seen running away from the scene. Forensic examination of the scene of the explosion will continue into the night . . .'

Sobbing Jo-Jo stepped back from the telly. Whoever had reported seeing three people running away was dead wrong because her mum hadn't come to the getaway car she waiting desperately in as planned. Wasn't answering her phone. She collapsed, crying like a newborn babe, in her mum's chair at the desk. She shook her head repeatedly, but she knew it was true.

Stella King was dead.

Jo-Jo covered her mouth with both hands, rocking forward and back, almost tipping the chair over. Hadn't she witnessed her mum's death with her own eyes? She'd waited in the second getaway car, waited for her mum to come. That was the plan and there shouldn't have been any mistakes, her mum didn't make mistakes. Her mum was meant to join her in the car after the job. So she'd waited and waited, smoking a half pack of ciggies. Then she'd heard the bang, waited for her mum and when she hadn't appeared knew that something was wrong. She'd pushed her foot to the pedal and driven at high speed towards the location of the other getaway car. As she neared her destination, she'd killed the speed and cruised along like any other car, just in case the cops were nearby. Her whole life had nearly stopped when she saw the blazing car. No one had to tell her that the reason Stella hadn't appeared was because she'd got into the first getaway car. Then she'd seen them, not far from the car. Daisy and Ricky running away. They were alive while her mum was dead.

Jo-Jo sobbed harder as the pain of her loss threatened to cripple her. There was only one way she knew how to deal with pain. She straightened. Reached for her handbag, which she'd flung carelessly on her mum's desk. Opened it. Rummaged madly inside, but couldn't find her razor. The movement of her hands became frantic, but still no razor. She needed release from her pain now or she would go crazy. She shoved her bag away. Held out her arm. Lowered her face. Sank her teeth into her flesh. Broke the skin. Tasted blood. She hadn't touched her arms in years, always careful to cut into places no one else would see.

She leant back, hoping that the pain would leave her on every long breath she took. But it didn't. The grief and pain got worse.

The tears bubbled back into her eyes. The grief tightened its grip on her gut. Just one more cut might sort her out. Make it all go away. As she raised the arm high again and lowered her head she heard a huge crashing sound from downstairs. She knew who it was. They'd finally come. But they wouldn't find anything to do with the bank job, she'd made sure of that. She stood up. Asked herself how her mum would deal with the cops raiding the brothel?

*   *   *

Shock had every last one of the women pinned to a seat inside the boat. Ricky and Daisy sat opposite them. Suddenly Misty let out a loud sneeze.

'Feckin' hay fever,' she said, as her hand hunted in her pocket. She pulled something out. A small vial. 'Can't believe I'm still carrying this around with me.' Daisy looked at the vial and remembered where she'd seen it before. In the club on that morning Misty had caught her in her office. Some drug called Midnight Blue. Misty chucked it on her second-hand table and searched for her hay-fever tabs. But before she could find them Jackie suddenly jumped to her feet. 'Did you just say that that bloody woman was your mum?'

Daisy clasped her cold hands together in her lap. 'Stupid me, right? I built this dream that my mother would be this decent woman who took up with Frankie and then left because she couldn't cope with that life.' Her voice was bitter. 'But my last name's Sullivan and it seems there's no way someone with that last name is going to have a parent who walked on the right side of the law.'

Ricky grabbed one of her hands and held it tight. 'Don't blame her,' he said to Jackie. 'This ain't her fault.'

'Hold up a minute, mate,' Jackie threw back, stabbing her finger at him. 'This ain't got nothing to do with you. You ain't a member of the family, so butt out.' She looked scornfully at their clasped hands. 'And I don't like the way you're touching my daughter. She's got a fella. A decent fella and it ain't you.'

But Ricky didn't let go of Daisy's hand, instead he looked back at Jackie defiantly. 'She's been through a lot, so if you want the full SP on what happened I'll tell you.'

Jackie took an outraged step towards him, but Misty's voice stopped her. 'Alright, get talking?'

So he told them, his words driving Jackie back into her seat. He finished, his breathing laboured, one of his palms rubbing against his arm.

'Jackie,' Daisy pleaded. 'Can we sort out Ricky's arm?' Daisy asked, 'Forget him.' Finally one of the other women spoke. Anna leant forward in her chair, her brown face showing both tiredness and concern. 'You need to be worrying about yourself.'

'No,' Daisy responded defiantly. 'I'm not going to forget about him . . .'

Suddenly her auntie Roxy's voice cut in quietly. 'Why don't I get some water and stuff to clean his arm up?' Without waiting for a response she stood up. Daisy sent her a tight smile of thanks.

'Have you thought what you're going to do when the cops come looking for you?' Anna asked as Roxy moved towards the kitchen.

Daisy shook her head. She'd been avoiding that question since the disastrous end of the bank job. Five people dead, with a bank manager who might be able to point the finger at her. If she wasn't already on the radar it wouldn't be long before she appeared. She worked in the law, she knew about these things

As she opened her mouth to answer she heard a deep groan next to her. She twisted her head to find Ricky clutching his chest. The other women bolted out of their seats at the same time Ricky slipped onto the floor unconscious. Roxy rushed back into the room.

'Ricky!' Daisy yelled, as she crouched down beside him. 'Why didn't you let me help him before? I should've checked him over before.'

'What's the matter with him?' Misty asked as she dropped to her knees beside Daisy.

Daisy looked her as if she was the stupidest person on earth. 'He's got a bullet hole in his arm . . .'

'No, I don't mean that, I mean his chest. He kept rubbing it.'

'Tommy King shot him in the chest.' She looked up at Misty with pleading eyes. 'I thought he was dead.' Her voice wobbled. 'Please don't let him be dead.'

Misty turned her head and nodded at Jackie. Jackie leant down and pulled Daisy to her feet. Misty turned back to Ricky. She shifted his upper body as she gently eased his tracksuit top from his body. Then she gently peeled back the dark T-shirt he wore underneath.

Her hands stopped moving as her head snapped back. 'Well screw me,' she whispered.

Daisy urgently pushed herself out of her adoptive mum's arms and stepped over to Misty.

'Is it bad?' she asked fearfully.

'Oh, it's bad alright,' Misty shot back looking up at Daisy. 'Come and have a look.'

Slowly Daisy moved around the older woman until she stood on the other side of the man who she'd reluctantly come to care for so much. Her fingertips pressed to her lips preparing herself for what she was about to see. She gazed down. Her fingers fell from her mouth in surprise. Instead of seeing Ricky's naked upper body he wore something black and bulky.

'I don't understand,' she said, switching her gaze from the unconscious man on the floor to Misty. 'You said it was bad.'

'And it is, my girl.' Daisy's expression grew more confused. 'Do you know what that is?' Misty pointed at the bulky item of clothing on Ricky's chest.

Daisy shook her head, the same time Jackie swore furiously in the background.

'That my girl,' Misty continued, 'is a bullet-proof vest. And do you know who wears that type of vest?'

Before Daisy could answer the voices of the other women spoke in unison.

'A cop.'

Forty-three

The 321X flight from Malaga airport to Gatwick had been in the air for fifty minutes. The woman in business class sat two rows from the front and three rows from the back. Her hands tightly gripped onto the armrest as she thought about what waited for her back in England.

Ricky's eyes flashed open twenty-two minutes later. His chest hurt like hell. He didn't have a clue where he was. Then the events of the day started to come back to him. The bank job. Tommy's double cross. A gun blast flinging him off his feet. He realised that his bullet-proof vest was gone. A large dark bruise sprawled across his chest from the impact of Tommy's bullet. Shit. A bandage covered the bullet wound on his aching arm. He started to struggle up, but froze when he saw what was aimed, point blank, right at him. A gun. And the person holding it was Daisy Sullivan.

'You've got a bit of explaining to do.'
    Neither Daisy's voice nor the compact pistol wavered as she spoke. Jackie and the others were outside. They understood this was one she had to do alone. She was mad. Angrier than she'd been in a long time. All the while she'd been falling under Ricky's spell he'd been playing her like a classical pianist. The tension between her and Ricky lay as thick as the swirling mist that settled on the canal outside. Ricky eased up. Daisy stepped forward.
    'I'm waiting.'

Without showing a shred of emotion Ricky swung his long legs over the side of the sofa. 'You read the papers don't you? Racism, poverty, poor education, it's a miracle any of us black kids stay on the right side of the law.'

'Yeah, take the piss, that's helping.'

Ricky settled back into the softness of the sofa as if he didn't have a care in the world. 'Why don't you put the piece away and then I'll tell you what I'm allowed to.'

'Cough up, "officer", I'm getting very upset.' Daisy's finger curled around the trigger

Ricky leant forward resting his hands on his knees. 'You might be Frankie Sullivan's daughter, but you ain't going to . . .'

He never finished because she dipped the gun. Pulled the trigger. The bullet slammed into the wall beside his head, the noise echoing against the cabin walls. The door burst open. A startled Jackie and Misty stood nervously in the doorway.

'Stay out of this,' Daisy yelled without looking at them or taking her eyes off an unfazed Ricky.

The two women continued to hover in the doorway. Looked at each other. Then retreated and closed the door.

'Want to know how old I was when my dad taught me how to use a gun?' Daisy said calmly. 'The day after my fourteenth birthday. You don't think I'd shoot you? A few weeks ago I wouldn't but I've been trained in a hard school since then. So don't rile me.'

Their blue and black eyes clashed. Suddenly Ricky leant back and began to speak. 'The name's Ricky Smart, as you know, or Detective Ricardo Smart. For the last two years I've been under-cover, investigating the Kings. They made a fatal error the day Tommy King murdered Elaine Matthews, daughter of Clement Matthews, a high-profile company director and close friend of the commissioner himself. We knew he did it but couldn't prove it. So my job was to get inside the Kings' organisation and find something that would bring them down for good.'

'But you were in prison.' She didn't lower the gun.

'All part of the set-up. I was "transferred" to Belmarsh while doing a bogus sentence and my job was to get friendly with one of

Tommy's cousins, Paul King. I looked after his back and Bob's your uncle, he's putting in a good word with Tommy for me to join the crew when I rejoined the outside world.'

Daisy lowered the gun by half an inch as she stepped forward, hitting the low table in her haste, jogging the vial of Midnight Blue. 'So all that stuff about your sister was a cover story?'

Ricky laughed, a humourless sound that sounded hollow in the room. 'No, that bit was true. Misty can verify that.' For the first time his gaze looked troubled. 'But I never told my superiors about my connection to the Kings. That was why I was so eager to take the job. You don't volunteer for Belmarsh just to get plus points on your service record, believe you me. Jenna did disappear twenty years ago and I'm sure that it's somehow linked to Stella King. So while I was finding the evidence on the Kings I hoped that I would find out what happened to her.'

'But if you told your people about the bank job surely that would have been enough for them to arrest the Kings?'

'Someone saying they're going to do something and actually doing it are two different things. We needed to catch them in the act of doing the job and anyway, as I said, I had motives of my own.'

'But the police weren't waiting for us at the bank.'

Ricky rubbed his hand across his chin. 'Stella's change of plans for the robbery caught me on the hop, so I didn't have much time to contact my handler, but I sent him a message. But the signal was shit, so the message obviously didn't get there.' He paused and gazed at her intently. 'Mind you, I'd been having a little battle with myself about whether I wanted them to turn up or not.'

'Why?' she cried, dropping her gun hand.

Ricky's hand dropped from his chin. 'Because if they'd come storming in I wouldn't have been able to get the deposit box, which I know has got something in it that will tell me what happened to Jenna. This was maybe my last chance to find out about my sister.' He shook his head. 'And maybe I could finally put her to rest if she was gone.' Daisy watched the sadness take over his face. She knew exactly what he was feeling because hadn't she been trying to put her Dad to rest for years?

Suddenly he sprang to his feet making her step back. 'What does it matter now anyway? The only person who could've told me about Jenna has been blown to bits. And the deposit box turns up empty.' He pushed his hand into his pocket and pulled out his mobile. 'I need to call my superior. Go ahead and pull the trigger because the pain is going to be nothing compared to the bollocking I'm going to get when he realises the game I've been playing.'

As he punched away at his mobile Daisy stepped towards him. 'You might not want to do that.'

Ricky's fingers stopped moving as he gazed at her. 'What?'

'If I could help you find out what happened to Jenna would you promise to keep my dad's name and Charlie's out of everything?'

He took an aggravated step towards her. 'How the hell can you help me? Stella's dead and the deposit box . . .'

'I heard you the first time. You've got to promise me before I say anything else.'

Ricky tilted his head, staring hard at her and weighing up what she wanted. He shifted his head straight. 'Alright.' He crossed his arms over his chest. 'So why don't you tell me how you're going to help me out?'

Daisy swallowed. Then spoke. 'The deposit box was empty . . .'

'Yeah, I know that.'

Daisy's eyes formed like blue ice as she looked him squarely in the eye. 'I know who has got the stuff that was inside the deposit box.'

Ricky took an incredulous step towards her. 'Who?'

Daisy whispered, 'Me.'

Forty-four

Daisy emerged onto the deck of the *Miss Josephine*. The darkness was well settled in. High-grade dance music pulsed from one of the neighbouring council blocks. Victoria Park, to the side, lay still and quiet. The five women on deck turned to face her as the cool evening wind laced its breath around them.

'Is he Old Bill?' Jackie asked, breaking the expectant silence.

'Come inside and we'll tell you all about it.'

She turned back into the warmth of the cabin, quickly followed by the other women.

'I've made you all some tea,' Daisy said waving at the table in the middle, where five mugs, half-filled with tea, sat next to Misty's box of extra strength hay-fever tabs. Ricky was already seated, lounging in the single chair by the far window. The women seated themselves while Daisy quickly passed each of them a mug. Jackie began to open her mouth but Daisy got there first. 'I know you all want some answers but I haven't had a drink in hours so if you don't mind can we just stop for awhile so I can take a breath.'

No one said anything back but the women let Daisy have her space. They sat there in silence. It was Daisy who broke the silence a good five minutes later with a bit of small talk. 'How's Uncle Schoolboy?'

Jackie's face screwed up at the mention of her husband's name. She averted her gaze from Daisy. 'Alright, I suppose.'

The other women looked at Jackie as she quickly tucked into her drink. Their expressions were troubled. Daisy knew that there was something going on between Jackie and her husband that wasn't quite right. What it was she didn't know, and now wasn't the time to find out.

So everyone drank in silence again, Jackie eying up Ricky with a you-don't-fool-me expression on her alert face. Misty shuffled forward, a perky expression lighting her face. 'You like my New York Mafia impersonation when I forced you two into the car.' Everyone looked at her. 'Get in the back,' she said huskily in her best gravelly *Godfather* accent, 'I frighten myself sometimes.'

No one spoke for the next five minutes. As soon as Jackie finished her drink she ploughed into Ricky. 'So, you a boy in blue or what?'

'I have that honour,' Ricky answered brazenly. 'Is your tax disc up to date?'

Jackie curled her lip. 'Don't give me any of your back-chat, sonny. I don't care what happens just make sure you keep my Daisy's name well out of this. Now piss off back to the Yard.'

Daisy leant tentatively forward. 'Ricky is a cop but he also needs to find out what happened to his sister. I can help him . . .'

'No way.' Jackie rapidly shook her head. 'I don't know or care who his sister is. You're back with us now and that's where you're staying young lady.'

'I knew his sister,' Misty joined in. The other women looked at her in surprise. She drained the dregs in her cup. 'She worked for Stella King. She went to work one day twenty years ago and never came home.'

'That ain't Daisy's problem,' Jackie persisted. She stopped when Roxy let out a huge yawn. Irritated, Jackie twisted to face her. 'I'm so sorry I'm boring you.'

'It isn't that,' Roxy continued, her voice groggy. She laid her cup on the table and settled back in her chair. 'I just feel so tired all of a sudden.' Her last word was quickly followed by another yawn. Her eyes fluttered closed as she eased her head back onto the back of the chair.

Jackie dismissed her and turned back to her adoptive daughter. 'You ain't going.'

'All we need is the rest of tonight,' Daisy pleaded. 'If we haven't found out anything by tomorrow we'll be—'

'You need to clear the wax out of your ears,' Jackie cut furiously in, her face taking on the red colour of her hair. 'You're stopping with us and . . .' Jackie's voice wobbled on the last word. She ran her hand over her eyes as she shook her head as if clearing it. 'I . . . I . . . I . . .' she stammered.

'You alright?' Misty asked, leaning towards her. Suddenly Misty wavered in her chair and fell sideways. She didn't get up. Jackie moved forward, but her head slumped against her chest as the mug slipped from her limp hand. She slipped out of her chair unconscious onto the floor.

Ricky shot to his feet, 'What the fuck . . . ?' but he never finished as he watched Ollie and Anna go the same way as Jackie and Misty.

'What did you do?' he demanded rushing over to Daisy.

Daisy calmly stood up. 'I put the Midnight Blue in their tea.'

Ricky grabbed her by the arms. 'You're nuts, do you know how dangerous that is?'

'Don't worry, it's only going to knock them out for a couple of hours. I checked it out on the Internet connection on my phone while I was making the tea. Apparently it's a nice way to come down after you've done too much E. If I didn't do it there's no way they would have let us go.' She gave him a pointed look. 'You do still want to know what I found in the deposit box?'

He gave the unconscious women one last look, then nodded at her.

Ricky moved towards Jackie. Bent down and started rummaging in her pockets. 'What you doing?'

'One of them has got my gun.' He moved on to a slumped Misty. Eased back on his heels when he found it stashed at the back of her trousers. Plus he had her car keys.

'Come on,' Daisy urged, already rushing towards the door.

She turned back when she realised that Ricky wasn't following her. Instead she found him looking at the sleeping women.

'I thought you wanted to find out about your sister?'

'Are you sure they're going to be alright?'

'They're east end birds. They'll be fine.'

Finally he moved towards her. She flung open the door, the cool wind lacing around her instantly.

'So where have you stashed the stuff from the safe-deposit box?' he asked.

Without looking around she replied, 'I'll tell you once we get inside the car.'

Her mum would have been proud of her. Jo-Jo smiled as she walked away from the police station. The cops had questioned her this way and that, but she'd kept to the 'I don't know nuthin'' line. Even the big cop, the one with the sharp suit and sharper eyes who'd been particularly interested in Ricky, hadn't worn her down. Then she'd gone in for the kill and played her trump card – shown them her scars. She'd got the effect she'd wanted. They'd all been stunned, uncomfortable. So she'd prattled on and on about being under the doctor for having mental health problems. Her voice had risen to high pitch hysteria until she knew they'd decided she was a nutter not a doer. They couldn't wait to see the back end of her.

She'd played her part brilliantly, but it had taken its toll. All she wanted to do was get to her place in Bow, so she could feel the touch of the razor's blade kissing the inside of her skin.

Less than thirty minutes later she shut the door on her sixth-floor flat. Leant against it for a while. Lowered her head and bit into her arm, just above her previous bite. Seconds later she was inhaling the stuffy, cool air as the blood dripped down her arms. Then she noticed the bag of money Billy had given her the other night. She smiled – at least that evil old letch was gone for good. She stood up. Walked towards the bag and gave it a vicious kick across the room. It skidded, falling on its side, making a pile of cash fall out. She smiled at it, her mind clearing as she began to make plans.

'So how did you do it?'

Ricky's question came a good ten minutes after they were cutting through London in the navy blue Ford Escort, the motor that the women had abducted them in. He'd insisted on driving despite his injured arm. She knew what he was talking about. How had she got the contents of the deposit box? She gave him a sidelong look as she ran her hands through the strands of her hair, fanning her face, which had escaped from the knot of hair at the back of her head. 'The day I went into the bank disguised as Charlie's daughter, of course . . .' Her mind whizzed back to the events in the small room in the bank . . .

Adam, the bank employee, came back into the room. Daisy's mouth ran dry, eyes sparkled when she saw what he was finally holding. Charlie's deposit box. She almost leapt out of the chair and grabbed it from him. But she remained in her seat. Her tongue flicked across her bottom lip. *Stay cool, stay cool.* The sweat leaked from under the itching blond wig onto her forehead. Did a circuit around her ear. Her breathing became shallow. Her eyes never left the deposit box. Then Adam started moving towards her. It was almost as if he were moving in slow motion. One foot slowly after another. Her body became more rigid as the box got closer and closer and closer to her.

Then Adam stood in front of her beside the desk. Her eyes moved eagerly with the box as he laid it on the table. In front of her. Her pulse was running so fast, it made her ribs vibrate. Then the movement of the man's hand beside her made her raise her head. She almost blew out a joyous puff of air when she saw it in his hand. The key. The key to all those secrets.

He held it out to her. She took it, hoping that he didn't notice her trembling fingers.

'I'll be waiting outside,' he quietly informed her, his voice echoing in the almost empty room.

He turned to leave. She grabbed the box with one hand, slotted the key into the lock with the other. That's when she heard them. Footsteps – click, click, click – coming quick-fire down the corridor. Instinct told her that it was Adam's manager. Maybe she'd rumbled that the power of attorney papers she'd held on to were fake? Maybes, maybes, maybes took over Daisy's mind.

Click, click, click, they were getting closer.

She had to act fast. She twisted the lock. Flipped the lid up. Didn't even look inside. She tore the handle of her bag off her shoulder. Shoved the bag on the table. Opened it.

Click, click, click.

Grabbed the deposit box and tipped the contents into the bag. She zipped her bag up. Placed it quickly back in the same position hanging from her shoulder. Slammed the box shut. Slotted in the key. And turned.

A female voice called strongly behind her, 'I'm afraid I can't let you have access to the box . . .'

'They all assumed,' Daisy ended her tale, still looking at Ricky, 'that because the key was still inside the lock that I hadn't had a chance to open it. After that it was easy. I left the bank, went home, got dressed. Hid the stuff. My dad taught me that you never keep everything together, always scatter it around, so that's why the deposit box papers were in my car.'

Ricky let out a low whistle as he took the car into a smooth right. 'But if you had the contents of the box why get involved with Stella?'

'Stella got involved with me not the other way around,' she flung back defensively. Her fingers rubbed against her left bracelet. 'I'd just got the stuff inside the deposit box when she stormed into my life. But I tell you this much, when you're hanging upside down in a tub of water fighting for your life you learn to think real quick. If I'd have backed out of her plans, Stella might've smelled a rat and turned the dogs on me and I know I would've told her that I had that stuff from Charlie's box. Everything rested on everyone believing that my trip to the bank was unsuccessful.' She quit rubbing her bracelet. 'All I had to do next was make sure that Stella believed me when she found the box empty in the bank. And Tommy, unwittingly, helped me to do that today. The plan was that after she left the bank empty-handed she'd go gunning for her mates and let me go. Why should she keep me? The deposit box coming up empty had nothing to do with me now did it?' She shrugged her shoulders. 'There was no way I was ever going to let them get anything on Charlie. I don't care if he was dead or not, that was never going to happen.'

'You played a dangerous game.'

'Well I wasn't the only one playing games.' He half shrugged his shoulders at that. Winced when the movement caused pain to shoot up his arm. 'The only thing I didn't figure out was that I was going to become part of a family that was riddled with jealousy and hate.' Her mind shot back to the bank again. This time to the image of Tommy and his dead associates on the floor.

'That weren't your fault,' Ricky said as if reading her mind. 'A bloodbath between Tommy and his mum was always going to happen. They were too much alike, apart from the fact she was smart and he wasn't. The bank job just turned out to be the place where it all went down. Tommy was right anyway, it was stupid to leave without the money.' He paused. Opened his mouth to say something, but she cut over him.

'I know what you're going to say. How could I have helped them take Miah's family hostage? That should've been the time I called the police.' She shook her head. 'You don't know how much I wanted to, but I couldn't because of what I found in the box.'

'Which was?'

She looked down at her hands and held her tongue. 'Was it something to do with my sister?' he persisted.

She heard the tremble in his voice. 'Let's get where we're going first and then you can look for yourself.'

Daisy knew all his fears about his sister would come tumbling out when he saw one of the items from the deposit box.

Ricky's mobile went off the same time he pulled the car to rest in Daisy's parking spot inside her apartment block. Ricky pulled out the phone. Stared at it, knowing he couldn't put off taking this call anymore.

He took the call. Listened to the blistering voice of his superior officer. Sighed. 'Yeah. I'm alright.'

'What the fuck happened? The bank's an abattoir . . .'

'Yeah I know. Looks like Stella King got blown up in the explosion. Too many things went wrong.'

'Too many things went wrong? I've got my superiors trying to kick my door in here and you're telling me too many things went wrong? We'll all be back in uniform after this. Why didn't you let me know that the day of the robbery had changed?'

Rick knew he either told the truth about Jenna now or buried the lie deep again. What a lousy decision he had to make. But he was a cop and he had taken vows to uphold the law whatever the situation.

'I did try to contact you, but the message obviously didn't make it. But you ain't going to like what else I've got to tell you . . .' So he told the truth about his sister. He didn't need to see Detective Inspector Bridges to know the man was almost hopping silly around the room.

When he finished his superior's words grabbed him down the phone. 'You're in so much crap, Smart. I can't cover this up for you, you know that . . .'

'I'll take my chances . . .'

'You're to report back to base right now.' The words were shouted.

'I'm afraid I can't do that.'

'If you're not back here in half an hour I will personally—'

Ricky's response was quick-fire and defiant. 'All I need is the rest of the night. There's more going here than this bank job. Whatever happened twenty years ago will give you more information against Stella King.'

'I don't need more information if you're telling me she's dead.'

'I'll come in bright and early tomorrow morning.'

'Smart . . .' Bridges warned.

'Do me one last favour sir. Make sure you keep Daisy Sullivan's name out of this.'

With the other man still blowing steam in his ear, Ricky cut the call. He held on to the mobile as he leant back in his seat, letting out a harsh puff of air.

'Is it "Goodnight Vienna" for you and the Yard?'

Ricky looked across at Daisy.

'If I'm lucky. Otherwise I really will be in Belmarsh this time.'

But he wasn't in the mood for smart talk, not while his whole career hung in the balance. He flicked his head towards Daisy when he felt the warmth of her palm on his knee. Their eyes met. Ricky felt his dick move. Shit, he didn't need a hard-on at a time like this. He didn't have the right to be feeling pleasure when everything he'd ever worked was dropping to earth with a bang right before his eyes.

Daisy quickly withdrew her hand and blushed. Ricky spoke as his dick fell back into line. 'I think it's time you shared what was in that safe-deposit box, don't you?

'Stay close by my side so no one can see your wound,' Daisy whispered to Ricky as they entered her apartment block back at Wapping. The security guard sat at his usual spot behind the desk in reception. He lifted his head as they tried to scurry past without making eye contact. But his voice stopped them.

'Miss Sullivan?'

Daisy whispered to Ricky, 'Keep going to the lift. I'll deal with him.'

As Ricky moved forward Daisy spun around with a smile on her face.

'A man went up to your apartment the other day . . .'

'Oh,' she quickly interrupted, remembering what Misty had told her about his visit to her home. Her forced smile grew wider. 'That was my uncle Michael.'

He leant back in his chair as he gave her a speculative look. 'A lot of your family coming to see you these days.' His eyes wandered in the direction that Ricky had gone in reminding Daisy that she had fibbed about Ricky being her brother.

'Wish I could chat,' she replied, in an off-hand tone. 'But I've got to run.' And without waiting for a response she turned around and quickly made her way to join Ricky at the lift.

Less than a minute later they entered her home. As soon as the door shut behind them Daisy let out a huge sigh of relief as she leant against the wall. She was back in her own space, which made her feel that much safer.

'So where is it?' Ricky's voice cut into her moment of peace. She pushed herself off the wall and walked briskly towards the main room. She flicked on the light switch without breaking her stride. Headed towards the TV. Picked up something that lay on top of it. Ricky sucked in his breath when she turned around and saw what she was holding. Her *Calamity Jane* movie video box. She was about to open her mouth to speak when Ricky marched towards her. When he reached Daisy he grabbed her shoulders, startling her, and moved her backwards towards the two-seatter sofa. He pushed her down. She landed with an oomph. He loomed over her large and serious. 'Let's get one thing clear from the get-go. You try any funny business and I'm going to forget that my dick has got a relationship with you.'

She tossed her hair back giving him a defiant look. 'Well you tell your very *little* friend,' she gazed mockingly at his crotch, 'that relationship is past tense . . .'

Before she could finish he swooped down and took her lips in a hard, controlling kiss. She groaned in protest for a few seconds, then relaxed and sank into the delicious thrill he sent zinging through her body. His hands caressed her breasts. She moaned. Caressed her belly. She moaned more loudly. His swift moving hands slid down her arms. She was so deep into the tailspin of passion he'd sent her in that she was wasn't prepared for his next move. He whipped the *Calamity Jane* video box from her. She shot half off the seat. He stepped back and dangled the box teasingly at her.

Then he plonked himself down beside her and opened the box. He turned it upside down. The contents fell on the sofa between them.

Forty-five

'Don't touch it.'

Ricky's voice was small. Quiet as if he were afraid someone else would hear.

Their collective breathing battered the room as they both stared at the items between them. Or rather stared at one of the items.

A gun. A Beretta.

'Do you think it belongs to Charlie?' Daisy whispered.

Ricky shook his head as he responded. 'Dunno. What we do know is that something happened twenty years ago that involved Stella, two men called Clarke and Johnson and a third unnamed party.'

Daisy cut furiously over him, 'Clarke and Johnson, Clarke and Johnson.' She rubbed the back of her hand over her forehead. 'I know I've heard those names before somewhere . . .'

'Look,' Ricky punched in.

She waved her hands in the air, her bracelets bobbing against her arms. 'Let me think. I've heard those names recently.' Her head shook from side-to-side. 'Jeepers, where was . . .' Her gaze slammed into him. 'Can't be. No . . .'

He leant towards her. 'Tell me.'

The blue of eyes covered with a sheen of disbelief. 'The day Charlie died two cops came to see him. Detective Sergeant Clarke and Detective Inspector Johnson.'

Ricky reared back as if he'd been slapped. 'What did this Johnson look like?'

Her hands gestured in the air. 'Tall. Designer suit. Handsome.

Was wearing a wedding ring so I'm guessing he's a family man and . . .'

'Black.' He ended. Before she could say another word he slammed his fist into the sofa. 'Bollocks.'

'I take it that means you know him?'

'He's only the cop all us black boys in blue look up to. He's a man who plays it by the book, though. There's no way he could be involved in this.'

'Two policemen called Clarke and Johnson came to see Charlie. Stella mentions two guys called Clarke and Johnson on the phone to another person who is clearly mixed up in whatever happened twenty years ago. That isn't a coincidence, Ricky.'

Ricky seemed incapable of speech – a first, Daisy thought – so she continued outlining what they knew so far. 'We know from Stella's conversation with this third person that they have a daughter. The only two people anywhere near this who we *know* have daughters are Randal Curtis and Priscilla Hopkirk.'

Ricky shook his head. 'Hopkirk's widow is out of the picture. I got my people to check her out and she's a regular orphan Annie.'

'And I'm sure you would have said that about Johnson five minutes ago so I don't think we can take anyone out of the picture.' She stopped talking because she knew her next words were going to shake Ricky up even more. But it had to be said. 'We also know that your sister went to work for Stella one night twenty years ago and never came back. And now we have a gun.' She looked hard at it. 'Which must have been used to do something . . . like shoot someone, that's what they're usually for.' He looked at her, eyes blazing, breathing ragged. 'Ricky, do you think someone shot her? That this has all been about covering up her murder?'

Ricky squeezed his eyes shut, dealing with the information she lay before him He shook his head. Reopened his eyes. 'I dunno, but I tell you this much, I ain't stopping until I find out.' He stopped, easing his breath back to normal. When he spoke again she knew he was back in control, back in Detective Inspector Ricardo Smart mode. He looked at the other items next to the gun. 'Let's find out what else we've got here.'

A torn piece of A5-sized card and a brochure of some kind. He flipped over the torn card to reveal the photo of a man. White guy, around forty, with thick bushy hair, laced with threads of silver, wearing a flashy suit, smile and a ring. Ricky peered closer. Titanium ring. Chunky. Celtic design.

'Who is he?' Daisy also peered harder at the photo as she threw out her question.

'Dunno, but . . .' Ricky left his words suspended in the air as his fingers flipped at his phone. He twisted his mobile around so that Daisy could see. She stared at another photo with torn edges with another man in it. 'I found that,' Ricky started. 'In Stella King's drawer the night I sneaked into her office. Remember the night you followed me.' Daisy nodded. 'And if I'm not mistaken.' Ricky picked up the photo on the sofa and lay it against the photo on the mobile. 'Both halves make the same photo.'

'Who's the man in the photo you found at Stella's?'

Ricky glanced up at her. 'Stella's husband, Stevie King. See how their hands shoot out.' He waved his hand over both photos. 'They're shaking hands, which means they were doing business with each other because Stevie King weren't a man who shook anyone's hand unless they were an associate.'

'If he was close to Stevie King why would anyone have ripped the picture apart? Kept it in a safe-deposit box? And what has this got to do with Charlie and my dad?'

'And my sister?' Ricky pointed to two people in the background of the photo of Stevie King. 'That's my sister sitting at a table with some guy.'

Daisy shifted her gaze, let out a soft puff of air. She wasn't staring at Ricky's sister, but at the man at the table with her. 'That's Randal Curtis.'

'Are you sure?'

She nodded. 'He's younger but it's Randy Randal, alright.'

'Tell me about him.'

'He was Charlie's partner in the law firm. Other than that, all I know of his background is that he came from a working-class London family. Had a son who died of a drugs overdose. And I think I heard once that his parents are still alive and that he's got a younger sister.'

'OK,' Ricky started. 'Let's look at the big picture here. In the frame with Stella King is Charlie Hopkirk. Both are dead. Then there's Clarke and Johnson, who may or may not be cops. We've got my sister who disappeared and a gun. We've also got two halves of a photo showing Stevie King and an unnamed man and behind them, sitting pretty, are my sister and Randal Curtis.'

'And that.' Daisy pointed to the final item from the deposit box. A brochure. She picked it up with her fingertips. The front cover was a picture of a huge stately looking home set in gorgeous grounds. She read out the name on the top of the pamphlet. 'Harding Hall. Looks like the brochure for a health farm or something.' She flicked through it. Nothing. At the back was a flap with folded papers inside. She pulled some out. 'This lot looks like the booking forms.' She stuck the papers back. 'Maybe Charlie just shoved it in the deposit box by mistake.'

She shoved the papers back inside and dropped the brochure back on the sofa.

'If the man in the photo is a Face in the underworld, Misty might be able to help us. She can give us chapter and verse on everyone from the Krays and Richardsons to the present day.'

'Well here's a steer for you, Einstein,' Ricky said in a tight voice. 'Misty ain't going to be opening her trap for at least the next few hours because someone doped her out.'

Daisy tugged at her lip as guilt flooded her, remembering how she'd drugged the very same people who had opened their arms and hearts to a fatherless fifteen-year-old kid. They would have been able to help her. She shouldn't have drugged them. *But they wouldn't have let you go with Ricky*, a tiny voice inside her mind whispered. They remained in silence, each other's brain rattling through a list of people. Suddenly Daisy dipped into her pocket and took out a white business card. 'I think I know who might be able to help.'

'Who?'

She avoided his gaze. 'I'll tell you later.'

'This ain't no game, Daisy.'

Her nostril flared in anger. 'I watched three people get gunned down today. Watched my mother get blown up. Betrayed Jackie, the only woman I've thought of as my mum. Most probably lost the best bloke a girl could ever hope to have. So I don't need you to remind me what a fucking mess I've made of my life.'

Ricky just shook his head at her rant and said, 'Get a carrier bag.'

She was back a few seconds later with a Waitrose bag. Ricky picked up the gun with his fingertips. Daisy stepped towards him, opening the bag. He dropped the gun into it, then took the bag from her.

'What do you plan to do?' Daisy asked as she retook her seat.

Instead of answering her Ricky pulled out his mobile and stood up, heading for the French doors with the incredible view over the river. 'Brett, it's Ricky.'

'Hey, long time, no hear.'

'I need a favour.'

'Is it a legal one this time?'

'I need you to check something out for me.'

'Sure, but it will have to be tomorrow because I've—'

'No, it needs doing asap.'

'No can do. I'm with the missus and she already thinks I'm giving my lovely assistant too much help with her career.'

'Which we all know you are. Do this for me and I'll join your rugby club.'

The man on the other end of the line was silent for a moment. 'You've got yourself a deal. Where do you want to meet?'

Ricky told him and ended the call. 'Who was that?' Daisy said.

'Forensic expert mate of mine. If anyone can find any evidence on the gun it will be him. Why don't you meet your mysterious friend to try and see if they can ID the bloke in the photo while I get the ball rolling about the gun.'

He grabbed the carrier bag and got to his feet. 'The night's moving on, so let's meet back here by nine at the latest.' He turned and briskly made for the door. As he reached it he suddenly twisted his head to look over his shoulder at her. 'You're right, Jerome is a good man, but you're going to have to eventually ask yourself what you're doing hanging out with me then?'

Her mind swung back to them doing the dirty in the car. Shit, if she turned up pregnant she didn't know what she would do. The look she saw on his face told her that he was thinking exactly the same thing.

As soon as he got outside Ricky hit his mobile.

'Ricky,' DI Bridges yelled. 'If you're not back—'

'I need you to check out a DS Clarke for me and DI Johnson . . .'

'What? Johnson? You've gone nuts. Perhaps we can use that to explain your behaviour at the disciplinary.'

'Believe me, in this case I wish I was. I think I'm onto something that could blow the whole Met apart . . .'

Forty-six

Ray-Ray Digby got out of his motor in the dimly lit car park in Stratford, East London. He turned to his associate, a bulky man seated in the driver's seat. 'Any funny business and you come out shooting, got it?'

The other man nodded. Ray-Ray straightened his jacket and hopped out of the car. He was in a jubilant mood after the news on the grapevine had reached him that Tommy and Stella King were over for good. Stupid cunts. No one did bank jobs anymore. East London was buzzing with the news that Stella had been blown to kingdom come. Fuck, he'd wished it had been him to light the fuse, but some other lucky bastard had got there before him. After Tommy King's hired gun had shot his younger brother, the Kings were marked for life in his eyes. Still, Ray-Ray had thought twice about taking on Stella King. And now he didn't need to anymore because someone had done him the favour. Then forty minutes ago he'd got the call asking if he was interested in taking out the thug who'd plugged lead into Johnny. Ricky Smart, that was the shooter's name. He was going to regret the day he ever tangled with the Digbys.

His mobile rang, dragging him out of his murderous thoughts. 'Yeah?'

'Go over to the large, plastic bin in the far right corner.'

'Look,' Raymond snarled. 'I don't do business with ghosts.'

'I hear that Ricky's saying he's going to take over the Kings' manor and the first thing he's going to do is put you and your business into "administration".'

'Yeah? We'll see about that . . .'

'If you do what I say it ain't going to happen. Now walk across the car park.'

Ray-Ray held onto the phone as he followed the instruction. Once at the bin he put the phone back to his face. 'Open the lid.'

'Open the lid? Why, did you miss dinner?'

'Just do it.'

He pushed the lid with one hand. Peered inside. On top of a black bag lay a small holdall bag. He pulled it out and pushed the phone back to his face at the same time.

'That's just to say thank you.'

He dropped the bag on to the grainy, concrete ground. Hunched down. Unzipped it. His breath sucked in when he saw what was inside. Neatly piled cash. He pulled the phone back up. 'Who the fuck are you?'

But he was talking to thin air because the line was dead. He smiled. It wasn't the only thing that was going to be dead that night.

Ricky spotted Brett Baxter as soon as he entered the Happy Duck pub. Brett stood out like sunshine on a winter's day. For some unknown reason, which Ricky could never figure out, his friend liked to wear porkpie hats, even when he was beavering away inside his lab.

'My man,' Brett called out as Ricky quickly eased opposite him at the table in the corner. 'I've got to get back or Bettina will be serving me with divorce papers.'

Ricky shoved the plastic bag across the table. 'I need you to do some tests on this right away.'

The other man peered inside and whistled. His gaze darted up at Ricky. 'Why act so clandestine if this is official police business?'

Ricky leant across the table, his voice dropping low. 'Let's just say, it isn't now but it will be later.'

'Um,' Brett let out, leaning back, with one hand still on the bag. 'Is this going to put me in the firing line?'

'Not if you do it right away.'

Brett shifted the brim of his hat with one hand and scratched his head. 'Do you want the usual tests? Possible DNA evidence? When it was last fired?' He shuffled forward peering back into the bag. 'Although I'll tell you now that it looks slightly old, which means I might not be able to lift anything.'

'Do what you can. Give me a bell asap. Thanks, man.'

Ricky eased to his feet and started walking away.

'That was bollocks about the rugby team, wasn't it? You aren't going to join at all.'

Ricky carried on walking, a smile settling across his face. Then he thought about what the gun might mean about why his sister never came home that night. Thought about DI Johnson . . .

Daisy glanced down at the white business card in her lap, taking her eyes momentarily off the road as she drove. Reread the name. This was a risky move, which was why she hadn't told Ricky who she was planning to see. But she didn't know where else to turn. Her shoulders relaxed back as her nerves eased down.

'I told you not to run.'

Daisy nearly jumped two feet out of her skin at the sound of the voice next to her. She swung her head around to find her dad in the passenger seat. Things were really getting bad if she was now seeing her dad without the aid of her happy pills. He wore black, from head to foot, even the leather gloves on his hands. His blond hair was tousled as if he'd been shoving his fingers through it. His blue eyes were shining and alert.

She turned her gaze back to the road as she took the car into a sharp right. 'I was staring at a no-win situation, knew I had a pair of legs and decided to use them,' she finally answered.

'We've all got choices . . .'

'I don't need to hear a shit load of psycho babble right now.'

'Mind your language, my girl.'

'Sorry, Dad. I just don't know how I got into all of this.'

He leant forward. Switched the radio on. The Mamas and Papas, already halfway through 'Dedicated To The One I Love', floated its dream magic inside the car.

'That's always the problem with you respectable people. She shot him a quick look on hearing his words. 'Too much looking back and too many regrets. This is one night you need to keep your mince pies looking forward.'

She let out an agonising breath. 'I could just keep driving until I find a police station and hand myself in.'

Frankie snorted. 'That's another thing you respectable people do, always full of guilt. You know what I always used to say? "Never complain, never explain."' His voice became hard. 'You need to do less thinking and worrying and more concentrating.'

The silence settled around them, until Frankie said, 'Who would have thought it? My girl fancying a copper.'

Daisy let out a huff and blushed at the same time. 'I do not fancy him.'

'Yeah, right.' He cocked his head towards her. 'And I ain't dead.'

They both looked at each other, eyebrows raised and laughed. It felt *so* good to laugh. Suddenly she was reminded of the days they had once spent together. Afternoons splashing and funning in the indoor pool of their huge Essex house; evenings together, as cosy as two bugs, on the sofa watching the box; nights spent bopping their lives away at the Hammersmith Palais. The tension drained from her as she remembered the good ol' days. Their laughter tickled away as they continued to stare at each other.

'I had real high hopes for you when you were little.' Frankie shifted in the seat to make himself more comfortable, his lips carved into a gentle smile full of memories. 'You weren't going to grow up to be a somebody like me.' Daisy ached as she saw regret touch his face. 'I wanted you to be decent. To live on the right side of the street. To never have to look over your shoulder.' Suddenly his voice blew soft and gentle in the space between them. 'I only ever regret two things in my life. Every time I turned up for parent–teacher evening at your school your teacher always looked like I was going to blow her head off. Always made me think that because they were scared of me they never treated you right.'

She'd always wondered why the teachers sometimes whispered when she strolled past. It wasn't until she was a teenager and

found out who he was she understood. 'And the second thing?'
she asked as the car drew into a well lit car park in front of a large
glass and steel building.

'That I just wasn't careful where I put my dick the night you
were conceived.' She gave him a sad look. 'Don't get me wrong, I
never once in my life regretted the day you were born. Only ever
regretted the womb you came out of.'

She nodded in agreement. 'Knowing that I was nurtured in Stella
King's womb for nine months doesn't fill me with joy either.'

'Stella?'

She quickly turned, catching the confusion on his face. What
was going on here? 'Dad?'

His face retreated to unreadable gangland villain. 'Remember
what I taught you about using a gun. You've been going around
without the safety catch on that gun you're packing. You don't
want to be shooting yourself, not on a night like this.'

She quickly switched her head back upfront as she eased the car
into an empty car park space. As she killed the engine she turned
back to question him some more about his earlier words about
Stella. But he was gone. And the radio was off. She eased forward
and pulled the gun from the back of her pants. Stared at it. Frankie
was right, the catch wasn't on.

Twelve minutes later the person she was after strolled out of
the building. Tall and straight, they walked in the opposite direction. Daisy grabbed the business card in her lap and jumped out
of the car. Taking long strides she followed the other person. The
person turned a corner. So did Daisy. As Daisy came around a hand
grabbed her by the throat and slammed her into the wall.

'What are you doing following—' Suddenly the other person
dropped their hand. 'Daisy Sullivan isn't it?'

Daisy leant heavily on the wall as she stared at the Deputy
Commissioner of the Met police, Barbara "Basher Babs" Benton.

Forty-seven

'What you bloody looking at?' Jo-Jo yelled drunkenly at the two women she passed. They whispered to each other and darted scornful looks at her as they quickened their steps. Jo-Jo tried to steady her unstable body as she threw at their backs, 'Think you're too good for the likes of me? Wanna know who I am? I'm Stella fucking King's daughter, that's who.'

But the two women hurried around a corner leaving her ranting and raving to herself. Defiantly she shoved two fingers in the air. Twisted back around and staggered towards Deadwood Hotel. She knew she was buzzing out of her head. She hadn't been on the gear for years, but the events of the day had tipped her over the edge. It hadn't been hard to track down a bag of C. She smiled. That was the beauty of London; you could get anything you wanted anytime, day and night. She entered the deserted and dark brothel.

'Mum,' she called out. Then she remembered that her mum wasn't coming home. Ever. The artificial feeling of numbness that the drugs and booze had injected into her system disappeared. Grief gripped her again. She leant her palm against the wall of the hallway and bowed her head as she started to sob. The image of the burning car flashed into her mind.

'Why, why, why?' she mumbled again and again. She hadn't even had the chance to tell her how much she loved her. Tell her about the things they would do together. Just them two, no one else. Shit, she needed to cut herself, to let this grief flow out of her body. She reached into her bag searching for her razor. Found it.

As she pulled it out she felt a presence behind her. Heard a shuffling noise against the floor. Knew that person was moving closer to her. Felt their heat grow stronger against her back. She whirled around, razor high in the air, and let out a terrifying scream when she saw who it was.

'I've never seen him before.'

Daisy sank back in her seat as a massive attack of deflation hit her at Barbara Benton's words. 'Just thought with your years of experience in the police you might've come across him.'

The other woman still fingered the photo Daisy had given her. They were seated inside Misty's car, still in the car park. The shadows of the deepening night slowly lengthened beside them.

'What's all this about?' Barbara's grey eyes darted up, as quick as her question.

Instead of answering Daisy hastily stuck out her hand for the picture. But the older woman didn't give it back. 'I could take it back to the Yard and see if it matches any faces in our computer records.'

'No, thanks.' Daisy tugged the picture back and shoved it back inside her bag.

Barbara pulled out a cigarette and lit up. She took a deep lug and leant back. 'I've been smoking since I was fifteen and every day since then I've been telling myself I'm going to give up. But that's what happens when something has got you hooked. You want to move on but you can't get away. So what's got you so hooked about this man in the photo?'

Suddenly the car felt like the tightest space Daisy had been inside. She twisted around desperate to get outside. 'I know who you are.' Barbara's words froze Daisy. The other woman carried on. 'Charlie told me all about you two years ago.' Daisy slowed and turned to face her. 'He knew how much Randal Curtis hated your dad and he needed someone inside the police to feed Randal false info if he started asking questions.'

Dazed, Daisy continued to stare, not sure what to do. Barbara leant forward and pulled out the ashtray and ground out her ciggie.

She faced Daisy. 'I don't know what's going on here but I suspect it's got something to do with Charlie.'

Could she trust this woman? Daisy mulled over the question. Made her decision. 'I'm worried that Charlie was mixed up with something he shouldn't have been. Something to do with my dad. Let's just say I found some stuff that includes a gun.' Daisy stopped, peering intently at the other woman's face, waiting for the shock to show but she saw none.

'Go on,' Barbara urged softly.

'A friend of mine is getting someone to check out the gun to see if it links to anything nasty.'

'Believe me, Charlie wouldn't have been involved in anything dodgy.'

'Don't you think I've told myself that?'

'Have you ever considered that Charlie might have been holding the stuff for your dad without realising what he had?'

'Why would he do that?'

'It's not uncommon for solicitors to hold onto things at the request of their clients.'

'But Charlie wasn't even my dad's solicitor.'

'I ran this case years ago. It was a child abuse case. We knew this scumbag had a child porn stash somewhere, but we couldn't find it. I turned this city upside down.' Barbara's tone was filled with determined grit as if she were involved in the case all over again. 'We had one hour left to hold the bastard. I reread his record again and again because I knew the clue was in there somewhere. And there it was, the name of his solicitor, which didn't match the name of the solicitor representing him. The bastard had changed the firm of solicitors who represented him right at the last minute. And do you know where we found all those disgusting pictures? Stashed in an envelope lodged with his original solicitor. Of course the solicitor didn't even realise what he'd been given.'

'Do you think that's what's happened?'

'I hope to God it is.' She stroked Daisy's arm, reminding her of the last time they'd sat in a car together and she'd held Daisy's hand. Daisy stiffened, this time wondering if there was some lesbian-thing going on. It wasn't as if this woman was married or had kids and stuff, Daisy reasoned. If it was true how was she going to get out of this one? She didn't want to offend this woman but girl-on-girl was definitely not her style. What was she meant to do? She breathed easier when Barbara removed her hand.

'Sometimes we think helping our friends is the best way. But sometimes it isn't because it puts us dead centre in the firing line.' Her hand came out and stroked Daisy's cheek. 'If things get dangerous you've got my number.'

'I'll be alright,' Daisy said as Barbara's hand dropped away. Barbara opened the door. 'Oh, yes, nearly forgot.' Barbara looked back at her, eyebrows raised. 'Good luck later at the gala dinner at City Hall with getting the keys to the commissioner's job. Oops,' Daisy's hand shot to her mouth. 'I didn't mean cell keys . . .'

Barbara laughed, a joyful high sound that surprised Daisy. 'If you get this all sorted out, why don't you come along and see me step into my new shoes? And Daisy.' Barbara looked drop cold sober now. 'Make sure you keep the safety catch on that gun.'

Daisy's jaw dropped. How . . . ? But before she could ask the other woman got out of the car and melted into the night.

Daisy pulled out the photo of the unnamed man. She still didn't know who he was. Her eye caught the time on the digital clock on the dashboard. She had less than half an hour to get back to Ricky.

The razor dropped from Jo-Jo's hand and clattered onto the wooden floor. She stared horrified at the tall person in front of her.

'Mum,' finally burst from her lips.

Stella stood in front of her daughter. She still wore the clothes she'd done the robbery in, but also had on a baseball cap. Underneath the cap was a black scarf that shrouded half of her face giving her a macabre phantom of the opera look. Her visible eye was bloodshot, but had lost none of its steely fire.

'Well it ain't the tooth fairy, is it?' Stella's words were slow and muffled as if she found it hard to speak.

The younger woman's terror intensified as she leant into the wall. 'You're dead, ain't you? You've come back to haunt me.'

Stella took a limping step forward. 'Don't be stupid.' Abruptly her words stopped as she peered hard at her youngest child. Her mouth twisted in disgust. 'You're tripping again, ain't you?'

Suddenly Jo-Jo launched her small body into her mother's arms. Stella clung on tight to her daughter, smoothing her hand over her hair as the younger woman cried.

'I knew you weren't dead,' Jo-Jo said excitedly. 'Not my mum. It's going to be just you and me now like it should be.'

Without warning Stella's legs went weak and she staggered back. Jo-Jo's arms tightened stopping her from falling.

'Mum?' Jo-Jo looked up at her concerned. She felt the tremble of her mum's body. Something was wrong.

'You need to help me upstairs.'

Jo-Jo knew this wasn't the time for questions. She folded her arm around her mother's waist and gently led her towards the staircase. Stella raggedly sucked in air as they took the steps slowly, one at a time. A few minutes later, a heavily breathing Stella still hanging onto her, Jo-Jo shoved open the door to her mum's office. She led her mum towards the sofa.

'Not there,' Stella said weakly. 'Put me in Stevie's chair.'

Jo-Jo propelled her to the other side of the room. Carefully she laid her mum in the chair behind the desk. With a small groan Stella sank down. She looked up at Jo-Jo, whose hand fluttered nervously in the air. 'Help me get this hat and scarf off.'

Nodding, Jo-Jo pulled the hat off and laid it on the desk. The scarf flapped around her mum's face like widow's weeds. She reached for the scarf.

'Gently,' Stella let out through gritted teeth.

Jo-Jo eased the material around the left side of her mum's face back. Stella's fingers dug into the arms of the chair as Jo-Jo did the same to the other side of the scarf. The material fell back. Jo-Jo clamped her hands over her mouth as she leapt back in horror. The right side of Stella's face was criss-crossed with cuts from where flying glass had cut into her flesh. The skin looked red and raw and as painful as hell. A deep cut sliced over the top of her right eyelid.

'Mum, I've got to take you to the ozzie.' Jo-Jo was almost hysterical.

'No you ain't,' Stella shouted, pain shooting through her head. 'You're going to clean me up and make Mummy look all nice and pretty again.'

Stella stared at herself in the mirror. The reflection wasn't pretty. Fuck, if she saw herself coming down a dark alley she'd run screaming the other way. But she was alive and that's what mattered. Her good eye closed as her mind skidded back to earlier that day. Back to the car. Back to the explosion. She'd been running like a mad woman, knowing the cops would be on the scene soon. The plan was that she should've headed straight towards the car with Jo-Jo in it, but she knew there wasn't time for that so she'd bolted to the car with Billy in. She'd twisted around when she'd realised Daisy had stopped. Yelled at her to get her arse moving. Carried on motoring forward, until she clearly saw Billy primed and ready to go in the driver's seat. So she'd run around towards the passenger's seat. Scanned her gaze over the car, seeing Daisy straighten up. She'd reached for the door the same time Billy's hand had touched the ignition key. And that's when she'd stopped. She didn't know why, couldn't explain it, but some sixth sense had held her back. Instead of moving forward she'd stepped back. And back. Billy twisted the key the same time she'd launched into the longest jump of her life. The next thing she knew she was lying on the grass, rolling in agony with her hair on fire and half her face feeling like acid was melting it down to the bone. But it hadn't knocked her out. She'd scrambled to her knees, blood running down her face, blinding her in one eye, and seen the burning car and debris strewn around her. She'd kept herself low as she moved away, pain twisting her mind, until she reached an underground car park. Straightening up she'd run towards a car and tried the handle, but it was locked. She kept trying until she found one where the owner had forgotten to lock it. Lucky for her a baseball cap and scarf with some magazines lay on the back seat. She'd snapped the cap on and wrapped the scarf around her head and got the fuck out of there.

That was the difference between her and the riff-raff. They rolled over and died but Stella King didn't roll over and die for anyone.

Her good eye flicked open. 'Mum.' She turned at the sound of Jo-Jo back in the room. Her daughter held a basin of warm water and some towels slung over her shoulder. 'I'm going to patch you up all nice.' Jo-Jo smiled as she reached the grim-looking older woman. 'Make you feel better again. I'll make your favourite—'

'Shut. Up.' Stella's voice was hard as she moved towards the sofa. 'Put *Calamity Jane* on.'

'What?' Jo-Jo stopped in her tracks.

'You heard.' Stella wearily sat down. Jo-Jo looked at her mum weirdly as she placed the basin and towels at the foot of the sofa. But Stella's gaze was locked faraway as she stared at the blank telly screen. A few minutes later Doris Day and friends were with them in the room. Jo-Jo dipped one of the towels in the disinfected water and leant across to wipe the blood from her mum's face. But Stella boxed her hand away. 'Go to the second last one in the scene selection.'

'But Mum?' Jo-Jo didn't like the look on her mum's face. Like she wasn't really there anymore. But she did what Stella asked. Flicked through the scene selections until she found the still image of Doris Day's Calamity Jane peeping through the branches of a tree shining radiance. 'That's it,' Stella said softly.

Jo-Jo pressed play. The sweet, honest voice of Doris Day swept into the room singing about her secret love. Stella started to sing along in her low, throaty voice.

'Mum – your face,' Jo-Jo pleaded.

Stella started speaking as if she hadn't heard her. 'I love that scene and you want to know why?' Jo-Jo didn't answer, just got more worried by the second as she watched her mother. 'My brother would play it to me . . .'

'Your brother?' Her mum was definitely in shock, she didn't have a brother.

But Stella didn't hear her again, just kept chatting along about some man that Jo-Jo had never heard of. Anxiously Jo-Jo reached forward and gingerly wiped through the deep lacerations and hanging flesh.

'They ain't dead you know.'

Stella flashed her good eye at Jo-Jo. 'Daisy and Ricky.'

'Ricky?' Stella leant up. 'But he got blasted in the bank.'

'I saw them running away. Together.'

Stella settled back down, a nasty expression twisting the good side of her face. 'Billy's dead. Tommy's dead.' She turned her damaged eye onto Jo-Jo. Her daughter cringed back. 'You're the only person I can trust. I'm going to tell you a story about something that happened here years ago. I know who tried to kill me. Who took the stuff in the deposit box and tonight you're going help me make sure that they pay with their lives. In the meantime I want you to get Daisy and Ricky back here.'

Forty-eight

Daisy was late. A good fifteen minutes late. She parked the car on a side street and then legged it to her apartment.

'Ricky,' she called as she advanced into the hallway of her home. No answer. She called out again. No come back. Cautiously she headed for the main room. The door was partway open. She used the tip of her trainer to push it wider. Hesitated for a nano second. Then shoved herself inside the room. No one inside. Where the heck was he? As her gaze danced around the room in confusion she heard a sound. Froze. A noise, ever so quiet, coming from her bedroom. She eased on tiptoes out of the room as she pulled the gun from the back of her tracksuit bottoms. One slow, careful step at a time she made her way towards the closed bedroom door. The sound came again. She shoved her head to the side, pushing her right ear forward trying to identify what it was. But she couldn't. She stretched the gun outward, in a two-handed hold, on a level with her chest as she eased forward. Her teeth twisted into her bottom lip. Her finger curved around the trigger. She stopped moving when she faced the door. Dropped one hand from the gun. Pulled the gun back as her other hand inched forward. Her hand touched the round handle. Curved around it. With a force she flung the door open. Rushed inside.

'Ricky,' she screamed as her gun dropped to her side.

She rushed over to her bed, where a glazed-eyed, sweating Ricky moaned, sprawled on his back. His eyes shone with the same intensity as the sweat shining on his forehead. She wasn't even sure that he was aware she was there. Her palm lightly touched his forehead. Shit, he was burning up.

'Ricky?' She placed her face closer to his. 'Can you hear me?'

He let out a laboured breath. 'You're going to have to take it out,' he croaked.

She leant closer. 'What?'

'The bullet.'

Her confusion deepened. 'What bullet?'

'The one that's taken up squatter's rights in my arm.'

Her gaze skidded to his arm. 'You said that the bullet had gone right through.'

'I lied.' He took in a sharp edge of air. 'You're going to have to take it out.'

Her gaze skidded to his face. He couldn't have just asked her to? No . . . he didn't mean. She looked back at his arm. 'That's it.' She shot to her feet. She shoved her hand in her pocket. Whipped out her phone. 'We're getting you to the nearest hospital.'

'You can't,' he croaked.

'Ricky,' she yelled, cutting over him. 'You've got to forget about your sister and think of yourself.'

'Don't do this to me. Please . . . Please.' His voice got fainter. 'Please.'

'Be serious.' She ran her hand over her face. 'I'm not Florence Nightingale, you know.' But there was no answer, only the laboured rise and fall of his breathing. How the hell did you take out a bullet? She wasn't going to be able to do this on her own. She stepped back from the bed as she shoved her mobile back into her pocket. Pushed her hand into her back pocket, just above the gun. Pulled out her bottle of pills. She opened it and peered inside. Three left.

She tipped the bottle over her mouth. A pill slid inside her mouth. She swallowed dry. Closed her eyes and waited. She reopened them a couple of minutes later, but no Frankie. She snapped her eyes shut again. Gave it another two minutes. Reopened them. Still no Frankie.

'Where the bloody hell are you, Dad?'

Ricky groaned. Shit, she knew she didn't have time to try and conjure up Frankie Sullivan. She was on her own. She'd have to do this herself.

How the hell was she going to find out how you took out a bullet from a body? It wasn't like she could phone NHS Direct and ask someone. She wiped her hand over her mouth. She looked down at Ricky then began pacing. Suddenly her hand dove into her pocket and pulled out her phone. Quickly she pressed the Internet icon. Activated Google. Typed in 'Taking out a bullet'. She blew out a huge sigh of relief when she saw that there were a number of sites with advice. She checked the first three and the advice was the same – if you weren't able to get to a hospital and the wound wasn't too bad and bleeding too much it might be more safe to leave the bullet in as it might be stopping the bleeding.

She rushed over to Ricky and gingerly moved his arm. He let out another groan. She looked at the wound. It didn't look that bad, but it was bleeding slightly. She checked back with the website for advice about stopping the bleeding.

'Right, got it,' she said as she nodded.

Gently she lifted Ricky's arm

'Sorry,' she whispered as he let out a long, agonised groan. She held the arm up with one hand and pushed her fingers into the pressure points in his armpit. And pressed. She held the position for a few minutes. Then inspected the wound. The bleeding had stopped. A tiny smile flittered across her lips.

'What are *you* doing?' another voice slammed into the room.

Daisy dropped Ricky's arm as she sprang to her feet.

Forty-nine

Like someone who had been found with their hand in the cookie jar Daisy stared at a shocked Jerome, who stood half in, half out, of the doorway. She was in trouble big-time now. But then that had been the story of her life lately.

Before she could respond he stepped fully into the room and waved his hand towards the bed. 'What is that man doing in your bed?' Jerome moved closer. 'Is that blood?'

'Help me bandage his arm and I'll answer all your questions after.'

He stood there for a few seconds looking from Ricky to her and back again. In the tense silence that covered the room she could almost hear his brain ticking away.

'OK,' he finally said. He carried on, his tone professional Jerome standing in front of a judge. 'Get that other pillowcase and tear it until you have a strip' As she followed his instruction he moved to Ricky. Took hold of his arm. Ricky was out cold. Without speaking Daisy bound Ricky's arm with the material. As soon as she completed the task Jerome said, 'Now you need to tell me why a man with a bullet wound has taken up residence with the woman I was planning to marry.'

Daisy pulled in a deep breath as her body went rigid on the bed. She was tired of lying. So she told him the truth, everything except the part about Frankie Sullivan being her old man. Jerome didn't display any emotion as she told her tale. Finally her voice stopped.

'Why didn't you come to me?' She couldn't meet his troubled gaze. She knew the time was right to tell him the whole truth.

Without raising her head she whispered, 'There's something else I've got to tell you . . .'

But she didn't finish because he cut in with the force of a knife, 'That you're the daughter of the deceased criminal Frankie Sullivan?'

Her head flicked up as her mouth flipped open.

'How did you know?'

Daisy's shocked question settled between them as they sat opposite each other at the dining table on the balcony that overlooked the river. The night air was cold with a real bite swirling in it. The video box with the evidence from the deposit box lay by Daisy's feet.

Jerome shoved his fingers through his hair. 'Charlie told me. He knew I was serious about you and I suppose his way of testing my devotion was to see how I'd react when he told me the truth.'

'I would've told you . . .' rushed out of her.

He grabbed her hand. Held on tight. 'I don't care about your family tree. I don't care that your adoptive mum and aunts might not be the first choice of people my parents put on their dinner party invitation list. I don't care that Jackie Jarvis's husband was once a drug dealer. Don't care that you've got a surrogate aunt-cum-drag queen called Misty McKenzie. In fact, I really like the ladies.'

An astonished expression swept her face. 'What do you mean, *like*?'

'I contacted them and they invited me around for tea one day. They're very nice people. I even went to see Miss Misty at her club on the day Angel died, after I left you sleeping at your place just to reassure her you were OK. They care about you. Just like I do.' He took her other hand in his and gave her a tender look. 'What you need to ask yourself is do you care about me?'

She tightened her grip on him as if she was terrified that if she let him go she might not ever see him again. 'You know I do.' A nervous smile rippled across her lips.

But he didn't return her smile. 'Do you love him?' Her palms stiffened in his hands. She hadn't been expecting that question. Before she could speak he rushed on. 'And please don't insult my intelligence by saying you love me in a different way. I saw you with him in a café in Soho.' She gasped at that.

'I was going to give you this.' He pushed his hand in the top pocket of his tailored jacket. Grabbed her hand and placed a beautiful sapphire ring into it. 'An engagement ring . . .'

'Sorry to break up the tender reunion, folks.' They both looked up to find a pinched-lipped Ricky standing in the doorway. His face had lost its glowing brown sheen and he held onto the door as if he was afraid to let go in case he toppled over. He stepped slowly outside, the ragged pattern of his hard breathing shooting into the wind. 'But this is going to have to wait because me and Daisy have got things to do.'

The two men stared at each other like knights about to do battle for the lady of the castle's hand. Daisy shoved Jerome's ring into her pocket.

'Daisy has told me everything, Detective Smart,' Jerome finally said. 'I strongly disagree with what both of you are doing.' Ricky let out a huff, but Jerome ignored him and carried on. 'But I might be able to help.' He turned to Daisy. 'You said you've got a photograph . . . ?'

Ricky leant heavily against the table. 'I don't think so, mate. The picture was taken when you were most probably still on nanny's knee in nappies.'

Jerome ignored Ricky's insult and held out his hand to Daisy. She looked up at Ricky. Finally he nodded. She pulled the photo out of her bag and passed it to Jerome. As soon as he saw it he sucked in his breath. 'I don't believe this.'

'You know who this is, don't you?' Daisy said excited, leaning across the table.

'Of course I do. I've been looking for him long enough, including jetting off to Spain. It's Maxwell Henley.'

'Who the fuck is Maxwell Henley?' Ricky flung out.

They all looked at the photo of the man as they sat around the table.

'I'm leading on a class-action case. A lawsuit, where five adults are suing Woodbridge council for abuse, including sexual, that happened to them while they were in the care of the council. One of the claimants is a member of the band Electric Star, which has guaranteed us lots of much needed media attention. Maxwell Henley was the leader of the council at that time and we suspect that he was involved in these abuses first hand.'

'So why haven't you got him?'

'Because he disappeared years ago. I heard he was in Spain, so I managed to find out where his villa was but he wasn't in residence. The woman who lives there claimed to know nothing about him.'

'And did you believe her?'

'That doesn't matter, what matters is she wasn't going to tell me if she knew anyway.' He looked back at the picture. 'Why is it torn?'

'We think that the man in the other half of the picture is Stevie King, the long dead husband of my mum, Stella.'

Ricky leant back in his chair, a thoughtful expression crinkling the skin around his eyes. 'So why would the leader of a council have connections with a big time hood like Stevie King? And what has this got to do with the disappearance of your sister?'

They all gazed hard at the photo that lay between them.

'There is one person I could ask.' Daisy and Ricky's gazes settled expectantly on Jerome as he spoke. 'She's been helping us with the case because she's a leading authority on child abuse. And lucky for us she knew Maxwell Henley. Barbara Benton.'

'But I have already . . .' sprang from Daisy's mouth. She shut it when she realised she'd have to confess to Ricky that she'd spoken to the commissioner elect of the Met police earlier that night.

Ricky peered hard at her. 'Don't hold out on us, babe.'

Resigned Daisy sank back into her chair. 'Barbara Benton. She's the person I went to see earlier to see if she could identify who was in the picture. She said she didn't know who it was.'

'You did what?' Ricky half erupted from the chair.

'Hold on a minute.' Jerome half rose in defence of Daisy.

Ricky flashed him a look of complete rage. 'Sit down, posh boy. This is between me and my partner here.'

The tension sizzled as both men remained frozen in their poses. Finally Jerome retook his seat, pushing his hand through his hair, settling every strand back into place.

'I met her at Charlie's funeral.' With a twist of his mouth Ricky eased back down as she carried on speaking. 'She gave me her card and said if I ever needed any help . . .' She waved her hand in the air when Ricky opened his mouth. 'I know it might seem to be a stupid move, but she might have known who he was. It was a chance I had to take.'

Ricky cursed furiously.

Jerome locked his fingers together across the table. 'You're both missing the big question here.'

'Which is?' Ricky responded sarcastically.

'I've already told you that Barbara knows who Maxwell Henley is. The big question is surely why she told Daisy she didn't recognise him?'

'No way.' Ricky shook his head after a pause. 'She's as straight as they come.'

Jerome leant across the table unlocking his fingers, 'I'm not suggesting for a minute . . .'

But his words stopped when Ricky's phone went off. He pulled it from his pocket as he stood up. He wandered over to the window. 'Bert, what have you got for me?'

'I couldn't find any DNA evidence. I suspect whoever used this wiped it clean. But I can tell you that it was last fired quite a long time ago.'

'Twenty years?'

'Maybe. I can't be that precise.'

'Thanks, mate.' Ricky winced as his arm began to ache. 'I need to get the gun back.'

'Ah.' Bert coughed. 'Now that is going to be a slight problem.'

'What are you talking about?'

'I don't have it. My boss demanded that I hand it over because one of the top brass wanted it.'

'Who?'

'I don't know.'

* * *

'I told you not to tell anyone about what we'd found – including the friggin' gun.'

Ricky railed at Daisy as they moved in the dark night towards the car, parked on the street around the corner from Daisy's home. 'You might as well have taken out a billboard ad.'

Daisy's long strides kept pace with Ricky's as she blasted back. 'Jerome has already said he isn't going to blab to anyone yet and you yourself said that Barbara is as straight as they come.'

'But she's the main man at the Met for Christ sake.'

'Maybe it wasn't her who requested the gun from your friend. It might be someone else.'

'Like who? The ghost of Dixon of Dock Green?'

Shaking, Daisy hunted in her pocket for her bottle of pills. She stopped as she undid the lid. Peered inside. Two left. As she tipped the mouth of the bottle into her hand she let out a loud 'ouch' when she felt fingers dig into her arm. She looked up to find Ricky gazing at her with his furious black eyes. 'You ain't still taking none of that shit? For Christ's sake, you might be pregnant.'

Thinking of carrying his kid made her feel giddy. She tried to wrench her arm away but he held on tight. 'I'm a fucking wreck, alright,' she yelled. 'I just need to calm down.'

He swiped the bottle out of her hand. 'That ain't going to help you.'

She trembled as she lunged at the bottle in his hand. But he pulled his arm back. 'Please Ricky, you don't understand . . .'

'When my sister disappeared, you know what I started to do? Drink. Bloody thirteen years old and I saw more of my local offy than I did of my school. And do you know why my life went bottle-shaped? Because I started seeing my sister.' Daisy stopped moving. 'She'd come to me as beautiful as the last time I saw her, talking to me, comforting me, telling me she was alright. Is that what's been happening to you? Every time you popped one of these?' He shook the bottle, the single pill making a dull rattle against the plastic. 'You get all happy and start seeing your old man?'

Quickly she averted her gaze, but he went in for the kill. 'I'm right, ain't I? He appears with a puff of smoke. As long as you've got the tabs you don't have to say goodbye to your dad.'

The truth of his words infuriated her. 'You're wrong,' she slammed out as she leapt towards the bottle in his hand. He danced out of the way, making her stagger into thin air. He started to speak – although to her rage-filled mind it sound like nasty taunting – as she righted herself. 'That stuff fucks up your mind.' She leapt, he moved. 'The first night I went undercover in Belmarsh, they stuck me in a cell with this deadbeat who was taking some heavy duty shit.' They did their antagonistic dance again. 'Every night he starts chatting away to Britney Spears, thinking she's in front of him, telling her to hit me baby one more time with her dominatrix whip.'

Daisy twisted her mouth. Right, she'd had enough of this. She lashed out with a powerful front kick and caught him dead centre in the balls. God knew what they must look like to anyone passing on the street, and for two people who were meant to be trying not to attract any attention they were doing a damn poor job of it. A loud whoosh erupted from Ricky's body as he fell to his knees. But he didn't let go of the bottle. She dived for it. He leant backwards. She landed on top of him pushing his weight backwards. He hit the ground, still in pain, and howled louder as she caught his wounded arm. But he was determined to hang onto his prize. He clasped his arms around her waist and rolled her onto her back. She kept the motion going and reversed their positions. Ricky yelped from the pain in his arm as they rolled like two kids slugging it out in the playground. Out of nowhere two beams of strong, white light hit them. Quickly Ricky glanced over her shoulder.

'Bollocks,' he shouted, his eyes going wide. She turned and saw what he was watching. The headlights of a black car headed towards them on the pavement. The wheels got larger as the car got closer. Desperately they untangled from each other's arms. The car wasn't stopping. Ricky rolled to the right. She rolled to the left. But the video box up her top made her roll awkwardly. The car clipped her leg as it roared past. She let out a screech of high pain. And that was the last thing she remembered.

Fifty

Dazed and in pain Daisy slowly woke up. She sucked in a harsh breath as a sharp pain stabbed her in the leg. The position of her body told her that she was lying down. Where she was she didn't know because her eyes were covered with a film of bleariness that obscured her vision.

'Easy,' a soothing voice above said. She rapidly blinked, flicking the bleariness away. Her vision cleared. The first thing she saw was a high, white ceiling with a huge chandelier decorated with what looked like crystal tear drops and with a light that made her blink some more. Where the hell was she? Then she remembered the car and the impact. Desperately, she used her hands to try to sit up. But someone else's hands got there first and gently pushed her back down. She twisted her head to the side and let out a sigh of pure relief when she saw who it was. Ricky.

He gave her a small smile, but the rest of him didn't look so good. His brown skin was unnaturally pale and his expressive black eyes were so filled with concern she thought someone had died.

He took her hand in his. 'Hey, how's my little kick-boxer feeling?'

'Like she's been run over by a herd of elephants.' Her voice was weak from both tiredness and pain.

They both smiled at each other as he squeezed her hand. 'Did someone try to kill us?' she asked.

'It's either that or you've got more than one jealous boyfriend who ain't too pleased about you running around town with me.'

Before they could say anymore Daisy heard the sound of a door opening. Someone else came into the room. Daisy lifted her head to look and when she saw who it was she froze.

Barbara Benton, kitted out in top brass police regalia, moved towards them. Daisy turned questioning eyes to Ricky and said, 'I don't understand?'

'Welcome to my home, Daisy,' the commissioner-elect replied as she perched at the other end of the couch.

Daisy rustled upright, wincing with pain. She looked from Ricky to Barbara. And back again.

'I never did tell you how I became a cop,' Ricky started. 'Some nosey woman helped me out of the gutter, saw my potential and mentored me.' He gazed at Barbara with a huge glint of respect and affection in his dark eyes.

The other woman picked up the story as she sent him a fond smile. 'I busted him on a marijuana charge, nothing major, just personal use, but the way he tried to dodge my questions made me realise that he had a savvy brain. And he knew the streets of London like the back of his hand. I told him if he started working for us he could do some good and make something of himself and he did. Eventually, he proved to be so good we made his membership of the service formal and overlooked all his very unfortunate and very long list of offences. You have to bend the rules sometimes, as I'm sure you know. Although whether we were meant to bend them that far I'm not so sure.'

Ricky's smile broadened. 'And on those long nights on my bunk in E-Wing, I sometimes thought I was better off smashed.'

Barbara pinned Daisy with her keen gaze. 'What matters Daisy is that Ricky trusts me enough to bring you here . . .'

'But it must have been you who took the gun,' Daisy slammed back despite the pain. 'You were the only other person who knew about it.'

'I hold my hands up. Of course it was me.' Her voice became stern. 'Tonight I'm going to be given the job of looking after the welfare of this city. As soon as you said the word gun and I suspected that it was in police custody there was no way I was going to let it back onto the street.' She raised her eyebrow at Daisy. 'I don't know if you realise but we have a firearms problem in this city.' She swiftly shifted her gaze to Ricky. 'Don't we, Detective Smart?'

'Barbara, you know I can't let this go. You of all people know how much my sister meant to me.'

'Ricky, you went undercover to do a job and you've done it. The Kings are out of action for good. Someone out there is trying to put you out of action for good as well. So why don't you now hand in all the other evidence that you've got? That.' She pointed to the video box on the floor between Ricky and Daisy. 'I take it has the contents of Charlie Hopkirk's safe-deposit box. Let the police deal with it.'

'I can't do that.'

'I'm your commanding officer and I'm *commanding* you to follow a direct order, Detective Ricardo Smart.'

They glared at each other, the younger cop's passion and defiance openly clashing with the powerhouse superiority of the Met's highest-ranking female officer. Barbara was the first to back down. 'I haven't got much time because I need to be at City Hall. This isn't finished, Ricky.' She stomped towards the door and left the room.

As soon as the door closed, Ricky pressed his finger to his lips, warning Daisy to be quiet. Silently he crept towards the door. Moved along the wide hallway towards the kitchen with the knowledge of someone who knew the house like his own name was on the mortgage papers. He found the kitchen at the far end tucked away in the right hand corner. As he leant against the wall outside he heard her voice. He didn't register what she was saying because he was too stunned that she was on the phone. The call might be innocent, but then again it might not. He wasn't taking any chances that she was on the blower to his superior.

Without saying a word Ricky carefully, but firmly, pulled Daisy up from the sofa, grasping both her hands with his and rocking backwards. She let out a yelp of pain as she stood on her injured leg. She almost collapsed on the floor. Ricky moved his hands to her waist, supporting her.

'You need to keep moving,' Ricky commanded as his gaze swung towards the window.

'What's going on?' Daisy leant on her good side, taking the pressure off her right leg.

'We need to get out of here now.' The expression on his face told her that it wasn't time for explanations.

He dropped her arm as he reached the long, draped curtains. Tore them back. Stared at the twin high windows. Reached for one of the handles but it wouldn't budge.

'I don't have time to pick the lock.' A swaying Daisy watched as he bolted for the couch she had recently vacated. Picked up an ornately patterned, mauve cushion and headed past a confused Daisy straight towards the windows. He pushed the cushion against the right window and raised his free arm. Fisted his hand as he swung his arm back and landed an almighty punch against the cushion. The window cracked, shooting shards of glass onto the immaculately maintained lawn outside. He moved the cushion back revealing a jagged, gaping hole. He pushed the cushion against the remaining glass making big chunks of glass fall outside.

Suddenly Daisy swung towards the door. 'I think she's coming.'

Without saying a word Ricky rushed to the left side of the room and grabbed a turquoise-and-white striped high-backed chair and ran with it towards the broken window. Positioned it underneath. Daisy didn't need to be told what to do. She leapt up, sucking her breath in as hot pain knifed her left side. Then she remembered the video box on the floor, with the contents of the deposit box.

She twisted her head at Ricky and said, '*Calamity Jane.*'

He swore and dashed across the room. She turned back around and gritted her teeth against the pain as she gripped the window frame and pushed herself through. Still hanging on she dropped to the ground. Her right leg gave way and she landed in a heap on the damp, cold grass.

'Ricky,' she heard Barbara roar inside as she started to pick herself up.

Daisy ducked and rocked when Ricky's body came spring boarding outside. He landed in a crouch position a few feet ahead of Daisy, video box clutched tight against his chest.

'We need to run,' he called to her.

'I can't.' She wobbled. 'My leg.'

He shot towards her. Gathered his arms around her. For the second time that day he lifted her, pain blasting through his arms and bolted down the dark street.

'I'm going to have to cut you loose, partner.'

Daisy stared with astonishment at Ricky as he inspected her hip and leg in the car. She lay prone in the backseat, the video box hidden under her tracksuit top as his gaze swept the bruise on her side. It was large, leaving her skin a remarkable marbled shade of purple entwined with black. Nothing was broken, but it still hurt like her first day in the fires of hell.

'What do you mean?' Her blue eyes blazed. She knew exactly what he meant, but he was going to have to explain it to her, straight to her face.

'This is the end of the road for you.'

She was furious. 'Now you've seen the contents of the deposit box you don't need me anymore. We had a deal. Someone tried to kill us less than an hour ago. Plus you're in no state to defend yourself.'

Before he could respond Daisy's mobile went off. Angrily she whipped it out.

'What?' she yelled with impatience.

'It's Jo-Jo.' Daisy's eyes swung to Ricky. She mouthed Jo-Jo's name to him.

'I'm really scared,' the younger woman said. 'I've got some information about some stuff that happened twenty years ago.'

'What? Tell me what you know.'

Ricky mouthed 'What?' to her, but she ignored him.

'Meet me at a lock-up that belonged to my dad. It's in Bethnal Green.' Jo-Jo gave Daisy the address and cut the call.

'What did she say?'

'That she's got information about what happened twenty years ago.' His body went rigid as his intense breathing filled the car and she knew he was thinking about his sister. She told him where Jo-Jo wanted to meet them.

'Come on, we need to turn the car around,' Daisy said urgently.

But he didn't follow her instructions. Instead he kept the car moving forward.

'What are you doing?'

But he kept his mouth closed. She peered out of the window suddenly realising where they were going. Into the heart of Wapping, where she lived.

'You can't take me home,' she pleaded.

He continued to ignore her as he swung the car into Wapping High Street. The car bumped along the cobbled road. Her mouth opened in surprise as the car shot past her building. Where the hell was he taking her? He hit the Shim-Sham-Shimmy Club and suddenly she understood. A line of clubbers waited outside, their clothes ranging from outrageous flares to shirts and blouses with flyaway collars to height defying Afros. It was a retro seventies disco night.

She picked up her pleading. 'Don't do this.' Her voice rose hysterically.

He got out of the car. Rushed around to her side. Swung the door open. She held onto the armrest with both hands resisting any attempt to move her. But he hooked his arms under and with his whole might pulled her into his arms. He carried her protesting out of the car, the line of people outside the club looking on with curiosity and horror. He dumped her gently on the cold pavement.

'Sorry, babe. This might be dangerous. I don't want you to get hurt anymore.' He shot her a grim look and dashed back to the car.

She tried to get up but her injured leg made her collapse back on the ground. She hit the ground with her fist and roared after him, like a mad woman, at the disappearing car, 'Ricky Smart, you bastard.'

* * *

'How could you have done that to us?'

It was Auntie Ollie who threw the damning question. Daisy stood looking at the pissed off face of Jackie and the calmer expression of Ollie in the Shim-Sham-Shimmy Club. The happy-go-lucky singing voices of the club's punters downstairs rocking along to Gloria Gaynor's 'I Will Survive' drifted upstairs from the dance floor. One of the club's bouncers dealing with the traffic on the door had recognised Daisy as she lay outside. He'd carried her to the room on the second floor. Plonked her on the black leather sofa. She'd got up ready to do a runner, but Jackie and Ollie had barged in before she could.

Aunt Ollie was right, it was a bad thing she'd done. But she didn't have time for regrets, not with Ricky facing the situation on his own.

'We don't have time for this. I need to help Ricky.' She strode towards the door, wincing from the pain in her leg.

But Jackie grabbed her arm. 'First flamin' decent thing that bloke has done is to leave you with us.'

Daisy tried to shake the smaller woman's hand off, but Jackie held on like a Rottweiler. 'You don't understand, I think he might be walking into a set-up. He hasn't got anyone covering his back.'

'Will you listen to yourself?' Jackie snapped. 'You really are beginning to sound like Frankie Sullivan's daughter.'

A suffocating cover of silence dropped in the air. Jackie laid her fingers across her lips as if she'd said something forbidden.

Daisy dipped her head. 'That's who I am. And always will be.' Her tone was quiet and sad. Before she could continue a furious Jackie grabbed hold of her again. Her eyes resembled green fire. 'Frankie Sullivan put you in this world, but you've made your own world for yourself, you hear me?' She shook Daisy. 'I don't ever want to hear you talk about your life like it's some sorta curse. You're amazing. The best daughter anyone could ever ask for, you get me?' She shook her again. This time the *Calamity Jane* video box tumbled from under Daisy's top and nose-dived onto the floor. The impact shot it open and its contents scattered on the floor.

Ollie rushed forward the same time Daisy bent to pick up the items on the floor. Daisy picked up the torn photo as Jackie asked, 'What's that lot?'

Daisy looked up at her, biting her lip. 'The stuff in Charlie's deposit box.'

'Hold up a minute, I thought that was still in the bank.'

Shame shone in Daisy's eyes as she kept her gaze steady on her adoptive mum. 'I had them all the time.' She waved her hand as Jackie opened her mouth to deliver, no doubt, a blistering tongue-lashing. But Daisy got there first. 'I know what you're going to say. But I didn't have a choice. I don't have time to explain at the moment.'

Suddenly Jackie's harsh breathing filled the air. Her eyes were glued to the photo in Daisy's hand.

'Where did you get that from?' Jackie's face was pale.

Daisy got to her feet and moved towards Jackie with concern. 'It's a man called Maxwell Henley, who was the leader of Woodbridge Council years ago . . .'

'He's a fucking pervert, that's what he is.' Jackie's voice shook as she ran her unsteady hand over her mouth.

'Tell me,' Daisy simply asked.

Jackie and Ollie exchanged looks. Ollie nodded. Jackie spoke. 'We haven't told you much about our lives as kids and I'm grateful you never asked. But for a time me and your aunts all lived in a care home. I can't even say its name because it makes me want to throw up.' She swallowed. Daisy limped forward and placed her arm around Jackie's trembling shoulders. 'These men would come and . . . well, it never happened to us. But one of the men I saw was that geezer in the photo.'

'Are you saying that Maxwell Henley . . . ?'

'Was one of the pervs who interfered with the kids? Yes I am.'

'What's this?' Ollie interrupted standing up. She held out the brochure that was inside the video box and some papers.

Daisy turned to her, arms still protectively around Jackie. 'Not sure. I don't know why Charlie would have had a holiday brochure in his box. And the papers are just the booking forms to fill out.'

Ollie shook her head. 'No, this is the Harding Hall brochure.'

'What?' Daisy's arm fell away from Jackie.

'Harding Hall. It's a well-known residential hospital for troubled teenagers. We often use them.' Ollie ran two high-profile organisations that helped refugees and asylum seekers, especially children who arrived in Britain unaccompanied by an adult. 'They really help some of our more traumatised teenagers.'

'But what's Charlie doing with it?'

'It might help if you read this.' She passed the booking forms to Daisy.

Daisy scanned one sheet. Then another. And another. She'd read this all before. Just booking forms. Her mouth opened wider and wider when she read the next page, papers she hadn't read before. And the next. She shook her head repeatedly mumbling 'Oh no'. She shoved the paper in her pocket as she rushed, half limping, for the door.

But Jackie grabbed her arm. 'You ain't going nowhere.'

'Ricky's gone to meet Jo-Jo.'

'And so what?'

Daisy pushed the papers at her. Jackie read. 'Blimey,' she let out a minute later.

'Please help me.'

Jackie turned to Ollie and calmly asked, 'You still remember how to use one?'

'Unfortunately, yes.'

'We still got them ain't we?'

Ollie nodded. Confused, Daisy watched as Ollie headed for the fireplace. She leant down and stuck her hand up the chimney breast. With a tug she pulled something out. A blue plastic carrier bag wrapped over with two strips of black tape. She moved towards the table. Laid the bulky bag on top.

She flicked her head to Daisy, her black eyes deadly serious. 'You still want us to help you?'

Daisy nodded.

Ollie pulled the tape off the bag. Unwrapped it. Opened it. Daisy sucked in her breath as Ollie calmly laid two things on the table. Two guns.

Fifty-one

It might be a set-up. The idea stayed at the front of Ricky's mind as he gazed at the lock-up hidden in the night shadows across the street. Mind you, he couldn't imagine Jo-Jo King having the brain-power to organise one. No, he decided, she must be running scared and needed someone to help her get out of this mess, so who better to ask than her long-lost sister Daisy. Plus she was expecting Daisy to come, not him. He checked out the street. Lonely, dark, not a living soul in sight. Still, he'd give it a few more minutes, see if anyone turned up who wasn't supposed to be there.

He waited a full twenty minutes, just to be on the safe side. Deciding that Jo-Jo must already be inside he cautiously moved towards the lock-up. The door was closed. Ricky's gaze darted over the building. He pushed with his foot at the metal door and it swung open.

The light was on. The room was rectangular, with a couple of rusty barrels lying idle against a wall with graffiti and a room that might have been an office at one time tucked in a far corner. A pool of dirty water settled in a dip in the concrete floor from a leak above. But none of that interested Ricky; what interested him was he couldn't see another living soul. He hesitated for a second. Ricky's training both in the force and on the streets had taught him that if you planned to meet someone and they weren't there when you arrived smell a rat immediately. 'Jo-Jo?' His voice echoed off the metal but he got no reply.

Could something have happened to Jo-Jo? He moved inside. Pulled out his gun and headed, one easy step at a time, towards the office. He called Jo-Jo's name again. No reply. He didn't like this one bit, but he kept moving forward. Reached the entrance of the office. Suddenly all the lights flicked off.

Something grabbed the front of his shirt and he was catapulted inside the room. He landed on his back as his gun flew from his hand. Before he could right himself something hard whacked him on the right shoulder. He let out a yell as pain screamed down the arm he had a bullet wound in. A boot stamped onto his chest holding him down. The lights belted back on. Two men stood over him, one packing a piece and the other with a crowbar that had just knocked Ricky for six. The man with the gun bent over him.

'You're getting careless, mate. I'm Ray-Ray Digby, by the way.' Ricky's eyebrows shot up in surprise. 'I see you've heard the name. Must've been when you plugged a couple of caps into my brother when you went strolling with Tommy King the other day.'

Ray-Ray turned to the man with his foot still on Ricky and ordered. 'Shut the door.' As he moved Ray-Ray settled the aim of his gun on Ricky's heart.

'Are you alright, there? You don't look too clever with that gash on your shoulder.'

Ricky faced up. 'I'm alright Ray-Ray, bit of a girly swing your mate's got there, if you don't mind me saying. I've had much worse.'

'Take the piss all you like, mate. You'll be laughing on the other side of your busted face a bit later and no mistake.'

Ricky laughed at him, 'You don't think I really came on my own do you? This is going to come as a surprise to you but I'm a cop.' Shock covered the other man's face. 'You and your boyfriend over there are toast.'

Ray-Ray looked at him for a few seconds. Then shook his head. 'I don't think so. We kept our eye on the street; we would've seen the Bill if they were lurking about. Nah, I think you're suffering from concussion, mate.'

Ricky looked to the door. He was shocked at what he saw. Ray-Ray's thug was walking backwards, his arms raised, covered by two very heavily armed women with another trailing behind. Jackie, Ollie and Daisy.

'Fuck me sideways,' Ray-Ray whispered.

'You will be if you don't put the gun down now,' Daisy Sullivan ordered.

'I've told you that someone paid me a hundred Gs to fuck over you and your girlfriend. We nearly got you as well when we tried to run you down earlier,' Ray-Ray Digby shouted.

He sat bound, stark naked, as did his associate on the cold, concrete floor. Jackie and Ollie stood to the side, their guns aimed directly at the men.

'Are you alright?' Daisy asked as she cleaned Ricky's latest wound.

'Sure.' They looked at each other. Then kissed. They only moved apart when they heard Jackie muttering with disapproval.

'Who paid you?' Ricky demanded, turning his attention to the cringing Ray-Ray.

'Want me to take off one of his nuts?' Jackie asked calmly as she lowered her gun in line with one of his testicles.

'I'm telling the fucking truth!' Ray-Ray's voice was desperate as he looked at the gun. 'Some woman. Just said she wanted you both out of the way.'

'What woman?' Ricky threw back, but Ray–Ray wasn't saying anything else.

Ricky was about to ask if she knew about Stella's brother, but Daisy got there first.

'You'd better read this . . .' Daisy handed him the document they'd found in the Harding Hall brochure.

PSYCHIATRIC REPORT

Doctor: A. Mitcham
Patient: Josephine Joanne King
Age: 15

History: Has been expelled from a number of schools because of violent attacks towards other children, including biting and punching others. In one attack she stabbed another child with a sharp pencil in the face. In another she constructed an electronic device and attached it to another child's chair which sent electric shocks through them. She is very good with her hands and has a special interest in making things and is adept at finding information on the Internet to help her. She admits this is how she found out how to make an electronic system. She refuses to discuss why she behaves like this or her emotional state. The school reports that none of the other parents will press charges because of the reputation that Josephine's family has in the community.

She also has a history of self-harming.

Diagnosis: Josephine refuses to discuss her issues or the source of her issues. She appears to be a normal girl during one-to-one meetings. But when her mother is mentioned she becomes very withdrawn and sullen. It is my professional opinion that she has suffered some type of childhood trauma and uses violence to try to get her mother's attention and love. It is also my opinion that if she does not get the required help soon her violence will escalate and she may seriously hurt someone, including members of her own family.

Family response: Her mother attended the session with her. She believes that her daughter is just like any other normal teenager and refuses to see the seriousness of the situation. She has dismissed my findings as 'social worker crap' and 'psycho-babble'. I have explained the urgency of her daughter's issues to her mother, but her mother refuses to consider any further support, medical or otherwise.

It is my opinion that if her mother does not do anything to address this situation, one day Josephine may resort to psychotic behaviour of an extremely violent nature, without warning, that may seriously injure people around her, including herself.

Further Treatment: She should be admitted immediately to
the centre for treatment. Her mother refuses to do this or
to admit her to another care facility.

'No way,' Ricky let out as he glanced at Daisy. 'Do you think . . . ?'

'She planted that car bomb?' Daisy finished. 'Yes. And God
knows who else she'll kill before this night's over. And it looks
like she's already tried to pay that scumbag over there to kill both
of us.'

'We need to stop her now.'

'Oi,' Jackie said. 'What are we going to do with these two likely
lads?'

Ricky pulled out his mobile and punched in a number. 'Sir,
it's me. I've got two blokes for you, you'll want to chat to them
about going around assaulting people.' He gave his superior
officer the address. 'I'm on the case with the other business . . .'
he continued.

'Clarke's dead,' the voice on the other end of the line informed
him.

Ricky took an involuntary step back. 'What?'

'I've heard it's suicide, but there's nothing official. You need to
tell me what's going on.'

'When I know myself I'll let you know.' And with that Ricky cut
the call.

He immediately turned back to Daisy. 'We need to find Jo-Jo
before she does anything else.'

They ran towards the exit.

'What about us?' Jackie called.

But neither Ricky or Daisy replied as they belted out of the lock-
up, Daisy limping as fast as she could on her bad leg.

Jackie flew after them, but Ollie's hand held her back.

'What you doing?' Jackie stormed at her mate.

'They need to do this on their own.'

'Are you mental or something?'

Ollie's hand dropped away. 'Can't you see that they fancy the
pants off each other? He'll make sure that nothing happens to her.'

Jackie pursed her lips, but didn't head for the door.

'As soon as we hear the police coming,' Ollie said, 'we get out of here as quickly as possible. If they catch us with these weapons we'll have a lot of explaining to do.'

Fifty-two

Jo-Jo hummed as she entered her mum's office. Her cheerful mood disappeared when she saw what her mum was doing. Back watching clips from *Calamity Jane*. Doris Day and Howard Keel, walking arm-in-arm, got into a stagecoach with a large banner that read 'JUST HITCHED'. Stella's husky voice filled the room as she sang along with Calamity Jane and Wild Bill Hickock singing 'The Deadwood Stage'. Jo-Jo didn't know what was happening to her mum, but she was acting like some of the people in that facility they'd put her in temporarily when she'd been a teenager. The one her mother had told her, 'It's them doctors that want treatment, love, not you'. Her mum's empire was falling around her ears and all she wanted to do was watch the same film, over and over.

Then she saw the gun that her mum fingered in her lap. A pistol with a silencer screwed on the front. 'Are Daisy and Ricky here?' Stella suddenly asked.

'No, Mum.'

Stella reared to her feet as she roared, 'What do you mean they ain't coming?' She waved the gun in the air.

Jo-Jo looked at the gun as a lump formed in her throat. Telling her mum bad news when she had a shooter in her hand was not a good move. And the bandaged half of her face added one hundred per cent to her dangerous look.

'I got it all sorted out.' Jo-Jo stepped closer to her mum. 'Don't worry, they're getting what's coming to them.'

'What are you chatting on about?'

Jo-Jo took her mum's arm and gently led her back to the sofa. She plonked herself down beside Stella. 'I got some mates to take care of them. They ain't going to be troubling you anymore. You won't believe it, but Billy gave me a hundred grand the other day to sod off, but I kept the money, Mum, to help you.'

'I told you to bring their arses here.'

'I know. But I took care of it. You just need to rest.' Jo-Jo smiled. 'I'm going to take care of you like I always do. You don't need anyone but me.' Her smile grew. 'They're all gone. It's just me and you like it should be—'

Stella's hand whipped out, grabbing Jo-Jo's shoulder and dragging her forward. Jo-Jo's smile shot off her face as she stared into her mum's menacing, steel gaze. 'It was you, wasn't it?' Stella's voice was soft.

'What?' Jo-Jo tried to get out of her mum's grip but couldn't.

'You planted that bomb in the car.'

Jo-Jo tried to desperately wriggle free as her frantic words filled the room. 'No, Mum. It weren't—'

Stella's mouth twisted. 'Don't fucking lie to me. That's why you wanted me to get into the second getaway car with you. To make sure I was safe, while the bomb got rid of everyone else. That way you've got Mummy all to yourself.'

'But none of them deserved your love, not like me,' Jo-Jo confessed, shouting, her words pumped with years of pent-up emotions. 'You kicked me out and gave it all to them instead. It was me you should have been loving, not them, they're scum and they always were but you couldn't see it.' Tears streamed down her face. 'Look what you made me do.' She reached for her trousers and rolled them up. Stella gasped as she saw the mass of criss-cross scars. 'You're *my* mum, mine. You should have put my name on the door not hers.' Jo-Jo shook as she cried.

A stunned Stella continued to gaze at her daughter's body. Shit, what a mess.

'That doctor was right,' Stella finally said. 'When you were little. You're bloody mental. I should've had you locked up in that nut house . . .'

Suddenly Jo-Jo flicked her face dead straight into her mum's face. Stella jumped back at the sudden rage in Jo-Jo's eyes. 'No, it weren't me that was bonkers, it was the babysitter. She'd bring blokes around. They'd take me and Tommy into the bedroom. Make us take our clothes off. Lie on the bed . . . I wanted to tell you years ago . . .'

'No!' Stella screamed.

Stella's arms flew out. Jo-Jo leant forward to fall into the embrace from her mum she'd waited years for. But instead Stella's hands circled her neck. Jo-Jo's disbelieving eyes bulged as her mum's hands tightened. Jo-Jo's nails dug into her mum's arms. She fought, but Stella's hold grew stronger. Stella slammed her youngest child into the sofa. She leant over. Increased the pressure. Doris Day's piercing voice burst into the room singing about the joys of the Deadwood Stage. Stella pushed down harder. Jo-Jo's eyes bulged as the tiny blood vessels in them burst. Her tongue lolled out of her mouth. Doris Day's voice pulsed higher. Jo-Jo's arms flopped by her side. Her scarred legs lay at an awkward angle. Her eyes stared lifeless at the person she'd loved most in the world.

Stella's shaking hands peeled away from her daughter's neck. She leant down and grabbed Jo-Jo's legs and held onto them as she moved back to her spot on the sofa. Gently she placed her daughter's feet in her lap as if Jo-Jo was having a nap. She twisted to face the telly. Looked at Doris Day as she cracked a whip atop the Deadwood Stage. Cried like she hadn't since she was fourteen years old.

Ricky and Daisy got to the brothel in record time. As they jumped out of the car Ricky didn't hear his phone ping. Didn't read the urgent text message from his superior officer:

```
Found out Stella King has/had an older brother.
Be careful
```

The woman on the flight from Spain got out of Gatwick's terminal at exactly 8.47 p.m. She still wore her sunglasses even though darkness greeted her outside. She didn't carry much, only a small overnight bag. She walked over to the taxi rank. Peered inside the black cab.

'Where to, love?' the cabbie asked.

She thought for a minute. Thought about going to Finsbury Park. No, she wasn't going to do that. Instead she answered, 'City Hall.'

Deadwood Hotel was dark. They crept towards the front door. Daisy didn't speak as Ricky took out his tweezers to unpick the lock. He worked quickly and silently. Click. The lock gave way. Ricky drew his gun. Hesitated. Then pushed the door. He twisted his head to Daisy. Nodded. Twisted back. Shoved the door wider. Eased inside. The hallway was empty, and surprisingly cool for a summer's night.

'Check the first room,' Ricky whispered, gun high and pointed forward. 'And I'll do the rest down here. Don't forget: Jo-Jo is dangerous.'

Daisy gave him a single nod. He left her, swiftly moving on his toes ahead. She pushed the door of the Meet 'n' Greet room. She held back as the door swung open revealing the room. Semi-dark, curtains drawn, no one in sight. Stepped cautiously inside. The room looked like she'd seen it before, all prepared and ready for the next group of men who would choose their woman for the night. Then she noticed a difference. A shovel leant up against the piano. A chill went through her as her gaze settled on the piano, just like it had done the one and only time she'd been in here before.

'Daisy, up here quick.'

Hearing the urgency in Ricky's voice she left the room and shot up the stairs. Reached Stella's office. She found Ricky inside gazing at the sofa. Gazing at the dead body of Jo-Jo King.

'Well, well, well. If it ain't the dynamic duo.'

Both of them looked around to find Stella standing in the doorway of one of the adjoining rooms. They gasped when they saw her. Saw the bloody bandage across her face. She held a revolver pointed straight at Daisy. Ricky automatically raised his gun.

'Put it down or Daisy's dead.'

Fifty-three

Ricky wavered for a second. Then dropped the gun. It clattered on the floor. 'Kick it towards me,' Stella ordered as she moved a few inches into the room.

He did what she said. She ignored the gun as she came further into the room. 'Don't worry about my Jo-Jo, she's just having a lie down.'

There was a strange glint in her wild, grey eyes that made Daisy think that Stella really believed what she'd said. She knew they were dealing with a Stella they had never seen before.

'Just having a little chat with Frankie.' They could see the photos of Stella and Frankie on the wall behind her in the small room. 'Thought I was a goner, didn't you?' she taunted them. 'You can't get rid of Stella King that easily.'

'What happened to my sister twenty years ago?'

Stella gave him a baffled look. 'Your sister? Got the wrong lady. I've never met your sister in my life.'

'Jenna Smart.' Stella sucked in her breath. 'I'm her younger brother.'

'Ricardo, of course . . .' Stella let out softly. 'Jenna used to chat about you. How her brother was going to be somebody one day . . .'

'And she was right,' he cut in. 'I'm Detective Ricardo Smart, so why don't you give me the gun because my colleagues will be here soon.'

'Colleagues.' Stella rolled her eyes. 'Oooh, get you. Jenna's little brother chatting all smart.' Then she laughed. 'Smart. Get it?'

Neither Daisy or Ricky responded. 'Don't play me for a complete tit,' she said. 'If the cops were coming they'd be here already. No, it's just us.' She slammed her gaze directly onto Daisy. 'Get moving and open the door. And, lover boy, you follow her.'

'Where we going?' he asked, his body going rigid.

'Thought you wanted to find out what happened to your darling big sister?' She waved the gun at them. 'Downstairs.'

Ricky was the first to move. Daisy cautiously followed him. They reached the top of the stairs. Halted when they heard Stella say, 'And no funny business or Daisy lands at the bottom of the stairs minus a head.'

She kept pace with them as they took the stairs. Reached the darkened hallway. Stood outside the Meet 'n' Greet room.

They entered the room that Daisy had left minutes earlier.

'Turn around,' Stella ordered once they were deep inside the room. They did what she asked. The blood on the bandage on Stella's face had deepened and spread.

'Mum, you need medical attention . . .' Daisy began.

'Mum?' Stella looked at her and laughed. The laughter soon fell away from her lips. 'Why don't you come over here and keep Mum company.'

It wasn't a question. Daisy kept her eyes nervously on the gun as she stepped forward. Stella's arm snaked out and grabbed Daisy around the waist and pulled her into her body. Cool metal touched Daisy's temple. The gun was on the side of her head. Daisy knew it would be easy to end this now. All she had to do was a quick three-step movement – jab Stella in the middle with her elbow, grab her gun arm and flip her over. But she didn't. Didn't because then Ricky might never find out what happened to his sister.

Before Daisy could continue to turn her decision over in her head, Stella ordered Ricky, 'Move the piano.'

Ricky moved across the room. Looked for a few seconds at the large piano. Then began to move it. It shifted easily on its wheels. He shoved it with all his might halfway across the room, up against a wall. He straightened and looked back at Stella. 'Go back to where the piano was and remove the floorboards.' He caught Daisy's fretful blue eyes. Looked away and moved back to the other side of the room. He crouched down and looked at the floorboards. Then he noticed that one had a little hole in it at the top. He slipped two fingers inside and pulled it up. It moved with surprising ease. He flung the plank of wood to the side. After that it was easy to remove the next one. The third. The fourth. The fifth.

'That's enough. You've saved me a job, see, I was getting ready to do this myself when you two arrived. I should've done it years ago. You're going to be needing that.' He followed her gaze to the shovel against the wall.

'What do you want me to do?' The agonised expression on Ricky's face told that he already knew the answer.

She pressed the gun deeper into Daisy's skin. 'Start digging.'

Now she knew that what happened twenty years ago led to a hole in the ground Daisy made her move. With lightning speed she slammed her elbow back. But Stella was ready for her. The older woman heaved her body back, never removing the gun from Daisy's flesh. Daisy sucked in her breath and froze. Ricky froze too.

Stella's snarled words tore through the tense air. 'I know all the tricks of the trade, darlin'. Frankie teach you how to drop kick the world with your hands tied behind your back?' Daisy didn't answer. She didn't dare with that gun at her head. 'Well, he taught me as well. Punters stopped trying to do me over in those early days on the street. Try that shit again and you won't be around to try any more moves.' She looked across at Ricky. 'Now dig.'

Ricky did what he was told for the next ten minutes. Sweat rolled down his face, not just from the hard work and the radiating pain in his arm, but also in anticipation that he might finally find out what had happened to Jenna. His heart slammed each time he pushed into the dirt knowing that he might be seeing the remains of his sister any second now. Suddenly the shovel hit something hard. He held the shovel back as he crouched down and used one hand to wipe the dirt back. He reared back when he saw the top of a metal box, of a similar size to a coffin. He opened the lid and coughed as dirt swam into his face. He looked down to see an assortment of bones, including a skull and ragged bits of decaying cloth. 'Jenna,' he wanted to cry out. Then he saw it. Something small, metal and round. He leant forward and picked it up. A ring.

Ricky stood up holding the ring. 'This didn't belong to my sister.'

''Course it don't, you tosser. That was just a little joke of mine.'

Ricky stepped closer. Daisy kept her eyes on the ring. She'd seen that ring before somewhere. Recently. But where? Who? W . . . ? Her mind skidded to a halt. She knew where. She knew who. She caught Ricky's eyes and read the answer in them.

She forgot about the gun and blasted, 'That ring belongs to Maxwell Henley.'

'Belonged,' Stella corrected calmly. 'I'd do it all over again, you know.'

'Why did you kill him?' Ricky went into Detective interrogating a suspect mode.

'Because of Daisy, of course.'

'What do you mean?' Daisy shot back, shocked by the words. Shocked that somehow she was involved in a murder she didn't remember.

'Both of you, near the door,' Stella ordered, ignoring the question. She shoved Daisy forward. Daisy, mind still reeling, moved to stand with Ricky at the still open door.

'Turn right and keep moving until you get to the stairs.'

They did what she asked. When they reached the stairs Daisy realised where they were going – to the room in the basement where Stella had almost drowned her. Daisy shivered as if she was back under water again.

The door slammed behind them. The lock clicked into place. Ricky rushed towards the handle. Thumped the door. It was locked.

'What do we do now?' Daisy asked as her eyes roamed over the room where her mum had shown her the delights of under-water entertainment. He didn't answer her. Instead he got out his tweezers and inserted it into the lock.

*   *   *

Stella sang 'Secret Love' as she got kitted out for the occasion – an off the shoulder, red evening dress that swung and swirled around her body; Roger Vivier lipstick-red 1950s stiletto heels. A wide-brimmed, floppy black hat with a heavy scarf underneath hid the injured side of her face. Scarlet clutch bag. Then she picked up the thing that completed her evening wear look. Her spray-and-pray accessory – an Uzi.

'Shit,' he slammed out as his fingers tried out their magic on the lock. It still wouldn't give.

'Let me try,' Daisy insisted. 'Your hands are shaking. You're upset about not finding out about your sister, although I'd be thanking God that that's not her remains downstairs.' She laid her hand on his arm. He stopped. Sighed. Looked at her. Nodded. Immediately she took the tweezers from him.

'You're trying to get the pins in the lock to . . .'

'I know, I know,' she answered, keeping her eyes fixed firmly on her task. 'My dad taught me.'

'Should've known.'

The lock wasn't easy. She drew in a steady breath. Kept her fingers on the tweezers moving, to the left, to the right, up, down. Once more to the right. Click.

'Done it.' She flung the door open. They sprinted up the stairs. Hearts racing, breath crashing in the air they stopped and looked around.

'We need to find out where she's gone.'

'But how?' Daisy asked.

'Her office.' Ricky was already running as he spoke. They dived up the stairs. First floor. Second. Hit the office with Stella and Daisy printed on the yellow door. Ricky kicked it open. The telly was on, showing a satellite news channel's live coverage of the gala event at City Hall and the guests arriving outside.

'Right,' Ricky said, eyes darting around. 'Check everything for clues where your mum's headed.'

So that's what they did for the next ten minutes. Nothing. Exhausted, Daisy held her hands on her hips as the pain in her leg made its presence felt again.

Ricky thumped his fist into the wall. 'Fuck, fuck, fuck.' Suddenly he stopped when he heard his phone ping. Text message. He pulled out the phone.

```
Found out Stella King has/had an older brother.
Be careful
```

Ricky stared thoughtfully at the message. Brother? He lifted his head to stare at Daisy. 'Did your mum have a brother?'

She shook her head. 'I don't know – in any case, I can do without meeting another long-lost family member.' Abruptly she changed the conversation. 'Have you still got my pills?' Ricky gazed back at her, eyebrows lifted, as she'd gone completely loco.

'This ain't no time to be getting into the twilight zone.'

She rushed over to him. 'I know you think I'm a nut, but every time Dad comes to me, he really does help me out. And if we don't get more information we won't find Stella.' She held her hand out.

Ricky shook his head. 'I must be going off my rocker as well.' He shoved his hand into his back pocket. Took out the bottle. Opened it. Lay a pill into her palm. She shoved it into her mouth. Swallowed. Spun away from Ricky. Closed her eyes.

A few minutes later she opened them. Smiled. There was Frankie sitting in Stevie King's chair with his feet propped up on the desk. He wore casual at-home clothes – black jeans, opened polo shirt and check slippers. Before she could speak he started talking.

'When I was eleven I took the beating of my life. Another gang – the Preston bunch, that's it – kicked seven bells outta me and my mates. We were running scared for days until a little bird whispers in my ear that I need to get on the box. Know what that means?'

Daisy ignored his question and cut in, 'Dad, forget that, I need—'

But he didn't let her finish. Just carried on. 'Get yourself down the gym and learn how to throw a punch. So we went down this boys' boxing club in Bethnal Green. That's where I met Billy Doyle. He used to coach the kids in between looking after Stevie King's back.'

'Dad.' Daisy's frustration grew.

Frankie eased out of the chair. Pushed back the blond hair that had flopped over his forehead. 'After I'd been on the box for six months the Preston gang couldn't touch me. Next time they crossed our path they were the ones picking up their teeth from the floor. I learnt every fighting move on the box . . .'

'Stop talking about being on the box! I need your help,' Daisy yelled.

'On the box, baby. It's all on the box.' Frankie's voice lowered into a whisper.

She continued to stare at him, shaking her head.

'Daisy.' She didn't hear the first call of her name. 'Daisy?' She half heard it now but didn't respond. 'Daisy.' This time it was a battle cry. She flipped around to find Ricky standing anxiously behind her.

'We don't have time for a séance, we need to shift ourselves.' He grabbed her arm.

She looked back at him as he marched her to the door. 'He just kept talking about how he'd learnt to defend himself. About being on the box.'

Ricky shook his head. 'The sooner you give those pills the push the better.'

'On the box. On the box . . .' She kept whispering as they reached the door. Frustrated she looked back at Ricky. Caught the telly still on in the background. Caught the image on the screen.

Abruptly she wriggled out of Ricky's grasp. She stepped away from him and pointed. 'On the box,' she said. He followed her finger pointed at the telly. 'Look who's on . . . the . . . box.'

The screen still showed live film of the gala event at City Hall. The camera closed in on guests arriving to witness the announcement of the first-ever female Met police commissioner. The camera settled on the smartly dressed figure of someone they knew.

Randal Curtis. Arms wrapped around his wife.

'You thinking what I'm thinking?' Ricky let out in an astonished voice.

'Must be. He was in the photo. The person Stella was talking to when we were hiding in her office has got a daughter, he's got a daughter. He was Charlie Hopkirk's partner. He must be the other person involved in this.'

'And, I suspect, Stella's older brother.'

'What?' Daisy's incredulous voice filled the room.

'Didn't you tell me that Randal Curtis was born to a working-class London family? He's the only one who can be her brother. He's the only one who fits.' Ricky muttered as if chatting away to himself. 'What if Stella's gone to get him to make sure that no one involved in Maxwell Henley's death is alive to tell the tale?'

Daisy and Ricky looked at each other. It was Daisy who broke the silence. 'We've got to stop her.'

They rushed for the door.

Fifty-four

The woman from Spain got out of the cab in front of City Hall. After she paid the driver she pulled out her mobile.

'It's me. I'm outside.' She nodded. 'I'll stay in the background until all the pleasantries are over and then we'll meet.' She nodded one more time, lowered the phone, but didn't cut the call. She made her way inside and was immediately stopped by one of the security men manning the entrance.

'Invitation, please,' he said.

'I don't have one.'

'Then I'm sorry, miss . . .'

'Someone important has asked me to come.' She passed her phone to him. He gave her a suspicious look before raising the phone to his face.

Suddenly his posture changed as if he was talking to royalty. 'Yes, of course.' He gazed at the woman in front of him as he passed her back her phone. Stepped out of her way. She drew in a huge breath as she made her way upstairs.

Stella entered City Hall. The entrance was empty. Her plan to get past the metal detector was simple. She moved towards the two security guards on either side of it. Pulled the gun from under her coat. Raised it. Pulled the trigger. Popped one in the forehead. Shot the other through the heart. They both fell dead by the time she walked past them. Calmly she walked up the eye-stopping spiral staircase as she pushed her gun snugly under her coat.

She made her way up the stairs, the blue and amber lit walls casting shadows over her. On the second landing she heard the rise and fall of voices, the laughter, the clink of glasses. She followed the sounds until she came to the open doors of a great room. The room was huge, filled with people sitting at round tables, partway through their dinner and drinks. On the fringes were waiting staff circulating among the tables. On the far side was a stage with the top table. And at the top table sat her target. Stella waltzed in. Swiped a champagne flute from a passing waitress. Shot the bubbly down her throat in one gulp. Placed the glass down, ever so carefully, on a windowsill. Then she began to open her coat.

Ricky crashed the red lights. Swung the car onto Tower Bridge like he was doing the final circuit at Brands Hatch. The river flashed past them on both sides like a gathering black storm. A car beeped its horn as the car wobbled onto the edge of the opposite lane. Ricky moved the steering wheel through his hands, bringing the car back under control.

'Maybe you should contact your cop friends.' Daisy hung onto the armrests, her eyes looking into dark city night through the windscreen.

'Believe me, there'll be enough cops there, including my superior officer.' He gave her a quick glance. 'Don't forget Barbara Benton is making history tonight. Everyone's going to be there.'

The sight of City Hall began to rise in the distance. The car hit the end of the bridge. Banged to a stop outside City Hall. The red carpet that had been laid out was long gone. No security guards outside.

'We stick out like a sore thumb,' Daisy said, looking down at her clothing. 'We aren't exactly dressed for the occasion.'

'This is going to do all the talking we need.' His hand dipped into his back pocket. He flashed his police badge at her like he'd pulled a rabbit out of a hat.

'Where on earth have you been hiding that?' she asked.

He answered her with a grin.

Without another word they ran towards the entrance. Saw the

metal detectors straight away. But no security guards. They went forward. Got within a few metres of the metal detectors when they saw the two bodies. Ricky ran towards them. Bent down over the first body he came to. Checked the pulse. He leant over and did the same to the other guard. He looked up at Daisy. 'They're gone. If we don't stop her, God knows who else she will shoot on her way to take out Randal Curtis.' He stood up at the same time a loud bang, bang, bang sound came from above. They didn't even look at each other. Just sprinted up the stairs. No one needed to tell them what that sound was. Automatic gunfire.

Stella laughed as she sprayed another round of automatic fire into the air. Chaos erupted. People screamed as they ducked and dived under the tables. Tables turned over, chairs flew. Those nearest to the exit crawled on their hands and knees in a desperate effort to get outside. Two cops sprang towards Stella. She aimed her gun at them. They dived out of the way as she hit the trigger. This sent more guests scurrying like mice towards the exit. Suddenly Stella's hand dove into her bag. Her hand came out shaped as a fist with something inside it. She held her arm high in the air. 'I've got a grenade!'

Her announcement was answered by more screams. People openly stood up, taking their lives in their hands and ran for the door. Stella just laughed. Looked at what she held in her hand. Her lipstick. She moved closer into the room searching for her target. Found them still at the high table on the stage. Sitting calmly while everyone else went mad around them. An arm came out from under the high table and grabbed the arm of her target. She heard a voice yell, 'You need to get down. We need to get you out of here.' But her target just shook them off. Remained rooted in their chair. Kept their eyes squarely on Stella as she advanced.

Stella pointed her gun directly at her target and shouted, 'Anyone left in here in five seconds I'm gonna pop.' The room emptied in a flash before Stella's eyes. But not her target who remained frozen on the stage.

Stella sauntered forward, gun still in the air.

'Put it down,' a voice roared behind her.

Calmly she turned around. Smiled at who faced her with a pistol in his hand. Johnson.

'Well, well, well,' Stella said sarcastically. 'If it ain't the cop on the edge.'

'I said: put it down.' He menacingly took another step towards her.

He should have never moved because before his second foot hit the ground Stella let loose with a round of bullets. They smashed into his upper body, spinning him around. His finger pulled back on the trigger shooting into the air as he collapsed on the floor. Stella left him there, bleeding and groaning his life away. She twisted back to the stage. Her target was still there. She moved. Reached the stage. The good side of her face dipped into a nasty expression. 'Who would've thought we'd meet like this after twenty years?'

There was one person who didn't panic and leave the room. The woman from Spain shielded herself behind a table that had over-turned on its side. She shook as she tried to breathe quietly.

A wall of people slammed into Daisy and Ricky as they hit the fourth floor. They rammed and pushed through the desperately escaping crowd, trying to get to the reception room. Trying to get there before Stella killed Randal Curtis, who they believed to be Stella's brother. Daisy used her elbows to barge through. A man, with his head bowed, as if shielding himself from gunfire, tripped as she pushed him. She grabbed on to him before he could fall. He steadied his balance and looked up at her. Daisy's mouth fell open when she saw who it was. Randal Curtis.

With relief she pulled him close to her. 'You managed to get away from Stella?'

He looked back at her both frightened and baffled by her question. 'Stella?' he threw back.

'Yeah.' Daisy nodded. She felt Ricky come to stand beside her. 'Stella King came after you. You know, what you did together twenty years ago. You're her brother aren't you?'

'I beg your pardon? I don't know what you're talking about.' He yanked himself out of her grip. Turned and fled down the corridor with everyone else.

'I don't understand.' Daisy looked up at Ricky.

A frown creased Ricky's forehead as his mind ticked away. 'What if it was never Randal Curtis she was after? Maybe he isn't her brother. What if she's after someone else here tonight?'

Before Daisy could respond more gunfire from the reception room tore through the air.

They burst through the doors. Skidded to a stop when they saw Stella, gun still in hand, talking at the front of the stage. When they saw who she was talking to neither of them could believe it.

The newly appointed commissioner of the Metropolitan Police, Barbara Benton.

Fifty-five

Before they could move Stella twirled around. Pointed the Uzi at them.

But it wasn't Stella who spoke but Barbara. 'Daisy, I didn't want you involved in any of this.' Her words echoed in the room.

'Get off the fucking stage,' Stella cut in. 'And you two get here.'

Ricky and Daisy stepped slowly forward.

'We have the place surrounded. Come out with your hands up,' a voice yelled on the other side of the door.

Stella yelled back in a don't-fuck-with-me voice, 'You step one foot in here and your new head girl is finished.'

They all remained tense waiting for a response. None came, but no one relaxed.

'I don't understand any of this,' Daisy stammered at Barbara.

'I grew up with Stella on the Caxton estate,' Barbara said. Both Ricky and Daisy were visibly surprised at this information. 'I was quite a bit older than her. I went one way and she went another. I tried to help her—'

'I came here to kill you, not hear a fucking story,' Stella interrupted threateningly. 'But since they won't be leaving alive either I suppose there's no harm in telling them.'

Silence. Then Barbara started talking again. 'My home life wasn't the best when I was young. My mum was an alcoholic and my dad . . . well, let's just say I met him once in my life and was glad he never appeared again. So I decided to become a cop and the one thing I wanted to do was to protect kids. Make sure they never had to go through what I did. Took a lot of convincing but I set up the first unit within the Met to deal with child protection. That's how I got to know Stella again. Back then knowing a few people in the underworld was important. Getting your information from the inside has always been crucial to policing. So myself and my two fellow officers in the unit, Clarke and Johnson, would visit Stella at her place in Finsbury Park.'

She saw the incredulous and damning look on Ricky's face. 'Stella was important. She gave us information about men abusing kids that we would have never got. Some of the girls who ended up in her brothel came from the care system. They told her things she passed onto me. We got into the habit of going to her place every Friday night. Having a drink, a bit of a chat. That's where we met Maxwell Henley—'

Suddenly a mobile rang. Stella's grip on the trigger tightened.

'It's OK,' Barbara reassured. 'It's mine.' The ringing continued as Stella decided what to do. Finally she said, 'You know what to tell them.'

Barbara nodded as she pulled the phone from her police jacket. 'It's all alright,' she spoke softly. 'Stay where you are. Please stay back.' She cut the call. Pushed the mobile back into her pocket.

She took a deep breath and continued with her tale. 'I knew he was the leader of Woodbridge Council, but at the brothel I found out he was also Stevie King's silent business partner. I could have told the authorities but I decided not to. Life's full of compromises and I turned a blind eye and I regret it to this day.'

'We did the right thing,' Stella belted out. 'We didn't have a choice.'

'But how can murder ever be right?' Ricky blasted.

'Let her talk,' Daisy cut in, pushing Ricky's inflamed question to the side, directing her words at Barbara. 'Stella said whatever happened involved me.'

Barbara shot Stella a look so furious Daisy thought she was going to jump off the stage. But she didn't. 'How could you say that to her?'

'It's time for the truth, every last bit of it.'

Barbara once again began to talk as if she was giving a statement. 'It was a Friday, twentieth of July, 1990. We went to Stella's
as usual that night. When we got there Stella and Stevie were
throwing a small party with Maxwell Henley to celebrate a new
business deal. And Frankie Sullivan was there having just got
out of prison. There were only two other people there, one of the
working girls who Maxwell had a thing going on with, and you,
Daisy.' Daisy swallowed, but didn't interrupt. 'You were asleep
upstairs in your room. I know me, Clarke and Johnson should have
left then but we didn't. We stayed for a round of drinks. Just settled
in and started talking.'

Stella waved the gun around. 'Then that bastard Henley says he
had to go to the Gents upstairs.'

The sound of a helicopter overhead filled the room.

Stella and Barbara looked at each other. Barbara resumed
speaking. 'Five minutes later he hadn't returned. None of us
thought anything of it. Johnson gave me the nod and I knew it
was time to go. But before I did I went to the ladies upstairs.' Her
voice began to shake. 'As I walked along the corridor I noticed that
the door to your room, Daisy, was slightly opened.' A shaky smile
rippled across her lips as she stared at Daisy. 'I always loved seeing
you. Sometimes I'd tuck you in bed on Friday night.' The smile fell
from her lips. 'So I thought I'd just look in on you. Kiss you goodnight. I walked up to the door. Pushed it open. And . . .' Her hand
covered her mouth as tears formed in her eyes. She shook her head,
not able to speak.

But Stella had no such trouble. 'She walked in on that cunt in
bed with you.'

Daisy covered her mouth, stunned. Ricky drew her into the
crook of his arm.

'You were four years old and that scumbag had his filthy hands
all over you,' Stella slammed out. 'I'm downstairs and the next
thing I hear is this scream. Didn't know it at the time but it was
Barbara screaming blue murder. We shot upstairs. Barbara had
dragged him out of the bed. Fucking hell, he had his pants around
his ankles. She was hitting him and hitting him. Daisy, you were

bawling your head off on the bed, so Clarke picks you up with your favourite teddy and takes you downstairs. He tells you to play with your teddy near the piano and comes back upstairs.'

'Henley was grovelling on the floor. Begging. Saying he didn't mean to do it. Couldn't help himself.' Barbara shook with every word.

Stella half lowered the gun. 'And all I could think about were the men my mum would bring back to our flat and make me go into the room with them. I was fourteen years old and all my mum cared about was the money I put in her drinks jar.' She touched her forehead with the tip of her fingers. 'I don't even remember where I got the gun from. I just shot him again and again and again. He was leaking blood everywhere. We didn't know but it was going through the cracks in the floorboards. All we heard was your scream, Daisy. So Frankie rushed downstairs to find blood dropping on you from above.'

Daisy's nightmares flashed into her mind. A girl playing with a teddy by the piano. A girl with blood dripping on her head. Oh God, it wasn't a dream. It was real.

'We had to decide what to do,' Barbara carried on.

But Ricky ripped into her. 'You should've taken it back to base.'

'No,' she replied coldly. 'That wasn't an option. If we had, all of our work – mine, Clarke's and Johnson's – would have gone up in smoke. There were still those in the force who thought that the child protection unit was a waste of taxpayers' money and if they found out what happened that night our work would've been wrecked. Maxwell Henley was evil and deserved to die. We did the right thing.'

'Murder can never be the right thing,' Ricky slung back.

'Think the same thing, do you, Daisy?' Stella asked. 'Think we should've let him loose to fiddle with more kids?'

The quick fire questions hit her like grenades exploding in her face. That man had been touching her. Putting his filthy flesh all over her. And those two women had saved her. But did that make it right? She just shook her head and didn't answer.

'We buried him under the piano. Kept the brothel closed for a couple months until the smell went away. Stevie put it about that Henley skipped town, gone off to his villa in Spain, which Stevie had given him as a welcome to the organisation present. He was divorced, no kids, thank God, so no one came looking for him.'

'So how did Charlie get involved?'

'Charlie was Frankie's brief,' Stella said. 'I told the others I'd destroy all the evidence, but I didn't, I gave it all to Frankie to deal with. He must've given Charlie the stuff to look after for him in a deposit box, no questions asked.'

'Why didn't Dad just get rid of the gun and photo?'

'Dunno. Mind you, knowing Frankie having stuff on people was his stock in trade. He always taught me that you never knew when you might need to hold something in someone's face to get them to do what you wanted.'

'But how did the doctor's report about Jo-Jo's psychiatric problems get into the deposit box?' Daisy threw out.

Stella shook her head. 'Over the years I would give Frankie other things to look after for me. I could trust him. I gave him Jo-Jo's report to make sure Stevie never found it. Stevie would've gone ballistic if he thought his daughter was a nutter. And Frankie must've given it to Charlie as well for safe keep–' Suddenly she stopped talking, her steel eyes turning deadly. 'How do you know what else was in the deposit box?'

Realising her mistake Daisy shifted closer to Ricky. 'You bitch,' Stella yelled raising her gun. 'You had the stuff in the box all the time.' Her finger curled around the trigger. 'I should–'

'What about my sister?' Ricky demanded. 'She disappeared that–'

A voice from the other side of the room cut in, 'I was the prostitute who was still there that night.'

They all looked over to find a woman standing in front of an overturned table.

'Jenna?'

Ricky's voice was faint as he stared at the woman recently arrived from Spain. His eyes devoured her as she made her way across the room. She stopped a few inches away from him.

'How's my boy been?'

'Jenna?' he repeated. But he couldn't move. Couldn't say anything else.

'What are you doing back here?' Stella screeched.

'I told her to come back,' Barbara announced. 'She contacted me the other day because some lawyer from England had been asking questions about Henley.'

'I'm sorry, Ricky,' Jenna said as if they were the only two people in the room. 'They forgot I was there that night. I stumbled into the room as they were burying Maxwell. They couldn't let me go because I'd seen too much. I was scared, really scared. So I did a deal with Stella – she would set me up in Maxwell's villa in Spain, with enough cash to last me years and I would never set foot in Britain again.'

'That's why I kept an eye on you, Ricky, when you were younger,' Barbara said. 'Jenna wanted to make sure you were OK.'

Jenna's hand reached out to him. 'You don't know how many times I wanted to pick up the phone and just hear your voice. I–'

But before she could utter another word two gunshots ripped through the air. Stella staggered back, blood pumping from the two holes in her chest. The Uzi fell from her hands as she collapsed onto the floor. The others looked up swiftly at Barbara. In her hand she held a Beretta that had last been fired twenty years ago.

All hell broke loose as the police stormed in and yelled for everyone to get on the floor. The only one who ignored their instructions was Barbara. She moved towards Stella's body. Knelt and gathered the other woman's body into her arms.

'She weren't all bad you know,' she whispered sadly.

It was then that the tears finally came and Daisy started to cry.

Fifty-six

The TV in the hospital room replayed the earlier dramatic scenes outside City Hall. Camera flashes lit up the dark as questions were thrown by the impatient media as they pressed around the new commissioner of the Met police as she was led away from the building by a cordon of her own officers. The bold headline running across the bottom of the screen read: QUEEN OF COPS VS QUEEN OF CRIME?

The media's questions came thick and fast:

'Is it true that Stella King is dead?'

'Did you shoot Stella King?'

'Is this related to today's earlier bank robbery in Canary Wharf?'

But the police around Barbara were having none of it. They pushed her forward, at the same time keeping the media well back.

'Need some company?'

Ricky glanced away from the telly towards the hospital door. He gave one of his cheeky grins as he nodded his head at Daisy. He'd stayed with Barbara until the police had arrived. ID'd himself to the officer in charge, but had not hung around so that his cover wasn't compromised. He hadn't wanted to leave the woman who'd helped turn his life around but he hadn't a choice. Instead his superior had made him go to the hospital to sort himself out. Ricky knew that the night was not over for him, there would be plenty of questions for him to answer. Just as there had been for Daisy and Jenna at Paddington Green police station. Both had claimed to be innocent guests caught up in the drama and Ricky's superior officer had backed up their claim.

Daisy hovered near the side of his bed. 'How you doing?'

He held out his neatly bandaged arm. 'I'll live.'

They looked at each for a while. Suddenly she launched herself at him and wrapped herself over his chest, careful not to hurt his arm. Their lips met in a full, long kiss. Then she looked up at him, her blue eyes tired and soft. 'What do you think will happen to Barbara?'

His good hand caressed her back as he shook his head. 'Dunno, but the time for lies is over. Where's Jenna?'

'At the club with Misty and the others.'

They lay secure in each other's arms until a voice at the door called, 'Daisy?'

They both gazed up to find Jerome standing nervously in the door. His eyes flicked between them. 'I'll be outside.' Then he was gone. Daisy let out a long sigh as she pushed herself to her feet.

She grinned at Ricky. 'I know this girl who wants to try your bangers and mash recipe . . .'

He grinned back. She twisted away from him as she pushed her hand in her pocket and found the ring that she knew she had to give back to the man waiting for her outside.

Fifty-seven

'It's negative.'

Ricky blew out a mega sigh of relief as he looked at Daisy who stood in the doorway. He sat with a newspaper at a table on the balcony that overlooked the river in her flat. Six weeks had come and gone since one of the most infamous nights in London's recent history. Ricky had kept his promise and airbrushed Daisy's, Charlie and her dad's name out of things. As far as the cops were concerned Stella King and Barbara Benton were involved in a crime that centred around evidence in a safe-deposit box that no one knew who it belonged to and involved in the murder of a council leader some said was involved in child abuse. Ricky and Daisy hadn't talked about the future much, except of the 'baby'. Now there was no baby.

'Pleased?' Ricky asked.

Daisy sighed as she plonked herself in the chair opposite him. 'Dragging a kid into an "are-they-aren't-they" situation just doesn't seem right. I think we need some more time to get to know each other.'

'Oh, I know all I need to know about you.' His dark eyes ran seductively over her. He flicked his gaze back to the newspaper in front of him. 'Look at this.' He spun it across the table towards her. She read the headline: 78% SAY BASHER BABS SHOULD BE LET GO.

She scanned the remainder of the article, which was an impassioned piece in favour of Barbara Benton, briefly the commissioner of the Met police, facing no charges. She might have been involved in a murder, but he'd been a paedophile for crying out loud. Paedophiles don't deserve to live, do they? Hadn't she done society a favour?

Daisy lifted her head, as the river breeze picked up. 'Think she'll get off?'

'Well, she's out on bail. And people seem to feel really strongly about this.'

'And what do you say?'

'You commit the crime you should do the time, that's what I would've said a month ago, but that would mean you and Jenna would now be deep inside Holloway for your part in all this mess.'

His reunion with his sister had been a private affair that he didn't really talk about. She'd gone back to Spain a week ago, but said that if Barbara ever needed her she would be back. She wasn't going to let the woman who had always been decent to and looked after her brother face the firing squad alone.

'Who would've thought,' Daisy started in a bittersweet voice, 'that there would be so many ghosts from our pasts waiting for us?'

Before he could say anything else a loud voice shouted, 'Yoo hoo!'

Ricky groaned. He knew who it was and wished she didn't have her own key. Jackie appeared followed by the cavalry – Misty, Anna, Ollie and Roxy. The women eyed him up. They were still uneasy around him, not too happy about having a cop dating one of their nearest and dearest. But they had brought up Daisy to be a decent person, which he was thankful for.

'You asked her to marry you yet?' Jackie said, hands on hips.

'A girl isn't going to wait for ever,' Ollie threw in.

'I know someone who can design a wicked dress,' Anna backed up.

'Father Tom says he's happy to officiate at the ceremony,' Roxy added.

'The club will put on the biggest spread London has ever seen,' Misty said with relish.

Both Ricky and Daisy groaned.

'You lot should become private detectives the way you know this city,' Ricky said as he stood up. The women all looked at each other and laughed.

'You'll have to excuse us, ladies, but me and Daisy have got one last ghost to lay to rest.'

'We have?' Daisy muttered, standing up.

'Lock up when you're finished, ladies.' He took Daisy's arm. 'You need to get your jacket because I'm taking you for a little spin.'

'Private detectives. What a laugh,' Jackie said, shaking her head as she and her friends settled themselves in for a long stay in Daisy's Calamity Jane decorated sitting room.

'Why not?' It was Ollie who threw out the outrageous question.

'Are you nuts?' Misty asked, kicking off her heels.

'Maybe Ollie's got a point,' Roxy said quietly. 'We did go away on holiday to think about our future. The club almost runs itself now.'

They stared at each other in silence. Then Anna broke the quiet. 'People do always seem to come to us to help sort out their problems. You know, the type of stuff they don't want to go to the cops with.'

Silence again.

'We don't have to make it official or anything,' Ollie finally said. 'Just a discreet office at the top of the club. Even Schoolboy can help . . .'

Jackie jumped in furiously at the sound of her husband's name. 'Leave him outta this.'

The others shifted their eyes away from her, not sure what to say. They knew there were problems in her marriage, but what they were she wouldn't say.

'And what are we going to call ourselves?' Misty scoffed, curling her long legs underneath herself, picking up a copy of *The Lady Killers*. She howled with laughter, but no one else joined in.

Suddenly Jackie leant back in her chair. 'The Lady Killers,' she said thoughtfully. 'I like it . . .'

*   *   *

Ricky's spin took Daisy somewhere she didn't want to go. The cemetery. She groaned aloud. She'd had enough of dead bodies.

'What are we doing here?'

He didn't answer. Just shot her a soft, but slightly serious smile. A few minutes later, the car breezed to a stop, past a few other people still paying their respects to a loved one. She knew exactly where he was taking her. She got out of the car. Met Ricky at the bumper. Hand-in-hand they strolled towards Frankie Sullivan's grave. The rose she'd laid six weeks ago had long since died. A wave of sadness swept her as she realised that there would be no more flowers from Stella.

'I don't really want to be here.'

Ricky pulled his hand away. His voice was solemn. 'It's time for you to say a final goodbye.'

Puzzled she looked at him. He said nothing as his hand dipped inside his denim jacket. Pulled out her bottle of pills. Rattled it. 'One left,' he said.

He placed the single pill in her hand. 'That's the last tab you're ever going to take.'

Her hand curled around the tiny, round object. This was so hard, but Ricky was right. It was time to get on with her life and say good-bye to Frankie Sullivan. But she didn't take the pill. She just closed her eyes. Slowly she began drifting. And drifting . . .

Then she opened them and stared with wonder at where she was. Back in the Hammersmith Palais, where her dad would take her dancing. The lighting was dark with soothing splashes of red in between like the light just before dawn. Four figures on the stage, shrouded in the shadows, crowded around the same tall microphone stand, one with a guitar and another with a tambourine. They stood like statues waiting. A huge grin erupted on her face when she saw who stood a few feet from her. Her dad. Frankie Sullivan, wearing a tailored tux, polished black shoes and white shirt. That's when she realised that she was wearing a huge, knee-length fluffy pink ball gown. He stretched out his arms to her. Grin growing, she moved towards him. Ended up in his arms, which closed around her waist. A guitar strummed from the stage soon joined by the single voice of a woman singing their song – 'Dedicated To the One I Love'. She leant her head against his shoulder. They began to move as the chorus of voices grew from one to four. They swept across the dance floor, their bodies moving in unison. Laughing they started to sing along. Over and over. Then the music fell silent. Frankie stepped back. Moved away. Further and further until he disappeared into the darkness of the dim light . . .

She was sobbing her heart out in Ricky's arms. He stroked her hair as her tears soaked his shirt, whispering, 'It's alright,' over and over again. They held on to each other in the soothing summer air. And she might be crying but she was alright. She felt Ricky's body tense. Looked up at him and realised that he was gazing over her shoulder. Abruptly he removed his arms from her and moved to stand in front of her grandmother's grave. His face wore an expression of such shock she became concerned about him.

'What's the matter?'

He gazed at her dazed. Looked back at the photo of her Gran. Back at her. He slapped on a smile, but it didn't reach his eyes. 'Nothing.' He reached for her arm. 'Let's get out of here.'

But she wriggled away from him. 'What's going on, Ricky?' As he opened his mouth, she cut furiously across him, 'And don't say nothing. Tell me what it is.'

He let out a deflated breath and rubbed his hand across his chin. 'This most probably don't mean anything . . .' She raised her eyebrow at him. 'But have you looked at your grandmother's photo properly?'

She stepped closer to him, not sure what he was asking her. Of course she'd seen the photo before. She peered at it and shook her head. 'I don't get it.'

'When we came here the other night I couldn't see the picture properly but I just caught the smile and it reminded me of someone.'

She looked again. Shrugged her shoulders at him.

'Look again just in case my eyes are playing tricks on me.'

She looked back again. And again. Her heart lurched. Suddenly she saw what he saw. The grin. The blond hair. The beauty spot.

No way. It couldn't be. Couldn't . . . Finally it burst strained and choked from her lips. 'She looks like Stella King.' She shot him a pleading desperate look. 'I don't understand.'

But Ricky did. And what he said next blew her mind. 'I don't think that Stella King was your mum. I think she was your aunt. Frankie Sullivan's sister.'

Frankie Sullivan's sister. The words drummed inside Daisy's head as she got out of the car with Ricky. It couldn't be true, she reasoned, because her dad didn't have a sister. If he had she would know about her. Wouldn't she? Although Daisy knew that she could have argued all day and all night about that one there was no argument about Stella being a dead ringer for her grandmother Millie.

She shook off the thoughts as she looked up. The last time she'd seen this house it had been dark and she'd been belting out of it via a window. Her tongued flicked nervously across her lip as she stared at Ricky. He took her hand in his, then they approached the front door. He rang the bell. Seconds later the door was opened by the still powerful figure of Barbara Benton.

Relaxing harp music played in the background from one of the other rooms as they sat inside Barbara's kitchen at the table set neatly in a corner.

'Is it true?' Daisy said abruptly. Barbara raised her eyebrows. Daisy swallowed. 'That Stella isn't . . . I mean wasn't . . .my mother?'

'What makes you say that?' Barbara spoke quietly but her gaze dipped away from Daisy.

'Don't bullshit us,' Ricky said angrily. Daisy reached out and took his hand on the table. Squeezed it. 'If anyone knows the truth you do. Plus Daisy deserves the truth after all she's been through.'

Instead of answering Barbara stood up slowly. Moved towards a drawer. Took out some ciggies. Lit one. Puffed for a few seconds. Then glanced back at them, the smoke dancing between them. 'Some things are best left alone,' she finally said.

'I need to know,' Daisy's voice was soft, but insistent.

'OK.' Barbara leant back onto the cupboard. 'I knew that Frankie was Stella's sister. She told me one day when we were kids, in confidence. He was older than her and was put into care just as Stella was born. That's why people didn't associate him with Stella. But they stayed in touch. When Stella hit the street he tried to rein her in, but Stella being Stella . . .' She let out a single punch of laughter. 'She wouldn't listen. When she got the brothel in Finsbury Park he would come visiting. And . . .' She swallowed. 'That's where I met him again.'

Daisy's hand tightened on Ricky's.

'It just happened one night.' Barbara's eyes got a faraway look as she remembered. 'We were drinking on our own in one of the back rooms. Laughing, swapping stories. And . . . well, one thing lead to another . . .'

Daisy shot to her feet. 'You aren't saying . . . ?' she cried out. Then it all slowly began to fall into place. How Barbara had told them that twenty years ago she would come to the brothel to kiss Daisy good night. The caresses and lingering looks Barbara had given her in the past that she'd taken for some girl-on-girl thing. Oh, it had been girl-on-girl alright – mother and daughter. Then she remembered what she'd heard Stella say on the phone: *'You want me to tell your daughter the truth and see the hurt written across her face?'* All the time they'd assumed it must be Randal Curtis or Charlie's widow and all the time Stella had been talking to the one person who claimed never to have had any children: Barbara Benton.

Barbara ploughed on. 'I found out I was pregnant a few months later and by that time Frankie was already in prison.' Daisy covered her mouth with her hand. 'I couldn't have an abortion, not with my Catholic upbringing. So I went away on some mythical police conference in Europe and had the baby. We agreed that Stella would bring her up as her own until Frankie got out . . .'

'But why didn't you keep me?'

Barbara stepped forward. Her face was riddled with anguish. 'I couldn't. My career was everything to me.' She took another step forward. Daisy shuffled back. 'But I loved you. Always came to tuck you into bed on a Friday night when I could. I didn't only come to the brothel to get information from Stella, I also came to see my baby girl. Of course, Clarke and Johnson never knew. That's why when I found Maxwell Henley in your room I went crazy. Couldn't believe what he was trying to do to my little girl . . .' Tears fell from her eyes as her mouth crumpled.

Daisy started crying as well. Huge, gut-wrenching sobs. Ricky's arms were around her in seconds. Held her tight. Barbara rushed towards her, but Daisy shouted, 'Don't come near me.'

'You need to leave her alone,' Ricky snapped. 'In fact we're out of here.'

He pulled Daisy on to her feet. Marched her through the long hallway towards the front door. Opened it. They were halfway outside when they heard, 'I'll always love you. Be there for you.'

Daisy froze. Twisted out of Ricky's arms. Turned back around. Stared her newfound mother right in the eyes. 'I don't know whether to believe you, but you know what, it doesn't matter because I've got a mum and her name's Jackie Jarvis. The best mum a girl could ever have.' And with that she turned back around.

'Will I see you again?'

Without answering and without Ricky's support she made her way back to the car.

Fifty-eight

Five days later, on an unseasonably gloomy August afternoon Randal Curtis burst into Daisy's office.

'Come with me, young lady, we are off to meet a new client.'

'Me?' Daisy said startled, standing up.

When she'd returned to work after taking some personal time off, Daisy levelled with Randal about who her dad had been, deciding that the time for secrets was over. He'd smiled kindly at her and told her not to worry about it. He'd taken over Charlie's role as her mentor and even told her that he'd been the one to advise Charlie's widow to meet Daisy to talk about the deposit box because Priscilla Hopkirk had been so worried that whoever had burgled her home might come back.

'Yes, you.' He puffed out his chest. 'I think it's time for you to move onto bigger and higher things.'

Daisy almost saluted him. She followed him to his office. A big case was just what she needed to help push the memories of the last few months to the back of her mind.

As they reached his office door, he spun to face her, making her stumble back. 'This is the big one. One that all the other firms are after. Think you can handle it?'

She thought of Charlie and everything he had taught her. She pushed her shoulders back. 'Yes, Mr Curtis, I can handle it.'

He nodded. Thrust the door open. Someone sat at his desk with their back to them.

Curtis swept into the room.

The person at the desk swivelled around. Daisy froze.

'This is my associate, Miss Sullivan, who will be assisting me with your case. And Daisy this is . . .'

But the person at the desk stood up stopping his words. Approached Daisy. Stuck out her hand. 'Good to meet you, Miss Sullivan.'

Daisy hesitated for a few seconds. Then took the hand of the woman she would be helping to defend.

Barbara Benton.

Her mother.